The Essential Jennifer Johnston

The Essential
Jennifer Johnston

review

The Captains and the Kings first published in Great Britain in 1972, *The Railway Station Man* first published in Great Britain in 1984, *Fool's Sanctuary* first published in Great Britain in 1987, all by Hamish Hamilton

First published in this edition in 1999 by REVIEW

An imprint of Headline Book Publishing

10 9 8 7 6 5 4 3 2 1

British Library Cataloguing in Publication Data

Johnston, Jennifer, 1930–
The essential Jennifer Johnston
I.Title
823.9'14[F]

ISBN 0 7472 7495 9

Typeset by Avon Dataset Ltd, Bidford-on-Avon, Warks

Printed and bound in Great Britain by
Clays Ltd, St Ives plc.

Headline Book Publishing
A division of the Hodder Headline Group
338 Euston Road
London NW1 3BH

www.reviewbooks.co.uk
www.hodderheadline.com

In memory of Gaga, Boodle,
Adelaide and Hamper Jack,
with thanks

Contents

Preface

I remember very well the first time, the first moment even, reading a page of a book by Jennifer Johnston. It was twenty years ago at least, when most other things are faded and forgotten. I was a very young writer in the arrogance and ignorance of first work, and I had heard her name. There was a book of hers lying there in the living-room of my mother's house. I was inclined to contemn it, as young writers like to do. I picked it up reluctantly. I needed to dislike it more than I needed to admire it, certainly, for that essential fuel of stoic stupidity that a young writer sometimes requires.

I began to read and I was immediately in cahoots with this Jennifer Johnston. I was immediately her friend, in the way a reader is suddenly, under the illusion of complicity and harmony that is the magic coat of perfect writing. I was, like the reviewers say, stunned, but stunned into affection and delight.

There is a special shock in reading an original writer for the first time, like the shock of a death or a birth. The same thing happened with Joseph Conrad, with Christopher Isherwood, with Trollope in their different times. I was arrested by – what is it? – the vigour, the miracle of life being contained in mere sentences, the leap of force and genius off the words, the rightness, the ringing trueness, all those things. But also, the complicity, the speaking directly, succinctly, and at the same time, discreetly, familiarly, strangely. The recognisable contours of the complete stranger's face.

A reader is grateful for these discoveries, a writer, a young writer, is indebted to them. The possible path is shown by its achievement before your eyes, a writer in your own time perfecting her art and using it not for display purposes, but to go down into, to hover over, to encompass, to forgive, the tangled colours of human life. To bring human birdsong into the realm of urgent understanding. All those things I recognised in those first minutes of reading. Such entire readability is next to Godliness.

Her early subject, not only on the surface but deep in her working heart, the subject that made her first books so vivid, new and bright, was the vanished and vanishing world of what used to be called the ascendancy in Ireland, for her part its minor officers and denizens, and the other people of Ireland where they touched against that dwindled and diminished species – a spectacular descendancy as one might say. It seems that that world struck the tuning fork for her, set the tune and the tone for her very prose. Though her subject has changed and varied across her subsequent novels, something of that vanished world is in all of them, in the very tenor of her prose, a cello tune playing darkly behind everything. All her books in that sense are catalogues of swansongs, sheet music for the ending of days and the difficulty of human days.

This volume gathers three significant books, the astounding *The Captains and the Kings*, the pristine and resonant *The Railway Station Man*, the unforgettable and highly controlled *Fool's Sanctuary*, billed as *The Essential Jennifer Johnston*. It is an honour indeed accorded only the best writers. And they are essential, three masterpieces in fact, and yet I am tempted to say that all her work is essential, if only because she has made it her business never to write or publish an inessential book. Every book is a spectacular experience for the reader, an encounter in a special country that is both Irish and Johnstonian, both here and there.

Often old age or aging is her theme, or its corollary and sister, vulnerable youth. Her subject though in the upshot is everything, and the mirror she has made to reflect everything is often a system of balances put under extraordinary stress. We watch her people rise and fall, and fall, like we might watch comets – not conscious always of their inexorable decay and yet affected by it and dazzled by the grandeur of the tail of light behind.

The music of that fall, that decay and interior grandeur, that magnificent isolation and essential human loneliness, that strange resilience, ignorance and knowledge, is known to her and serves all her purposes. It is not necessary to say that the results are universal, because she has been recognised these several decades as a classic Irish writer, living and breathing though she may be. The reputation is unassailable. But she has gained this reputation not by spurious means of social relevance or historical aptness, but by sheer force of the joy that she has given her readers. And those that approach her books stay neither casual, academic, or critical. Their official natures and seeming uniforms are sloughed off by simple pleasure in her artistry. I stress this fact because so much of Irish literature is in constant danger of being official.

There is nothing official about Johnston, she is subversive, conservative, innovative and deeply traditional all at the same time. She is solitary and unique but completely integrated into the general geist and flavour of her country. She is in a way the most benign of Irish writers, in the way Tolstoy was the most benign of Russian. She is helpful to the emergency and healing of the heart. She does the air good for having breathed of it, and she has done the general good health and will of Irish writing and writers a ferocious service, forcing the stakes high. It is not a time of sloppy prose with a figure like Johnston around.

She has made the business of prose writing in her time a serious matter — both its smile and its sorrow — and upped the ante of excellence, in the way Seamus Heaney has made Irish poetry both pinnacle and revelation. I would set her with Heaney in the firmament of Irish writers, because she has his individuality, his lovely power, and his searing conscience.

One can go in praise of Jennifer Johnston because she is beyond praising. Her work rises out of the ashes of a past and passing time, and stands in its depiction of sorrows as, ironically, a vindication of the business of being alive. If a person can be alive in the same quality of prose that Jennifer Johnston imparts to her subjects then truly life is worth living because it sings so well.

Sebastian Barry

The Captains
and the Kings

The two guards left the barracks at ten past four on the afternoon of September 20. The barracks, a small white house, was set in a terrace of similar houses, the only distinguishing features being a small sunburst over the door, signifying Garda Siochana, and a tall white flag pole on the roof for use on ceremonial occasions, which were very few and far between. They cycled slowly along the village street with the sun behind them and their shadows, black on the ground, always that unattainable length in front of them. Guard Devenney was the taller of the two men and the older and the least ambitious. For nearly twenty years he had lived in the village. His kids had been born and reared in the barracks and were all gone now, bar one. His wife had evolved from a tender girl, with soft nunlike white skin, into a woman of enormous proportions with a greying moustache fringing her upper lip. He knew everyone for miles around. He knew their weaknesses, he knew when to blink the eye. Guard Conroy was new to the job, new to the country, a Dublin man, with high hopes of quick promotion back to the hard, grey city streets again, where there was a bit of gas when you were off duty and the possibility of some real crime when you were on. The street curved sharply at the end of the village and their shadows moved round to the left-hand side.

'I don't like it at all,' said Devenney, more or less to himself.

Three children sitting on the edge of the pavement watched them go by without interest. There was no one else about. All indoors, no doubt, with nothing better to do but yak about what didn't concern them. Guard Conroy grunted in reply. He didn't believe in committing himself. Back at the other end of the village the level-crossing gates clattered shut behind the Dublin train. Smoke hung over the fields for a while, before melting.

'It's the sort of business goes sour on you. Heads fall. And I'll tell you one thing, it's never the Superintendent's head, nor the Inspector's neither.'

They rode on a while, in silence. The tyres of their regulation bikes crackled on the road.

'The law's the law,' said the younger man, for something to say.

'Ah, maybe. But trouble's trouble, just the same.'

It was hot for September, an Indian summer. The chestnut leaves were turning and the tops of the trees were gold against the clear turquoise sky. On the lower branches the leaves were still a tired green and the chestnuts hung in paler clusters, almost ready for dropping. It was the best part of a mile to the gates of Kill House and the two men were sweating by the time they arrived. They stopped outside the gates on the gravel sweep and each took a handkerchief from some interior pocket and wiped his face and neck. Guard Devenney even removed his cap and ran his handkerchief round the band inside before he put it back on his head.

'Well, here we go so.'

*   *   *

It was late May. The few remaining daffodils that fringed the avenue were turning brown and papery. The leaves were curling at the top. The early rose bushes in Clare's formal beds were covered in buds, which would begin to open with another couple of days' sun.

Since Nellie's death almost six months before, Mr Prendergast had taken to living more or less completely in the study. Books on the tables (where his father used to display his adequate collection of duelling pistols), on some chairs even and also in piles on the faded Chinese carpet. The piano sat in the middle of the room and in one corner there was a divan that he and Sean had carried from upstairs, in case of some unmentionable need. The two long windows faced south-west across the terrace at the wooded hills, and behind them the gaunt blue mountains constantly changed from one elusive colour to another. As the evening thickened, he would sit in his chair by the window and watch the green quivering lights spring up across the valley as people lit their lamps, and the moving fingers of light from cars on the main road below. It was almost his only pleasurable connection with the world. He would drink his first evening glass of whiskey as he watched and then, when he rose and crossed the room to switch on his own lights, he would refill his glass and settle down to read for the rest of the evening.

During the last few months of Clare's illness he had formed the habit of driving down to the church to play the organ. As the house became enclosed by the half light each evening, he had become obsessed by her eyes. For four months she had lain, propped up by pillows, in her bed, one side of her face pulled down into a sour little grin, her right arm useless, a cashmere shawl covering her thin shoulders. He would arrive in her room each afternoon as the clock on her mantelpiece chimed three and, picking up whatever book happened to be at hand, he would sit in the wing chair and read to her for an hour. The book was then closed and put away. He would move to the end of the bed and force himself to smile down at her.

'Anything you want, my dear?'

One eye stared coldly up at him, the other drooped as if in sleep.

'You're looking a little better today. Quite distinctly better. Have you up and about soon. Come the summer and you'll be out enjoying the garden again.'

He would bow and leave the room. He found it all most disconcerting, almost disagreeable. The memory of her eyes stayed with him until he left the house and drowned such thoughts in the vast chords of Bach.

He played the organ more often in the daytime now, as he found his eyes were giving him trouble in electric light. It was time he took himself to the oculist for new glasses but he preferred to live without them than make the journey to Dublin and back. From the moment of his marriage to Clare until his mother's death, his life had been spent in continuous movement. He had never stopped anywhere long enough to become accustomed to its rhythm. The moment a feeling of familiarity began to creep over him, or a new acquaintance seemed to have the audacity to be becoming a friend, then the trunks were packed, servants dismissed, tickets booked. They would move on. Clare's only pregnancy had been an irritating hiatus in his life. They had returned to sit it out with her family in North Oxford.

The atmosphere had affronted him. The roads upon roads of red brick, high-gabled houses, the smell of newly cut grass, the politesse over teacups, the indestructible goodwill of the English middle-class. After several weeks he had gone upstairs one afternoon and packed a suitcase.

'What are you doing?'

Clare had arrived home early from her daily walk.

'It should be obvious.'

'Are you going away?'

'Yes.'

He was embarrassed by the situation.

'I, ah, feel I'm wasting my time here. I thought I'd have a look at Sicily. Perhaps get in a few music festivals round the place.'

'You could go up to concerts in London from here.'

Her eyes dazzled with tears. He looked away from her, continued to pile neatly folded shirts one upon the other. 'I'm sorry, Clare. I can't stay here.'

'What will I say to mother? She'll think it's all most peculiar.'

'Say anything you like.'

Silently she watched him fasten his suitcase.

'You would have gone before I came home?'

He nodded.

'It would have been easier.'

'For you perhaps.'

'Quite.'

He picked up his case and leant forward to kiss her formally. 'Well, goodbye, my dear.'

She moved her head out of his reach. 'I don't understand.'

He ignored this. 'You'll be perfectly all right. After all, what could I do?'

* * *

After their daughter's birth they moved on again, leaving the child in the care of both her grandmothers. Neither lady had anything in common, apart from Sarah. Even this, they felt, wasn't a strong enough reason for them to become involved in the exhausting processes of communication, so the child shuttled between them, in the care of a good, old-fashioned nanny who knew her place and stood no nonsense, either from children, or interfering adults.

Her parents made it their business to visit Sarah at least once a year. They made responsible decisions about her education. They followed her scholastic career with interest and a certain amount of pride. She was a clever child. They sent her presents, not extravagant, for they were not flamboyant people, but interesting, sometimes beautiful, objects from every corner of the earth.

The war caught them in Mexico, where they stayed for a couple of years and then moved on to the United States. There they continued their nomadic life until the war was over. In 1946 they came cautiously back to Europe to find tired people desperately trying to build a new world. It seemed, at that time, as if it might be going to be a world in which there would be very little place for people like the Prendergasts.

One evening, as they sat in North Oxford surrounded by bleak post-war people and problems, ration books and a scarcity of domestics, a telegram arrived to say that the old lady was dead. She was being driven to dine with some friends by her man, Sean. Snow lay thinly on the higher hills and the roads between the black hedges sparkled with frost. Sean, exhilarated by a drop too much before setting out, drove just too fast on to an icy patch and the car went into a skid. They went off the left-hand side of the road into the ditch and hit a telegraph pole. Sean was unhurt but the old lady was dead. Her ringed hands were clasped, as usual, in her lap but her neck was broken. There was no sound anywhere but the humming of the telegraph wires and the drop of snow falling from the branches of the trees.

Surprisingly, they settled down. They didn't mix much; in fact, withdrew gently but firmly from the social ramifications created by the past. Clare and Sean had taken at once to each other and had thrown themselves, for their own different reasons, into the reshaping of the old lady's garden. Mr Prendergast took to reading. He wandered through books as he had wandered through the world, never quite grasping what it really was that he was looking for. He never read one at a time, always a pile were tumbled by his chair or bed. He roamed from author to author, century to century, prose, poetry, biography, essays, philosophy, history. He read, with fluency, books in French and struggled through German ones. Parcels arrived regularly from London and Dublin and he would tear the paper off like an impatient child and then carry the books into the study, where he would pick one of them at random, almost throw himself into a chair and start reading.

For pleasure, he played the piano. As a young man he had had reasonable talent but through the travelling years he had played little and his fingers had stiffened, and he played now with more than average skill but with caution.

Sarah intruded seldom. When her grandmother died she had been in her last term at school. Her hair lay in two plaits on her grey uniform coat. Her face was like marble, white and still.

'So, you're off.'

Clare seemed to flutter in the hall behind him, like a moth in a cobweb.

'We haven't had much time for conversation. You've never told us why you've picked on Cambridge.'

'I thought it was time for a change of scene.' She wasted no words.

'We, ah, your mother and I have decided to stay on here for a while. At any rate. Straighten things up. We actually thought we might settle down here.'

'Oh.'

'You wouldn't think of . . . ?'

She shook her head. 'No. I think not.'

'Your mother, perhaps . . .'

Sarah looked briefly across his shoulder in her mother's direction. 'I think we'll all manage all right.' They kissed each other's cheeks. She went down the steps and got into the waiting taxi. The way she moved reminded him of his mother.

In order to keep the house alive old Mrs Prendergast had sold the land, hills, fields, bogland and wood to men who had been her husband's tenants and labourers. She watched with ironic eyes the golden and purple weed flowers creeping up through the corn as the years passed and barbed wire filling the gaps in walls. To keep himself and Clare alive, Mr Prendergast had closed the house room by room, floor by floor. Rows of unused keys hung on the wall by the kitchen door, under the coiled and silent bell springs. Only Nellie remained, indoors, and Sean, in the garden. After several years the book parcels dwindled and finally stopped altogether. Now he was alone and, it seemed to him, the way that he had always wanted to be.

Approaching nine o'clock and after his third glass of whiskey, the old man found his eyes sore and heavy and he threw his book down on the floor by his chair. He watched, for a moment, a furious fly beating himself against the window, bewildered by what seemed to be the sudden solidification of the air. He pushed himself out of the chair with a certain amount of trouble and went over to the piano. He sat pulling at his fingers, cracking the knuckles, trying to press the stiffness and swellings out of the joints. His head nodded as the fingers pressed. There was no point in looking for music. He would have to play what was in his head. He could hear it there, played to a perfection that he could never reach, or have reached, even before his fingers became so tired. The bell rang, a great jumping clatter of sound. He could see in his mind's eye the tarnished bell jumping on the end of its spring. Number one, the left-hand bell of the long, numbered line, high up on the damp wall below. Number two was the drawing room, three, the dining room, four, this room, father's study. There were only two things father had rung his bell for—turf and his boots. He had always refused to burn coal in this room and from September to May each morning the ashes were raked through and a neat pyramid built in the hearth. He could remember the fascination of watching the dry turves catch and the timid first flames crawling up the inside of the structure.

The bell clattered again and, whoever the unexpected guest might be, he was banging now with the huge iron knocker. The old man got up slowly and crossed the room. Sometimes, now, in the evenings, if he moved too fast or incautiously, cramp knotted the muscles in his calves so inextricably that he had to sit, motionless, in his chair for up to half-an-hour. 'Coming, coming,' he muttered irritably in reply to the hammering. 'Coming.'

He opened the door and found a boy on the step. As far as the old man was concerned he could have been any age between a large seven and an under-nourished, under-privileged seventeen. Tight coiled springs of orange hair covered his head.

'No need to batter the door down.'

The eyes that peered up at him were honey-coloured, secretive. The face pale, already fatigued by living.

'Who might you be?'

The boy didn't answer. He pulled a white envelope out of his pocket and offered it.

'Hey?' Mr Prendergast ignored the letter. 'Can't you speak?'

The boy stared down at his black shoes, which looked as if they had been contorted into their particularly alarming shape by a hundred pairs of feet.

'For heaven's sake, boy, I'm not going to eat you! Hey? I don't often eat boys. Never Celts. They're stringy.' He looked down at the outstretched hand, the bitten nails, the envelope. 'I joke,' he muttered to the air.

It was almost dark and he knew that the last rays of the sun now painted the chimney stacks away above their heads. The air was sweet and moist.

'Look at me, hey, boy.' The boy looked up. 'You know my name?' The boy nodded. 'What is it, then? Let me hear you say it.'

'Mr Prendergast, sir.'

'Splendid. That's the first hurdle over. At least I know you're not a deaf mute. Now, tell me your name.'

'Diarmid, sir.'

'A splendid name.' The boy's mouth stretched slightly in a smile. 'An historical name. Tell me, Diarmid, what do you know about the Diarmids that have gone before? If anything, hey?'

'I don't know, sir.'

'You don't know what?'

'I don't suppose I know anything much.'

'That's honest, anyway. There's many a man goes to the grave without admitting as much.'

'I'm not too keen on school, like. I don't go much . . . I mean . . . you wouldn't let on?'

'I wouldn't. What do you do when you're not at school?'

For the first time the boy really smiled. 'I keep out of the way, sir.'

'A wise precaution.'

They both looked at each other, weighing up carefully what they saw.

'Come in,' ordered the old man. 'There's a rising mist.' He stood back and let the boy pass him. Then he closed the remaining light out. The hall was large and very dark now, like a cave. 'Straight across. I presume you have another name.'

'No, just Diarmid.'

'A tribal name, at least. You must belong to someone.'

They came into the study and the old man groped on the wall for the light switch. Illuminated, he stood, his head shaking slightly, looking at the boy with a mixture of interest and embarrassment, wondering why he had invited him in. 'Diarmid . . . ?' he asked.

The boy was staring round the room. Outside, a gold pencil line divided the black sky from the black earth. In a moment that, too, would disappear.

'Oh, Toorish. It's like a shop in here. Are all these things yours?'

'Mine? Yes, yes, they're mine all right. I take it you're connected with my late housekeeper in some way. Miss Nellie Toorish.'

'Yes,' said the boy vaguely, still trying to come to grips with the room. Suddenly he remembered the letter and held it out once more towards the old man. 'This,' he said.

'Ah, yes. Thank you.'

Mr Prendergast took the letter and inspected the writing on the envelope, leaving the boy free to edge round the room touching things, picking up a book, a dusty Meissen figure, a photograph, examining them with fingers and eyes. It was only when he came to the piano and touched the bottom note that the old man reacted.

'Ah, no,' he said. 'The hands must be clean. Otherwise the notes become grimy, unpleasant to touch. Come.' The boy stood by the piano, listening to the fading growl of A. 'Diarmid Toorish. This way.'

He spoke sharply. The boy followed him out of the room and down the passage to the kitchen. The old man filled the sink with hot water, placed the Sunlight soap to hand and fetched a towel from behind the door.

'There.' He pointed to the sink and then to the boy's hands, just in case any mistake might be made. 'Wash.'

Mr Prendergast opened the letter while Diarmid washed his hands and then dried them on the towel, leaving long grey streaks as he rubbed. The old man waved the half-read letter in his direction. 'So Nellie was your aunt.'

The boy nodded and began edging towards the door.

'I'm surprised she never taught you the importance of clean hands.' He hung the towel up on the back of the door again, looped over a printed overall that had been Nellie's and a greasy Burberry that had been there for ever, unworn, unclaimed. This had been the flower room before circumstances had made it necessary to close up the basement. A glass door led out on to the flight of stone steps that arched over the area and down on to a sanded path.

'I never seen much of her. She didn't get along with Mam.'

'She had a strong personality.'

The boy wasn't interested. He held his hands up in front of the old man's face and perked his head in the direction of the other room. 'May I . . . ?'

'Run along.'

The words were neatly placed on grey lines, each loop meticulous, each bar neither too long nor too short.

Dear Sir,
begging your pardon for troubling you. My husband, J Toorish Groceries ltd, is the brother of the late Miss Nellie Toorish, RIP, as you will know, and we wondered if you would have a place for the boy in the garden, as he must leave school come June, being then almost fifteen. He can read and write, but much more for him I cannot say as he hasn't spent much time on his studies. He has no great wish to go into the shop, but I'm sure he'd learn the gardening easily. One thing to be said for him is he's honest.
yours truly
Kathleen Toorish (Mrs)

*   *   *

In the study the boy was touching the piano notes, singly at first, then in discordant combinations.

'Ah,' said the old man with irritation. He folded the letter and put it into his pocket. As he entered the room, the boy looked up and smiled.

'No, no, no, boy. You go and sit down Anywhere. I'll play something for you. It must please the ear. Make yourself at home. Just a minute.' He went over to the window and picked up the whiskey bottle from beside his chair. He looked vaguely round for glasses. 'In the kitchen, by the sink.'

They both stood looking at each other.

'Well, jump to it.'

'But what, sir?'

'Glasses, for heaven's sake, boy. Upside down, draining. And some water.'

Diarmid moved.

'A jug . . .'

'I'll find something, sir.'

'For God's sake stop calling me sir,' muttered the old man, unscrewing the top of the bottle. The need for a drink suddenly became so great that he quickly took a short, guilty swallow. The boy came back, balancing three glasses, one filled with water.

'I couldn't see a jug handy.'

'Splendid. A fellow of initiative. Here, just a little for you. Fill it up with water. When I was your age I was a veteran drinker. My father believed in teaching a man to hold his drink.'

'My father's a pioneer.'

'Poor, misguided fellow . . . The trouble with us, as I see it—Celts in general, I mean—is that we tend to exaggerate. We exaggerate the limits of both liberality and frugality. Other examples spring to mind.' He looked at the boy's blank face and waved him to a chair. 'Sit down, boy, whatsit. I'll play you something. Then we'll discuss your mother's letter. I suppose.'

He shut his eyes to play and visualized the notes of a Nocturne rising and falling on the empty page of his mind. The boy sat in the chair by the window holding carefully in his hands, as if it were alive, the faded, brown silk tassel on one end of the silk rope that tied the curtain back.

'Frederic Chopin,' said the old man, turning round from the piano, 'born in 1810. He was a Pole. Poland is a country with a history not unlike our own. Tragic and violent. I don't know when he died but it's immaterial. He was comparatively young. How do you like your drink?'

'I don't mind it.'

'And the music?'

'I didn't mind that either.'

'Well.' He got up slowly. Every joint ached if treated roughly. 'To business. I suppose you know what is in your mother's letter.' He took it out of his pocket and waved it round in the air for a moment.

'No.'

'Your mother thinks it would be a good idea if you came and worked in my garden.'

Diarmid looked up at him, totally surprised. 'Garden?'

'Mmmm. I suppose they think that Sean can teach you something. Misguided. Sean is . . . well . . .'

'Barking.'

'Well, I suppose you could put it like that. Only when the spirit moves him. Spirits, I should say. That's beside the point. I haven't the money to pay another hand.'

'I don't want to be a gardener.'

'Well, that seems to sort out that problem.' He poured himself another drink.

'I always thought I'd like to be a soldier. I suppose they wouldn't take me yet a while.'

'I think you're possibly a little young.'

'I thought the British army.'

The old man was suddenly tired of the whole thing. 'I think it's time you went home. High time you were in bed.'

Reluctantly the boy got up. He swallowed the last drains of the coloured water and looked around the room, trying to find some reasonable excuse for staying. A glass-topped table caught his eye. He moved towards it.

'Are those medals?'

'They are. Let me see now . . .' He felt in his pocket and found a two-shilling piece. 'Here. I'll write a note to your mother in the morning. Don't feel up to it now. You come up sometime tomorrow and collect it.'

The boy paid no attention to the coin. 'Yes. I'll do that. You can tell me about the medals then. OK?'

'I suppose so.' He put the money back into his pocket and brought the boy to the hall door.

* * *

The old man had forgotten his visitor by the time he reached his bedroom door. Until Clare had become ill they had shared, for traditional if no other reasons, the large room that had been his parents', the master bedroom, with the western view out over the valley. Then he had moved, without regret, into a smaller room at the end of the passage and had never bothered to move himself back. Through the window you caught glimpses, beyond the elms, of a lake created by his grandfather. No one had bothered with it for years and the patch of water was slowly being crushed by weeds and rushes. Soon there would be no echo of the sky, fair or foul, to be seen amongst the green.

Sometimes, on the landing, his feet would automatically carry him to the door of what he now thought of as Clare's room. Only the feel of the cold, unused handle in his palm would remind him and he would turn away. Clare's body had shrivelled on the bed until it had become impossible for life to continue any longer. In the last few weeks of her life her body had hardly crushed the pillow or creased the sheets. He had never touched her then, never taken her hand or bent to kiss her grey cheek. Nellie had lifted her like a baby, had insisted on sharing, with the nurse they had had to call in towards the end, all the personal chores that he preferred not to know about. When Clare finally died, Nellie had nearly gone mad with grief. She had apparently believed, for some reason the old man couldn't grasp, that this humiliating state of suspended animation was better than death.

He had felt a sense of huge relief, as if a rock that had been tied to his back had suddenly been removed. He had taken his walking stick and gone striding down the avenue to the village where he had sent a telegram to Sarah. 'Your mother died this morning. Father.' He handed the form across the counter to the post-mistress and she counted the words in silence. She made several cryptic signs on the form and then put the pen down. She blessed herself. 'God rest her soul.'

'Amen.'

'Four and six. You could have phoned it and saved yourself a walk.'
He laid a half-crown and a florin down on the counter.

'It's Nellie would miss her, I'd say.'

She crooked her hand around the money and swept it into the cash drawer. 'A sad day.'

'Yes.'

He was hypnotized by the blueness of her eyes through her glasses. What more could she want? Why would she not let him go?

'A nasty shock a telegram like that would give you.'

'She's been expecting it for some time,' he excused himself.

'Just the same, a mother's a mother.'

'Yes. Well . . .'

'I'm sure you've a lot to do. Arrangements . . .' she dismissed him, recognizing his inability to come up to scratch.

He left the post office feeling that he should have come out of the conversation better.

He slept little, three hours at the most. Some nights he was almost certain that he never slept at all. Inside his head pictures came and went, snatches of conversation or music, faces he found the greatest difficulty, if he succeeded at all, in putting names to. It was all like turning over the pages of some friend's photograph album. Here were people he believed he had never given a second thought to, places that had left him cold, irritatingly crowding out of the dark crevices of his mind and causing him irritation because they insisted on being labelled. When the effort to remember became too great he would sit up and switch on the light and read until the words, merging and unmerging in front of his inflamed eyes, became meaningless marks on the page and he would doze off, his head slumped on his chest, his mouth ungainly open. Discomfort would wake him and the process would start again. Now, though, he was no longer angered, as younger people are, by the evasiveness of sleep, merely resigned.

The morning after Diarmid's visit Mr Prendergast got up early and put clean sheets on his bed. He folded the old ones carefully and put them into a pillow case, along with four shirts and three pairs of underpants. Sean would take them away with him when he was going and bring them back clean in a few days. Outside, the lake was hidden by a grey mist being drawn up from the grass by the early morning sun. Tea and toast was all he ever had for breakfast. As he ate it he read the *Irish Times*, which a boy from the village dropped through the letter box every morning at seven thirty. The tin teapot he left bubbling on the stove as Sean, if he came, always needed a good strong mug to clear his head. If there was no sign of his arrival before the old man had finished the paper, he would know that the gardener was having one of his bad days and he would empty the mess of glutinous leaves into the bucket. This day, though, Sean banged on the door just as Mr Prendergast was folding the paper into a suitable shape for reading the leader columns. He continued to fold and, after a moment, the irritable banging was repeated. He propped the paper against the milk bottle and went and unlocked the door.

' 'Morning, Sean.' He sat down again and, leaning forward to focus, began to read.

'Sir,' was Sean's contribution.

The gardener looked as if he should have been a jockey, small and bow-legged, with a brown check cap that never came off except, presumably, if and when he went to bed. What could be seen of his face was red and swollen from exposure to the weather and alcohol. Sometimes the flesh round his eyes swelled up to such an extent that it seemed impossible for him to see through the slits that were left to him. His mug was waiting by the stove. He poured himself the full of it and stirred in three spoons of sugar. He carried around with him, like a travelling salesman carries a suitcase, a smell of alcohol and general decay. As it reached Mr Prendergast he took out a handkerchief and banged at his nose impatiently, as if his nose was inventing the smell.

Sean sucked a mouthful of tea in and held it in his mouth for twenty seconds or so before letting it slip noisily down his gullet. 'It's great old weather,' he said, 'great, so it is.' The old man unfolded the paper and cast his eyes over the letters to the editor. 'A couple a days a this and them roses will be bursting out.' He sighed dramatically. 'God rest her soul.' He repeated the tea-drinking operation. 'I hear that young fella a Toorishes was up here.'

The old man put the paper down on the table. 'Yes.'

The two men looked at each other.

'Well?'

'Well, what?'

'What did you say to him?'

'I see. You know. You are perhaps . . .'

'I just heard,' said the gardener sourly.

'It's out of the question.'

The gardener looked a shade brighter. 'I wouldn't trust him as far as I could throw him. That's just personal, mind you.' He scratched at a cheek with his brown horny nails.

'I appreciate that. You should realize better than anyone else how impossible, impossible . . .' he emphasised the word by banging on the table with his knuckles '. . . out of the question. You know what I mean. Financially.'

'That's all right, then,' said the gardener, rinsing his mug out under the tap and leaving it upside down on the draining board. 'I'll be off so. There's a pile to do at this time of year.' He went out, leaving behind him for a while his strange, unwanted smell.

Dear Mrs Toorish,

I regret that I am unable to help you by giving employment to your son. In the past, as you no doubt recall, we had gardeners and under-gardeners in abundance. Now, alas, times have changed and it is as much as I can manage to pay Sean Brady the few pounds that I do. I also feel, in all fairness to your son, who seems, on a very short acquaintance, far from stupid, that you should discuss with him any plans you may be making for his future.

I remain, etc etc formalities and so on.

He re-read it and grimaced. Most of it was irrelevant but, just the same, he folded it and pushed it into an envelope. It would surely give offence, he felt, licking the flap, put a quick stop to anyone else around thinking that maybe he was a charitable organization. He put the envelope on the mantelpiece, propped against what he had always considered to be an excessively vulgar Dresden parrot, to await Diarmid's return.

* * *

The bell jangled just as Mr Prendergast and Sean were finishing their lunch. Many years before Clare had decided that Sean, if he were not provided with one hot meal a day, would all too soon rot the inside walls of his stomach with too much undiluted alcohol and she would be without a gardener and ally. So Nellie, much against her will, had been ordered not only to provide him with a meal but to make sure that he ate it. Nellie, being someone to whom all the intricacies of social distinction were an open book, pursed her lips and said nothing but did as she was told. Since her death the old man had continued with the routine and he and the gardener sat in almost total silence, one at each end of the kitchen table, and ate in rotation the three different dishes that circumstances had forced Mr Prendergast to teach himself to cook. For all the interest either of them took, he might have saved himself a lot of trouble and merely taught himself one.

The bell rang.

Mr Prendergast turned over a page. The book flat on the table by his plate was *Sodome et Gomorrhe, Part One*. He preferred to read it in French as, in spite of the perfection of Scott Moncrieff's translation, he preferred to interpret the subtleties of Proust's prose for himself. Across the table Sean chewed as he stared out of the window. At first, in self-protection, the old man had offered him books and newspapers but the gardener had brusquely shaken his head without saying a word. It was only then that he remembered how Clare had sighed, years before, over the fact that Sean couldn't read. She had toyed momentarily with the grand idea of teaching him but the gardener hadn't the will to learn nor she the drive to teach. His own comments at the time he could no longer remember but he was sure they had been effectively demoralizing. Each day, as he placed the book carefully by his plate, taking care not to damage the spine as he flattened the pages, he would look across the table at the gardener. 'If you'll excuse me . . .'

'Fire ahead,' Sean would say.

'It's the bell.' Sean leant across the table towards his employer who had heard nothing. Nose always stuck in a book, he thought with contempt, or banging away at that old piano. No time for a soul. Hardly a civil word out of him in the course of a day. 'Mawnin', Sean, Evenin', Sean,' in his bloody West British accent. Not like herself at all. There was a real lady, even if she was English. Never a cross word, always kind, even during his bad moments. And he'd been in a queer bad way when they came first, owing to—well, best not thought of owing to what. That's when the head starts, when the eyes get tight and hot and the sound of humming wires grows and grows, filling the whole body. She took him in hand, right from the start, never a cross word, even in the winter when the day came round, never a frown, she knew what he was going through. Put his hand in the fire if she asked, only to ask and he would. 'It's the bell,' he repeated. 'I wonder who that would be now?'

The old man, disturbed by the sound of his words, looked up. He focused his eyes with difficulty. 'What's that?'

'No one calls here.'

'Thank God.'

'It's the bell.'

The bell jumped and twisted on its spring.

'Well, well,' said the old man, closing his book. 'I suppose you wouldn't like to go and see . . .'

'I'm the gardener,' refused Sean, reasonably.

'Quite.' Mr Prendergast got up and went to open the hall door.

Diarmid let go of the bell. 'You told me to come back.'

'Have you never heard of patience? I seem to remember yesterday also you . . .' He indicated the bell with his hand. 'We . . . ah . . . surely had words on the subject then. Hey, boy, what?'

'Right you be, sir. A nod's as good as a wink. Next time I'll stand outside and whistle. Here. Looka. I washed my hands this time.'

He held his hands up above his head, the startling pinkness of the palms towards the old man. He peered at them and nodded. 'You'd better come in.'

He stepped aside and the boy went past him through the door and straight across the hall to the study. At the door he turned and jerked his head, asking permission to go into the room.

'Go ahead. If you don't mind amusing yourself for a few minutes, I'll just go and finish my lunch.'

When he went back into the kitchen Sean was rinsing his plate under the tap, scratching the congealed food into the sink with a cracked nail. Mr Prendergast sat down and opened his book once more. Shining drops splashed off the plate and scattered on to the floor.

'Leave it, leave it, Sean. I'll do that.' He always had to do it, anyway. There was always this farce. Sean barged the plate down on to the draining board, wiped his polluted finger on his trouser leg, adjusted his cap, paused for a moment in his journey across the room to see if the old man would tell him who had been at the door, and then marched out and down the steps. Mr Prendergast watched his ungainly progress.

The treads of the steps were so narrow that the normal foot, even when placed sideways on them, overflowed dangerously. He watched how the sand from the path scattered out from under the heavy feet, some of it on to the edges of the grass, which was ragged with uncared-for springtime growth. He was heading for the potting shed where he would have a little smoke, probably a little drink, possibly a little sleep, at any rate strengthen himself for an afternoon's work out in the weather.

While the kettle was on the boil, the old man tidied up the kitchen, rewashing Sean's plate with his own, drying them carefully and putting them away. Then, reaching down two cups, he made some Nescafé and carried it into the study.

Diarmid had opened the display table and was standing by the window with a medal in his hand. As he heard the old man come into the room he asked, without turning round: 'Is this yours?'

Mr Prendergast crossed the room and looked over his shoulder. The boy had square hands with short, thick fingers and badly bitten nails. The knuckles were swollen and scarred from winter chilblains. Hands of an unmitigated plainness but they held the medal with enormous care.

'No. That one was my grandfather's. A noble fighting man. The Crimea, I think that was. Yes. That's right.'

'Oh.' The voice was slightly disappointed.

'Ever heard of the Crimea?'

'No.'

'Tttt. What do they teach children in schools these days?'

'It's like I told you. I don't go much to school.' He threw his head back and laughed loudly. 'Maybe they're all learning about the Crimee, or whatever you said, this very minute. I doubt it, though. They never teach you anything interesting. What did he do?'

'Who?'

'The fella got this.'

'I've no idea. Killed a hundred Russians with his bare hands, no doubt. He was rather a flamboyant gentleman.'

'Flamboyant?'

Mr Prendergast put down the coffee cups and took a miniature from the table. He held it out for the boy to look at. 'Here.'

Tiny diamonds glittered round the frame.

'They don't wear clothes like that now.'

'It's probably just as well, they'd be a bit conspicuous on the battle-field. The whole technique of war has changed since then.'

'I could see myself in that.'

'Shot dead by a long distance marksman with a telescopic lens. Drink up your coffee before it gets cold.'

'But what sort of thing would you have to do? That's what I'd like to know.' He transferred his attention back to the medal again.

'A moment,' said the old man. He went over to the bookshelves and peered at a row of peeling spines. 'Drink it up,' he repeated rather irritably.

The boy paid no attention.

He took down a copy of Tennyson and blew along the top. Dust drifted away like a wisp of smoke. 'Listen to me, now. This is what you want to know.' The skin on his hands was almost as dry and transparent as the rustling pages. He stood by the fireplace and began to read.

> Half a league, half a league,
> Half a league onward,
> All in the valley of death . . .

The boy stared out across the terrace at his own valley. On the higher slopes the golden flame of the gorse was spreading through the stone-spattered fields. When he was quite sure that the old man had finished, he moved over to the table and carefully put the medal back where it came from. 'Volleyed and thundered . . .' he whispered.

'Well—? What did you think of that? Isn't that what you were after?'

'Which of them is yours?' Diarmid looked down at the relics.

Mr Prendergast put the book down and went over. They looked like tombstones lying there on uncared-for green velvet grass.

He touched a cross with one finger. 'That one?'

'Yes.'

The metal was cold, made, he felt, from the cold metal that killed. 'I never knew you were a soldier.'

'A temporary fit of madness. A situation arose when it was impossible . . . a lot of people died. It was to have been the war to end all wars.'

'Were you very brave? What did you do?'

The old man picked up the cross and put it into the boy's hand. 'I was young. When you're young you think you'll never die. It makes you act in a reckless way. Even when everything around . . . everyone . . . Some people call it lack of imagination, others, courage.'

'You must have done something.' The boy's voice was impatient.

'I survived. That, I suppose, is worth commemorating with a bit of decorated metal.'

'You're a terrible old cod.'

There was a moment's rather frightening silence and then the old man began to laugh.

'An old cod. That's a good one. Nobody's ever called me that before.'

Weakened by his first laughter in years he groped for the sofa and sat down. The room seemed to tremble with alarm. The boy, embarrassed by his own words, turned over the cross in his hand and stared at the back of it. The laughter came in short jerks. Mr Prendergast clutched at his chest; the unaccustomed exercise was causing him a certain amount of pain. Discomfort, as they would insist on calling it nowadays.

'You have a point. That's just about what I am.'

'I'm sorry,' muttered the boy without looking up. 'It just slipped out. You made me mad by being so . . .' he thought for a moment '. . . fancy. I like to understand.' He smiled suddenly looking directly into the old man's face. 'Cannons to right of them, cannons to left of them volleyed and thundered . . . I understand that OK.'

Mr Prendergast leaned back against a cushion. His head was throbbing and his heart seemed to be pulsing in a space that was far too small for it. 'I am too old for laughter.'

Diarmid picked up the nearest cup of coffee and carried it over to him. 'Here.'

'Thank you, boy.' He straightened himself with effort and took a mouthful. It was pretty disgusting and barely luke. Much better to drink tea, really, than this ersatz rubbish that always made you slightly queasy as it plunged into the digestive system. Before, Smiths of the Green had posted a pound of Continental Roast beans once a fortnight and Nellie had ground them, as the need arose, in a green, box-like grinder with a brass handle. As she turned the handle, the house was always filled with the friendly smell of coffee beans. Now there seemed little point. He noticed, as he put his cup down, the boy's fingers caressing the surface of the medal. 'Put it away,' he ordered abruptly. 'It's not something I really care to be reminded about.'

The boy nodded. He put the cross away and shut the top of the case. 'It's a great gadget, that. For putting things in. Like a museum. I went to a museum once, and I up in Dublin with my auntie. They had cases like this all over the place. A lot of coins and things like that. Do you find coins interesting?'

'I can't say I do.'

'She didn't want to stay long. It was only because it was raining we went in at all.'

'Perhaps you'll go again some day.'

'I never liked my auntie.'

It was the time of the day the old man usually spent sleeping. About an hour he slept, sitting in the high-backed chair by the window, his head dropped on his chest, his mouth fallen open, so that when he woke his neck was always stiff and his mouth was filled with a taste of stale air. He could now feel his eyes becoming heavy. A yawn arose inside him. It was well past his accustomed time. He waved a hand towards the mantelpiece. 'The letter for your mother. You'll find it up there.'

'No bother yet a while,' said the boy. 'I can't go home just yet. Amn't I meant to be at school?'

'I must sleep. Old age . . .' he began, almost apologetically.

Diarmid smiled. 'I won't bother you.'

'I don't know what I should say.'

'I wouldn't bother saying anything.'

'Save my breath, hey?'

'That's right.'

Surprisingly, the old man went asleep.

He slept about his statutory hour. He lifted his head with difficulty and stared at the pearl-like strings of cloud moving slowly across the sky, then at the boy in his chair, his head bent in concentration over the copy of Tennyson. He looked up as the old man moved.

'You've slept a long time. It's near on four. I'll have to be going soon.' He shut the book.

'Don't you expect to be discovered some day?'

'There's not much they can do. Only hit me. I'm used to that.' He grinned for a moment. 'My father hasn't a very strong arm.'

'The so-called authorities tend to have stronger arms than parents.'

'Ah, who cares.' He put the book on top of a pile that the old man had left beside the chair at some time or other. 'So, if you'll give me the letter for Mam, I'll be getting along.'

'Of course.' Mr Prendergast got up slowly.

The boy watched, his face wrinkling up with the old man's effort. 'I'd hate to be old.'

'Some people think it's better than being dead. There's no alternative.'

'What do you think?'

Mr Prendergast took the letter from the mantelpiece. He stood looking at it for a moment. The all-enveloping, unconquerable shakes were creeping over him again. 'I'm pretty tired these days.'

'Tired of being alive?'

'I think, rather, tired by being alive.'

The boy came over and took the letter from the trembling hand. 'You could always do away with yourself.'

'The idea doesn't actually appeal to me.'

'Sammy Ryan hanged himself the other week. My friend saw him just after they'd cut him down. His face was black. He was a bit wanting. Mam said it was a mortal sin.'

'I think I'll take my chance with the rest.'

'What did you say in the letter?'

'That is between myself and your parents. If they see fit . . .'

'They. She, more like. He can't even switch on the TV without her allowing him. "Morris, do this; Morris, do that. Morris, fetch in the coal, wouldya. Morris, don't put your shoes on the covers. Morris, wouldya punish the child. Morris . . ." Ah, hell.' His eyes were hard golden stones.

'Well, I think . . .'

'Last evening when I got home she was in the front room. Her head was bulging with big iron curlers.' He waved his hands around his head descriptively. 'You always know Thursday. Curlers. Ready for confession on Fridays. "Where were ya? What kept ya? What did the old fella (that's you) say?" '

'I really don't want . . .'

Nothing was going to stop the boy. His body had become possessed by the metal-headed fury. The old man resigned himself.

' "If he said nothing what kept you so long? The piana. Nellie said he was always banging on that, true enough. No, you can't watch TV. Get on up to bed, I'm sick of the sight of you." ' He came to himself once more and looked apologetically at Mr Prendergast. 'It's like that,' he said.

'We all have our problems.'

'I'd better go.'

'Yes.'

'Can I come and see you another day?'

'I suppose, if you want to . . .'

'It won't be over the weekend. They make me work in the shop on Saturdays, and Sunday's there's Mass and I have to stay at home after that because my Granny comes.'

'Run along home, boy. I've had enough for one day.'

Weary of conversation, Mr Prendergast sat down at the piano, clenching and unclenching his hands to try and make them fit for playing. The boy let himself out without another word.

Once out of sight of the windows of the house he stopped and, taking his penknife from his pocket, he carefully opened the letter and read what was inside. It was not a difficult operation, he had done it many times before.

✿ ✿ ✿

Friday was the night for choir practice. Mr Prendergast pulled himself together with a strong drink before going round to the yard and getting out the car. The windscreen was yellow with age. He took his handkerchief from his pocket and rubbed the glass in front of the steering wheel. It made very little difference. Sean's bicycle leant against the yard wall still, but there was no sign of the gardener himself. Mr Prendergast backed carefully out of the garage and turned in the yard. The cobbles were covered with a fine coating of moss. The window of what had been the harness room had been without glass for many years. The evening ground mist was filtering its way between the tumbledown buildings. The old man hadn't noticed desolation since his settling in.

It only took a couple of minutes to get to the church but these last few months he had preferred to drive. He felt less vulnerable, as if he were not really leaving the house at all. The rhododendrons were purple and white and crimson, massive flowers with stamens held out expectantly. They sickened him. One day, he had always threatened, he'd have them all burnt down, rooted out. The inevitability of nature disgusted him, the ever-turning wheel. Clare had always been emotionally moved by it, had made idiotic breathless remarks in springtime. He thought suddenly that a surprising thing had happened during the course of their lives together. At the end he had known less about her than he had thought he had known in the beginning. Things had got lost on the journey, rather like the odd suitcases, or rugs, his father's racing glasses, all things that had mysteriously disappeared in the course of their travelling.

He turned sharply in at the church gate, scraping the front mudguard along the granite wall. 'Damn.' At the vestry door he got out and looked at the long white scrape on the paint. Little glitters of mica lay on the wound. 'Damn.'

The Rector materialized beside him, like some rather unpleasant spirit in his cassock which, much to the old man's disapproval, he had taken to wearing in the street. Ridiculously flamboyant, almost verging on High. Mother would have spoken strongly. She had taken a very strong stand when some Rector with advanced ideas had changed from

The Church Hymnal to A and M, or was it vice versa? Whichever it had been, mother had adamantly refused to move with the times and all members of her house who attended the Church of Ireland took their hymn books from the hall table each Sunday and would spend most of the service fluttering through the gold-edged pages trying desperately to find the words they were supposed to be singing. The old lady herself never opened her mouth in church, except to speak, with great clarity, the expected responses. She would pray with her gloved hands placed palm to palm, like a Botticelli angel, and her pale face lifted slightly heavenward.

'Well, well, well, old man. Damaging church property?'

'I think, rather, that church property's damaged my car.'

'Took the corner a trifle sharp, I fear.'

'Mmm.'

'No great damage done, though.' The Rector inclined, rather than leant, towards the mudguard. 'One's eyes start playing up as one gets on.'

'My eyes are perfectly all right.' He had all his life lied to James Evers.

The Rector put his hand on the old man's shoulder and drew him towards the church. 'We wouldn't like to lose our organist.'

Mr Prendergast wrenched his shoulder free from the Rector's grip. 'If you'll excuse me, I came early to put in a little bit of practice.'

His footsteps echoed in the empty church. The Rector stood by the door watching as he settled himself at the organ, switched the light on, rubbed at his fingers for a moment. He shut his eyes so that he couldn't see the watching figure. Pretentious blithering fool, in his fancy dress. Incompetent shepherd of a dwindling flock. Ten on a good day. His hands reached out and the first notes of a fugue touched the unused air. Son of a local Bishop, always asked to nursery tea and then later to tennis. Not enough gumption to do anything but follow in father's footsteps. Never yet managed to preach a decent sermon. Too ironic to come back and find James established here, of all places. Clare had talked gardening with them and done the expected good deeds. Chatted over teacups. All dross. Why torment yourself with face to face confrontations? Why try to communicate? This terrible post-war urge.

Everything that had to be said was there, on the bookshelves, dancing on the staves, on canvas. Find your own salvation there. If that was what you felt the urge to do.

Eileen Evers clattered in to the music. She came at him from behind and leaned her tissue paper cheek against his. She smelt faintly of witch hazel. He took his hands from the keys.

'Charles, dear.' She straightened up, the salutation over.

He turned towards her and smiled with civility. Every Friday evening it was the same. They eyed each other like boxers.

'We must get together and have a good chat sometime soon.'

He smiled thinly in reply.

'Why don't you come back with us this evening and have a bite? Pot luck. Please do. James would be so pleased.'

The old man lifted his hands in a helpless gesture. 'I must decline.'

'Nonsense, Charles.' Her voice had become slightly shrill and domineering. 'Why must you decline? You become more and more ridiculous every day. Of course you'll come.'

Silently he shook his head.

'We worry about you.'

'I assure you there's no need.'

'After all, you are one of James's oldest friends. And, of course, dear Clare.' She sighed.

'Absolutely none whatsoever. How many times do I have to say it?'

The door at the other end of the church creaked and voices could be heard. Mr Prendergast reached for the hymnal with relief. Mrs Evers, with a charming smile, turned to meet her husband's parishioners.

The Rector himself came out of the vestry and switched on the lights in the choir. Some narcissi at the foot of the pulpit, that had looked and smelt so sweet last Sunday, drooped pitifully. The old man played a few experimental chords and then folded his hands in his lap and waited until the choir was ready to begin.

'And how is dear Sarah? What's the news from London these days?' The Rector spoke to him in the porch as he was hurrying out. Down the other end of the village the bell of the Catholic church struck nine times. Automatically the Rector took his watch from his pocket and looked at it. He adjusted the minute hand a fraction. 'Irritating.' He put the watch back where it had come from. His Christian hands were long and pale against his cassock. Fragile with age. They could have been the hands of a musician, thought the old man, if only the old fool had had anything stirring in his head.

'I hear from Sarah very seldom. She leads a very busy life.'

'Surely a visit from her is overdue?'

'It's not much fun for her over here. She doesn't really know anyone. There's, ah, not much to do. Young people like . . .'

'It's her home.'

The old man looked startled for a moment at the severity of the Rector's voice. 'Oh, no,' he said. 'It's never been that.'

'Well, you know what I mean.'

'She'll come if she wants to.'

'Why don't you drop her a line?'

They had reached Mr Prendergast's car. He opened the door. 'I think she's as well off where she is.' He hesitated, not quite liking to get into the car with the Rector still fluttering beside him. 'I like to be alone.' He said it as an explanation, not a rebuke.

The Rector pursed his lips and shook his head slightly. 'Of late, my old friend, you have become, how shall I put it . . . ?'

'Put it how you like. I am old, James. We are both old. We have a right to behave as we wish. No longer to be bound by . . . ah . . . conventions.'

'But friendship?'

'Think clearly, Rector. At no time in our lives has there been friend-ship between us.' He got into the car and groped for the key in a panic. The engine began to vibrate. He reached out and closed the door between the Rector and himself. The white, Christian hands hung limp, like the dead flowers at the foot of the pulpit. Behind him the windows flushed and flamed, reflecting the western sky. He edged the car gently forward.

Eileen came out of the porch and stood beside her husband. He spoke some quiet words to her out of the corner of his mouth. She raised her hand, cheerfully high, and waved to Mr Prendergast.

I'd better be careful, he thought as he approached the gate; another bump and they'll have my licence removed.

✻   ✻   ✻

It was several days before Diarmid turned up again. The door stood open and he walked in without waiting for a yes or no. He dawdled his way through the hall. A grandfather clock that had stopped a few days after Nellie's death caught his fancy. He opened the case door and set the pendulum swinging. The figures on the face were brass and the ornate hands pointed permanently to twenty-five past three. There was a sound from the kitchen. Quickly he shut the clock. The pendulum moved slower without his helping hand. He went on down the passage to the kitchen.

The two men sat at the table, Mr Prendergast behind the paper, Sean, unprotected, chewing with great care. His teeth gave him trouble. They seemed to have shrunk in their sockets and sometimes it felt dangerous to eat. He looked over at the boy as he came in. The old man put the paper down on the floor.

'Well, well, well.'

'Hello.'

'Would you look what the wind blew in,' said Sean disagreeably.

Diarmid ignored him. 'I've brought you this.' Carefully he took from his pocket a large, luminous-looking duck egg. The shell was patterned like the moon's surface with ridges and bumps. He held it out towards Mr Prendergast.

'Well . . .' repeated the old man.

'Who'dya pinch that from?' Sean mopped round his plate with a piece of sliced loaf.

Mr Prendergast took the egg gingerly into his hand. It had a smear of mud or excrement on it.

'A duck egg.'

'Not a duck or a hen, if it comes to that, to be seen around your back yard, anyroad,' commented Sean through the bread and gravy.

'It's a present.'

'So I gather. I am most touched and grateful. I used to be very partial to ducks' eggs. It's been a long time. Thank you, boy, hey.'

'Scallawag. It's a good larrup on the backside you need, not thanks.' Sean got up and carried his plate over to the sink. He dropped it in with a clatter.

'Never mind him.'

'Oh him; sure, why would I mind him?'

'You steal one flower out of my garden and you'll mind me. Or go bringing your friends up and galloping over the place. Let me warn you. Here and now.'

His eyes were really bad today, the old man thought; sunk right back into his head, rimmed with moist red. He must be coming up for one of his turns. As if the old man's thought had reached him the gardener groaned slightly, a disconcerting noise, and then took from his pocket a handkerchief of sorts and wiped, most carefully, one red slit and then the other. He examined the handkerchief with interest and groaned again before returning it to his pocket.

Diarmid paid no attention to the groans. 'You're not the boss around here, anyway.'

' "Mind the garden, Sean," the mistress said with her dying breath,' lied the gardener.

The boy looked unimpressed.

Mr Prendergast put the egg down carefully on a saucer. 'I think we've had enough.'

'And mind it I will, 'till I drop in me tracks and there's some that appreciate what others do for them and some that don't.'

'Oh, I do. I couldn't have managed without you.'

The gardener smiled fiercely in the general direction of Diarmid, pulled his cap down over the sad, red, slits of eyes and went out into the garden. They watched him go down the steps in silence.

'He has turns. His life hasn't been all it might have been. You mustn't pay too much attention to him.'

'He's an old sod. I don't know how you stick him round the place.'

'Ah, well yes,' said the old man. 'How long . . . ?'

'I had in mind to stay till school was over. If it's all the same to you.'

'I have no plans.'

'Will I put the kettle on for coffee so?'

'That would be very kind.' He began to clear the table. 'What was your mother's reaction to my letter?'

'She said nothing to me at all but I heard her say to me Dad, "I might have saved the ink."' He lit the gas. 'They're in a right way, now. They don't know what to do with me at all.'

'They must be worried.'

'Worried in case they can't get rid of me. They think if they have me in the shop I'll be getting into trouble, dipping my hand in the till, adding up the bills wrong, eating and not earning.'

'I think you exaggerate.'

'They say as much to my face. My father should know the ropes, anyway. Doesn't he nick the petty cash himself a half a dozen times a day. She keeps him very short, I suppose he's not to be blamed.'

'And you?'

'Huh?'

He had to stand on his toes to reach the Nescafé tin which was on a shelf above the stove.

'You. Would you, ah, be carrying on like that?'

'I don't steal money.'

'Just things like duck eggs?' suggested the old man.

'Where will I find a spoon?'

Mr Prendergast handed him one out of the basin. The boy dried it carefully before measuring the powder into each cup.

'I'll take it back if you don't want it.'

'Oh, no. I didn't mean that. I was only making a dirty crack.' He looked at the boy frowning, as he worked the coffee and a little milk together with the spoon.

'You look like a little old man, frowning away there.'

The boy looked up at him and smiled. 'And you're behaving like a little boy, making dirty cracks.'

They both laughed.

'I only pinch things because I like them. Not because I need them. Isn't that all right?'

Mr Prendergast reached for the whiskey bottle and poured a small tot into each cup. 'It improves the taste. I refuse to make pronouncements on the rights and wrongs of stealing.' He put the bottle away and took a large bunch of keys from a hook near the door. He peered at the labels. The writing on some of them was so faded that it was impossible to read more than a letter here and there.

The kettle boiled and Diarmid filled the cups with water. The smell of warm whiskey rose with the steam.

'Bring the cups, boy. I've something to show you.'

The first flight of stairs had tarnished brass rods holding the carpet in place. Nellie used, once a week, to slide each one out from its slots and polish it golden and for a while the hall and stairway would smell of Brasso. She sang always as she did this job. Sometimes now, as the old man climbed the stairs, her voice came into his head. 'Come back to Erin, mavourneen, mavourneen. Come back, machree, to the land of your birth . . .' The cloth would squeak as she rubbed it up and down the rod and the smell of the polish flew up your nose and made you sneeze if you happened to be passing.

The top flight had only tacks which held the remaining rags of carpet to the floor. Up at the top, the long passage between the locked doors was lit by two half-moon windows, one at each end of the passage, perfectly symmetrical. Long creeper fronds tapped against them now, incessantly, impatiently, wanting in . . . The light in the passage was constant twilight. The smell was musty and all the time the tiny noises made by unused rooms brushed your ears. The end room on the right had been the nursery. Three windows to the south-west caught the afternoon sunlight in tangles of spiders' webs. Everywhere that dust could lie was filmed with grey. The chairs were sheeted. A large grey bear with one eye stared down from the top of a cupboard.

'It was the nursery. The playroom,' he explained, seeing the boy look puzzled. 'Look.' He opened a cupboard. Inside on the dusty shelves, neatly stacked as if only yesterday some creaking, crackling nanny had tidied them away, were boxes of soldiers and equipment. Each box was carefully labelled, spidery thin-nib, black writing, starting to fade now after many years. Black Watch, Lancers, Gurkhas, Field Artillery, Red Cross, Foot Guards, Dragoons, Légionnaires. Miscellaneous. 'My brother and I were great collectors.'

The boy moved to the cupboard and opened one of the boxes. He stared, fascinated, at the soldiers.

'We were very proud of them. Mind you, they're a bit out of date now. It must be almost sixty years.' He nodded to himself and whispered quietly '. . . or more.'

Diarmid was lining some men up along the edge of a shelf.

'. . . More. A bit more than sixty years since the last ones were bought. He was older than I.'

'What was his name?' He didn't sound really interested. He opened another box.

'Alexander. After my father.' The boy picked out a galloping horseman. 'That's an Uhlan. Ever heard of them?'

'No.'

'A very famous German regiment. There's a book downstairs. It will tell you all about them. We'll have a look later.'

'Thanks. Where is he now?'

'Who?'

'Alexander. He must be very old. Or is he . . . ?' He paused discreetly.

'He's gone a long time ago.'

'Gone?'

'1915.'

'Oh.' He began to root in another box.

'I was on leave when we heard. It was in the summer. Nobody liked opening telegrams in those days. I was here, so we knew . . .'

'Knew what?'

'Knew it was he.'

'It might have been something else.'

'It never was.'

Mother and Father had been out, somewhere, couldn't recall, irrelevant, anyway, and the telegram had lain on a silver salver in the hall for several hours. He had gone to his room and lain, waiting, on his bed. Alexander's voice sang in his head—'Röslein, röslein, röslein rot, röslein auf der heiden . . .' And as he heard the car door slam and his mother's laughter on the steps, the singing stopped. He ran down the passage to the bathroom and vomited into the basin.

'Your hands are shaking.'

'I must sit down a minute. It's . . . the stairs.'

The boy pulled the dust sheet off the nearest chair. A grey cloud rose into the air. Imperceptibly it settled again, this time also on the intruders. Mr Prendergast lowered himself into the chair. He clasped his shaking hands between his knees in the hope that the pressure would force the convulsive movements to stop. No thought of Alexander had entered his head for years and now it was as if the young man was there, inside his mind, tearing down walls expertly built by time.

'Wer reitet so spät durch Nacht und Wind? Es ist der Vater mit seinem Kind . . .' As the walls fell, the song grew louder. The old man's fingers trembled now for the piano. He had never mastered the accompaniment then.

'No, no, boy.'

'I'm sorry. I'll try again.'

'You must practise. I keep telling you.'

'I do. But when you sing, it eludes me. Listen, I can do it.' He played a few phrases.

'It won't do. Honestly, Chas, it's terrible. Mother'll have to play.'

'Alec . . .'

'Not a word. Mother.'

When Mother moved it sounded as if someone was unwrapping a parcel of tissue paper. She came in from the garden at Alexander's call. She always came at Alexander's call.

'Well? What is it?'

'You must play for me. He is impossible.'

She swept Charles off the piano stool with a hand. 'You must practise more, my darling.' She sat down in his place and quickly began pulling her rings off and clattering them into a porcelain bowl on a table nearby, as if they were worthless pebbles. When her hands were bare she opened and closed her fingers several times and smiled up at her son. The old man felt the burn of jealousy in his stomach and remembered the smell of burning leaves that drifted past him as he stepped out of the window into the cool evening.

'It must have been autumn.'

'What?' Diarmid was staring up at him from the floor, where he was sitting surrounded by boxes.

'I'm sorry. I was very far away.'

'Sometimes I think you're a bit gone, you know.' He examined each man with care before putting it on the ground. 'I never seen soldiers as good as these before.'

'They don't make them like that nowadays. There's a shop in London that would give you a lot of money for these, in fact. If you go over to that cupboard by the window you'll find a book called . . . *Famous Battles* . . . something like that. It's full of maps and plans. We . . . he and I used to recreate them . . .' he gestured with his still shaking hands. 'All the floor was our battlefield. We used to take it in turns to have the winning army.'

'That would be a great idea.'

'Somewhere there's a box full of generals, field marshals. Even, if I remember aright, Le Petit Caporal himself.'

'Who's he when he's at home?'

'One of the greatest generals of all time. A rogue, mind you. A villain, rather. Alexander, Caesar and Napoleon Bonaparte. If you hand me down that box up there in the corner, I'll show you.'

The boy put the box on the old man's knee. He sat down on the floor again and watched Mr Prendergast's hands carefully as he picked his way through the great men of war.

'Yes, indeed, I suppose these probably have a considerable value nowadays. The Lord Protector. I'd forgotten we had him.' He held him out, warts and all, in his fingers towards the boy. 'Alexander had great admiration for Cromwell. It was one of the many subjects on which we differed.'

'Is that Cromwell? Can I see?'

'I thought that name might strike a chord in your peasant skull.' He handed Cromwell over to the boy.

'He was an ugly-looking git, anyway. Why did your brother like him?'

'He liked efficiency and order. He thought that perfection could only be achieved through discipline.'

The boy thought about that. 'I suppose that's what's in the back of their minds when they larrup you at school.'

'I doubt it, boy. I doubt if much is in their heads at all.'

'I'd laugh to see Mr Moyne's face if he heard you say that.'

'There. That's Napoleon.' The Emperor stood, feet slightly apart, the hand stuck between the coat buttons, shoulders hunched, his peasant face brooding, in the palm of the old man's hand. 'He was a giant.'

The boy looked startled. 'A giant?'

'Metaphorically. A giant among men. He ruled almost all of Europe until one day he went too far.'

'What happened?'

'As a general, he overstretched his lines. As a man, he misjudged the character of his enemy. They were desperate and cunning. They lured him deeper and deeper into Russia, stretching his lines to the limits. They knew that, inevitably, Nature would be on their side. He thought he'd won the prize and then, literally overnight, they broke him. They say he got into his coach in Moscow and didn't get out until he reached Paris. That's romancing, of course. But he was lucky. Thousands and thousands never saw France again, let alone Paris.'

'Was that the end of him?'

'The beginning of the end. He was a hard man to finish off. Beaten in the end by an English army with an Irish general . . . a bit of help from the Germans.' He peered into the box. 'I don't recall that we had him.'

'And if he hadn't gone to Moscow, he'd have gone on ruling almost all of Europe?'

'I don't suppose so, really. It was just a matter of time. With time every tyrant's thinking becomes clouded. Had he thought more clearly he might have conquered Ireland, but he was preoccupied with things he thought were more important.'

'I might be a general.'

'You never can tell. It's an advantage to have been to school from time to time. Acquire some knowledge. It always comes in handy.'

'I can read, can't I? I can teach myself. What I want to know, not just what they decide they want me to know.'

'Unfortunately, we don't necessarily know what we need to know until it's too late. Like I said, if Napoleon had known more about the Russians, he'd never have gone all the way to Moscow. Into the trap.'

Diarmid took Napoleon from the old man and examined him closely. 'One thing I do know, anyway, is not to stretch my lines too far.' The old man laughed. 'I don't think much of his uniform.'

'He was never a flamboyant dresser.'

'That man downstairs, in the picture, was he a general?'

'No, alas. Merely a flamboyant dresser.'

'Flamboyant.' He tasted the word in his mouth, like a new piece of food.

'Peacocks,' suggested the old man.

The boy put Napoleon carefully on the shelf, not on the floor with the commonalty. 'I'll have a look at them all first and then, tell you what, we'll have smashing wars. Like you and he did.' He went back to the boxes.

Mr Prendergast watched him for a while then fell asleep, a sleep without dreams, without alarms. When he awakened, Diarmid was standing on a chair replacing some boxes on the top shelf. His face, hands and adolescent wrists were caught in the gilding sunshine. Benvenuto, thought the old man. Pure rascal.

'You snored,' said the boy.

'My wife always used to say so.'

'If my wife snores, I'll kick her out of bed. The noise coming out of Mam and Dada's room would waken the dead.' He stepped down from the chair. The old man saw that his face was streaked with dust.

'You're filthy, boy. What's the time? You'd better wash before you go home or your mother'll wonder what you've been up to.'

'Tomorrow will you show me that book?'

'What book is that?'

'The one about battles.'

'I suppose so.'

'I might come up a bit earlier.' The old man started to push himself up from the chair. 'You wouldn't mind, would you? Here, let me give you a hand.'

'I can manage, boy. I am not totally incapacitated yet. Though no doubt my time will come.'

'But would you mind?'

'What time you come? That's entirely up to you.'

'I could do a few things for you.'

'I don't think that . . .'

'Around the place, like.'

'It's very kind of you . . .'

'There's always things to do.'

The boy looked at Mr Prendergast and laughed as he watched him straighten himself carefully.

'We all grow old,' said the old man, with reasonable good humour.

39

'I won't.'

'Permit me to laugh this time.'

'What happened to him?' The boy nodded his head towards Napoleon. 'Did he die a hero's death?'

'No.'

'Oh.' The boy was taken aback.

'He was exiled. He spent the last six years of his life a prisoner.'

'He could have killed himself.'

'He could. You seem obsessed with the idea of people killing themselves. It is, as you know, a mortal sin.'

'It's always there for you to do. If you don't like the sort of life you have to live. Have to.'

'Your life is supposed to be in the holy hands of God, for Him to do what He likes with it. You are not supposed to take these decisions for yourself.'

'What's the time?'

The old man took his watch from his pocket. 'Getting on for five.'

'Mother of God, I'll be murdered. She'll ask me questions.' He put his hands over his ears, as if to protect them from the battery of shrill words.

'What'll you say?' He gave the boy a gentle shove towards the door.

'I'll think of something. I'm a great hand at inventing.'

They walked along the passage. A fly buzzed somewhere, caught irrevocably in a spider's web.

* * *

'I got kept in, Ma. I'm sorry I'm late.'

'Your tea's ruined. What were you up to this time? Nothing ordinary, I'll be bound.'

'It was spelling, Ma. I hadn't . . . I'd forgotten me stint.'

'The same old story. Wait till your father hears you were in trouble again and he'll give you what for.'

* * *

There was a distinct smell of mice, the old man thought. Perhaps a cat. But what, in the end of all, did it matter if the mice took over. When he was a child the passage had smelt of beeswax and friar's balsam. Both he and Alexander had been chesty and small lamps filled with friar's balsam had burned in their rooms during the winter. Somehow, even though the windows were wide open all through the summer months, the heavy smell had always lingered in the passage. He wondered why he had stayed on in this white elephant of a place after Clare's death. He should have taken something more compact, more suitable to his way of living. Sarah, at the time, had suggested that he move to London but the idea hadn't appealed to him. Didn't appeal to him now, either. Nor did the idea of the tentative and probably painful gestures that would have to be made if he and his daughter were to create even the most formal relationship.

'I think, in fact, I'd be safer to say I went along the river with Mick and never looked at the time. Mick is my friend, only I'd never trust him with my life.'

'Can you swim?' asked the old man.

They stood on the steps. There was a little breeze which lifted Diarmid's hair gently from his forehead and let it fall again. The rooks were having their afternoon fling and the sky seemed full of their ungainly bodies.

'I've never tried. We just fish a bit and throw stones. Skim, you know, if we can.' He skimmed an imaginary stone across the grass and through a rose bed.

'We used to swim in the lake.' He nodded over beyond the trees. 'In the summer we used to spend nearly all day down there. We had a boat and we used to take all our clothes off and dive in from it.'

The boy looked him up and down. The old man realized with embarrassment that he was trying to visualize what he must look like naked.

'A long time ago.' he said, in the direction of the rooks. 'We were boys.' Diarmid nodded. 'If I got Sean to cut the rushes back a bit in places, you and your friends could use it, if you wanted. With the summer coming on.'

'That would be great. I'll cut the rushes, though. I'd like to do that, if you want them cut.'

'I can always get Sean . . .'

'I'd like to.'

'You'll need a sickle.'

'I'll get one of them all right.'

'I'm sure if we asked Sean . . .'

'I wouldn't ask that git for anything if he was the last person left on earth.' He held out his hand. 'I've had a great afternoon.'

Formally and awkwardly they shook hands. Diarmid, with a wave of both arms, leapt down the five steps at once and ran down the avenue. At the bend he turned and waved again but the old man had gone into the house and closed the door. The boy whipped across the grass, bending low as he ran. He took his penknife from his pocket and cut three newly opened rose buds. The outside petals were brilliant red and the hearts were yellow. As he went on down the avenue he examined them closely. Their smell was very sweet.

'Flamboyant,' he whispered and put them carefully inside his jacket.

* * *

'That one is here again.'

It was already eleven thirty and Sean had only just arrived. He had brought the groceries from the village and left them on the kitchen table. Hearing the sound of the piano, he had put his head round the study door to announce this piece of information.

'I thought you weren't coming.'

'I'm not feeling too good.'

You could smell the drink from him. Each time he moved the smell intensified and then faded slightly until the next gesture. His clothes must have steeped all night in whiskey, thought the old man. He got up from the piano.

'Do you want a cup of tea?'

'I didn't like to let you down.'

'I appreciate that. I do, indeed.'

'I couldn't keep tea down.'

'Coffee, perhaps?'

'Nothing.' The humming of the wires always started gently but it inevitably filled his head with a sound that nothing could drown, not even alcohol. 'Couldn't bloody keep anything down at all.'

The old man looked out of the window. The haze that had covered the valley in the early morning had almost completely lifted and everything dazzled in the sun.

'We're really in for a heat-wave.' The gardener only grunted. His head was splitting. 'Well, if you won't have a cup of something . . .'

'Amn't I after telling you, that one is here again.'

'Who?'

'That Toorish boy. I seen him nipping through the rosiedandrons and I coming up the avenue.'

Mr Prendergast sighed. 'Just leave him, Sean. He'll co no harm.'

'I'm sorry I interfered.' He withdrew, his face sick and angry. By lunchtime he would be in a black mood and round about five he would grope his way from side to side down the avenue and along the road to his hovel, that was the only possible name for it, and that would be the last time that anyone would see of him for up to a week. Sometimes it had even been two weeks and he would come back thin and crazy-looking, his hands shaking so much that he was hardly able to lift the fork to his mouth. Nellie had always raged on and on at him as he sat there opposite her, desperately trying to eat, for the sake of peace, but the old man left him alone to recover his equilibrium as best he could.

Mr Prendergast took his blackthorn stick from the hall stand and went outside. It was safer to take it these days if he intended walking any distance at all. He walked slowly down the avenue and branched off along the path through the rhododendrons that led to the lake.

Diarmid had taken his trousers off and thrown them on the grass. He was standing up to his waist in water attacking the rushes. The sickle flashed like the sun on the water as it rose and fell.

'Good morning, boy.'

The boy looked up at him. 'It's muddy.'

'Always been like that round the edge. It's clear further out. Aren't you cold?'

'No. Look what I found.'

He moved slowly along the bank. Under the streaks of mud the old man could see that his legs were white, like they'd never before seen the light of day. He threw the sickle on to the grass and, stooping, gently pulled aside the rushes and uncovered a nest with three eggs in it.

'A moorhen,' said the old man.

'She went squawking away as if the devil was after her.' He laughed. 'Right enough, I near chopped the head off her.'

'She'll be back.'

The boy covered the nest again then climbed out of the water on to the grass. He shook like a dog and a thousand drops of shining water whirled away from him.

'Are you stopping?'

'Jaysus, no. I've only started.'

'You can have some lunch later, if you like. I doubt if Sean'll be wanting any today, so there'll be a chop going begging.'

'Great.'

Above them a lark's voice rose and fell in unphrased song. The old man looked pointlessly up to see if he could catch sight of the bird. He was many years too late.

'Like I said, I can't swim, though.' He bent down to poke some mud from between his toes.

'That's a bore.' Somehow he'd thought that all boys could swim. Everywhere he'd ever been, water had always seemed full of swimming children. He couldn't remember a time when he hadn't been able to swim. 'Old motorcar tyres are a help.'

'Yeah. That's a great idea all right.' He picked up the sickle and slithered into the water again. 'Give me a shout when you want me up at the house. I'll carry on with this. It's a job you could be for ever doing.'

'Herculean. Don't overdo things, Hercules.'

He was glad of his stick on the way back to the house. He was constantly irritated by his increasing lack of mobility, by the discomfort he suffered in his bones. He was frightened, not of death, which now was so inevitable that it was like waiting for a visitor who never told the time of his arrival but you knew was on his way; rather, by the thought that one day he would be unable to get out of his bed and would be forced to lie, like Clare had done, wasting away. Imprisoned. He struck angrily at the grass with his stick. If he could strike the ground open and be swallowed, how splendid. No debris. Alexander had been hit by a shell. Very little debris there. Miscellaneous fragments, not worth gathering up. Mother had insisted that an empty coffin be buried with full pomp, here, in the churchyard. She had sent him packing the next day, unable to bear the sight of him. She had looked at him, he remembered, as if she'd thought that somehow it was his fault. Even a year later she still wore black. It was a colour that had always suited her. After the war was over, uniform in moth-balls, neatly folded into the black tin trunk in the attic, he had left home. 'A travelling man.' He'd once heard one of the maids describe him thus. 'Though I am old from wandering through hollow lands and hilly lands . . .' It didn't apply. He had merely been routed, weakling that he was, by a lady in black, whose diamonds flashed with grey splendour each time she moved her hands. The mica in the granite steps flashed ferociously up at him, baiting him. He wondered what Sarah had done with the rings. Clare had never worn them. Her hands had been too . . . no, it was her personality that had been colourless. She had been too retiring to control such jewels. They would have overpowered her. They had lain in their boxes until after her death. He had taken them from their velvet boxes and laid them all on the table in front of Sarah. She picked one up and slipped it on to her finger. In his head his mother's laughter glittered like the stones.

'It's not me. I'll never wear them.'

'Take them, anyway. They're yours. Sell them if you want to. What good are they doing anyone shut up in a drawer? Hey? You may have children.'

Sarah laughed shrilly. The sound set his teeth tingling.

'That's unlikely.' She took the ring off and put it back in its box. 'But if you really want me to have them . . .'

'I never want to see them again.'

Had he said that, he wondered, or merely thought it?

A horn blew. He stopped on the top step and turned round to see who was arriving. A small green car, being driven with extreme caution, came round the bend. It was too late to take cover. The Rector's hand moved in blessing or salute. The car, narrowly missing the bottom step, stopped in a series of diminishing jumps. It coughed. The Rector stared at his hands for a few moments, as if he were surprised to see them side by side on the steering wheel. He was wearing a grey flannel jacket. His TCD scarf hung limply around his collared neck. He had left his cassock somewhere else. He got out of the car and coughed like an echo. 'Ah-ha . . .'

'There's not much in it as far as bad driving is concerned.'

'We're not getting any younger, my friend.'

'Are you coming in?'

'If I may.'

He climbed up towards the door, his spindle legs buckling under him slightly as he moved from step to step. In the hall he peered round, worried, judging.

'I live as I live,' said the old man shutting the door. 'I'll make you some coffee if you like.'

'Thank you, Charles, that would be most acceptable.'

They moved in silence towards the kitchen. The shopping that Sean had brought earlier still lay on the table. The old man put the kettle on before beginning to clear away the groceries.

'You manage?'

'I manage.'

'We worry about you, Eileen and I.' He sat down and folded his hands in his lap, as if he were about to start praying.

'I had hoped that I made my position clear to Eileen the other evening.' He put two cups without saucers down on the table. The Nescafé tin was already there. He measured a heaped spoonful into each. 'I apologize for this. I find real coffee too much of a problem.'

'We drink this all the time,' said the Rector gloomily. 'I don't find it agrees with me at all.'

'If you put a little of this in it takes the harm out.' He reached up to the shelf for the whiskey. 'Will you join me?' He could see by the Rector's face what was turning over in his mind, what he would be saying to worried Eileen during dinner that evening.

'I? No, thanks. Ah, hum. You know how women are once they get an idea into their heads. If I've told her once, I've told her a thousand times there was no need for worry. If anyone can manage on his own, I said, it's Charles. But she insisted, nonetheless.'

The kettle boiled. Mr Prendergast made the coffee. Let him get on with his own mission. He'll get no polite help from me. The Rector moved his hands in a strange nervous gesture and then reclasped them.

'I pray for you.'

'Oh.' He was disconcerted. 'I suppose I should say thank you.' He pushed the coffee and the sugar across the table.

The Rector stared into the swirling brown liquid with distaste, though whether it was for the situation he was in or the coffee it would be hard to say. 'You don't have to.'

'Well, I will. Thank you.' He poured a goodish measure of whiskey into his cup.

'No matter what you say, I've always considered us to be good friends—no!' He unclasped his hands quickly and held one of them up, like a policeman in white gloves, at a crossroads. 'You were about to speak.'

'Yes. I . . .'

'Don't, I beg of you. No more unconsidered, splenetic words. I know you value your solitude. I appreciate . . . sometimes, indeed, I have envied . . . yes. But we would feel so happy if you would visit us from time to time. There is so much behind us and, in this world, so little left. We would value it . . . Old friends become rare as . . .'

'Oh, very well,' said the old man, trying hard not to sound too splenetic. 'I'll come and visit you from time to time.'

The Rector looked relieved. He lifted up the cup and took a scalding sip. 'Capital.' He smiled triumphantly across the table. 'Eileen will be so pleased. Why don't you come back with me now and have a spot of lunch. Pot luck.'

'I regret. I am already committed.'

The Rector's face lost its smile. 'I don't want to press you.' His words were like cold stones of hail beating on a winter face.

In the distance the door opened and shut. The Rector, mouth pursed with disapproval, raised his cup once more. The old man, moving at his own top speed, went to the kitchen door and down the passage to the hall. Diarmid stood quite still by the door, half alarmed. He was still wearing only his shirt and held his trousers socks and shoes in front of himself self-consciously. He jerked his head towards the door and the car outside.

'Upstairs, third on the right. You'll find a towel in the hot press.'

Without a word, the boy ran across the hall and up the stairs, leaving a trail of mud and drips behind him. The old man returned to the Rector with a slight smile.

'My lunch guest.'

'I'd better be off.'

'There's no rush. Though I'm sure you've other calls to make. In the, ah, course of your parochial duties.'

The Rector stood up. He pushed the half-finished coffee across the table. 'Nothing is as it used to be.'

'It's called evolution.'

James Evers brushed the remark aside impatiently with a flutter of his fingers. 'When I was a young man the Church was the backbone — no, more than that — the nerve centre of a healthy society.'

'That's how you saw it. A narrow view, if I may say so.'

'We never saw eye to eye.'

'Precisely.' They moved slowly out of the kitchen.

'And you'll come and see us,' pressured the Rector once more. 'Drop in. Have a drink or something, if you won't come for a meal. A chat with Eileen. She gets perturbed.'

'No need.'

The Rector looked down at the floor. 'Your guest was very wet.'

'Mmm.'

He waited on the steps until the car had disappeared.

*　*　*

The sun marched majestically through the rest of May and the first couple of weeks of June. Clare's roses had never been better. Each morning as Diarmid passed through the garden he cut an armful and the hall and the study smelt sweet and reminiscent of youth.

Sean didn't reappear for ten days and then he spent most of the day shivering in the potting shed, hiding from the sun. He seldom spoke but if his eye lit on Diarmid his face became stiff with hate.

The boy cut back the rushes at the edge of the lake until there was a wide channel through which he would push a tyre out into the middle, where his feet couldn't touch the bottom. He would splash around out there for half an hour or more. As the days passed his naked body turned from white to pink and then, gradually, a very pale brown.

Sometimes the old man would put on his panama hat and take his stick and walk slowly down to the lake. He would lower himself gracelessly on to the grass and sit there reading until his back became insupportably sore; then he would, with Diarmid's help, get himself to his feet and go slowly back to the house again. Sometimes he played the piano or sat by the open window reading or sleeping and would suddenly find that Diarmid had silently arrived and was sitting near him, motionless in the golden light. He almost always brought a present when he came. Another duck egg or two thick slices of rich fruit cake, a slab of yellow butter with the imprint of a flower on it and tiny salty beads of sweat lying on top. Once a music manuscript book; another time a honeycomb. Mr Prendergast asked no questions, accepted with a smile and shared, when possible the gifts. The main part of their time, though, was spent up in the nursery, the floor covered with soldiers, maps and books. There they observed military formalities, saluted each other and addressed each other with military titles.

In the evenings, after the boy had gone and the heat and brilliant light were draining away from the garden and the growing fields as the tide patterns its way out across acres of wet sand, the old man sat by the window, his drink by him on the floor, and realized the beauty of peace.

As June continued clouds began to trouble the sky and black shadows passed from time to time over the house and garden. A sharp wind rippled the water of the lake and made bathing little pleasure. The boy became daily more remote, withdrawing into unhappy thoughts of his own.

'What's bothering you, eh, boy?' The old man sat at the piano. The words had been in his mind for a long time. The boy moved uneasily in his chair, squirming like a fish that didn't like the taste of the hook. 'Hey?' Mr Prendergast turned round and looked at him, demanding an answer.

'They're going to send me away.'

'Away?'

'I listen at doors. I read their letters. I know they're conniving. Is it terrible to do those things?'

'It's certainly socially unacceptable. Maybe you have misinterpreted things.'

'Got things wrong?'

'That's it.'

'No. I'm not an eejit.'

'I'm aware of that. Where are they intending to send you? A school somewhere?'

'Not on your nellie. To Dublin. They're looking for a good job for me in a shop up there.'

'You're very young. Are you sure?'

'I have this auntie.'

'Ah, yes. The lady of the museum.' He turned to the piano and very softly played the first phrases of a fugue with his right hand.

' "Mary can take him for a year or so. 'Till he's old enough to fend for himself." ' Mrs Toorish's voice minced into the room. ' "After all, she's little enough else to do. She'll be glad of the extra coming in each week. Whatever, anyway, he'll have to go out of this, we can't have him idling around here another minute. He'll never come to anything at all if we don't get him out of here soon." '

'Honour thy father and thy mother that thy days may be long in the land which the Lord thy God giveth thee.'

'That's the Bible.'

'Exodus twenty, twelve. It was quoted constantly to us in our youth.' The left hand came striding in. 'You're very young,' repeated the old man, over the music.

'You keep saying that.'

'When I was your age . . . what does that matter. When I was your age, indeed.'

He concentrated on the music for a while. Chords swelled and faded. The walls seemed saturated with the sound. The boy put out his hand and held the old man's shoulder gently. He could feel through his fingers the movement of the bone in its socket, the movement of the music. When the fugue was finished they were silent for a moment.

'Yes,' said the boy. He put his hand back into his pocket. The old man turned and looked at him.

'You've all your life in front of you. Dublin's as good a place to begin life as any. Better than most, probably.' He nodded, thinking aloud. 'I've travelled the world over, boy, and I can't think of a better place to start from.'

'You didn't start as apprentice to a grocer.'

'True.'

'Anyway, I didn't think much of Dublin when I was there before. It's maybe changed since your day. Not my auntie.'

'Maybe you've got it all wrong. They'll have to discuss it with you.'

'Divil a bit of discussing. "Tomorrow your Dada's taking you to Dublin and I'll have no lip out of you. If you don't like it you can lump it." And the next day she'll hand me the case and shove me out the door with him and that'll be that. I bet she won't even come to the station and wave . . .'

The old man got up and went over to the window. He stared out at nothing, but out of the side of his eye he watched the boy fidgeting restlessly with a button on his jacket.

'I enjoyed the train ride. There and back. I came back on my own. A lady bought me a cup of tea in the restaurant car.'

'That must have been nice.'

'It was OK. You need money to be a traveller.'

'I certainly got through quite a bit. But there are those who can make a profit out of it.'

'I want to be a soldier.'

'It seems to me it's all just a question of getting through the next few years until you're old enough to enlist.'

Sean appeared on the path below the windows with his wheel-barrow and started scuffling weeds with a regular rhythm, developed over the years to use the least effort. Scratch, scratch, the blade pushed the weeds in small heaps in front of him on the gravel. He didn't look up at the window.

The boy ducked down behind the big chair, his fingers touching the ground, stooped as if he were about to begin a race.

'What are you doing? What on earth . . . ?' Diarmid poked his finger towards the window. 'Foolishness. Utter.'

But the boy stayed where he was, relaxed a little, down on to his knees, a finger traced the faded complications of the carpet. 'They catch you before you can do anything about it and put you in a cage.' He looked up at the old man. 'That's what it looks like to me, anyway.'

'What a strange child you are. In all the best stories the hero runs away.' He regretted it the moment he had said it but Diarmid didn't seem to be listening. 'You could almost say that I had run away and where did it get me?' He put his hands out wide to embrace the room.

'So, you're off?'

A sod of turf slipped in the edifice and sparks chased each other up into the blackness of the chimney. Mother reached out from her chair and rang the bell. The diamonds and the sparks became confused in the blackness of his mind. Her hand returned to her lap and lay motionless beside its partner. Father, older than his years, was crumpled upon the sofa. His face, devoured by the years, hid a mind that had almost ceased to function. *The Pilgrim's Progress* lay open on his knees, as if he had just laid it down for a moment; in reality he carried the book round with him from room to room, chair to chair, all through the long day, without it occurring to him to read a page or even a few lines.

'Yes. The car is waiting.'

She sighed. Her hair was still golden, a halo round her unsaintlike face. 'You will never make anything of your life.'

He bowed slightly towards her. 'Thank you for a mother's blessing.'

She laughed, throwing her head right back against the chair, almost joyfully. Father moved on the sofa and muttered something under his breath.

'He,' she said, when the laughter stopped.

'Yes, yes. I know what you're going to say.'

A maid came in and went over to the fireplace. In the afternoon they wore dresses of dark brown stuff, with pale coffee-coloured aprons. She knelt down and began to rebuild the fire. Mother and son watched in silence. The girl rose after a few moments and rather nervously wiped the turf dust from her fingers with the corner of her apron.

'Will that be all, ma'am?'

Mother gestured with a hand and the girl left the room. As the door closed, Charles spoke:

'Well, goodbye.'

'Goodbye.' The word was thrown out with indifference. He moved towards her and bent to kiss her cheek, but she put up a hand and brushed his leaning face away.

'Spare me.'

He felt the heavy weight of hatred that he knew so well gathering in his stomach. Without a word he turned away from her and went over to the man on the sofa.

'Goodbye, father. You'll be fit again soon.'

An uncaring smile moved the old man's lips. Charles put a hand out and touched his father's shoulder in farewell.

'He would have become a man.'

'I am a man, mother, believe that.'

She threw her head back again and laughed. The sound of her laughter followed him out of the room, followed him for ever.

'I want to stay here,' said Diarmid.

'Impractical.'

'Right here.' He pressed his two hands down on the carpet, as if he were trying to make a hold for himself that no one could drag him out of. After a moment he looked nervously up at the old man.

'Have I annoyed you?'

'No. No, of course not. Bemused, rather.'

'Bemused,' repeated the boy, almost under his breath.

The gardener coughed and turned his back on them, stooping to grapple with some harmless daisies on the edge of the grass. The first rook launched itself from a branch and called mournfully down to its slower-witted companions. There was a general black stirring amongst the trees.

'It would merely lead to trouble.'

'I wouldn't mind.'

'I don't suppose you would. I have spent my life trying to avoid trouble. With a certain success, I must admit.'

The boy jumped up from the floor suddenly and threw his arms around the old man's neck.

'Look here, boy . . .' He looked down at the head pressed painfully against his ribs, felt the child's desperation impinging on his own private personality. Gently he put up his hands and tried to unknot the fingers laced at the back of his neck.

'Please.'

The old man groped behind him with a hand until he found the arm of a chair. He fell backwards into it and the boy came too, not loosing his grip for a minute. His face was now pressed against the drooping flesh of Mr Prendergast's neck.

'Please,' he murmured again.

'This is ridiculous. You're strangling me, boy. Consider. You're too old to be . . .'

The boy let go and crouched back on his heels, looking anxiously into the old man's face. 'Please.'

'Have some sense, child.' He rubbed the back of his neck which seemed to have taken the whole weight of the boy and was now aching. 'You can't come and live here. For one thing your parents wouldn't allow it.'

'They don't want me.'

The old man thought for a moment. 'I don't think it's quite that. They want you to be qualified to make your way in the world. Earn. Acquire knowhow. That's important, you know. I'm sure that they have your best interests at heart, no matter how things look to you.' He scarcely believed it himself as he said it. The thought of Sarah came into his mind. His heart, he recollected, had merely been filled with immense relief as he recognized the fact that here was a person that needed no propping or pushing from him, who preferred her own advice to that of others. Quickly he pushed the thoughts behind the nearest dusty curtain.

'You can't stay here,' he announced with authority.

'OK.'

To the old man's surprise the boy got to his feet. There was no arguing look on his face, merely blankness.

The other rooks had followed their leader now and the sky above the trees was filled with the rising and falling of black wings.

'It's time I went.'

'Yes.'

The old man groped around on the floor with one hand for the whiskey bottle. It wasn't within groping distance. He let the matter slide. He was tired. He couldn't think of anything to say. 'It was a wild thought. Panic. You didn't really mean it.' Wrong, weary words.

'I'll be seeing you,' said Diarmid coldly and left the room.

'Tttt.'

He was annoyed by the situation and with himself for having allowed such a situation to arise. Exasperated that even now, at the fag end of his life, after all his precautions, someone could touch him, make him feel uneasy pain.

Below in the garden Sean, panting each time he stooped, began to fill the barrow with weeds. Diarmid strolled around the corner as if he owned the place and crossed the path just by where Sean was working. He walked across the grass and, taking his penknife out of his pocket, began to cut a selection of roses from the nearest beds. For a moment Sean watched in silence, not believing his own eyes.

'Hey!'

The boy paid no attention. His knife cut obliquely through the green wood.

'By Jesus, I'll fix you.'

Sean picked up the rake, which leant against the half-full barrow. The old man pulled himself up out of his chair and went over to the window. He pushed it open and the sweet warm smell of summer evening gardens surrounded him.

'Sean. Leave him be.'

Sean didn't stop or look round. 'I warned him.'

'No matter, he's doing no harm. I told him he could bring a few flowers home to his mother.'

The gardener turned suddenly and walked back to the barrow. He threw the rake in on top of the weeds. 'You're the boss.' He picked up the handles of the barrow and wheeled it off down the path.

Diarmid watched him out of the side of his eye, then folded the knife up and put it into his pocket. With a sudden violent movement, he turned towards the house and hurled the roses at the window where the old man stood and then ran off down the avenue. The roses lay scattered on the lawn, red and yellow, flame and pink, colourful waste. Mr Prendergast waited until Diarmid was out of sight and then he went slowly out into the garden. With difficulty he picked up the fallen flowers and brought them into the house.

✳   ✳   ✳

He felt Clare's presence as soon as he entered the room. Any time that she had come into this room, she had balanced herself on the corner of the sofa like an awkward guest, rather than making herself at home in one of the armchairs. She was there now, her head bent towards a dark sock stretched over a mushroom. The silver splinter in her other hand glittered as it moved through the wool. She sighed as he passed her. She had never liked sewing. Without a word he sat down at the piano. His back was adamantly towards her but he could hear, from time to time, her sighs. A familiar exasperation prevented him from playing. He flexed his fingers in preparation but couldn't bring himself to place them on the keys.

'To what do I owe the pleasure,' he paused on the word, rather like Diarmid might, tasting its insincerity, 'of this manifestation?' It was the sort of question he had plagued her with over the years. As she had grown older and less wounded by his grotesqueries towards her she had ceased to try and answer. There was silence in the room.

'A surfeit of alcohol might, I suppose, cause hallucinations.' He began, after a moment's consideration, to play with great precision a pavane. A rhythm, he decided, of suitable dignity for a moment like this. He played quietly.

A warning of approaching death? He shook his head in answer to his own question. The angel of death would be unlikely to arrive with socks to darn; of course, you never had much sense of occasion.

In the autumn of 1919 he had returned to Oxford to finish his studies, interrupted by the war. Clare's father had been a don with musical inclinations who had offered an open invitation to him to use the piano whenever he wished. Clare had always been around, little more than a child, but filled with a soft and tranquil admiration for him that was irresistible. The horror of the war he had survived hung about him like a thick cloak. He was incapable of throwing it off, seemed rather to rely on its denseness to protect him from the demands of living people. He had tired very quickly of university life, finding the self-confidence of the very young tedious and the desires of those whose lives, like his own, had been disturbed by war, to start climbing the ladder of success as soon as possible frightening. He was unable to find in himself any seed of either confidence or ambition. As he had left home that last time he had, in fact, been filled with anger that

Alexander, the potential man of achievement, had not been the one to survive to face the hateful world. Taking Clare by the hand, he had begun to run. Now he realized that, in all their years together, he had given her nothing, only a child that he had not allowed her to enjoy. She had slowly died of starvation. In her whole life with him only her garden had been an act of defiance against his indifference. He was suddenly shaken by anger. Not against himself but against Clare that she had denied her own right to existence. He turned from the piano to speak to her once more but the sofa was empty.

'I am old,' he complained to the emptiness. 'I should not be tormented by the past like this.' He got up slowly and went to search for the whiskey bottle.

*   *   *

One day the good weather was gone. A wind from the west tossed the arms of the trees and forced Clare's rose bushes to dance ungainly dances. Shreds of pink, yellow and red chased each other over the wet grass.

Sean arrived at his usual time and shut himself in the potting shed without coming into the house for his cup of tea. When he did come into the kitchen at lunchtime, a smile lay on his face like a slice of moon in a turbulent sky. He was not given to smiling. It made the old man slightly uneasy. Sean sat down at his place in silence and smiled at his waiting meal. Mr Prendergast opened the paper.

'It's all over the town.' He always referred to the village as the town.

'What's that?' asked the old man, more out of politeness than interest. He moved the paper slightly to one side, so that he could see Sean's face.

'They're getting rid of the little brat at long last. It's one decision they'll not regret, anyway.'

'I haven't the remotest idea what you're talking about.'

'That Toorish brat. He's off to Dublin first thing in the morning. If they had real sense it's to an institution he should be going.'

Mr Prendergast put the paper down on the floor by his chair. 'I've never found him any trouble.'

'Well, you're the only one for miles. Traipsing in and out as if he owned the place. Picking the mistress's roses. Giving out cheek.'

'I don't understand why you get so worked up about those roses. Flowers are for picking.'

'She and I made that garden what it is.'

'I'm not denying it.'

'And not for the likes of him.'

The old man looked silently at his plate for a moment. The paper on the floor sighed with boredom. 'Better that he should appreciate than no one. However, how do you know, anyway?'

'Amn't I after telling you. The whole town has it.'

'You never go near the village.'

'I do when it suits me.' He began to eat his lunch. He turned the fork upside down and packed the food on to it unusually energetically.

The old man couldn't bear to watch. 'It seems to me . . .'

Sean pointed the loaded fork across the table before shoving it into his mouth. He spoke with difficulty through the food. 'You only see what you want to see. Have a good look around the house before you say too much and see what he's laid his hands on. Cast your eyes round.' He chewed triumphantly.

'I think you're forgetting our relative positions. Taking liberties.'

'I certainly wouldn't want to do a thing like that.' He leant forward towards the old man. 'Everything'll be all right when he's gone. Just like it was before. You'll see. Just the two of us and a bit of peace.'

Mr Prendergast picked up his plate and took it over to the sink. He felt a cold lump forming in his stomach as if he had swallowed a large, cold stone. He recognized the feeling with alarm, like diagnosing an unpleasant illness. He remembered the same physical symptom from his childhood. It was hatred . . . He swept the untouched, dead pieces of food off his plate into the bucket with a fork. He couldn't bring himself to speak to Sean. So it had been with Alexander, the feeling you wanted to pull the stone out of your gut and crush someone with it.

Sean's chair scraped on the linoleum and his boots tapped across the room to the door.

'I didn't want to upset you,' he whined, knowing too late that he had pushed his luck rather far. 'Sir.' He coughed a little, waiting for some reassurance, grasped the handle and opened the door. 'I only thought I ought to warn you, like. He went out, at last, into the fine rain that was now drifting rather than falling through the blue air.

Mr Prendergast left the dishes to soak in the sink with the tail-end of a bar of Sunlight soap to cut the grease. He went upstairs to the old nursery and had his sleep in the chair by the rain-pearled window. Swallows scraped and twittered under the eaves, coming to grips with their northern world. He slept for a long time and awoke stiff and melancholic. Slowly he tidied the soldiers away into their boxes and put the dust covers back over the furniture. The room was asleep once more. The child had, somehow, halted for a while the inevitable, dreary process of dying. Now, as the last grey cover went over the last chair, he could feel the process beginning again. He locked the door and went downstairs.

It was choir practice evening. He put the nursery key back on its hook. His legs and back ached from stooping. He couldn't think of anything more disagreeable than playing hymns for an hour and un-doubtedly being worked over by the Rector.

*   *   *

'This evening we simply won't take no for an answer.' Her hands fluttered like butterflies around his shoulders, her cheek brushed his. He stopped playing and turned his head slightly towards her so that she might get the breath of whiskey from him and, perhaps, falter. But not Eileen. Her hands came to rest on his shoulders.

'Eileen . . .'

'Not a word. We have made up our minds. We'll carry you off in our car and James can run you home. We never eat till after choir practice. The girl leaves us something cold. You couldn't expect her to stay in. You and James can have a . . . nice big drink and a good chat.'

'If you insist.' He was too tired to argue.

She removed her hands from his shoulders and, for a moment, he thought she was going to clasp them but she decided against it. In earlier years she had been given to expansive gestures of this sort. Never appealing, he remembered.

'That's settled, then. I'm so glad.'

Her hands fluttered around him again but, before she had time to touch him, the first ladies chattered into the church.

They captured him when the singing was over and walked, one on each side of him, as if they thought he might escape, take to his heels across the weed-splashed gravel and out of the gate. The Rector's cassock flapped in a ridiculous fashion round his legs and his shoes needed a good polish. Politely the old man refused to sit in the front seat but they insisted, almost pushed him through the car door. His own car looked forlorn by the vestry door as they drove away.

'You'll have to have a word with the Brown girl,' said Mrs Evers as the Rector paused nervously in the gateway, ducking his head quickly this way and that to make sure that nothing would take him unawares.

'There's nothing coming,' said the old man irritably. The Rector continued to duck.

'I like to make absolutely sure,' he muttered. 'It's a blind corner.'

'She hasn't been coming to choir practice as regularly as she might. Do go on, dear. We can't sit here all night.'

The car moved across the road in a series of little jumps.

'Perhaps you, too, James, should take to shanks's mare.'

'I'm sure there's a young man involved. I haven't asked, mind you, but I would suspect. But I do think if she's going to continue to sing in the choir she ought to come to practice.' She tapped her fingers impatiently on the back of the seat waiting for him to speak. 'Don't you?'

'Quite,' answered the Rector automatically. He rubbed at the windscreen fretfully with the back of his hand. 'Can't anyone ever wash this windscreen?'

'It's on the outside,' said the old man. 'Flies and the like. Summer flies and dust, bird droppings, too, sometimes. Sean gives mine a rub from time to time.'

'We haven't had a man for years.'

'It would come better from you than me.' The Rector appeared to hear his wife for the first time.

'What would?'

'A word to Joanna Brown. Before things go any further. The young slip from the church, if allowed. Have you got your bobby dodgers on?'

'No need.'

'That car had.'

'Tttt.'

'Someone mentioned to me, just in passing, that the young man wasn't altogether suitable. How is dear Sarah?'

'I presume she's all right. She doesn't correspond. We don't.'

'She used to write to Clare. I remember how pleased she used to be to get her letters.'

'It's a duty she doesn't feel bound to continue with me.'

The rectory was Victorian, an agglomeration of peaks and towers, turrets and tiny spires, Gothic windows and expansive bays, surrounded closely by giant rhododendrons and, in the summer, a mist of midges.

'It's too wet, alas, for you to come and give us some advice about my borders.'

'My dear Eileen, you know I've never been a gardener.'

'I thought that a little of Clare's knowledge might have rubbed off on you.'

The Rector stopped at the hall door and bowed his head over the steering wheel for a moment, as if he were saying grace.

'I'm afraid not.'

'The back of my neck is stiff,' complained the Rector.

'You will insist on sleeping with the window open.'

'Tttt.'

They got out of the car, each one with difficulties of his own, and went into the hall.

Eileen turned the light on. The light hanging in the centre of the hall was covered by a shade of multi-coloured glass, which made the walls and furniture multi-coloured also. The three old people took on the look of over-elaborate stained glass. They stood awkwardly for a few moments, not quite knowing what to do next. Then Eileen gave one of her charming laughs and almost clapped her hands again. 'It's so nice to have you here at last.' Her face was marbled green and red. 'Run along both of you into the sitting room and have a drink. I'll join you in a minute.'

She looked at her husband as she laid a delicate stress on the word 'drink' then, like a demon in a pantomime, she disappeared into a dark hole in the wall. The Rector gestured to the old man to follow him into the sitting room where a turf fire smoked wearily on the hearth.

'Take a pew.' The Rector laughed, then stopped abruptly and watched while Mr Prendergast lowered himself into an armchair that in the distant past had given more support to brittle bones. 'Sherry? Whiskey?'

'Whiskey.'

Only the Rector's unpolished shoes and the whisper of the fire broke the silence.

'It must be several years . . .' The Rector came across the room and handed him a glass. Pale amber, too pale amber.

'Not since Clare . . .'

'That's right. We miss Clare. How stupid of me to say that to you. You must know about that. She was such a . . . tower of strength.'

James Evers could no more pour a drink than preach a sermon, that was for sure. The old man got up. 'Do you mind?' He went over to the cupboard where the bottles were. He smiled back, disarmingly, at the Rector over his shoulder. 'A drink must be a drink.'

'Go ahead, old man. Help yourself.' He wandered round the room looking for nothing. 'A tower of strength,' he repeated.

The old man took a sip of his drink. An improvement. 'You surprise me. She always seemed remarkably diffident to me. Almost nervous. Too nervous.'

'No, no, I assure you. You've only to ask Eileen. A very font of wisdom.'

'Fount.'

'Fount,' said the Rector irritably.

The old man took another sip and looked out of the window. It was almost dark. The rain had stopped but the wind stirred the rhododendrons. The green leaves moved like a thousand wings. 'Why don't you cut those bushes back a bit? They're crushing the house.'

'There's no view from here, anyway. Not like over with you.'

'How can you breathe with them all pressing round you like that?'

'We don't notice it.'

'My mother planted them all over the place. An appalling Victorian vice. I always wanted to root them out but Clare liked them. Rhododendrons.' He spoke the word with contempt.

'Ireland wouldn't be Ireland without its rhododendrons.'

'What utter rubbish.'

'Tell me one thing, Charles.' The Rector poured himself a small glass of sherry. He splashed a few drops on to the front of his cassock and rubbed at it with disgust.

'Yes?'

'This withdrawal.'

'You wouldn't have so many flies, either. Midges. In the summer. I always remember the midges here in summer evenings. It's all that shrubby mess right up to the house.'

'There seems to be something – well . . . a little, don't take me amiss . . . unnatural about it. As an old friend I feel I can speak to you like this.'

'All round the tennis courts, flies. Drive you insane. Walking through your hair in thousands. I don't suppose you keep the court up these days, though.'

'We feel, Eileen and I . . .'

The old man turned round from the window. 'I do not wish to discuss my way of living. Or dying.'

A nervous giggle burst from the Rector. 'Dying doesn't come into it, old man. You've many years ahead of you yet. Please God, as the . . . ha-ha . . . others say.'

The old man sighed. 'At some point in our lives we cease to grow and start to decay. It's an inescapable fact. I passed that point more years ago than I would like to say. I would like to die as I have tried to live, in private.'

'Alone?'

'If you prefer to put it that way, yes, alone.'

'All in the dark,' said Eileen, switching on the light as she came in. 'I'll have a tiny sherry, James. Do look at that fire. You've let it almost out.' She ran to the fire in case it died before she got there and threw herself down beside it. The bellows blew a golden hole in the centre of the turves.

'Ah, Eileen.' The Rector was relieved.

'I expect you're both starving. I'll drink my sherry quickly and we can go in.'

'We were just . . .'

'Quite,' said the old man. He jerked his head towards the whiskey. 'May I?'

'By all means.'

'We were just . . . ?' asked Eileen, sitting back on her heels and looking up at them. Her finger tips had become white with turf dust.

'Well . . . ah . . . yes . . . talking about Clare, actually.'

'Dear Clare.' She rubbed her fingers on her skirt.

'I was saying to Charles that she was a tower of strength.'

'Indeed she was.' She took a little swoop at her sherry and spilt some down the front of her dress. 'Oh, dear.'

'You're so clumsy, Eileen,' moaned the Rector.

'Arthritis.' She held her gnarled fingers out towards the old man. 'It's very hard for me to get a good grip on things sometimes. Occasionally I break things. James gets so angry.'

'I don't.'

'Yes, you do.' She wagged a finger at him. 'Frequently.'

'One has so little left.'

'We've given all the silver to George and Hilda. Not that I suppose they use it. People don't these days. I'll have to ask you for a hand up.'

The Rector gave a hand to his wife and she got slowly up. There was a crackling of bones, like dry sticks being consumed by fire.

' "Come away, come away, Death, and in sad cypress let me be laid." ' For no good reason, Alexander's voice was in his head. No interference, a clear line from Paradise. There were no cypress trees in the graveyard. Three chestnut trees shaded the leaning stones. In the spring the pink candles glowed as sweetly as the pyramids of candles the others lit in their churches in supplication and appeasement.

'Charles.'

The Rector's voice startled him. 'Oh . . . ah . . . yes?'

'Where were you?'

'I'm sorry. I drop off sometimes. Like a horse, I must be able to sleep on my feet.'

The Rector's wife put her arm through his and gently pulled him towards the door. 'We'll go and eat.'

They walked in silence through the multi-coloured hall to the dining room. Cold meat and beetroot sat gloomily on three plates, longing to be eaten. They all sat down and the Rector bowed his head and muttered a few Latin words. Mr Prendergast carefully placed his glass in the exact centre of a lace mat on the table, slightly to his right. The Rector took the lid off a dish; steam billowed up into his face.

'Ah. King Edwards. Our own. I guarantee they're delicious. Help yourself.' He handed Mr Prendergast a spoon and pushed the dish in his direction.

'Thank you.'

'Beetroot always reminds me of graveyards,' said Eileen, chopping nervously with her fork.

'I don't know why we have them so often.'

'They're easy to grow and difficult to sell. I sell a lot of the garden stuff down in the village, you know. Helps make ends meet. But really one finds they only want cabbage and carrots, perhaps some onions now and then, or cauliflowers. Terribly dull. They've so little imagination. Since I've had to give up golf I like to have some excuse to spend time out in the air.'

'I didn't know you'd given up your golf.'

She waved her hands towards him without speaking.

'I'm sorry.'

Disarmed by this second of sympathy, she plunged. 'Have you never thought of going to live near Sarah?'

'I can't say I have.'

'A nice little flat in Kensington or somewhere. Central heating. That's what would appeal to me. Not the constant struggle in the winter here to keep the circulation moving. Sarah could pop in. It's not right you being all on your own the way you are.'

'I haven't the faintest intention of moving to Kensington.'

'You could probably get a fair price for the house if you went the right way about it.' She leant towards him confidentially. 'I'll tell you something. If James dies before me, and please goodness he won't, I shall go straight over to George and Hilda. I know they'd want it.'

'I am perfectly happy where I am. In my own home.'

'I don't want to interfere . . .'

'I've often wondered since that day how your lunch guest got so wet.' The Rector, tactfully, was changing the subject.

'Swimming.' The old man's voice was ice cold. He stood up. 'I will be going now. It was kind of you to invite me but I would appreciate it if, in future, you would . . .'

'Quite,' said the Rector.

Eileen was distressed. 'But Charles, you mustn't be angry. Believe me, we only have your interests at heart. And one tends to think of Clare, of what she would have wanted.'

'Clare would agree with me. I should be allowed to get to hell, or wherever, in my own way.'

'Charles. Sometimes you say such terrible things.'

'No need for outrage. I appreciate your . . . ah . . . thoughtfulness. If you'll excuse me now, I think I'll be getting along.'

Eileen was crying unashamedly into the beetroot.

The old man sighed with exasperation. 'It is the incompleteness of women that drives me mad,' he said to no one.

'I'll drive you home,' said the Rector.

'I prefer to walk, thank you.'

'Clare was so devoted to you. All those years, never a word against you, never a complaint, and you were never the easiest . . . You sound as if you hate her. It's so unfair. Ungrateful.'

'What should I be grateful for? She gave me nothing.'

'Devotion.'

'A dog can do that.'

The Rector's religious hand touched his sleeve. 'I'll drive you home.'

'She gave you a child.' Her voice was becoming shrill.

'We're too old for this kind of conversation. Now, if you'll excuse me . . .'

'It's raining,' said the Rector.

'I'll go along the back lane. It won't take more than ten minutes. A little rain never hurt anyone.' He looked at Eileen rubbing at her eyes with her napkin. 'I appreciate your interest. I merely . . . I can't explain . . . words . . .'

She nodded bravely at him over the starched damask.

'Goodnight.'

'Goodnight.'

'Goodnight, James.'

'Goodnight, old man.'

'Sunday, morning and evening.'

'Quite.'

The back lane passed the yard gates of both the rectory and Mr Prendergast's house. Along one side was an embankment, on top of which ran the railway line, now unused the narrow gauge hidden by brambles and cow parsley. In his childhood, the old man recalled, if there were anyone on board for the house, the driver would stop the train just above the yard gate and a couple of the men would be waiting in the lane to help the visitors down the crude steps that had been cut in the bank. This saved a tedious drive to the nearest station and gave both the visitors and the Prendergast boys a feeling of enormous importance, as if the whole railway system was run especially for them.

'How good it is,' Alexander had said to him one afternoon as they watched the little balls of smoke jerking up into the sky before the engine got under way again, 'to be people of privilege.' They used to walk for miles, one on each shining track, arms outstretched to balance, stopping every ten minutes or so and kneeling down, ears to the rail, listening for the vibrations that meant a train was on the line. Then they would slide down into the long grass of the embankment and wait until it went past. Goods trains rolled slowly along the track leaving a smoky, dungy smell behind in the air and usually the sound of worried sheep or cattle. Sometimes it was possible to climb on to the last truck and sit there, rocking from side to side, feet dangling, watching the rails and sleepers unfolding behind you, until you became bored, or you were getting too far from home. Alexander, usually preoccupied with his own thoughts, might as well have been on his own really, except that, every so often, at some bend in the lane or some fence that had to be climbed, he would pause, tapping one foot impatiently on the ground and humming to himself until the younger boy had caught up with him.

The old man was drenched by the time he reached home. He climbed up the back steps and in through the kitchen door. He was concentrating so hard on removing wet shoes and stuffing them with paper, shaking and hanging up his coat, mopping at his face and neck with a towel, boiling a kettle for a hot whiskey and a hot water bottle, working hard, in fact, on the survival routine, that he never felt the imperceptible change in the atmosphere that tells you that there is someone other than yourself in your normally empty house.

✻   ✻   ✻

He slept later than usual and lay for a few minutes after waking, conscious only of the deep aching in his bones, across his shoulders, down his arms, even his ankle joints felt as if he would never be able to use them again. He thought about a flat in Kensington, warm towels on a rail in the bathroom, a lift with wrought-iron gates, only a short walk, leaning on a rubber-tipped stick, to the public library, deference from men wearing gloves and rows of ancient battle ribbons, outside clubs and theatres, men of the old school who knew a gentleman when they saw one. Sarah would visit him once a week and they would both be faced with the almost impossible creation of a relationship which neither of them were exactly eager for. He opened his eyes, preferring the reality of the wreck of his bedroom. Outside the sky was a pale wet blue, the branches of the trees stretched sideways with the wind. Another day to see through. More rain would come, more petals would blow on to the grass, more chords from the piano would stroke the air, another night would wipe the colour from the sky. I could end it now, he thought, if only I was not afraid of what I might find.

He got himself out of bed, partially dressed himself and shaved the white stubble from his chin. He had all his own teeth which he cleaned each day with care but his gums bled with the pressure of the brush and the globs of blood on the white basin made him feel ill. A door banged somewhere and he stood still, his razor in his hand, listening, mildly surprised. There was no further sound, so he continued to scrape his face, stretching the skin carefully between the fingers of his left hand. The manifestations around him recently had not been ghosts of the door-banging, chain-rattling kind, merely pointing fingers of the past. He hoped vaguely that they weren't going to change their tactics and become uncomfortable to live with.

He went downstairs and put the kettle on and lit the grill for toast. He opened the kitchen door. The air smelled of wet grass. Sean was weeding within calling distance. 'Morning, Sean.'

'Good morning. You're on the late side. You had me a bit uneasy.'

'Overslept. I've the kettle on, if you're feeling like tea.'

'I'll be with you in a minute.'

He paused on the top step, scraping the mud off his boots before he came in. 'It's not like you to sleep in.'

'I think maybe I'm getting a cold.'

Sean collected his mug and sat down. He stirred in three teaspoonfuls of sugar, clattering the spoon against the sides of the mug. 'At this time of year?'

'You can catch colds at any time of year.'

'I don't feel too good myself.'

'We're getting on.'

'Sometimes I feel there's not long left in it for me.' He gave a melancholy sigh, blew on his tea and proceeded to suck it into his mouth.

The old man spread some marmalade on a piece of toast. He couldn't bring himself to sit down with Sean so he moved nervously around the kitchen as he ate it.

'There's ructions below.'

'What is it this time?'

'What you might expect. Didn't the boy run away in the night. Neither sight nor sign of him to be seen anywhere.'

'My goodness,' said the old man uneasily. 'I wonder where he's got to.'

'You might well ask,' said Sean.

There was a long silence. Sean bided his time, staring at the leaves whirling round on the top of his tea. The old man thought about doors that bang in the morning and wondered what to say next. Silence, he decided, was the best line to take.

'I wouldn't say he'd be a hundred miles away.'

'He'd hardly have had time . . .'

'You know well what I mean.'

'I don't think so.'

'I'm not blind, you know.' He drank some more tea. 'Don't think I haven't seen what's been going on.' He stared the old man maliciously in the face. 'I've eyes in my head.'

'I really don't know what you're talking about.'

'No?'

'No? If you've finished your tea . . .'

'I haven't.'

Mr Prendergast turned his back on the gardener and buttered himself another piece of toast. It wasn't going to be a day like any other.

'I always used to wonder to myself why you and the mistress never got on.'

'I don't want to hear any more of this sort of talk. You may go now, whether you've finished your tea or not.'

Sean pushed the cup across the table with a tip of one finger; it left a trail of brown liquid behind it. 'You're not natural.'

'You're fired.'

'Ha-ha-ha.'

'I've taken enough of your insolence and laziness over the last few years. I'm not taking any more.'

'Laziness?'

'That's what I said.'

'Who made that garden what it is?'

'My late wife.'

'And my work. My hands. My humping earth on my shoulders from here to there. Never a night I didn't go to bed tired out in every bone.'

'It was your job.'

'I was hired as a chauffeur.'

'And a good job you made of that, if I may say so.'

The gardener screamed and clutched his head between his earth-grained hands. 'May God forgive you.'

'He has a lot to forgive us both for.'

'To throw that in my face.'

'I'm sorry,' said the old man, surprising himself with his gentleness. 'But you've been trying hard to make me angry. You may not realize what you've been insinuating . . .'

'Not a word but the truth has passed my lips. Insinuating, is it? The truth. I seen it for years and I never recognized it till now. And if it's sacking me you are, the guards will be only too pleased to hear the truth.'

'If you don't get out of here this instant . . .'

'What about my wages?'

'I'll send you a cheque.'

'And the pension she promised me when I retired?'

'You should have thought of that before you started on this madness.'

Sean picked his cup up from the table and threw it on to the floor. It broke in four pieces and thin streams of brown tea snaked across the linoleum. He got up and walked to the door without a word. He opened it and stood quite still, quite silent, looking out at his garden, at the wind-stirred rose bushes, her shrine, his appeasement, his only life. The old man ignored him. He bent down, with pain, and picked up the broken pieces of china. A question came into his mind. He dropped the pieces, one by one, into the bucket. His head throbbed with the stooping.

'Not natural, you said?'

'That's right.'

'What precisely am I to understand by that?'

'You can understand what you like. Others will have no trouble in knowing what I mean.'

The old man pushed a laugh out of his throat. It would have fooled no one. 'I take it you're accusing me of some sort of immoral behaviour.'

'Unnatural.'

'You must really be mad. You'd better go. Don't worry, I'll send you a cheque.'

'Taking into consideration . . .' He suddenly sounded unsure.

'Absolutely nothing. Get out. Now.'

'It's a mercy she's dead.' He closed the door behind him softly with an unexpected element of civility.

The old man watched him down the steps and along the path to the potting shed. His feeling of anger was completely swamped by a feeling of great relief at having finally got rid of Sean. The garden could go to hell for all he cared. It was merely a relic of the past. Once Sean was out of sight he turned to look at the hooks where the keys were hanging. The nursery key was not there. He turned on the tap and squeezed out the floor cloth under it and, stooping down, wiped the mess of tea and unabsorbed sugar from the floor. He rinsed the tea from the cloth and took a cup down from the shelf above his head.

'I've brought you a cup of tea.'

The boy had taken the soldiers out of their boxes and the floor was a battlefield once more. Over by the window two armchairs had been uncovered and pushed together to make a bed. The shelves where the boxes had been were piled with food, arranged as if in a shop. A pyramid of apples, some tomatoes in a small box, a couple of boxes of processed cheese, some tins of evaporated milk, a neat arrangement of tinned fruit, a tin opener hanging from a hook, three sliced loaves in cellophane wrappers and about a pound of unwrapped butter sitting tidily on a white plate. The boy looked up as the door opened. He had been moving a group of Scots Guards. He didn't speak. The look of confidence on his face was barely skin deep. His eyes moved restlessly, like oil beads on water.

'You've settled in very nicely. Perhaps I was wrong. Maybe you are officer material, after all.'

'I can stay?'

'There seems very little alternative.'

The boy got up and made a rush at the old man. He threw his arms around him. 'I knew you'd let me stay.'

'You've spilled the tea.' He pushed the cup into the boy's hand. 'Drink it before it gets cold.' He went over to inspect the commissariat. 'You would appear to be intending to stay for some time.'

'That's right. No one will think of looking here.'

'I wouldn't be too sure about that, if I were you.' He sighed and settled himself down in one of the chairs. 'Well, first of all you'd better tell me what happened. The truth, mind you, not some hysterical invention created to pull the wool over my eyes.'

'It was just like I said and you wouldn't believe me.'

'It wasn't that I didn't believe you, it was just that I didn't see what I could do about it.'

'When I got home yesterday afternoon, she had the master there and the whole thing just blew up. Boom.' He stared at nothing, remembering. The cup in his hands tilted so that the tea ran right up to the edge and quivered there.

'Mind your tea.'

'What?' The boy looked down at the cup and straightened it. He sat down on the floor again and put the cup on the ground in front of him.

'Boom,' said the old man.

'Yes. She screamed like a pig was being killed and he went on and on about me as if I was some kind of a criminal. My father locked the shop and joined the party. Reprehensible, the master said. I suppose you know what that means.'

'Yes.'

'It was easy enough to get the meaning, anyway, even if you never heard the word before. As if he cared whether I went to school or not, any of us for that matter, as long as he gets his money. I told him, too.'

'Unwise.'

'He came up behind me and did what he always does at school when he's in a bait. He gathers a little handful of hair, tight in his fingers, and pulls till it comes out. You can't stop from crying out.'

'Boy . . .'

'So in the end they decided I must go today. It wasn't even soon enough for them.'

'Your father . . .'

'Him. It's as much as his life is worth to speak out of turn. He's sometimes not too bad on his own. I've never understood why people get married.'

'I can't help you there.'

'You should know.'

'I can't remember.'

'That's old age for you.'

'Maybe I never knew.'

'Anyway, you said the thing to do was run away . . .'

'Oh, God . . .' groaned the old man.

' . . . So, I ran away.' He gestured at the food on the shelves. 'He'll have a right job to get his books square this month.'

This was no time for jokes. 'And what, might I ask, is your ultimate plan?'

'I hadn't really got one. I hadn't thought much, beyond getting away. It was as lucky you weren't here last night or you might have sent me home.'

'Indeed, I might.'

'I thought maybe we could go to England.'

The old man started laughing.

'What's so funny?'

'Everyone seems determined that I should go to England. I don't mind where you go, boy, but I'm staying here.'

'What's there here?'

'You forgot my age. Anyway, I don't find it so disagreeable here.'

'I thought you didn't like it.'

'It's where I've spent more years of my life than any other place in the world. Youth and old age . . . senility, some people seem to think. Well, Colonel Toorish, so this is it?'

Diarmid jumped to his feet and saluted. 'Yes, sir.'

'A state of siege.'

'Is that what it's called?'

The old man nodded. 'There's just one alarming thing, Colonel, which may interfere with your plans. There has been a spy in the camp.'

'You know what happens to spies.'

'Under the circumstances execution is a little impractical.'

'We must put him out of action.'

Mr Prendergast thought about this for a while. He had suddenly started to enjoy himself. 'That might be arranged. Like everyone, he has an Achilles heel.'

'What's that?'

'I'll tell you another time. I'm going out for a while. Possibly a couple of hours. Get some food and things like that. Whiskey. You never can tell how long a siege may go on for. Some have been known to last for years.'

'God, that'd be great, wouldn't it?'

'I'd rather it didn't myself.'

What am I doing? Why am I behaving in this irresponsible way? 'It'll only end in tears, Charless.' Nanny sat by the fireplace endlessly sewing, snipping the thread between her yellow teeth, crackling with starch as her arm moved up and down. Once, when he had asked her why she called him Charless, she pulled him against her apron and kissed his hair. 'Isn't it your name, child dear?'

'I'll lock you in and take the key.'

Suspicion pushed all other emotions off the boy's face. 'You're not going to renege on me, are you?'

'What did you come here for if you didn't trust me?'

'I do.'

'I shall lock you in and take the key with me. I'll lock all the outside doors, in fact. Just to be on the safe side.' He took the key from the inside of the door and put it on the outside. 'Do you want to . . . you know . . . before I lock the door?'

Diarmid blushed, most un-colonel like. He shook his head.

'I'll be off, then.'

'It seems like you don't trust me, either.'

'I want to make sure. You might just be tempted to go downstairs and you never know you might meet someone.'

'There's no one to meet.'

'You can't be too careful.'

'If I promised?'

The old man thought of Sean's mean face. 'This time I'd rather be certain.'

The boy shrugged. 'Just as you please,' he muttered ungraciously.

* * *

Downstairs, Mr Prendergast locked the kitchen door. There was no sign of Sean moving in the garden. He collected five bottles of whiskey from the cupboard. That should put him right out of commission for several days. Three remained. Better get another half dozen. Never do to run short of booze in the front line. He felt in his pocket to make sure his cheque book was there. The car keys. He suddenly remembered that the car was at the church. 'Damn.'

Walking stick. A box. Impossible to secrete five bottles of whiskey on one's person. Or basket, perhaps. Keys. He'd already checked. A sure sign of nerves, checking and rechecking. Basket and stick clenched in one hand he went out of the hall door. He carefully closed it behind him, making sure it was locked.

A hole was blown momentarily in the solid grey cloud that hid the sky and a shaft of light passed across the façade of the house, startling the mica into trembling life. A great flower of happiness was growing inside him and as he stood on the top step he began to sing in his old man's voice:

'Voi che sapete . . .'

He went, still singing, down the avenue and cut off through the bushes, along an overgrown path that led, eventually, through the graveyard to the church.

He put the bottles carefully on the front passenger seat and then went round and settled himself into his own seat. The car was slow to start. The night in the open had done it no good. For about five minutes it made offensive coughing noises. The old man stopped pulling at the starter for a couple of minutes and just sat staring at the wheel. He wondered how he would treat the arrival of his old friend the Rector. The melody of 'Voi che sapete' wound itself through his thoughts. When he tried the starter again, the car engine came to life at once.

He drove to Sean's cottage. Hovel was a better name for it. Four thick stone walls, splattered with discoloured whitewash, held up a thatch that no one had tended for many years. The door and one small window let a minimum of light into a room where a couple of hens pecked hopefully at the mud floor when they got tired of pecking in the stone yard between the door and the road. The hovel crouched for support against a slightly larger building, now derelict. The slate roof had caved in in places and long green shoots of grass and weeds grew up through the holes, looking for the sun.

Clare had wanted to move the gardener into some unused back part of the house but the old man had been adamant about that. Sean on the premises was out of the question. The argument had meandered on for several weeks, he remembered, but had gradually petered out, like all Clare's arguments. She had little stamina.

He crossed the yard and, taking the bottles out of the basket, left them standing in a row, like soldiers, just to the right of the door. The hens showed no interest in the operation. They knew there was nothing in it for them. It was a neat plan, he thought, as he got back into the car; reasonably expensive, but guaranteed to keep Sean out of circulation for several days. A breathing space.

He drove to Roundwood, about fifteen miles away, where he cashed a cheque in the bank, bought several days' supply of ham and some whiskey, filled the car with petrol, in case of emergencies, and bought a toothbrush for Diarmid who, he decided, had probably been too obsessed by food problems to think of toothbrushes. Probably never brushed his teeth, bloody peasant that he was. Eight faces out of ten in the whole country filled with rotting teeth. Finally, he went into the hotel and stood himself a large whiskey.

'Well, oh well, oh look who's here. If it isn't Charlie Prendergast. Thought you were – ha-ha-ha-ha-ha – dead years ago.' A small man with a moustache focused two watering eyes on him with the greatest difficulty. 'Could have sworn we sent a wreath or something.'

Mr Prendergast smiled coldly, an almost dead man's smile. 'Clare.'

'By God, you're right. How bloody awful of me. People go so quickly these days. Hard to keep track. What? Never see you out and about anywhere. Become a bit of a recluse, hey? Can't say I blame you.' He pushed his drink along the bar until it stood companionably beside the old man's. 'Still living in that great big place?'

Mr Prendergast nodded.

'My dear fellow, you have my sympathies. We sold up a couple of years ago. Couldn't keep the place going at all, what with one thing and another. Bloody place needed reroofing. Can you imagine? I mean to say.'

They both stared at their drinks for a moment, thinking of acres of lead, tiles, timber, guttering. The man with the watering eyes sighed and pulled at one side of his moustache.

'Sold it to a fellow from Dublin. Business type. Nouveau. Very nouveau. Vous comprenez.' He winked across his glass. 'Goes up and down every day. Must be mad. Actually, taken all in all, he's not a bad chap. Eldest daughter hunts. Pity to see the old places going. We built ourselves a bung. All mod cons. Just outside Annamoe. Marjory's happy there. How do you manage to keep it on, hey?'

'I only use a couple of rooms.'

'I expect your girl'll sell it when you're gone. Once they get out they never really want to come back.'

'I suppose so.'

'Knock that back, old boy, and have another.'

Mr Prendergast obliged. Why not, after all? You might as well start an adventure drunk as sober.

'Two more of the same there, Barney.'

'Right you be, sir.'

'I've a boy in the States, another out in Ghana. He was at the Bar but decided there was no future in it, so up sticks and off he goes to Africa. My God, I said to him, all the whites are pulling out of Africa now, my boy, not like it used to be. Bloody fine place it used to be, too. What do you want to go poking your nose in for –? I said.'

'But he went.'

'Sure enough. Told me to mind my own bloody business. Something like that. You know the young. Always know best. Mind you, to give him his due, he seems to be doing very well out there. Next thing you know he'll come back with a black wife. Hahahaha. Marjory's face. Oh, ah, this'll interest you now. My youngest girl's married to Connolly Fitzherbert's boy. Remember old Connolly?'

'Haven't given him a thought for years.'

'Still going strong. Better shape than you or I. Doesn't do too much of this.' He flicked at his glass with a fingernail. The barman looked over from the other end of the counter. 'A bit deaf, though. You used to see a lot of him, didn't you? Played golf together, hey?'

'That was my brother. Alexander.'

'God, yes. Of course it was. Alexander. Yes, Handicap about five, I remember. He went in the Dardanelles, didn't he?'

'Gallipoli.'

They drank in silence for a moment. Their heads filled with the soft booming of distant guns, names, voices, faces of the past.

'Ah, yes,' sighed the man with the watery eyes.

'Quite,' sighed Mr Prendergast.

'Things have changed a lot since then.'

'True enough.'

'You know, now I've never said this to a soul before, but I'd never have believed we'd have made a go of it the way we have.'

The old man looked at him, puzzled. 'We?'

'You know, the Irish. Dev and all that lot. I bet you never thought back in 1916 that things would turn out like this.'

'I never gave it much thought.'

'Neither did I, old man.'

They both started laughing.

'How about another?' asked the old man when they had recovered.

'Why not?'

'The same again, Barney.'

'The same it is.'

It was quite some time later. The man with the sore eyes must have been having difficulty in seeing, only threads of blue showed among the folds of skin. Mr Prendergast's hands were as steady as two rocks. He felt on top of the world.

'I feel on top of the world.'

'Capital. Nothing like meeting old friends. A quiet drink or two. Tell you what, old man, why don't you come back to the bung and we'll give Marjory a surprise? Hey? How about that?'

A thought nudged Mr Prendergast. He shook his head. 'Can't.'

'Why ever not? You said you spend all your time playing the piano. Highly ad . . . mirable. Come and play our piano for a change. Nothing I like better than a bit of Chopin. Hasn't been tuned for years. Marjory insisted on bringing it. Damn foolishness, I said, but you know women. Anyway, come along.'

'I have an appointment somewhere,' said the old man vaguely.

'Keep up your tennis court still?' asked the new old friend, surprisingly.

Mr Prendergast thought about the tennis court with difficulty. 'Good God, no.'

'Remember those tennis parties the old lady used to give? Remember them, hey?'

'I can't say I do. I never enjoyed them. I remember that much.'

'You never were much of a chap for sport.'

'I suppose not. Never been gregarious.'

'Not like Alexander.'

'No.'

'Ah, dear.' The thin blue lines disappeared for a moment. He rubbed a finger up and down his cheek. 'The flower of England's youth and Ireland's, too.'

'Just water under the bridge.'

'I suspect you're a cynic. Are you a cynic, hey?'

'I don't think so. I find it hard to be very enthusiastic about the human race.'

'A cynic. That's what I'd call you. Have another drink?'

The old man shook his head. 'I think not, thank you. I fear I have delayed too long as it is.'

'Just as you wish. I won't press you. I'll just stay and have one for the road. May as well be hanged for a sheep as a lamb, hey?'

'Give my regards to . . . Marjory.'

'Barney. She'll be delighted . . . surprised, really, I suppose. Drop in, old man, any time you're passing. Anyone'll tell you where the bung is. Give us a bit of Chopin. Ah, Barney. Sure you won't change your mind?'

'Positive.'

'One of the same ilk, then.'

'Right you be, sir.'

Mr Prendergast drove the car with great care just out beyond the edge of the town. He stopped by the side of the road and switched off the engine. He felt definitely the worse for wear. Strange it was, he thought, as his capacity for drink appeared to be limitless in the emptiness of his house that he should be so affected now. Couldn't even remember the fellow's name. Remembered his place, though. A grey building, remarkable for its numerous chimney stacks which pushed great fistfuls of chimneys up into the sky. In the winter, when the smoke twirled up from most of them, the place had taken on the look of some sort of power house, rather than a dwelling. In latter years Clare had visited them from time to time and had usually come home with precious cuttings which she and Sean had nursed with love and stimulants until they began to thrive. The thought of Sean sobered him. He must get home. The boy locked up. He would drive very slowly and with great care. He must get home. Tucked right in to the left-hand ditch and then neither he nor anyone else would come to any harm.

*　*　*

It was well after five by the time he reached home. The hours had slipped through his fingers like wet soap. There was no sign of Sean for which the old man was thankful. It was going to be a beautiful evening. The solidity of the clouds had broken, the wind had blown itself out, the earth sighed contentedly beneath his feet. Indoors it was cold, evening, grey and dirty. He bolted and chained the hall door behind him carefully. The three flights of stairs seemed like Mount Everest. An almost impossible feat, to be celebrated at the top groping in one of the boxes and opening one of the bottles. Down the passage Diarmid rattled the handle and banged with his feet on the door.

'Coming.'

His head was shaking violently and the whiskey trickled out of the corner of his mouth. He breathed deeply in and out, trying to collect himself. This ridiculous way of carrying on, he thought, will be the end of me. I am too old for adventures. He took another drink and was surprised to see, out of the corner of his eye, Alexander, dressed for tennis, crossing the landing below. His whites were, as usual, immaculate. He smoothed his yellow hair back from his forehead with his right hand—a gesture he had frequently used, a self-satisfied gesture. He ran down the stairs, the rubber soles of his shoes squeaking slightly against the edge of each step. The old man replaced the top on the bottle and, bending cautiously down so as not to upset his equilibrium, he put it back in the box.

'Coming.'

He called louder this time, exasperated by the continuing rattling on the door. He felt unable to lift the boxes, so he left them at the top of the stairs for Diarmid to collect.

'Where were you?'

'I said I'd be a couple of hours.'

'You've been all day. I thought you'd had an accident. I thought . . .'

To the old man's horror the boy's eyes overflowed and tears ran down his pale cheeks. He turned his head away. Mr Prendergast put his arm round the boy's shoulders.

'I am sorry. I became involved in an irrelevant episode.'

'You've been drinking. That's what you've been doing. I can smell it off you.' His voice had become shrill and hysterical, like his own imitation of his mother. He pulled himself away from the old man and wiped at his face with his shirt sleeve. 'Anyroad, I'm bursting.' He ran out of the room.

'Take care,' called the old man after him, seeing in his mind's eye the strange meeting that might take place between Alexander and Diarmid.

'What of?' called back the boy.

'Nothing. Don't mind me.'

*　*　*

It was impossible to get away from the smoke. Even if the wind got up, it merely seemed to blow more smoke in your direction, never blow your personal smoke away. The sun, red through the smoke, was sliding down behind a few torn trees. The men's eyes stung, their throats itched, their bodies stank. The only thing that didn't taste of smoke was what you swallowed from the furtively uncorked flask. In the not very far distance a village smouldered. From time to time a dry beam would catch and send a spray of sparks up into the overcrowded sky. A field ambulance bumped along a narrow lane. In a ditch lay the bodies of six horses, waiting with eternal patience for a man with a spade and time enough to dig a large enough hole. The earth quivered as shells landed. Men moved through the smoke about their business, too tired to think that they might be taking their last step. Some of them played cards, some slept, some read crumpled letters, some sat and stared at the sky, now almost dark, but glowing with the reflection of a burning world. Some were just dead. When it was dark they would attack; out of the comparative safety of the trenches, across the fields and through what remained of the wood. The objective was the smouldering village, a push of about half a mile. For several days the tension had been mounting. Reinforcements had been filtering in. Diversionary tactics planned. The enemy at every moment had been under observation.

'Damn,' said a voice in the darkness.

'What's up?'

'I can't see a thing. We'll have to postpone the attack till the morning. First light.'

'Oh, sir . . .'

'I can't even see where my advance group have got to. I could have sworn I stationed them here by this chair.'

'Church.'

'Quite. Church, I meant.'

'We could turn on the light.'

'No. Better not. It could be seen down on the road. We don't want anyone snooping around. Things have gone so well. Send a dispatch rider off to HQ, will you, and let them know the form.'

'Right you be, sir.'

The dispatch rider set off along the lane, after the field ambulance, past the horses.

'I'm hungry, anyway,' said Diarmid.

'It's late.'

A cloud moved away from in front of the moon and white light lay in squares on the battlefield.

'You see. It would have been a massacre. No one can hide in that light. They have really got us where they wanted us. From the heights there.' He got up with difficulty from the floor.

'A massacre.'

'Death to many.'

'I know what it means.'

'I've seen it happen.'

'When you got your medal, was there a massacre?'

'I suppose you might call it that. I do wish you didn't want to be a soldier.'

'You were.'

'I had to be. I've never stopped regretting it.'

'I won't be massacred. I'll be the one who does the killing.'

'Precisely.'

'Wonder what it feels like to kill someone. Sometimes I dream about it. Someone you really hate.'

'Soldiers seldom hate the people they kill.'

'I bet I'll win more medals than you.'

'This is an abominable conversation. I thought you were hungry.'

'So I am.'

'Help yourself, then.' He waved a hand towards the shelves. 'I'll go down and make some coffee.'

'I'll come with you. I'd like to do that.'

'You know I'd rather you didn't.'

'Please. This once. I'll keep away from the windows. Please.'

The old man sighed. 'If you insist. I don't like it, though. Come on then, boy.'

He was glad of the boy's help climbing the stairs again. The firm hand under the elbow taking a little of the weight that now and then almost became too much for him. They brought up a jug of Nescafé which they laced with whiskey. It washed down the bread and ham adequately and made them both feel sleepy.

'Are you going to lock me in again?' asked Diarmid as the old man began to collect his things.

'I think it's best.'

'I don't like it.'

'I'm not trying to make a prisoner of you. You do understand that, don't you? It's really to keep other people out. Someone just might come prowling around. You ought to trust me. I am only trying to do what I think is best.'

'I don't like it. You wouldn't like being locked in, either.'

'I suppose I would take the circumstances into consideration. Tomorrow we'll think up some better scheme. It's just that I like to feel in control, boy. You know, this way nothing can take me by surprise. Tomorrow we'll . . . I am tired now. This room is becoming oppressive.'

'I only came because you were my friend,' whispered the boy.

'Thank you. Get some sleep now. Remember we have to take that village in the morning.'

Diarmid smiled. 'Yes, sir.'

They saluted each other and the old man closed and locked the door. He carried the key downstairs and put it on his dressing table beside a dusty pile of pennies and halfpennies. His bed was unmade. He always tried to remember to make it in the morning. He hated the wrinkled greyness of the sheets, the uncouth pillows. He sat down on it, nonetheless, and bent to unlace his shoes. Normally he put them carefully on shoe trees each night but now he couldn't be bothered. He let each shoe drop to the floor as it came off his foot and he lay back against the pillows. This had been Alexander's room. When he had come in here to sleep, at the beginning of Clare's illness, he had found a blazer, a tail coat and an army greatcoat hanging in the wardrobe. There had been nothing in any of the pockets, save the white grit of ancient moth-balls. He was surprised that they had been overlooked by mother. She had been so thorough with regards to everything else. Trunks had been neatly packed and sent off to some charitable organisation in Dublin. Not even a pair of socks, neatly rolled, had remained in any of the drawers or a handkerchief with an ornate 'A' embroidered in one corner. His papers had been burnt. His golf clubs, tennis racket, cricket bat, all had left the house for some unknown destination. So much debris. Unattached property. The bed became a boat, rocking him towards uneasy sleep. Mother had always eaten paper-thin brown bread and butter every afternoon at four and taken China tea from a massive silver pot, strained through a strainer into an opaque cup. After Alexander's death she had eaten it on the move, pacing round the drawing room, from one window to another, staring angrily at the unsympathetic sky, at the hateful, constant rebirth of nature. From the piano to the fireplace, her glittering fingers clamped round a fragile piece of bread, she strode every afternoon for over forty years, her mind absorbed by the past, by one man's brief and beautiful life. Her skirts, which had only been mildly shortened during the passing years, flicked against the legs of occasional tables and the fluted columns supporting potted plants or cascades of sweet-smelling garden flowers, according to the season, and her words flicked like whiplashes against the ears of any guests foolhardy enough to call between the hours of four and five. Father, who never went into the drawing room unless there were evening guests, would refer to 'your mother's post-meridian perambulation', but he never laughed when he said it or even smiled. His eyes would droop sadly at the corners and he would fidget nervously with his moustache and then, having let you know that he realized all too well what went on around the house, he would lower his head like a man entering a tunnel and dash on about his business. Debris, rocked from the back of his mind by the waves between wake and sleep. It had been his father's decline into illness that had driven him irrevocably away. The terrible vision that entered his head of having to live with someone who felt love and hate as strongly as she did. His father had protected himself by withdrawal behind a barrier of gentle dignity and silence. He had the strength that his son lacked. Useless debris. Clare's waiting eyes. The flashing of rings on pale hands. If only there was some way of disposing of the debris, leaving the mind neat and ordered, but more and more now the mess, the past, kept breaking through the barriers.

'Wer reitet so spät durch Nacht und Wind?'

His fingers struggled with the notes. It will be, it must be, even acceptable this time. There was no complaint. Exhausted, he fell asleep.

*   *   *

He was awakened by banging. It's the boy, he thought, struggling to open his eyes. Every morning they were held closed by thin ribbons of glue-like substance. When they were finally open he realized that it was well day and that he was lying on his crumpled bed fully dressed save for his shoes. His head was splitting and someone was banging. Not the boy. Not possibly the boy. It was the door knocker making the house tremble, making his head throb. Could he answer the door in his socks? It was something he'd never done before but he'd have to do it now if he was to do it at all. He wondered about ignoring the whole thing. True, whoever was there would go away all right but anyone prepared to make that appalling noise would surely come back. It was merely putting off the evil hour. He sat up and survived. He reached out for the whiskey bottle on the table by the bed. Kill or cure. It was an instantaneous, though, he realized, temporary cure. He tucked his unpleasant shirt securely into his trousers and made his unsteady way out of the room and across the landing. There was no sound from upstairs. May it stay like that, he prayed, and he could do without interference from Alexander also. To meet him, immaculately dressed for civilized life, on the stairs at this moment would be the last straw. For a moment the knocking stopped and he could hear the crackling of his own prehistoric bones; then, whoever was at the door began to batter once more. As he started the unlocking process the knocking stopped and the knocker breathed heavily, shuffled his feet and cleared his nervous throat. It gave a certain amount of courage to the old man, who opened the door with a small flourish. The Rector stood outside.

86

'Well, hello,' said the old man. 'What's all the . . . ?'

The Rector visibly disapproved of the sight that met his eye. He cleared his throat again, then swept his hands out wide, away from his body, and let them fall to rest, exhausted, against his black clerical mackintosh. 'May I come in?' He was obviously suffering under a great strain.

'By all means.' He opened the door wide enough for James Evers to squeeze his way through. 'What can I do for you? We seem to be seeing rather a lot of each other these days.'

'It's complex. If we might sit down.'

They crossed the hall and went into the study. Mr Prendergast opened one of the windows. A mean little wind hurried in and set things rustling and rattling. He put a hand to his head to steady it.

'I apologize for the deshabille. I . . . ah . . . was asleep.'

'Quite.'

The Rector placed himself carefully in one corner of the sofa; his eyes scurried here and there furtively, looking for evidence. He took a deep breath. 'You'll have heard the rumours.'

'Rumours?' To be calm was the important thing.

'The Toorish boy has disappeared.'

'Sean did mention something to that effect. I never pay too much attention to what he has to say, though. Sometimes he's not quite at himself. It all goes back to the accident, you know. It plays on him on occasions.'

'The child has run away from home.'

'Oh, dear. I'm sorry to hear that.'

'His parents are, needless to say, distraught.'

'Of course, but I hardly see . . .'

'Father Mulcahy came to see me . . .'

'Oecumenism.' No time for jokes, bad jokes in particular. A terrible sign of nervous tension.

'As usual, you are going to mishandle this.'

The old man turned quickly but Alexander was certainly not visible behind him.

'I hardly think this is a joking matter,' said the Rector, sour as a lemon.

'I agree.'

They eyed each other silently.

'In what way can I help you?'

'There are other rumours that you have not heard.'

'I haven't seen Sean for several days.'

'Sean says that you sacked him.'

'That's true but irrelevant. He's been a thorn in my side for years.'

The Rector didn't speak. He seemed to be gazing past the old man out of the window at the waving branches and the soft hills, but he saw nothing.

'James,' said the old man gently, 'you came here to ask me something.'

'Rumour has it that the boy might be here. Informed rumour.'

'What on earth would he be doing here?'

'Sean has been spreading malicious and . . . ah . . . I must say . . . scandalous stories far and wide.'

'Sean, indeed.'

'So Father Mulcahy, a decent fellow, really, felt compelled to come and see me. He . . . ah . . . came around last night. Of course, I assured him that what he'd heard couldn't possibly be true. Yes.'

'I suppose I should thank you. Though I'm not absolutely certain . . .'

'We were both agreed that I should, at least, come and tell you what people are saying.'

There was a long silence.

'I always told you you were a fool,' whispered Alexander.

'Am I to take it that people are accusing me of being a . . .'

'Quite,' said the Rector hurriedly.

'I can assure you . . .'

'No need. Absolutely no need, my dear fellow.'

'I won't deny that the child came up here from time to time. He swam in the lake, browsed a bit among the books, listened while I played the piano. He was never any trouble. On the contrary, in fact.'

'He should have been at school.'

The old man waved his hands helplessly in the air. 'Boys.'

'Quite.' His fingers roamed for a moment on the surface of the sofa. 'I fear you have been . . . ah . . . perhaps, careless.' The hand moved to his head and the fingers wandered among the remaining silver wisps.

'I admit, certainly, to a certain, well, negligence. I suppose that's what one must call it. I just let things be. I made no serious enquiries about things.'

'With no thought for the consequences?'

'Consequences never entered my head. The boy was happy here. He appeared to appreciate some of my finer points. I could only let him be.'

'Is he here at the moment?'

'Have you any idea why he left home?'

'Ah,' said the Rector irritably, 'the usual sort of thing, I suppose. I think they didn't see eye to eye with him about his future. A brat, I suppose, who thought he knew everything. Father Mulcahy wasn't very explicit. It was just this disturbing element . . .'

'Which is ridiculous.'

'I agree. I said so. Unequivocally.'

They looked at each other, each seeing for the first time the pain written on the other's face. In the garden the birds filled the air with painless song. The Rector hauled himself to his feet.

'He's not here, you say?'

The old man gestured wearily towards the door. 'You are at liberty . . .'

The holy hands waved a negative. 'I'll be on my way. It's all been most unpleasant. Forgive me for . . .' he searched for the right word, '. . . intruding.'

They walked in silence across the hall. Mr Prendergast opened the door and the Rector stepped out into the bird-song.

'It's going to rain.'

'Probably.'

'That's a west wind. Always brings rain. Well.'

'Well?'

'I knew it would be all right. I said to Father Mulcahy that it was all a wild goose chase. The boy'll turn up soon enough. Bad pennies always do. By the way, I haven't said a word to Eileen.'

'Might upset her.'

'Quite. Well.'

He held out his hand. The old man shook it briefly.

'Goodbye, old man.'

'Goodbye.'

The old man shut the door and stood in the hall until he heard the car drive off.

* * *

Upstairs, all was not well. The boy sulked on his improvised bed.

'It's all hours,' he complained as the old man entered the room.

'Querulousness will get you nowhere. Have you never learnt to sleep with the window open, boy? The atmosphere in here is appalling.'

Without speaking, the boy got up and opened the window.

'I heard a car.'

'Alas, yes.'

'What's happened?'

'It was someone looking for you. The hunt is up.'

The boy's face changed. A look of excitement and delight chased the sullenness. 'Is that a fact?'

The old man nodded.

'Who was it? What did he say? It wasn't Mam, was it? What did you do?'

'Take your time, boy.'

Diarmid came across the room, skipping over soldiers, the barricades, the gun emplacements, the field ambulance and took hold of the old man's arm.

'Was it the guards?'

'Heaven forbid. It was Mr Evers.'

The boy looked puzzled. 'The Protestant minister? What's it to do with him?'

'I happen to be one of his flock. Father Mulcahy thought it more tactful for him to come. Bearding the lion in its den, you might call it.'

'And you hopped him out of it, quick?'

'Well, I wouldn't say that exactly. I think he left reasonably satisfied.'

'Isn't that great. They'll never find me at all.'

'I wouldn't be too sure. They're none of them fools, you know. Have you eaten?'

'Not yet. I was waiting for you. I get the creeps up here all by myself sometimes.'

'You'll never make a good soldier if you get the creeps too easily.'

'It's only being locked in like that. I hate it.'

'Well, you can come down later and help me carry up a mattress. I'll sleep up here tonight.'

'You're a great old stick.'

'Thanks. What do you want to eat?'

The old man mainly watched while the boy had ham and baked beans and thick slabs of bread and soft butter. He then opened a tin of pineapple chunks which he mixed with condensed milk and washed down the lot with a can of Coca-Cola. The old man had a quick strengthening nip of what was in his pocket. Diarmid lay back in his chair at last and held on to his stomach.

'God, that was great. The best meal I ever had.'

'I've known better, I must admit.'

'In the trenches?'

'I must admit that meals in the trenches were not of a very high standard.'

'What would you have, like?'

'Diarmid, sometimes you push me too far. I simply can't remember every appalling thing that happened in my whole life. It was . . . It was fifty-five years ago, or thereabouts.'

'Ah, go on, try. I'm sure you could remember if you tried. I'd like to know.'

The old man closed his eyes and tried, obediently, to think about meals in the trenches.

'If one had to be left,' his mother's voice was clear and cold, like the frost the night she died. 'I can't understand why . . .' Her basic manners prevented her from speaking the remaining words. At that moment, he remembered, her fingers cracked as she twisted her rings viciously.

'There is very little justice.'

'What?' asked Diarmid.

'Corned beef,' invented the old man. 'Quite a lot of corned beef. Roly-poly pudding and fruit cake sent by ladies in Hampshire to fill the cracks.'

'I'd like that.'

'Under other circumstances, perhaps.'

'We were going to attack at dawn, sir.'

'So we were. Someone had blundered, eh?'

'It looks like it, sir. Will I give the order for the attack to begin?'

'A small reconnaissance party, I think, first. I don't like it when the enemy is too quiet. A few reliable men.'

'Sir.'

He saluted and picked up his field telephone.

The war game continued until the evening, attack and withdrawal, smoke and confusion and pain. No one had time to bury the horses. Then they went downstairs and dragged a mattress up to the nursery and some pillows and blankets. The prospect of a night on the floor didn't please him but there seemed to be no alternative. While they ate their supper, the old man started in on the story of the Golden Fleece and the boy listened until his eyes would stay open no longer.

'That'll do for now.'

'Oh, no. Please go on.'

'You're asleep. I'll tell you more tomorrow. We'll find a book downstairs, fill in the gaps. A lot of it escapes me now. You go to sleep though, now, boy.'

After a while, when Diarmid had dozed off, the old man opened the door quietly and went downstairs. The piano needed tuning. He must send for a man from Dublin. This escapade must be brought to a reasonable end. Tomorrow. The priest, a man he had always recognized to be a man of integrity, was probably the person to approach. In all conscience I cannot throw the boy to the wolves. I will have to fight. That's tomorrow. He played the opening bars of the Erl King. His fingers had stiffened over the last couple of days and were grimed with dust from the floor.

'Wer reitet so spät durch Nacht und Wind? Es ist der Vater mit seinem Kind . . .'

He half whispered, half sang. His fingers laboured.

'No, boy. No. No. No.'

He played on.

'Er hat den Knaben wohl in dem Arm, er fasst ihn sicher, er hält ihn warm.'

'Oh, for God's sake, Chas, stop murdering Schubert and come and have a game of tennis.'

The old man shook his head. You can't play tennis in the dark. You do not exist. Let my hands fumble in peace. He continued to sing. A shadow fell across the page as he leaned forward so that his eyes could make out the crowding notes, a hand placed another book on top of the Schubert.

'If you insist on strumming, let's have something you can play. Something charming and sentimental.'

His hands paused. Alexander moved from between the page and the light. How I hated you, thought the old man. How strange that, in all these years, this is the one emotion that I remember. What sickness of spirit have I suffered from?

'Play, boy. Get on, can't you?'

His hands began to play once more and, behind him, Alexander, in his prime, began to sing.

> Birds in the high hall garden
> When twilight was falling,
> Maud, Maud, Maud, Maud,
> They were crying and calling.

Two days later he had left for the front.

'Bravo.'

Mother always came when she heard him sing, or so it seemed. She had stood motionless in the doorway until the song was over. He heard the rustling of her dress as she crossed the room and kissed Alexander.

'You are in good voice today, my darling.'

A lover's, caressing voice.

The old man picked the book from the ledge in front of him and threw it across the room.

'What are you doing?'

Diarmid came into the room. His face was pale and half alarmed. 'I woke and missed you. I heard the piano. Are you all right?'

The old man was sweating and a pulse throbbed over his right eye, sounding like a drum inside his head. He stared at the boy.

'Can I get you something? Coffee? A drink? An Aspro?' The latter being his mother's prop in times of crisis.

'No, no. I'll be all right.'

'You look terrible. You're not going to die on me, are you?'

'Not just this moment.' He spoke almost regretfully. He held his hand out towards the boy. Diarmid came over to him and laid his own hand in the palm of the old man's.

'Look, boy, I may as well say it now, we've got to look at things straight. Both of us.'

'You're not sending me back, are you? I won't go. I can tell you that much.'

'Sssh.' He pressed the boy's hand to stop him from speaking. 'Just listen a while. Tomorrow morning I shall bring you down to Father Mulcahy. Preferably to your parents, I think. A man with whom we could discuss . . .'

The boy's face was in shadow and it was impossible to see what his thoughts were, but his hand in the old man's was like a stone.

'You must understand me. I will bring you. We will talk. We will all come to some agreement. I should have worked all this out before. A reasonable agreement. It should be possible to arrange for you to go away to school somewhere for another couple of years. A decent school. You'll find lots of things you want to learn in a decent school. I am prepared to give financial assistance. Between us all we must be able to find some acceptable solution.' He put a hand momentarily on Diarmid's head. 'You know as well as I do that staying here won't get us anywhere.'

'I like it here. I want to stay.'

'I think the time has come for us to be sensible about the whole thing. You mustn't be afraid. You'll never make a good soldier if you're afraid of a confrontation like this. We'll drive down in the Ford. You'll see. Everything will be all right.' The words were not convincing the boy. He was very tired. He could only repeat them time and time again. 'Everything will be all right. We'll drive down in . . .'

The boy pulled his hand away and went over to the window. 'You silly old man. I thought you were my friend.'

'I shouldn't stand in the window, if I were you. Someone might see you.'

'It doesn't matter any more, does it?'

'In a way, yes, it does.'

Diarmid moved from the window to the display table. He looked down at the medals.

'Well, what about it? Will you do as I say?'

'There's nothing else I can do, is there? There's nowhere for me to go. I thought you'd help me. Take me to England or somewhere, anyway, that no one could find us.'

'Tir na n'Og. Mind you, they tend to send you back after seven times seven years, which has led to problems in the past. No jokes. This is neither the . . . it's not possible, boy. I'm only sorry that I've been so slow about the whole thing.'

'Can I have your medal?' He had opened the case and taken out the Military Cross.

'You can have them all, if you like. They're no use to me.'

Diarmid put the medal in his pocket. 'I only want this one.'

'You'll probably get one of your own some day.'

'Grocers' assistants don't get medals.'

'I've told you. Everything will be all right.'

'You don't know them. Everything'll be the way they want. I know.'

'Look,' said the old man, exasperated, 'I promise you, everything . . .'

'. . . will be all right.'

'You're a cheeky little brat.'

'And you're a silly old man.' His still childlike voice was shaking with a determined effort to keep from crying.

There was a very long silence. The furniture, the books, the dead roses on the mantelpiece, all waited. A fly, awakened by the light, buzzed angrily for a moment and then slept again. The old man wondered where the whiskey bottle might be. He groped behind him with one hand, trying to find the piano so that he might lever himself up. He caught a knuckle on a corner and gave a little gasp of pain. He tried again and this time grasped the edge and pushed without success.

Diarmid turned and came over to his side. His eyes were red-rimmed but there were no tears. He put a hand under the old man's elbow and helped him gently to his feet.

'Thank you.'

'You wouldn't give me the money and let me go to England on my own?'

'No, boy. I'm sorry.'

'I didn't think you would. I doubt if I'd have been brave enough to go on my own, anyway. Otherwise, I suppose I'd have gone right away in the first place.'

'I suppose so.'

'You'll take me back?'

'Yes.'

'You won't . . . ?'

'No, boy. I won't throw you to the wolves if that's what you're worried about.'

'OK. So.'

The old man was relieved. 'That's the boy.' He touched Diarmid's arm.

'I don't feel happy, though.'

'No more do I. But I do believe it's the only thing to do.'

They stood beside each other, just touching, without speaking, for quite a long time.

'Come,' said the old man at last, 'we'll have a drink on it. Life is filled, boy, with uneasy silences. The one thing you'll grow to realize, if you've any sense, is that silence, even uneasy, is better than speech. All this communication stuff they go on with nowadays is rubbish. Dangerous, misleading, rubbish.'

'I haven't a clue what you're talking about. Not that that's anything new.'

'One day you'll know.'

'Everything?'

'Alas, no.'

'Even after reading all these books.'

'Possibly they only confuse you. I've always found it impossible to leave them alone, though. My mind is like blotting paper. Sucking up other men's ideas but producing few of my own.'

'Then you must know a lot.'

'I forget a lot. I've forgotten what my wife looked like, among other things.'

'You're codding.'

'I'm not given to cod. The occasional passing joke. Not cod.'

The boy let his eyes move slowly across the morass of old grey face. 'I never know whether you're a little touched or not.'

'No matter. Let's go and celebrate the beginning of a new life.' The boy grimaced. 'I'll do my last bit of fighting for you. No medals this time, though.'

Arm in arm they left the room.

Sean moved across the terrace until he stood by the window, peering into the empty room. 'I have you.' His voice was blurred with drink and triumph. 'I have you on your hands and knees. Dirty old sod. Mam.' He looked up to where the mistress watched him, from beyond the stars and moon. 'Forgive me for the dirty word but I'll fix him for you.'

He shuffled back over the terrace and down the steps. He moved for a while through her rose beds. She had a little rubber mat, God love her, on which she used to kneel to weed. He had never been great on weeding but she never expected it of him and would kneel, like a woman in the chapel, completely absorbed, only her fingers moving. His eyes were burning in his head. He pulled his cap down over them to protect them from the damp night air. In the far distance a car changed gear, otherwise there were no night sounds. He set off for the village, his boots leaving dark tracks on the dew-pale grass.

'It's as if I'd never known her.'

It was a good couple of hours later and the two of them leant sleepily against each other on the old man's mattress.

'You've said that before.'

'Alcohol makes one repeat oneself. Forgive me.'

'Yer.' The boy yawned. 'I wish I'd never known my mother.'

'It's not my mother I'm talking about. It's my late wife, Clare.'

'I know. I only said I wish I'd never known my mother. I'm sure your Clare would have been pre . . . fer . . . a . . . bell.'

'I never wanted to be a parent.'

'I hear them fighting through closed doors. She always wins. I even heard him cry once. You ever cry?'

'I don't remember.'

'He's harmless. Fecks the odd couple of dollars from the till. Where's the harm in that? Isn't it his money, anyway? He looks so scared when he's doing it, I always feel like hitting him. For God's sake, if you're going to do it, do it and enjoy it.'

'Never had to worry about money. I mean, not really worry. Not enough for, well, you know, flamboyance . . .' (the boy nodded, recognizing the word) 'but enough to get by on. See me out.'

'I cry.'

'You're a child still.'

'It's not so much the things they do to me. It's the things I see. Do you follow?'

'Keep your eyes shut.'

There was a silence while they both emptied their glasses and the old man refilled them. Then the boy laughed.

'I see you as a mad old man and the funny thing is, I like you. Why is that?'

'I suppose because you must be a mad young man.'

'I don't fall for your advice.'

'Advice? I never advised anyone, boy.'

'You've just told me to keep my eyes shut.'

'It's the only way to live, without too much pain, I mean. Believe you me, the great thing is to protect yourself. Keep yourself out of the way of the slings and arrows of outrageous fortune.'

'Have a heart.' The boy's face was flushed and his eyes swollen with tiredness.

'Shakespeare. To be or not to be, that is the question. Whether it is nobler in the mind to suffer the slings . . .'

'. . . and arrows.'

'Quite . . . of outrageous fortune. The greatest man.'

'I just don't know what you're on about.'

'Believe me, boy, neither do I. I used to be reasonably collected. But I think of late,' he rubbed at his forehead with a certain degree of petulance, 'senility is setting in.'

'Senility?'

'Mental decay owing to advancing years. It happens to the best of us.'

'I'm almost asleep.'

'And I.'

'I thought I'd never sleep, thinking about tomorrow. But . . .'

'The magic power of alcohol.'

'You never said a truer word.'

In the long silence they drifted towards sleep. Young and old breathed at different speeds, on different levels. The black windows stared at them. Someone moved and a glass was overturned. The comforting smell of whiskey filled the room.

*   *   *

The bell on the Catholic church struck four and hurrying after it, trying desperately not to be left behind, the slightly deeper bell on the Protestant church. It had always been the same. No matter what adjustments the verger made to the clock he had never succeeded in encouraging it enough so that one day it might beat its rival by a neck and amaze the village.

Five minutes later Mrs Toorish opened the nursery door and looked into the room. Behind her Mr Toorish, Father Mulcahy and Guard Devenney breathed heavily in the passage. A silver pearl moved slowly down Guard Devenney's right cheek. The band of his uniform cap was soaked with sweat. He wiped the palms of his hands nervously on his trousers. Mrs Toorish screamed.

'Mother of God. Mother of God.'

She ran across the battlefield, disregarding the gun emplacements, the barbed wire, the redoubts. Soldiers, guns, horses were scattered by her best navy court shoes. She had taken care to dress herself suitably for her visit to the big house. She dragged at the arm of the still sleeping boy. He lay curled like a small animal in the warmth of the old man. The smell of whiskey grabbed at the woman's nose.

'Drink.'

She screamed again, only this time she didn't quite make it and only a sick whisper reached the ears of the men in the passage. The priest followed her into the room.

'Drunk. Drink everywhere. Oh, my God.'

The three men were silent, even their heavy breathing seemed to have stopped. The old man, totally confused as to what was going on, dream or reality, struggled painfully to sit up, to grasp the situation. The more he grasped, the more unpleasant the whole thing became. The mad woman, in an incongruous hat, dropped the boy's arm and began to hit Mr Prendergast in the face and chest with her soft, pink hands. It was like a nightmare. He hoped it was one. He dodged and struggled to get away from the damn woman, from her fists, from whatever dreadful, incomprehensible words were pumping from her mouth. As he moved he became conscious of the boy who had uncurled himself and was lying stretched on the floor, crying. His hands were clenched over his ears to keep out the sound of his mother's voice.

He put a hand down and touched him on the shoulder. 'There, there,' he whispered, like a mother to a child that had fallen in the road. He recognized the inadequacy of the words but was helpless.

'Take your dirty hands off my child.'

'He's frightened.'

'Frightened of his own mother, is it? Of you, more like, you dirty old . . .' She paused, even in her rage not liking to say the word with Father Mulcahy behind her in the doorway.

'He's confused. He was asleep. He doesn't understand what's going on yet. Give him a little time. Your behaviour is alarming.'

'I don't want to hear what you have to say.'

'I have very little to say. I'm not quite sure what you're doing in my house, uninvited.'

He had managed to get himself to his feet and was desperately searching for some rags of dignity to cover the humiliation that he was feeling. For the first time he became aware of the three men in the door. He bowed abruptly towards the priest, ignored Mr Toorish and addressed the guard.

'Ah, Guard Devenney, I take it you have a warrant. May I see it, please.' He held out his hand with all the authority of an officer and a gentleman. The guard fumbled in his pocket but merely pulled out a neatly folded handkerchief which he pushed up under the peak of his cap in an effort to stop the sweat running into his eyes.

'It's like this, sir . . .'

'The warrant.'

'Well you see . . .'

The priest spoke. 'Guard Devenney has no warrant. He's here at my request.'

'Information was laid . . .'

'Information was, as Devenney says, laid as to the whereabouts of the child.'

'If Guard Devenney has no warrant I would be pleased if he left my house at once. All of you with him. Have you never heard of the law of trespass?'

The priest turned a stern eye on the policeman, who was edging out into the passage. 'Stay where you are . . . Have you, Mr Prendergast, ever heard of what the law says about kidnappers?'

'I haven't kidnapped anyone.'

'I warn you that that may be the least of the charges against you, when all's said and done.'

'I think, Father, you're speaking out of turn.'

'We are all upset. I am here in support of this distracted woman.'

'I appreciate your position but I would be glad if you'd all leave the house. None of us can possibly think at this moment. Tomorrow morning at, say, eleven. Perhaps you would be good enough to come back then. We can discuss with clearer minds, perhaps . . .'

'There's nothing to discuss,' said Mr Toorish, speaking for the first time. 'We've nothing to discuss with you.'

The priest put a hand on his arm. 'I think . . .'

At this moment Mrs Toorish swooped like a hawk and dragged Diarmid to his feet. 'Has he hurt you, son? Has he touched you?'

The boy covered his face with his hands and continued to cry.

'He's drunk,' said Mrs Toorish with disgust, 'I can smell the drink on him.'

'My God, tonight,' muttered Mr Toorish. He picked at a loose thread on his coat. He, too, was dressed in his suit. The guard had faded from the room and could be heard shuffling his boots in the passage. This sort of affair tended to blow up in your face. He saw stormy interviews with the Super, maybe even the County Inspector, looming ahead. Invisible was the only thing to be.

'Come here to me, Diarmid.'

The priest spoke reasonably but the boy never moved. Father

Mulcahy clicked his fingers with impatience. Mrs Toorish gave the boy a push towards the door.

'Didn't you hear Father Mulcahy . . . ?'

'Leave the child alone, can't you, woman. He's frightened and he's tired. Tomorrow morning we can . . .' Mr Prendergast touched the boy's shoulder as he stumbled past.

'Don't touch him,' screamed the mother.

The boy uncovered his eyes and looked around at the situation. The old man took a handkerchief from his pocket and handed it to him.

'Thanks.'

The priest took the boy by the shoulders and shook him gently. 'What have you to say for yourself, Diarmid Toorish, worrying the life out of your good mother like this?'

'Nothing, Father.'

'Not even "sorry, Father", hey?'

'No, Father.' He spoke the words so softly that only the priest could hear.

'Tch.' The fingers pressed warningly on the boy's shoulders.

'I'm not going home.' He looked up and stared the priest straight in the eye. 'I'm not going home. I mean it.'

Mrs Toorish began to cry. Dear God, dear boy, thought the old man, this is no time for heroics.

'So you're not. What do you intend to do with yourself, then, might I ask?'

The boy shook his head. 'I don't know.'

'You can't stay here, you know, and I'm sure you don't want to spend the night with Guard Devenney.'

'Is that a threat?' asked the old man angrily.

'My heart is broken,' sobbed the mother.

Guard Devenney, hearing his name mentioned, appeared like a ghost in the doorway, ready to vanish at a moment's notice.

'Let me handle things in my own way.'

'You're trying to intimidate the boy. Could he not spend what's left of the night, and God knows it's not much, with you?'

'When a man gets thrown from a horse, Mr Prendergast, you know as well as I he has to get straight back up again. It's better he goes tonight with them.'

'I'm not going home.' It was said this time with less conviction than before.

'You tell him,' suggested the priest.

'Off you go, Diarmid, with your mother. I'll see you in the morning.'

'You wouldn't make me.'

'Alas, boy, I have no alternative. No one will harm you. You have Father Mulcahy's word for that.'

'Yes,' said the priest. He looked around fiercely. 'No one will harm you.'

The group of them suddenly went quiet. Their faces were grey and exhausted, without energy or courage. They stood looking helplessly at each other. Outside, in the passage, the guard cleared his throat nervously.

The old man took his watch out of his pocket and looked at it, just for something to do. No one else seemed to know what to do or say next.

'Well. Yes. Eleven. How about eleven? We should be able to clear everything up then.'

The priest nodded. He pushed the boy before him out of the room. He said something to the guard that Mr Prendergast couldn't catch and then their feet started moving away, along the passage. Mr Toorish darted out of the room like a startled bird. He needed their protection.

'Fuck you, Mr Prendergast,' shouted Diarmid. His last heroic gesture. There was the sound of an almighty slap. Mr Prendergast closed his eyes. Mrs Toorish, who had remained standing in the centre of the room, made a sudden dash for the door roughly pushing the old man to one side as she went.

'Wait. Don't leave me here with him.'

It was all over for the time being. The sound of steps disappeared, descended. In the distance Guard Devenney coughed. The hall door banged.

☆ ☆ ☆

'Messing about,' said Alexander, 'forever messing about. You'll never get anywhere if you go on like that. Maybe the army'll teach you a thing or two.'

Mother laughed. The silver, beautiful laugh of a scornful girl.

'I shall go to my bed. It has been too long a day.'

'My bed, I believe, you sleep in these days . . .'

'Your bed, my dear Alexander, is six feet deep. Somewhere that is forever England.'

'Unkind.'

'I don't deny it. I have known little kindness in my life.'

'And practised less.'

The old man smiled sourly. 'I know my faults. I don't need to be judged by a . . .'

'Anyway,' interrupted his brother cheerfully, 'you've stuck your neck out now.'

'And you'll laugh when they cut my head off.'

'Dear Chas, it's nothing to what they did to me.'

'Water under the bridge.'

'Go to bed.' Alexander's voice was gentle. 'You'll know it all tomorrow.'

The old man felt the brush of a hand across his shoulder and then he was alone.

'I ought to be able to die.'

He never slept all night. The blackness of his room became grey and then blue. The chairs, book-littered tables, trousers, coats thrown with disregard here and there around the room turned from shadows into unhappy possessions. The birds, in the greyness, chattered to each other for a while and then were silent until the sun coloured the garden with golden early light and the grass was streaked with the long shadows of the moving trees. He lay on his back, tense with exhaustion. Sweat lay on his forehead like the beads of dew on the grass outside. His hands were clenched together as if he were praying.

A ludicrous situation that, in the end of all, the fag end of his life, he should be accused of being a sex maniac. There were almost elements of comedy in that. In his way of life passion had been an irrelevance, a trap for the uncautious man, creating unnecessary links between human beings. A form, to his way of thinking, of slavery. His desire for Clare, if it had ever existed, had been transitory. He had used her body from time to time as a means of relief rather than for the attainment of joy.

After the conception of Sarah it had been finished. It was ludicrous. It must, at all costs, be kept from Sarah. It would blow over. Not soon enough. Perhaps it was a nightmare and he would wake up and find his disordered life was calm once more. To tangle with the Church, the Law and the local grocer all over the head of one small boy. Ludicrous was the only possible word. He repeated it several times aloud. The empty room was filled with the sound of the one word and he was reminded of the way Diarmid repeated words after him, planting them in his brain. 'What will they do with you now, little soldier?' He pushed the bedclothes aside and sat slowly around on the edge of the bed. His eyes were hot and encrusted. His heart pounded like an engine being driven too fast. Maybe he had a slight fever. At the very thought a rush of sweat burst out from under his soft hair and ran down the crevices of his face. He rubbed at his face with the back of one hand and groped for the cureall with the other. As the alcohol ran down his throat he felt more collected. He must shave, have a bath. The smell of his own sweat revolted him. Clean clothes. Put oneself into the right frame of mind for the coming interview. A suit, he thought as he stood up, is indicated. An old regimental tie, perhaps. The brave diagonal stripes covering a hollow man. If he could find it. Must be years. He made his way unsteadily to the bathroom.

*　*　*

He was at the piano playing Scarlatti when he heard the car arrive. He looked at his watch. Ten thirty. They were rushing him. He continued to play until the bell rang. Apart from his tie he made a poor figure. Since he had last worn this suit he seemed to have wasted and it hung around him as if he were a child dressed in his father's clothes. The sickness had left him now and he walked across the hall with what he hoped were the steps of a sane and confident man. It was neither the priest, the guard, nor the grocer on the step. It was the Rector.

'Oh,' said the old man, taken aback. 'Forgive me, James, but this is hardly the best moment . . .'

'Don't be ridiculous.' The Rector put a hand on his chest and pushed him back into the hall. He closed the door behind him. 'This is all most distasteful. I had to come. The place is alive with most horrible rumours. May we go into the study?'

'Of course.'

'I hardly know what to say.'

'Perhaps it would be best if you said nothing.'

'Why did you lie to me the other day? That angered me.'

'I evaded your questions. It really all seemed so pointless. What could you have done? I have been foolish, I admit that. Almost insane, I suppose.'

'Venal?'

The old man laughed. 'Of course not. I haven't evaded that question. I'm surprised you even asked it. You've known me a long time.'

'Acquaintances. As you have so often pointed out yourself.'

'Well enough to know the answer to that.'

'It's surprising the things you discover about people from time to time. Especially with regards to . . . eh . . . matters of an intimate nature.'

'Why have you come?'

'Duty . . . Eileen . . . as I said, I find it all most distasteful. There has never been . . .'

The old man held his hand up, like a policeman on point duty. 'No need to proceed.'

'If I felt I could help in any way, but . . .'

'Quite.'

'I . . . ah . . . would strongly advise you to go to England. On a visit. Extended. Right away, before they take any action.'

'Running away in the face of enemy fire, hey?'

'Whatever way you like to see it. I must look at it from the point of view of my congregation. There will be a scandal. It will be very unpleasant, very damaging for all concerned. Some good, ah, and well . . . People will be offended. If you disappear it may come to nothing. So many tales. People have short memories.'

'I have done nothing scandalous.'

'Who will believe that?'

'You?'

The Rector waved his hands distractedly.

'I don't really care one way or the other. I am distressed that the child should become embroiled in such unpleasantness. I shall do my best to straighten things out. This needs an element of good faith from the other side, though. If they possess such a thing.'

'Sarah, perhaps . . .'

'Absolutely no. I must insist, James, that under no circumstances . . .'

The Rector ran a nervous finger round the inside of his collar. 'If you really refuse all advice . . .'

'Certainly all that has been offered to date.'

'Then there's one last thing I'm afraid I must say . . .'

'Go ahead. We haven't much time.'

'I hope you won't take it amiss.'

'I'm sure, James, I will take it in the spirit in which it is given.'

'Until this . . . ah . . . yes . . . is all cleared up, I feel it would be best for all concerned if you allowed Eileen to take over your duties, vis à vis the choir. It might become an embarrassment to you.'

'Ah, yes. Of course.'

'I must think of my parishioners. If it was purely a personal matter, believe me. I have my duty.'

'Get on home, Rector. You've done your dreadful duty. Your God will forgive you. Do go home now, there's a good man, and leave me in peace. I have nothing more to say to you.'

He crossed the room slowly and stood at the window with his shrunken back towards the Rector.

'Ever.'

The Rector stood for a moment and watched while the old man pulled a flask out of his pocket, unscrewed the top and put it to his mouth. The man is mad, was written on his judging face. He shrugged slightly. Eileen was going to be very upset about all this. He tried to think of something appropriate to say, decided against it and left the house as quickly as he could.

The room was quite still. Mother would never have tolerated a situation of this kind. No one knew better how to keep them in their place. Mother would never have changed with the changing times and all, bar a few of them, would have bowed before her arrogance.

'Mother,' he implored, tucking the flask back into his pocket. But she had never come before. He wondered, irrelevantly, what Sarah had done with her rings. He had been offended by her casual acceptance of them, by the way she had thrown them into the bottom of her bag. The garden looked neglected. The grass had not been cut since Sean left and a fine summer growth of weeds was starting to crowd the rose beds. Money was the only thing these people understood. He could make a good offer. Things could be sold. If not stocks, objects. The house was full of unwanted objects of no little value. After all, what would Sarah care? She had more than enough for one. And those rings, unused in the bottom of a drawer, no doubt. She had her mother's hands, practical hands, without distinction. What do I care about her, anyway? I gave her life. An established place among the more serious middle classes. He remembered the proprietorial pride suddenly with which he had read the telegram she had sent them on receiving the news of her double first. For some reason he hadn't even tried to explain to himself, he had pushed the telegram into his pocket and omitted to tell the news to Clare for several days. He had groped in his pocket at lunchtime and brought out the folded paper. He unfolded it and placed it on the table by his knives. It must have been about this time of year. The windows were open in the dining room and the buff paper stirred under his fingers. He had tried to smooth the creases out, erasing the evidence of delay, but then realized the foolishness of that and pushed the telegram across the table towards Clare, who was peeling ringlets of apple skin on to her plate. She waited until the apple was bare before picking up the paper. She had stared at it for a moment and then handed it back to him.

'I haven't got my glasses.'

He took the telegram, folded it once more and put it back in his pocket. 'It's merely from Sarah to say she's got a double first.'

Clare didn't say anything. She sliced through her apple, with a small silver knife. He had never been able to understand why she didn't eat an apple in her fingers like most other people in the world instead of treating it with the irritating reverence only due to more exotic fruit.

'A most admirable academic achievement.'

'You said merely.'

'Just a manner of speaking. Telegrams can be so final.'

'I'm delighted,' said Clare formally, as if she was uninvolved. 'Mother would have been so pleased.'

He didn't bother replying.

'Wouldn't she?' Her voice was plaintive.

'I beg your pardon?'

'Mother. So pleased?'

'I never could stand your mother. Damn Bloomsbury female.'

During the long pause that followed, Clare cut her apple up into even smaller pieces.

'I suppose it means she'll have no difficulty in getting a good job.'

'No problems at all. All sorts of doors open to her.'

'She won't have to rely on getting married, then.'

He reached across to the fruit bowl and took an apple. Shining red and green, one of the early crop from the orchard, with a sweet fresh smell. He bit into it angrily with his perfect teeth.

The clock on the mantelpiece struck eleven. He clasped his hands in front of him, rather as the Rector might have done, and turned away from the window. Pulses beat in all sorts of strange places in his body. As he turned, the door opened and Father Mulcahy came into the room followed by shadowy Mr Toorish ducking his head this way and that, adding up things and translating them into money. Courage, thought the old man, do not leave me now.

'Your door was on the latch,' said the priest, 'so we took the liberty.'

'Good morning. Your punctuality is scrupulous.'

Mr Toorish muttered something incomprehensible.

'Won't you sit down.'

The three men sat down and stared at each other for a moment.

Mr Prendergast cleared his throat. 'Well, let's get down to discussion.'

The priest spoke sadly. 'I'm afraid there's nothing to discuss. We probably, in fact, shouldn't be here. But we had agreed . . . The boy has made a statement. To the guards.'

'Yer.' Mr Toorish fidgeted as he spoke with some coins in his pocket. Ill-gotten, no doubt, from the till, thought the old man. But, in spite of wry thoughts, panic was creeping in.

'He's confessed. Yer. It's all written down. In black and white.'

'Confessed?'

'That was what I said.'

The old man gave a disbelieving laugh. 'I'd be interested to know to what crime he has confessed.'

'He's confessed everything. He signed a statement at the barracks last night. The guards'll be on their way to take you in soon.'

'But . . .'

'That'll be enough, Toorish,' said the priest.

The old man put his hand to his head and looked at them in amazement. 'I really don't know what you're talking about. You gave me your word . . .'

'In good faith. It never occurred to me . . . What can you do?'

'Have you seen the statement?'

The priest nodded. 'I went to the barracks on my way here. It's . . . well . . . fairly damning.'

'Oh.'

'He has admitted to being under your influence. He has admitted to accepting presents from you, mitching from school at your request, drinking alcohol here in this house with you. Running . . . ah, naked in front of you, letting you touch him . . .'

'In particular places.'

'Toorish, please. You encouraged him to leave his parents and then locked him in the room upstairs . . .'

'I don't want to hear any more. You realize, don't you, that this is the most fantastic distortion.'

'You used him for your own corrupt purposes.'

'What utter rubbish. The boy wouldn't even know what you were talking about.'

'He signed it all. In the barracks. Only a few hours ago. They'll . . .'

'Toorish.'

He began to rattle the coins again. 'He says my son's a liar.'

'You know as well as I do that your son is not exactly an angel.'

'I had hoped that I might be able to do something for the boy.'

'Yer, and we all know what that was.'

'Toorish.'

'Sorry, Father.'

'I would just like, if you'd bear with me for a few minutes, to put things in perspective.' He looked anxiously at the priest.

'Go ahead.'

'I . . .'

'Hold your tongue, Toorish.'

Mr Toorish continued to jingle the coins, if not to speak. His face was fatigued and mean but there was a distinct air of triumph about him that someone else other than himself was on the receiving end of trouble. This would take the wife's mind off the petty cash all right.

'My version. You may believe it to be distortion if you like, but I should like you to hear it. The boy came here first with a message from his mother. Something about working in the garden, if I remember aright. Isn't that so, Toorish?'

Mr Toorish moved his head uneasily but didn't say anything. He wasn't going to commit himself. The coins were silent in his pocket.

'He seemed genuinely interested in me and my belongings. Totally uninterested in school. A bit of an original, I thought. He took to coming up here to visit me. I admit to being at fault here. I suppose I should have sent him away with a flea in his ear. I didn't. That's the crux, really. He came to talk, listen, read, just be about. I admit I enjoyed his company. I suppose I must have been lonely without, so to speak, realizing. Hardly a crime.'

He got up, unable to sit under their watching eyes any longer. He walked over to the window. Mother would have disposed of them long since. She would have rung the bell for Helen Peoples, the parlour-maid, to come and show them out.

'Well . . .' began the priest uncertainly.

'He didn't want to be a grocer. Apart from anything else, it didn't appeal to him as a way of life. I'm not expressing myself very well, I'm afraid. You must appreciate . . .'

'Yes, yes.' The priest looked apprehensively at Mr Toorish out of the side of his eye.

'He came up to ask me would I give him enough money to go to England. I told him to go home and talk to his parents, that running away at his age would get him nowhere. Something on those lines, anyway.'

The jingling started again.

'Would you stop.' Father Mulcahy turned angrily on his companion who pulled his hand out of his pocket as if he'd been hit.

'Quite,' muttered the old man. 'I told him to go home. I wanted neither part nor parcel of his problems. I assure you, at that moment I was prepared to wash my hands of the child.'

He made a feeble handwashing gesture. This is ridiculous. I am justifying myself. I am whining. I am frightened.

'He came back without my knowing. Established himself. What could I do. I was his friend.'

'He has signed a statement. Isn't that enough for you? What are we listening to this for?'

'I presume the law knows as well as I, you, Toorish, and I . . . how easy it is to obtain statements from frightened people.'

Father Mulcahy sighed. 'There are very unpleasant implications in that remark.'

'I am not a perverted man.'

'There is also a witness.'

Mother and Alexander crossed the lawn on the way to the tennis court. She had her arm through his and smiled up into his face. It was the day before . . . They had drunk champagne by the tennis court and late that night they had swum in the lake. It had been full of stars which lay, he remembered, in his cupped hands, like the bubbles in the champagne glasses.

'A witness?'

Mr Toorish began to laugh.

'How can you have a damn witness?'

'You see, me bucko, we have you where we want you. There was Sean Brady watching every move you made and you never knew. He saw your mauling and your conniving and not ashamed to tell either.'

'Enough, enough,' said the priest wearily.

'You really are amazing.' He put a hand against the wall to steady himself. The world was spinning.

'Not a bit afraid of those that might think they were his betters.'

The priest put out a hand and touched Mr Toorish gently on the arm. 'Please.'

Mr Toorish shrugged the hand off ungraciously. 'There's no reason to stay. He's got the picture now.' He stood up.

'There's just one thing I'd like to know before you go. The boy? What will happen to him?'

'You'd like to know, wouldn't you?'

'I thought it was best if he left here as soon as possible . . .'

'There's no need to speak a word, Father.'

'I'm not too sure that this man is the kind of devil you're making him out to be.'

'Isn't there the statement? Don't you tell me a kid could make up that sort of thing.'

'With judicious questions . . . who knows . . . In this country, thank God, every man is innocent until it's proved otherwise.'

'About the boy . . .'

'I have arranged for him to go to the Christian Brothers in Cork. They will take good care of him for a year or two. From now on, late though it be, I shall take a concerned interest in his welfare. I feel, Mr Prendergast, that I, too, have been lax in my duties.'

'I couldn't see him before he goes?'

'I'm afraid that's out of the question.'

'He has made a very serious accusation behind my back. I would like him to make it, if he will, to my face.'

'That will be for the law to decide. In time. He's leaving here this afternoon. I shall take him to Cork myself and see him bestowed.'

'That's something, anyway.'

They looked at each other with a glimmer of understanding.

'Hmm.'

The priest stood up slowly. 'I used to be a bit of a pianist myself once.'

'Indeed.'

'When I was a curate. My duties then were not so time-consuming and, I suppose, I had the energy of youth. I must confess I sometimes stop and listen when you're playing the organ. Thank God, anyway, for Bach.'

'Amen. I don't play like I used to. My fingers are stiff these days.'

'Old age comes to us all. I've often wished we had an organist like yourself. Owen Doherty is hardly an artist. Mind you, that's just between these four walls.' He paused. They had both forgotten Mr Toorish whose mean eyes shifted from one to the other, like someone watching a tennis match. 'Perhaps, when all this has blown over, we might, ah, look out some duets. What with your stiffness and my lack of practice we might be well matched.'

'Do you honestly think, Father, that all this will blow over?'

The priest thought for a moment. 'No. I don't suppose it will. Their blood is up. Were you ever a hunting man?'

'My brother.'

'Ah, yes. Before my time. I heard of him, though. A great man, by all accounts. There's this . . . well, it's hard to put into words . . . feeling of excitement that sometimes happens. Closeness. To the humans and animals alike. A sudden single-mindedness. No obstacle is too great. Their corporate mind is on one thing, the kill. And when that happens, God help the fox.'

'You don't sound as if you liked your flock, or should I say pack, very much, Father.'

'I understand them. I try to love them. I have very few illusions about the human breed, Mr Prendergast, or about my own inadequacies as a guide. But I do try to love them. I find there's very little more I can do . . . I've wished many times that you had been one of mine. The thought has often been in my mind that I could have helped you.'

'Maybe I didn't need your help.'

'We all need help. There has never yet been a human being that didn't.'

The old man went over to the glass case. He opened it and stood for a while looking at the contents. He picked up the medals first and then, after a moment's hesitation, the four miniatures. Only dark patterns lay on the velvet when he closed the case again. 'Here.' He held them out to the priest. 'Give these to the boy. He's the only one has any interest any more. This one is reputed to be by Teniers.' He held up a smiling young man. 'He might get some money for it in years to come.'

The priest hesitated to take them.

'What's that?' Mr Toorish came to life at the sound of the word 'money'. He moved towards the two older men, his hand groping in his pocket once more for the comfort of the coins. 'What's that?'

The priest accepted the offering into his hands. 'This one, you say?'

'Yes. I'd say a couple of hundred. Who knows. It might come in useful sometime.'

'I'll see he gets them.'

'Money,' squealed Mr Toorish. 'Is money changing hands?'

'A handful of military medals.' Father Mulcahy waved them in front of his eyes.

'There's no use trying to buy me off. The whole thing's in the hands of the law.'

'Don't worry,' said the priest. 'Leave it all to me.' He stowed the medals away in his pockets and then the miniatures. He pulled a large white handkerchief from his breast pocket and carefully wrapped it round the possible Teniers.

'Thank you.'

'I insist on being told what's going on.' He rattled the coins savagely.

'He was interested in those medals. That's all. I thought he might like to have them.'

'I don't know that it's right. My wife . . .'

'You can discuss it later with Father Mulcahy. Now, if you'll excuse me . . . I think there's little left to say . . . I don't feel quite myself . . . I would be grateful if you'd go.'

The priest put out a hand to touch him and thought the better of it. 'Have you no friend would come? I myself would call . . .' Mr Prendergast didn't seem to hear. '. . . Could see you through?'

'I will be all right, thank you. You have been kinder than might have been expected.'

'I'd say the guards will be here quite soon.'

'They've asked me to stop playing the organ in the church.'

'I understand that.'

'You seem to understand a lot.' His voice was cold.

'Without understanding there is no forgiveness. Without forgiveness there is no grace.'

'Bah.'

'You have a hard road in front of you, my friend. I shall pray for you.'

'Thank you.'

The priest turned to go, pushing Mr Toorish in front of him across the room. As they reached the door the old man spoke again.

'I loved the boy. Do love. Yes.'

'There's an admission for you. Did you hear that, Father? Out of his own mouth.' He looked at the priest with admiration in his eyes. 'Didn't you work him up to that well. I thought you were reneging on us with all those soft words but, by God, you were working him up. We have him for certain sure.'

'In the name of God . . .' Father Mulcahy raised his fist as he shouted and it looked as if he was going to hit the man as he had hit his son the night before. He let his arm fall to his side and laughed, embarrassed. 'May God forgive me. You see, I too, have my problems. Thank you for saying that, my friend.'

'Oh, do go away,' muttered the old man. He needed a drink desperately but didn't like to produce the flask in their presence.

'Yes.'

The two men left the room. Mr Prendergast lowered himself into his chair by the window. He waited until he heard their voices in the garden and then he pulled the flask from his pocket and drank deeply from it. He lay back in his chair and the late summer sun shone full in his face. He closed his eyes, which otherwise watered in the brilliance of the golden light. He only moved to raise the bottle to his lips from time to time and lower it again. He was still there four hours later. The sun had dropped behind the trees and its rays now gilded the ceiling. Dust danced lazily in the golden light. No squad car had arrived. No guard with notebook and ballpoint pen. No Alexander, no mother, not even Clare. No one disturbed his peace. A wasp crawled slowly across the window. Maybe the priest and that terrible little grocer had been creations of his tired mind. Last night also. How long could it all go on for? He must have some rest. Peace. Darkness, so that he could open his eyes without the pain that seemed to be splitting his head in half. He made his way over to the piano. Books of music were in piles all over the top. Some fell on the floor as he searched. Eventually he found Chopin's Nocturnes. He began to play. He felt as if he had never played like this before. The music came leaping out from under his fingers and filled the world.

*   *   *

The two guards heard the sound of the piano as they came round the last corner before the house.

'He's there, anyway,' remarked Guard Conroy.

'True enough.'

'He's a great hand on the piano.'

'I thought yeez were never coming.'

Sean stepped out from behind a rhododendron bush. He was looking very old and very mad. He peered up at them both from under the brim of his cap. Devenney put a foot on the ground.

'What are you doing hanging around here, anyway?'

'I've been here all day, waiting to see he doesn't get away on you.'

'If we need your help we'll ask for it. Get away off now and don't be hanging around here.'

'Have it your own way. He could a got into the car and driven away all the time you've been coming.'

Guard Conroy circled round and came back to see what was going on. 'Trouble?'

'There's always trouble with him around.'

Sean backed away from them into the bushes once more. The two guards looked at each other and shrugged.

'He's been banging on that piano for near on an hour now. As if he didn't care. That'll show you the bad is in him.' Sean's voice came out of the bushes.

'If you don't get out of here double quick,' said Guard Devenney, pushing off with his foot, 'I'll have you inside for trespass.'

The hall door was wide open. They knocked, as a formality, but didn't wait for an answer. They walked across the hall towards the music. The old man never heard them come into the room. They both stood in silence, listening. The younger man glanced at the other with embarrassment.

'Mr Prendergast.' His voice made no impression. 'If you'll excuse me, Mr Prendergast.'

The old man took his hands off the keys. His head was shaking gently back and forth. He turned round to face the two guards.

'That was as near perfection as I will ever achieve. Ever have . . . ever.' He peered at them, screwing his eyes up to thin lines. 'I presume you exist. I think I have been waiting for you. Yes.' He suddenly looked slightly puzzled and his hands went to his side.

The older guard spoke. 'If you wouldn't mind coming down to the barracks, sir, there's a couple of questions . . .'

'By all means. Clear things . . .'

He stood up, painfully, slowly, his hand still on his side. His fingers almost clutching.

'Indigestion.'

'We can wait till it passes, sir. There's no need to rush yourself.'

'Sit down again. A minute or two.'

Guard Conroy was alarmed by the way the old fellow's face seemed to be collapsing in front of his very eyes.

'Can I get you something?'

The old man shook his head. But the effort to do even that was too much.

'Ah . . .'

The two guards rushed to him. He gestured to them to keep their distance.

'Leave me.'

He fell. His shoulders shuddered for a few moments and that was all.

'Oh, my God,' said Guard Devenney. He took off his cap. Conroy bent down and touched the old man's body.

'He's gone all right.' He took his cap off, too; then, not quite knowing what to do with it, he put it on again.

'You'd better ring the barracks and the doctor, I suppose. Yes.'

As he spoke, Devenney took his notebook out of his pocket. He looked at his watch and began to write. After a moment he realized that Conroy was still fidgeting in the doorway.

'Well, get on, can't you?'

'The telephone . . . ?'

'Search for it, man. If you can't find a telephone in an empty house you're not fit to be in the force.'

Conroy left the room. Guard Devenney finished what he had to write and put the notebook back in his pocket. He looked down at Mr Prendergast.

'Well, I don't know . . . I just don't know. You poor bloody old sod, you've saved us a pile of trouble, anyway.'

The
Railway Station
Man

Isolation.

Such a grandiose word.

Insulation.

There was the connection in the dictionary staring me in the eye.

No place alone or apart; to cause to stand alone; separate, detached, or unconnected with other things or persons; to insulate.

The good old OED puts things straight for you.

At this moment, as I write these words, the sky is huge and quite empty, no blemishes, vapour trails, not even the distant flick of a lark's small body.

They used to eat larks' tongues. A great delicacy I've read somewhere in a book. At least we're spared that now. The larks can sing. They have their own peace in the empty sky.

I am insulated from the sound of their song and other realities by the thin panes of glass that form one wall of this studio that I have had built on the hillside just above my cottage. That also sounds grandiose.

To be accurate, and it is in the interests of accuracy that I am struggling with these words instead of colours, textures, light and shade, visual patterns, Damian thought up the idea, and then set to work to build it for me out of three tumbledown sheds. I wanted the sea imprisoned there for me alone. Spring, summer, autumn, winter, to be able to watch it change. Morning and evening, insulated from its reality. Crack, shatter, scatter angry shards and splinters. Ploughing wind driving furrows through glasslike deep grey waves. I can watch. I know that to watch is my isolation. I have no other function.

I dream sometimes of catastrophes.

I remember occasionally in the daylight the shuddering of the houses when the explosion happened. Windows then, taken by surprise, cracked, some even splintered to the ground and for days the smell of smoke lingered in unexpected places.

But now, here, the glass holds.

Over here it is bare. No one visits. Sometimes the cat startles me as he pads across the floor and rubs himself against my leg. He doesn't much like it here though. He will pad for a few minutes, stare with almost unbearable arrogance at the canvases leaning against the wall. If the sun is shining he may sit in its warmth by the window for a while but sooner or later he will retire to the cottage, the comfort of cushions and the purring machines that keep us both warm and clean and fed.

I have an easel now. I bought it for a lot of money after my first exhibition. I thought perhaps I might then feel more like a real artist, no fly-by-night enthusiast. I don't use it very often. I have become accustomed to crouching, hunkered down on the floor, but I suppose as I get older, less flexible, I will be glad of the easel. Its cross-shape gives a certain class to the studio. Damian approves of it.

The cottage is quite high on the hillside. I look west from the windows across rough fields, scattered stones and squat bushes, over the peaks of the dunes to the wide bay. A bare rocky headland to the south and to the north a long spit of sand. There is no sign from here of the village nor of the little harbour from which the fishing boats set out on tranquil summer mornings. How romantic that sounds. That is when I am impelled to stand by the window and watch, when the half-dozen boats, Enterprise, Cailín Bán, Girl Josie, Queen of the Sea, Mary Lou and Granuaile slide across the early morning sea. The grey days, the buffeting days, I don't bother to watch out for them, then they look ugly and disturbingly vulnerable. The village is much the same as any other village in this part of the North West, the houses and shops clinging to the sides of a blue-black road. You swing into the village past the new Church, vulgar, triumphant and quite out of place in the almost stark landscape. Three or four shops, a couple of pubs, the licensed betting office, a few cottages, the Hotel and at the far end of the village the new estate, two neat rectangles of houses sprouting aerials from every roof. In the summer Sweeney's shop and Doherty's sell buckets and spades and brightly coloured plastic balls, picture postcards in revolving metal frames and both shops have installed machines for making whipped ice cream. In the hollow between the village and the dunes there is a caravan site, which takes a hundred caravans, permanently placed and discreetly hidden from the road. A great source of prosperity.

If you look with care you can see scattered through the surrounding fields the pattern of the village as it used to be a long time ago. Falling gables and piles of rubble are linked by the vestiges of tracks through the rocks and the whin bushes. A few cottages still stand, re-roofed with slates and with glass porches built to keep out the wind. These are, by and large, the homes of holiday people from Dublin and Belfast, England even. Though you cannot see the sea from the village you can smell the salt on the air and the heavy smell also of the seaweed that is washed up on great patches of the sand in the winter storms. On wild days you can hear the crash of the waves and the grinding of the stones as they drag along the beach.

About two miles out of the village on the side of this same hill is the railway station.

Since the closure of the railway in 1940 the square stone house had been uninhabited, the windows had been broken in the signal box and the wooden steps had rotted as had the gates at the level crossing.

Brambles and scutch had grown up on the permanent way and the platforms were covered with thick grass and weeds. That was until the Englishman bought it about three years ago and he and Damian restored and refurbished it until you would never have known that it had suffered nearly forty years' neglect. It is now derelict again and the weeds are beginning to take over once more. The engine shed by the level crossing was almost demolished when the explosion happened, and part of the gable wall of the house itself was badly damaged. No one has bothered to rebuild, or even shift the rubble, nor I suppose, will they ever . . . The buildings stand there, and will presumably continue to stand there until they fall down, as a derelict memorial to the deaths of four men. Violent, and to use Roger's own word, 'needless' deaths.

Who is this woman with the cat who lives on the side of a hill and watches the fishing boats on tranquil summer mornings?

I had hoped not to have to explain. Explanations are so tedious for the writer as well as the reader, but having explained the place I feel I should also explain the person; sketch might be a more reasonable word . . . sketch the person.

My name is Helen. Not the name I would have called myself if I had had the choice, but I have learnt to live with it. Two rows of wrinkles circle my wrists. My body is still smooth and pale, spotted quite nicely here and there with brown moles; in spite of that I don't get much joy from catching sight of myself in the glass, just too much flesh and pride.

I was born on a Sunday in 1930. The day of the week always seemed important to me. The child that is born on the Sabbath day, is bonny and blithe and good and gay. I at least had that over most of my friends.

My life was filled with safety.

We heard about the war on the wireless. The names in that distant game stuck in our heads, El Alamein, Monte Cassino, Dunkirk, Leningrad, Arnhem, Hiroshima, Ypres, the Somme, Balaclava, Waterloo, Culloden, Agincourt, Crécy. Nearer to home Drogheda, the Boyne, Wexford, more names. Words in books, newspapers, on the air, once more into the breach dear friends, we shall fight on the beaches, and gentlemen in England now abed have nothing to offer but blood, toil, tears and sweat. Just words. We received small wooden chests of tea from America at regular intervals and delicious pounds of yellow butter from friends in the country and there were no more banana sandwiches at parties. These were realities.

I drew and painted. That's really all I can remember positively about my education. My attitude to the whole process of learning was one of passive resistance. Something inside me didn't want what they were offering me. I didn't make any fuss about it. I didn't break their rules, I merely slept most of the way through more than ten years of education. My lethargy tired them out and in the end they just left me to sit in the back row and draw. My pockets were always full of pencils, finely sharpened leads, that snapped if you pressed too hard on the paper, and stubby rounded soft leads, almost grey on the page and soft enough to smear when you rubbed the lines with a warm finger. The art teacher didn't like me doing that. She liked perspectives, neat lines, colours that matched and stayed inside confining lines. Her greatest aspiration for us seemed to be that we should be able to draw perfectly a cardboard box. 'Just so,' she used to say as her pencil flicked across the paper, straight lines, angles, height and depth. I slept again.

I had great expectations when I finally persuaded my parents to let me study at the College of Art, expectations that revelations might occur, both artistic and spiritual. I needed a revelation of some sort at that moment. Of course no such thing happened. I didn't have the gumption nor the energy to realise that we have to create our own miracles. It was like being back at school. I retreated into my sleep once more. I left the College of Art with a dismal record and a confused dislike of art in any form. I remember quite clearly one summer night about a week after my final term had ended, when I carried all my sketch books, my canvases, the framed pictures that I had hanging on the walls of my room, down to the bottom of the garden, beyond the tennis court, and burnt them. I had to make several journeys through the house, up to my room and down the stairs, across the hall and out the side door. The raked gravel crunched under my feet. The sun was only just visible over the high escallonia hedge that protected us from our neighbours. I neatly stacked the whole damn paraphernalia of my life into a pyramid and lit it with pink-tipped Friendly Matches. As the papers curled down into ashes the smoke curled white up past the top of the hedge and disappeared. The sky shone, a deep blue, as if it had been enamelled by some old Italian master. Three gardens away they were playing tennis. I could hear their voices and the plocking of the ball. I stood by the fire until nothing remained but a pile of shifting ashes, the heart dying. The sun flashed in the western windows as I walked back to the house. My mother was standing in the drawing-room door.

'What were you doing down there?' she asked. 'Your face is all covered with smuts.'

'Burning things.'

'What things? I hope you didn't damage the grass.'

'Just a whole lot of rubbish. Stuff I didn't need any more.'

'Not clothes, I hope. I always like to send clothes to the jumble sale.'

'Not clothes.'

Soon after that I got engaged to Daniel Cuffe.

I remember no rapture. Perhaps, though, that is because of the passing of time, rather than the fact that it didn't exist. The snapshots I have of him are like pictures of some past acquaintance, I am not stirred in any way by seeing him sitting on a beach, or standing by a flower bed in my parents' garden, his eyes screwed up slightly in the evening sun.

When I first married him he was a teacher of mathematics at Kingstown Grammar School. I see from the snaps that he was quite a nice-looking man, with large eyes and a friendly smile. If he were still alive he would have run a bit to fat, in the way that men who have been athletic in their younger days do as their lives become more sedentary. He would probably have lost quite a lot of his hair by now, and he might have had the usual Irish trouble with his teeth. He had a good singing voice.

'Did you not see my lady, go down the garden singing.' I remember that, his *pièce de résistance*. 'Did you not see my lady out in the garden there, rivalling the glittering sunshine with her glory of golden hair.' Somewhat complacently I used to think he was singing about me, my glory of golden hair, but I don't think he had that gallantry in him.

We rented a small flat on the ground floor of a Victorian house down behind Blackrock. From the front windows you looked out across a low wall and the deep railway cutting to the sweep of Dublin bay. It was all urban landscape, but beautiful none the less, always changing with the light and wind, blue, grey, green, and evening, smokey purple and the squat houses lighting up, chains of light rimming the dark sea. At night the sky above the heart of the city glowed and lighthouse signals flashed. The Bailey light, the North wall, the South wall, Dun Laoghaire and through the misty summer nights the fog horns moaned to each other. Distant painful music. There were seldom strongly defined lines, for the most part roofs merged into the sky, walls seemed to grow from the earth; the sea, the sky, the hill of Howth all seemed to be part of each other, shading and shadow, no hard edges. A few days each year were so clear, bright that then you could see the realities of granite, slate and glass, the distant sea walls became three-dimensional, Howth moved closer affirming its solidity. On these days people would look at the sky in amazement, shake their heads and say, 'It's going to rain.'

They were invariably right.

Jack was born during that time. Eight pounds four ounces, all faculties intact. I suppose I was happy and anxious. All young mothers are anxious, most of them are probably happy, niche found, creativity fulfilled, something to love bundled fretfully in their arms.

There was also a little girl. She died soon after birth, a victim of warring blood. I remember quite sharply the pain of watching her die, not because I loved her, there hadn't been time for that, but because of the fact that she had been offered no choice but death. I don't mean to swoop into sentimentality, merely to state the facts, and though the fact of her short existence has no bearing on what happened eighteen months ago, her conception and her death are a part of me.

About ten years later we moved from Dublin to Derry where Dan became the head of the mathematics department in a large grammar school. I remember so little of those years. It's probably just as well or otherwise I might bore you with tedious domestic details. It is a curious reflection on more than twenty years of marriage that all I remember with clarity was the ending of it, and even that memory is electric still in my mind for what most people in the world would consider to be the wrong reasons. It was shortly before Christmas in 1975 and I was alone in the house. I was sitting in front of the fire. I could feel the heat spreading through me. Around me on the floor were the Christmas cards. Daniel always complained that I left them too late for politeness. He was out visiting the parents of one of his sixth-form pupils. I even remember the name of the boy. George Cranston. His father was an Inspector in the RUC. My shoulders had been stiff for days and the warmth was mellowing them. The bell rang. I put the top on my pen and placed it carefully on the floor beside the unwritten envelopes and got up and went and opened the door. A policeman and a policewoman were standing on the step.

It's strange how immune you always feel to violence, devilry. Snow mixed with rain feathered their caps. In the car parked in the driveway behind them some sort of a radio crackled.

'Yes?' I said.

'Mrs Cuffe?' he asked, moving his hands nervously as he spoke.

'Yes.'

'May we come in a minute?'

'Of course. It's a horrible night for standing on doorsteps.'

I moved back into the hall and they came in through the door. He took off his cap and banged at it for a moment with his hand. Snow drops sprinkled onto the carpet and melted. The policewoman closed the door and they stood looking at me as if waiting for me to speak first.

'I'm afraid we have some bad news for you . . .'

'I think,' said the woman, interrupting him, 'we should go into the fire. I think you should sit down.'

'Bad news.' The words didn't have any meaning to me as I spoke them. 'What's bad news? I mean – I think you'd better tell me here. Now.'

'There's been an accident. Your husband's been shot.'

I laughed.

'Cuffe's my name. Helen Cuffe. You must have got the wrong person.'

The policewoman took me by the arm and pushed me into the sitting room. I looked at the piles of envelopes and cards on the floor.

'I was writing Christmas cards . . .' I gestured towards them.

'Your husband has been shot,' she said.

'Dan?'

'Yes.'

'But how? Why? Dan?'

'He was with Inspector Cranston. Leaving his house. They were . . .'

'Yes. That's where he was. He went to see George Cranston's father.'

'It seems like they were trying to get the Inspector, but they got . . .'

'Dan?'

'Your husband has been injured.'

'Is he . . . is he all right?'

'They've taken him to the hospital.'

'Is he all right?'

'We don't know any more than that. That's all we were told.'

'Shot.'

I wanted to laugh at the absurdity of it, but I didn't think they would understand.

'Would you like to get your coat?' The policewoman touched my arm. 'It's cold out. We'll take you on over to the hospital.'

I nodded and went towards the hall again.

'Nothing like this has ever happened before. To me . . . to us . . . I feel a bit confused.' I pulled my coat out of the press in the hall. 'Are you sure . . . ?'

'Yes. Quite sure.'

The policeman took the coat from me and held it while I fumbled my arms into the sleeves.

'I don't think anyone would want to shoot Dan.'

The policewoman held my bag out towards me.

'Is your key in this?' she asked. 'You'll need your key.'

I nodded and took the bag from her hand. Forty-seven pounds that bag had cost me, I thought at that traumatic moment. I remembered how I had lied to Dan about the price. I smiled at the thought. They watched me smile. I wondered what I should be doing, saying.

'I suppose you're used to this sort of thing?'

They edged me across the hall.

'It's bad times, Mrs Cuffe,' said the constable opening the door. The snow still whirled in the wind. A rotten, stinking night to be shot.

'Will I turn out the lights?' asked the woman.

'No.' I got into the back of the car. 'I hate the dark. I hate coming into a dark house.' I remembered that I hadn't got a handkerchief and wondered would I need one. Uncheckable tears flow in the cinema. Maybe at any moment that might happen. I had no precedent, nothing to measure up to. It was cold. The flakes shone under the street lights or whirled black in the shadows. Uncouth gaps in the street's façade meant war. Snow whirled in the gaps, lying now on the roads and on the birds sleeping along the railing by the river, heads folded down into their bodies.

The soldiers on the bridge peered into the car and nodded us on.

'Why would anyone shoot Dan?' I asked again as we drove up the hill towards the hospital. I asked it just to break the silence. They didn't reply. Why should they. I knew the answer.

I laughed.

'Maybe it was a dissatisfied pupil.'

They didn't move. Their heads remained stiff, staring out of the windscreen. Didn't smile, gesture. My hands were so cold in their silence. We drew up at the entrance for the ambulances.

No Parking, it said. Ambulances Only. A tall man was standing at the door. I knew the moment I saw his face that Dan was dead.

We took him to Dublin and buried him beside the little girl in Mount Jerome. He had had no choice either, I thought, as I stood by the grave, but then, I told myself, we none of us have that choice. Dan's mother clung to my arm as if she needed my support. My hands were still cold. That is the one thing I know I remember. All the rest is a vague jumble in my mind. Did I feel sorrow? Anger? I hope I felt both of these emotions, but I'm not very sure. My hands were cold. No matter what I did over that two weeks I couldn't warm them. I would wake in the mornings to find these two cold hands clenched across my warm breasts. They felt as if they belonged to someone else. One of my teachers at school had had flat white hands. They looked always as if no blood moved through them. If she touched me I used to find myself shivering with some kind of panic. I was worried by the thought that my hands might become like hers.

I worried about Jack. He seemed curiously unperturbed, rejecting almost contemptuously any comfort that I held out towards him. He stood beside his grandmother at the funeral in his school suit, wearing Dan's black tie. His face was very white, but quite composed. He used to go up to her room in the evenings after dinner and I could hear their voices rumbling on, laughing even at times, being comfortable with each other. The day he went back to school I got on the bus and returned to Derry.

The house was just as I had left it that evening. Two piles of Christmas cards on the floor in front of the dead fire, a fine dust on all the furniture. I threw the cards in the dustbin and cleaned out the fireplace. Somewhere not too far away there was an explosion, the floor trembled under me, the windows rattled. I knew at that moment that what I had been hiding for the last few weeks from myself as well as the people around me was an amazing feeling of relief, liberation. As I cleared out the fireplace I wondered about guilt and decided against it, where was the point or the time for guilt. In the distance the fire-engines raced to a fire, ambulances, army vehicles. Glass cracked and split. The flames burst out through windows flickering into the street.

I was startled by my own happiness. The first thing I did after I bought this cottage was to build a small glass porch onto the front, not so much to protect me from the wind, but so that I could walk past packed shelves of plants each time I used the front door. On summer evenings when I water the geraniums they release a warm sweet smell that clings to my hair and clothes. That is the full extent of my gardening activity. I have never had any aptitude for weeding, grubbing, digging. There is room in the porch for one wicker chair. This has become the property of the cat. He curls and stretches on the two green cushions, digging his claws in and out of the covers, which have become feathery and pock-marked with this treatment.

I sold everything that had been in the house in Derry, apart from my books and, of course, Jack's curious mess. It seemed the right thing to do. A lot of people turned up at the auction and pawed with a certain evil excitement through the labelled contents of the house.

Jack never really moved in here with me. He preferred to take on the role of visitor, making quite short and almost formal visits to see me. Most of his holidays he chose to spend with his grandmother in Dublin. I think he must have recognised, without any words being spoken, my reaction to the death of his father and possibly been deeply hurt by it. I hate to think that I caused him pain. Maybe I merely bored him to the bone. Perhaps if he had been allowed to live we might have grown into some kind of understanding, a closeness.

Who can ever tell?

He could hear her shuffling round the kitchen. Her clogs or rope soles flapping as always at the heels. The murmur of her voice as she talked to the cat. The inscrutable yellow eyes would stare back at her as she spoke. Then they would close, a slow curtain falling. If he shut his eyes and dug himself further under the clothes, he could pretend maybe that this was a dream. I am not in Knappogue, the back of beyond, I am wrapped in my bed in number eleven, Trinity College, Dublin. Warm and comfortable city sounds thrum in my ears. People breathe in the next room, cough, piss in the lavatory down the passage, try to spit hangovers out of their heads with the toothpaste. Sometimes when his eyes were shut he could remember his room in Derry. That was his pride, his safe joy. When he had had to rip the posters and the pictures from the walls, exposing the pale patterns underneath, he had felt such desolation. He had had to empty all the drawers and the shelves, pack into cardboard boxes all his books, records, tapes, papers, throw out old clothes, the past's broken toys. He had felt so vulnerable as he stood there in the dusty, empty room with the pale empty patterns on the walls.

'It'll be all right Jacko,' she had said behind him. 'We'll put the whole thing together again. Everything will be all right.'

'I don't understand why you're leaving here.'

She had laughed and left the room.

She was like that. Inscrutable was a word he had often applied to her.

He could hear her now, coughing. She smokes too much, he thought. She stubs out her cigarettes on plates and saucers. Dead butts and ash beside the crumbs or forlorn in the spilt tea. Filter tips float eternally in the lavatory. Father had hated that. He would rant and rave a bit and tell her she would be dead before she was fifty. She just used to laugh, bend down over the lavatory and pick the butt out with her pinced fingers.

'I'll see you out,' she had once said.

She had been right.

He heard her going out of the back door.

The bottom of the door scraped on the kitchen tiles. It had been like that ever since she moved in. She never seemed to notice that you have to push the door quite hard to open it, nor the noise it made as it scraped on the floor. It gritted his teeth. He supposed that perhaps he should do something about it, but he always felt that doing odd jobs around the place committed him to the house in a way that he didn't wish to be committed. She had run out of cigarettes. The early morning pattern. He could never understand how it was that smokers allowed this to happen so frequently. She would prowl around the house looking for the hidden cigarette, a half-smoked one in a saucer somewhere, one shoved into the back of a drawer. The car was always the last hope. Sometimes she would find one, a box even, lying on the shelf under the dashboard. If she didn't she would get into the car, just as she was in her dressing gown, hair uncombed, and drive to the village. Of course if he were up and about he would offer to go for her. But he wasn't. He was tucked in his bed listening. There, the car door banged. The engine coughed a little, as she did so often, before it started. Probably a piece of red dressing gown trailed out under the door as she drove away.

She would never have lived like this if father had been still alive. He had been a neat, well-ordered man. He believed in tradition, in keeping up appearances. 'Within the structures,' he used to say to her, 'you can be vague, careless, introspective, anything you like, Helen, but you must keep within the structures. Otherwise things fall apart.' He had, of course, been a mathematician.

Father had felt she needed protecting from some destructive demon that he could see inside her. He had tried to explain it to Jack one afternoon as they played golf at Portsalon. Pillars of driving rain interrupted their play, sweeping relentlessly down the lough. Five minutes later it would be over and the grass would sparkle and steam under a hot bright sun.

'Your mother'll be getting wet,' he had said as they stood under a tree near the fourth green. 'I bet she hasn't a coat or a scarf or anything with her.'

His voice had been filled with irritation.

'I told her it was going to rain, but she didn't listen, she just went off down the beach with her hands in her pockets . . . She doesn't mind getting wet. She never has. She used to say the rain made your hair curl. I remembered laughing when he had said that. She had the world's straightest hair.

'She gets stiff. After all she isn't twenty any longer. It's silly not to take care of yourself at her age. At any age. She's never had much sense.'

He had looked out through the leaves at the rain. Jack didn't say a word. He had really been talking to himself.

'I sometimes wonder what would have happened to her if she hadn't married me. Drift. She'd have drifted.' He had turned to Jack and spoken almost angrily.

'What's she up to now? Down there. Miles away on the beach. Wet. Soaking wet. What's she up to?'

'She can't be up to very much,' Jack said.

'In her head. Bring a friend, Molly, Jean, someone you can chat to while we play golf. Have a drink in the bar with. Company. Not a bit of it. She just laughed and said she'd be okay on her own.'

'She likes being on her own.'

Dan had been silent for quite a long time. The rain was almost over.

'I have given her so much. I can't damn well work out what else it is that she wants.'

'I don't suppose she wants anything, Dad. I think you're just being a little paranoid.' It had been a new word in his life. He was rather pleased to find an opportunity to use it. Dan laughed.

'Come on. The rain has stopped. Play can be resumed.'

That had been the end of the summer holidays before Jack had gone back to school, before his father had been killed.

'And all is dross that is not Helen.' Christopher Marlowe, 1564–1593. Prodigy. Prodigious progidy. Political activist and poet, like Patrick

Pearse, d'Annunzio. Heros. Bobby Sands. His heroism was beyond
doubt but Jack didn't think that, had he lived, he would have stood up
to the scrutiny of the literati.

None of them shut their eyes to keep out reality.

No time to do that if you are to become a prodigy . . . or even a hero.

> Oh thou art fairer than the evening air,
> Clad in the beauty of a thousand stars,
> Brighter art thou than flaming Jupiter . . .

Helen.

He wondered what they thought when they had called her Helen.
Had they seen all that?

'And all is dross that is not Helen.'

Or had it been just another name?

He thought he too would like to die at twenty-nine, prodigiously
full of living.

☆   ☆   ☆

She called him for his breakfast after she returned from the village with
her purchases, not just cigarettes, but also milk for his Cornflakes and
the *Irish Times*. He always washed and dressed before he sat down to eat
his breakfast so she had almost finished the paper and her second piece
of toast when he arrived into the kitchen.

'The tea's still hot.'

'Mmm. Lousy day.'

He poured some Cornflakes into his bowl and then some milk. He
sat silently looking down at it for a while.

'I hate Cornflakes.'

The last time he had been to stay he had eaten Cornflakes several
times a day. She said nothing.

'Really hate them.'

He sighed.

'Soggy, tasteless, cardboard. That's what they are, cardboard.'

'Appalled, stunned, sickened, outraged,' she read the words from the
paper. He got up and took his plate across the room to the sink. A grey

curtain of rain hid the view from the window.

'God what a bloody day. How can you stick it here when it's like this, mother?'

'Five times on one page the word outrage. The whole country is outraged.'

He held the plate of Cornflakes poised over the bowl with holes in it that sat in one corner of the sink.

'What are you doing with your Cornflakes?'

'I'm throwing them away. I hate them.'

'Now I'm outraged. Give them to the cat. Waste not, want not.'

'I don't believe the cat likes them either.'

He scooped the mess into the bowl.

'What's everybody outraged about this time?'

He put the plate in the sink and turned on the tap.

'The usual.'

Water bounced into the plate and sprayed up at him.

'You mean the fight for freedom continues?'

'You're splashing water all over the floor.'

He fiddled with the tap.

'Jack. You're making the most awful mess.'

He turned it off.

'I don't mean any such thing. I mean a man was alive yesterday and now he's dead. That's not fighting for freedom.'

'None of those words mean anything any more. Overworked. Demeaned. Anyway, why get worked up about a man's death? We all die. We're all here one day and gone the next.'

He clicked his fingers.

'It's the snatching, playing God . . . that's what is the outrage . . .'

'An overworked word. Anyway what do you care? What does anyone care? A handful of people feel sorrow, fear, pain. Something. Otherwise it's just words, news. Manipulated words. Pictures of tight-lipped people on the television screen. Not nearly as affecting as a good play. To get back to Cornflakes . . .'

'Have some toast.'

'It's cold.'

'I'll make you some more.'

She didn't move, though. He looked at her for a moment and then sat down again.

'Don't bother. I really don't mind cold toast.'

He began buttering.

He always put too much butter on his toast; the thought of heart disease never worries people in their twenties.

'No home-made marmalade?' he asked, taking the lid off the jar.

'No.'

'You always used to make marmalade.'

'I have no time.'

'I'd have thought you'd have had all the time in the world.'

'Have some tea?'

He nodded and pushed his cup across the table . . . she filled his cup and then poured out some more for herself.

'How long are you staying?'

'Just over the weekend. I really should go on Sunday evening, but I may wait till Monday morning. It all depends . . .'

He took a large bite of toast.

'Depends on what?'

'The weather. If the weather turns good, I may not be able to tear myself away. Have you any plans?'

'I never make plans. I thought of clearing out a lot of the junk in your room. I'm sure you don't want it any longer. There's a jumble sale next week and I thought most of it could go to that.'

He laughed.

'My precious belongings. You have a nerve.'

'You brought everything precious to Dublin. What's in there now isn't even worthy of the name of jumble.'

'I suppose I can't stop you.'

'Not really.'

'If you make a pile . . . several piles . . . I'll . . .'

'Did you know that the station has been bought?'

'No. Who . . . ?'

'A couple of months ago. Some Englishman. I haven't come across him yet. I thought I might walk over this afternoon and say hello. He's doing the place up. He has one of the Sweeney boys working full time.'

He was buttering another piece of cold toast.

'Damian Sweeney.'

'There are so many Sweeneys. I never know which is which. He won't eat sliced bread according to Mrs Doherty. She has to keep him a pan loaf twice a week when the breadman comes.'

'The Englishman or Damian Sweeney?'

'Don't be silly. Haythorne. Hawthorne. Something like that his name is . . . according to Mrs Doherty. I used to have to go to tea with horrible Haythornes when I was a child. I do hope he's not one of them. He wears a black patch over one eye, Mrs Doherty says. I like the sound of that. Pirates and things. Will you come with me?'

'Where to?'

'To spy on Mr Whatsisname.'

'No. There's a couple of things I have to do. Anyway, it's raining. You don't mean to go plodding off there in the rain do you?'

'Rain'll make my hair curl.'

He smiled somewhat sourly.

She poured herself another cup of tea and got up. She wanted to be on her own.

'I'm going,' she said to him.

'Far?'

'Just out to my shed. I must work. There's so much work I have to do.'

'Why don't you get dressed?'

'I'll get dressed in my own good time.'

She picked up the cigarettes and put them into her pocket.

'You smoke too much.'

She walked to the door and then turned around and looked at him.

'Yup,' she said. 'I do. I enjoy it. I just love puffing all that poison in and out of my lungs. Anything else?'

He shook his head. She left him sitting there staring into space.

* * *

It was about two miles uphill all the way to the station house. The road could have been better. It was years since the county council men had been along with the loose stones and the tar machine. Not much need really as the road was little used. The occasional farmer with land high on the mountain would pass that way with his sheep, either on the way up to their mountain grazing or on their way down to the market. Sometimes tourists would come over the shoulder of the hill and stop their cars to look down at the ocean and its burden of small islands. No one, either farmer or tourist, ever gave the station house a second look; in those days, that was. Now it has become a part of the local folklore.

The red-brick house had been built in 1903, solid, functional, tailor-made to suit the network of lines that stretched out through the hills and along the coast, opening up for the first time access to the world, for the inhabitants of the tortuous and desolate coastland.

The house stood, squarely, facing out towards the distant sea, behind it the two platforms and the weed-filled track and then the hill, treeless, bleak. The signal box was at the right-hand end of the up platform about fifty yards from the station house. Two or three of the wooden steps had rotted away, and a couple of panes of glass were missing, but the box itself appeared to be in very good order. The white-painted words, Knappogue Road, could still be seen faintly beneath the window. The old goods shed was at the far end of the down platform, beside the unused level crossing.

The rain had settled into a misty drizzle, but from time to time a slight breeze stirred, which soon might shift the clouds. The hedges were still filled with wet shining blackberries, and she made a note in her mind to come up with a couple of baskets the next dry day. They never tasted good if you picked them in the rain, their sweetness somehow dissipated with the damp. She and Jack could carry a basket each. She laughed at the thought. He wouldn't do that. He doesn't seem to have that line in his mind leading back to early days. We can't seem to find that comfort between us, she thought. I suppose that is what parents and children should have, some form of comfort, if nothing more. It seems quite hard to achieve. She wondered why he had come down to visit her.

A blackthorn tree marked the end of the hedge. Beyond it the road widened and the station house stood there. The right-hand half of the green door was open and she walked across the road, up one step and into the flagged hallway. The air was musty and damp; over twenty years of dead mice and spiders. Even though it had all been scrubbed out and the walls painted white, the smell remained. The door onto the platform was open, letting a draught run through the hall. She walked over and peered through the window into the ticket office. A cheerful fire was burning in the small fireplace. A gate-legged table and a couple of chairs were piled with books. A duffel coat hung on the door that led out on to the platform. She could hear the sound of someone sawing wood.

'Yes?'

The voice came from behind her. She jumped.

'Can I help you?'

'I didn't hear you coming.'

A tall man with a patch over his left eye was standing in the middle of the hall. His empty left sleeve was tucked neatly into the pocket of his tweed jacket. He was altogether very neat, apart from the fact that he was wearing old tennis shoes, in the front of both of which his toes had made small jagged holes. Or perhaps the mice, she thought. Unlikely. He didn't look the sort of man who would let the mice at his shoes.

His voice was neat too, when he spoke again.

'If you're enquiring about trains . . .'

She began to laugh.

'It will be a while yet before they will be running.'

She stopped laughing.

'There's still a lot of work to be done before we're operational.'

'I . . .'

'As you can see.'

His voice was dour, unwelcoming.

'Where did you want to go?'

She didn't know what to say.

'I believe there is a reasonable bus service. You can get without too much trouble to Letterkenny and Donegal town. After that . . .' He shrugged. 'There are connections.'

She laughed again, because she wasn't sure what else to do. A little nervous laugh.

'Oh no. It wasn't that. I live here. I just came to see . . . to . . . Someone told me your name was Haythorne. I wondered . . . I used to know Haythornes back in Dublin. Ages ago. I thought perhaps . . .'

'Hawthorne,' he said, and left it at that.

'Oh.'

After a moment she held out her hand towards him.

'Mr Hawthorne. I'm Helen Cuffe.'

He didn't move.

'I live in the cottage down the road. Just before you get to the village.'

There was silence except for the sound of the saw somewhere out along the platform.

'I just thought I'd come up and see if there was anything you . . . It must be difficult to manage here. If you'd like a meal . . . or something.'

She felt her face going red.

'I am quite good at managing, thank you.'

Two puckered scars ran from the eye patch down to his chin, pulling his mouth very slightly to one side.

'I seldom go out in company.'

Bugger him, she thought. She turned away from him and began to walk back across the hall. I seldom go out in company either. Bugger him.

'Mrs Cuffe,' he called after her.

Helen stopped but didn't turn around.

'You're wet.'

She nodded.

'Or is it Miss Cuffe?'

'Mrs.'

'Did you walk all the way up here?'

'Yes. For the good of my health. I want to live a long, long time. Goodbye, Mr Hawthorne.'

'Goodbye, Mrs Cuffe.'

When she got out into the rain, she said, 'Bugger him' again, out loud.

Towards evening the rain stopped, as happens so often on the west coast. The clouds lifted and the sky became a delicate washed blue. The distant sea, a darker blue, looked turbulent; white foaming waves licked and curled around the islands. The sun softened by mists moved downwards towards the edge.

Helen sat on the step outside the porch and watched the colours change. The shadows of the trees and hedges below her grew longer and darker. Real excitement always filled her at this moment. All nature's changes are otherwise so imperceptible, this hiding of the sun by the world's edge shocked her by its speed and its awful simplicity each time she watched it happen.

Jack appeared from nowhere and stood in silence beside her. 'What time's dinner?' he asked at last.

'Any time you want it. I hadn't thought about it yet.'

'I thought I'd go down and have a drink in the village.'

'You can have a drink here and save yourself the trip.'

'See some action.'

Helen laughed.

'There hasn't been action in Knappogue since 1798. I doubt if there was any then either.'

'If that's all right with you?'

'Sure. Go ahead. We'll eat about half past nine. Unless the action is too exciting, then you send me a message by carrier pigeon.'

'Right. See you.'

Surprisingly, he bent down and kissed her on the top of her head.

*　*　*

Eight high plastic stools along the bar. All empty. Two jugs of warm water and some pickled onions in a jar. The smell of beer, cigarettes and turf dust. The turf dust must be my imagination, he thought, as nowadays no one uses the real thing any longer, neat stacks of clean briquettes beside each fireplace. No dust, no smell, no fleas. Rather tired flames flickered round the structure in the grate and across the room, high on the wall, the TV set flickered in reply.

Do not leave me oh my darling –

Mr Hasson must have seen it before. He stooped, arms outstretched along the bar, over the *Democrat*, his bi-focals slipping slowly down his nose, unable to sustain their normal position owing to the tilt of his head.

— on this our wedding day . . . ay.

Mother will be watching it, a half-smile on her face. As she cooks the dinner she will speak the lines with the actors.

Jack thought how irritated he would be if he were there.

Across the hall Mrs Hasson was supervising the laying up of the tables for breakfast. The white cloths hung in stiff points. Each side plate had its folded napkin. This evening one dahlia stood on each table in a silver cornet-shaped vase.

Mr Hasson looked up from the paper as Jack reached the bar. In the background Mrs Hasson adjusted a silver cornet a fraction of an inch and the men leaned against the pillars of the station, blue morning sky waited, they waited, the long silver tracks waited.

'How's Jack?' asked Mr Hasson, as if they were used to meeting every day. He pushed his glasses back into place again and began to fold up the paper.

'Great, thanks. Everything okay with you?'

'Mustn't complain. The Mammy keeping well? Just down for the weekend? She'll be glad of the company. Give her a lift.'

Want to bet?

Jack thought of her face as he had walked in the door the evening before, quite unexpectedly, like someone being pulled sharply from the safe web of sleep. Pleased, yes, finally pleased, but her mind taking quite some time to reach that pleasure.

'And dear old dirty Dublin? Same as ever?'

'Much the same.'

'Dangerous. Maire McMenamin from Gortahork had her car broken into and all her clothes taken. In broad daylight. Not a stitch or stim left to her. You want to mind yourself up there. Drugs and drink and kids stealing money.' He laughed suddenly and reached for a pint glass. 'That's what they say on the wireless. Guinness?'

Jack nodded.

'They say nowadays it's safer in Belfast. Troubles and all. What would you say to that?' He held the glass carefully angled under the tap.

'It's not as bad as the papers make out.'

He paid no attention.

'I wouldn't go near the place at all now. There was Mrs Hasson only last week wanted up to Dublin to look at the shops. Not at all, I says to her. What can you get in Dublin you can't get just as well in Donegal town? And the price of petrol. And you could lose your life. Have the car smashed up. Lose your life in the night walking down O'Connell Street. That's what I said to her. Wasn't I right?'

'Did she go?'

'Of course she didn't go. Why would she go whenever I told her not to? Save your money I said to her and away on to Lourdes next year with your sister Kathleen. The two parishes is getting together and forming a group.'

He slowly let go of the handle and looked at the glass. 'Wasn't I right?'

'If she wants to go to Lourdes . . .'

'Of course she wants to go to Lourdes. Hasn't she been on at me for years about it, and the group has always gone at the wrong time. Right in the middle of the tourist season. Caravans full. The hotel full. People in and out for meals at every hour of the night and day. How could she go then? I mean to say. Answer me that?'

'How indeed.'

He pushed the glass over to me.

'There's a new priest here, Father Mulcahy, and I said to him, Listen here, Father Mulcahy, I said to him if that Lourdes trip was at a more expedient time . . . see what I mean? A nod is as good as a wink. Father Collins, not that I'd a word against him, was never very amenable to suggestion. July suited him, so July it had to be. Let's start with this new young fellow the way we mean to go on. Let's have a bit of flexible thinking. That's what I said. Wasn't I right? After all, if you look at it another way, Mrs Hasson works for this parish like no one else. The backbone you might say she is and I wouldn't mind who heard me say it and it's only fair she'd get a chance of a trip like that. Wouldn't you say so? And her the backbone.'

'Definitely.'

He looked pleased.

'That'll be one pound and five pence. God be with the days Guinness was one and six a pint. I don't know how the young fellows can afford to drink at all these days. The politicians have the country ruined.

Ruined into dire straits. Wouldn't you say? One and six. And that was real money. Silver was silver. They stole the money out of our pockets when they changed all that. Daylight robbery.'

Jack handed him the money.

'I took the pledge at the age of sixteen and never broke it. Forty-seven years. Think of that now. Think of all the money would have flowed out of my trouser pocket in all those years. Mrs Hasson will take a drop from time to time. A wedding or such like. A glass of port or a nice brown sherry, but never a drop has passed my lips. My old mother, God rest her, always used to say . . . Good evening sir.'

Jack snatched his glass from the bar and fled to a small table by the fireplace. A tall man in a tweed suit walked across the room. He wore a black patch over one eye and his left sleeve was empty. Mr Hasson folded away the paper.

'Good evening, Mr Hasson. A better evening.'

His voice was English. An Oxford and Cambridge sort of a voice, quite low, quite pleasant.

'Just what we were saying, sir, before you walked in the door. A Scotch, sir? What a fine country we'd have, sir, if only we had the weather. Paradise I'd say it'd be.'

'Full of happy tourists?'

'That'd be the way, sir.'

'Hmmm.'

He turned away and looked at the screen.

A lonely man walked down the street. People waited behind the windows. Watched.

'Ah, yes . . .' he said, nothing more.

Mr Hasson poured a large Scotch in silence. When he had finished he put it on the bar and pushed the water jug along beside it.

'Good man. That's the ticket. No water thanks. I like it just as it is. I hate your dream of tourists. So here's to the rain.'

He took a drink, then he walked across the room to the fireplace. He stood looking down at Jack for a moment.

'Mind if I join you?'

'No . . . I . . . of course not.' Jack gestured at the chair across the table.

'Thanks.'

He put his drink down on the table and pulled the chair round so that it was no longer facing towards the television set. He sat down.

'Seen the damn film seven times,' he said. 'But maybe I'm disturbing you?'

'No. I've seen it twice.'

'I've always thought it was a bit over-rated. Mind you,' he laughed abruptly, 'I've never seen it with two eyes. Maybe it's better with two eyes.'

Jack shut one eye and looked at the screen for a moment.

'It seems much the same.'

The man held his hand out across the table towards Jack.

'Roger Hawthorne.'

Jack took it. His fingers were cold. He wore a gold signet ring on his little finger.

'Jack Cuffe.'

He withdrew his hand quite abruptly and they sat in silence.

'I suddenly felt the need for company,' he said at last. 'A sickness from which I seldom suffer. I am not the most . . . Just occasionally . . . a great urge to see a face, hear a voice. I haven't seen your face before around here, have I?' He paused and looked at Jack carefully. 'Perhaps I was rude to your mother earlier in the day. Your mother? Your aunt, perhaps.'

'My mother. She said she might go and visit you. I don't suppose she minded. She's sometimes quite rude to people herself.'

'Gregarious was the word I was looking for. It's strange isn't it the way words elude you from time to time. Play hide and seek with you. I am not the most gregarious of people. Your mother walked through the rain.'

'She doesn't mind the rain. She hates driving.'

'I walked down here myself this evening. It's quick coming down. Healthy. I sometimes regret my foolishness when I'm walking home. I have a specially converted car.'

'Oh.'

The gun battle flickered behind his head. Beyond the door Mrs Hasson was calling to someone in the kitchen. Mr Hasson unfolded the paper again and spread it once more on the bar.

This is intolerable, Jack thought. I will have to go.

'Are you interested in the railway signal system?'

'I . . . not really. I don't know very much about it.'

'What a pity. You could have come up and looked at my box. It's really in amazing working order after all these years.'

Mr Hasson looked up from the paper and winked at Jack over the man's head.

'It's criminal the way they've neglected boxes all over the country. England too. If they'd even kept up minimum running repairs it would have saved them so much money in the long run.'

'I can't see . . .'

'They'll have to open the branch lines again, you know. The day is coming very soon. I just thought you might be interested.'

'Well . . .'

'I have been very lucky really. The box itself has taken a bit of a beating . . . some steps gone, a bit of rot. Nothing though that I can't cope with. I have this chap giving me a hand.' He laughed. 'No. More, much more than that. We'll have it in first-class order very soon now. Everything in working order. Damian Sweeney. A really very interesting young man. In other times he would have made a most superior cabinet maker. Marvellous hands . . . imagination. A craftsman. It's good to meet a real craftsman.'

His eye looked sadly at the smouldering briquettes.

'So few people,' he said. 'So few people.'

His eye moved from the fire to Jack's face. He protected himself by taking a gulp of beer.

'Perhaps you know him?'

'Not really. I came across him when my mother moved here first. We had a bit of a barney.'

'I take it that means a fight? Fisticuffs.'

Jack nodded.

'He called me a West British bastard.'

'Ah, yes. Yes.'

'So a bit of blood was drawn. Nothing serious. I don't really live here. I just appear for a few days now and then.'

'He holds a piece of wood in his hand as if it were alive. We don't talk much. We just work together. It is a very good feeling.'

Jack wondered what Damian was up to, working for such an oddball.

'Perhaps you would allow me to buy you another drink?'

'I . . .'

'Seeing as how I have imposed my company upon you.'

'That's very kind of you.'

He nodded and called over his shoulder to Mr Hasson.

'Could we have another drink for this young gentleman here please, Mr Hasson?'

'Right away, sir.'

'You've bought the railway house?' Jack asked rather foolishly.

'Throw a couple of bits of turf on the fire for me, would you, Jack, there's a good lad.'

He got up and took some turf from the basket and placed them carefully on the fire.

'It has taken me several years to find the place. This possibility of perfection.'

Jack wiped his fingers on the leg of his jeans and sat down again. The man didn't seem to have noticed his movements at all.

'I had a splendid station in Northumberland, but they wouldn't let me stay there.'

'Why not? Who . . . ?'

He looked at Jack and smiled.

'They didn't think it was seemly.'

What an odd word, Jack thought. One half of his face was seemly, fleshed out, quite precise in its good looks, the other half a travesty of seemliness.

Mr Hasson came out from behind the bar with my drink in his hand and plodded across the room. He put the full glass down on the table and picked up the empty one.

'Jack here's at Trinity,' he said. 'Trinity College Dublin. A famous seat of learning. Maybe you've heard tell of it?' He spoke slowly and with great precision as if he were speaking to a child, or a foreigner. Jack felt himself blushing.

'A very famous seat of learning indeed,' agreed Mr Hawthorne.

When he smiled the scar down his cheek puckered and the skin over his jaw tightened with the strain. 'I had thoughts of going there myself once. My mother was Irish. It seemed appropriate at the time, but my education, that is my formal education ended somewhat abruptly at the age of eighteen. I was misguidedly led to believe that my country needed me.'

Mr Hasson winked at Jack again.

Grace Kelly was standing there crying.

'We are very foolish when we are eighteen.' Mr Hawthorne looked at Jack. 'You, I take it, have passed that foolish age.'

'He's a very clever fellow,' repeated Mr Hasson, moving away from the table. He tapped his head with his finger in case Jack hadn't got the message.

I must face a man who hates me – the music crescendoed –

'I'm in my third year.' – or lie a coward, a craven coward –

'What . . . if I may be inquisitive?'

– or lie a coward in my grave.

'Politics and economics.'

'Didn't I say he was clever?' Mr Hasson stepped in behind the bar and lifted his eyes to the screen. The serious shooting was about to begin.

'Little did she think in them days she'd end up a princess.'

The man, Roger Hawthorne, smiled again.

'Is that interesting?'

'I thought it was going to be . . . but . . . I'm not quite sure what I'm doing there.'

'It's breathing space.'

'Or a waste of time.'

'I presume you're quite intelligent.'

Jack laughed. 'Quite.'

'Then the time probably isn't being wasted. I have spent almost half my life in hospital. One sort of hospital or another. From the age of nineteen. That is wasting time. They sew you together, mind as well as body and try to make you acceptable to society. Be thoughtful of the feelings of others. Don't show people your scars. Be a good brave boy.'

Oh hell, Jack thought.

'It's all right. You don't have to worry. I'm not going to show you my scars. Any of them.'

He took a long drink. 'For how long are you here?'

'Just a couple of days. I come down from time to time to see my mother. She's alone.'

'Oh.'

'My father's dead.'

'Oh.'

'He was killed in the North. Derry. We used to live there. 1975.' He always felt that it was best to get that over.

'Oh, I see,' was all he said.

After quite a long time he spoke again. 'You must come up and look at my box.'

'Box? . . . oh, yes.'

Damian.

'Yes. I'd like to do that.'

'Come tomorrow. He's working seven days a week at the moment. He should have finished the steps tomorrow. Damian that is. If you feel like it come tomorrow.'

He stood up abruptly. 'I have imposed myself upon you for too long. Forgive me.'

'Please don't . . . I . . .' He indicated my glass of beer.

The man moved his mouth in a slight grimace. He nodded towards Jack and picked up his glass. He turned away and walked across the room to the far end of the bar. Jack noticed as he walked that his head was pulled slightly to the left as if the left-hand side of his body was slightly shorter than the right.

It was all music now and a happy ending.

What should I do if you leave me?

He pulled himself up on one of the black plastic stools and indicated silently to Mr Hasson that he would like another drink.

Do not forsake me oh my darling on this our wedding day. Do not forsake me oh my darling . . .

Jack swallowed down his beer as quickly as he could.

'Goodnight,' he said as he left the bar.

'Night, Jack,' said Mr Hasson cheerfully. He gave a final wink as he spoke. Roger Hawthorne didn't say a word.

* * *

She was sitting apparently staring at the reflection of herself in the dark window of the sitting room. The reflection of the warm room was like a blind keeping out the darkness and yet at the same time meshed with the darkness.

'You missed *High Noon*,' she said, standing up as Jack came in.

'No. I got *High Noon*. I'm thinking of starting a campaign for the suppression of *High Noon* in public places and *Casablanca*, come to think of it.'

'I thought you were well reared.'

'*Stagecoach* and *Maltese Falcon*.'

'You're quite disgusting.'

'And Cornflakes.'

She went into the kitchen.

'Such foolishness . . .' she said as she passed him. 'Come and eat. No Cornflakes tonight.'

He followed her in and sat down at the table.

'I met your friend.'

'Who?' she asked, taking things out of the oven. 'Open that wine, like an angel. I have no friends.'

'The station man. Mr Hawthorne.'

'Oh, him. Hardly a friend.'

'Damn, the cork's broken.'

'Well, don't mess about with it, push it in. Push it in, Jack. Where did you come across him?'

'In the hotel. He also was rather bored by *High Noon*. He sort of apologised for being rude to you.'

'Fancy that.'

She put a plate of food in front of him. She had always had the idea that a good mother's function was to feed her young.

'I think he's probably a bit mad. He wants me to go up and look at his signal box. Mother, I'll never wade through all that.'

'Try,' was all she said.

She took the wine bottle out of his hand and pushed her fingers down the neck moving the remains of the cork to one side so that she could splash out a first glass without too much trouble.

'Your father always mucked up the corks in wine bottles too.'

'Cheap wine has cheap corks.'

'Rubbish. He just had a somewhat insular attitude towards wine, so he didn't take care. All you need is a little care. Put the corkscrew in straight for starters. Look at that.'

She picked up the corkscrew and waved it under his nose.

'Okay. Okay. I get the message.'

She sat down and looked at the food in front of her. She had given herself almost as much as she had given Jack. No wonder she was getting fat, he thought. Fat and crabbed. She grinned at him suddenly.

'Tell me more about your man above. The Long John Silver type.'

'I don't know much more. He just seems to have this thing . . . fantasy . . . madness . . . I don't know which, about signal boxes. He said he had a station in England somewhere before he came here. A bloody Capitalist with more money than sense, if you ask me.'

She usually went a little red in the face when he said that sort of thing. Blushed for what she considered to be his crassness. He always resented that. She didn't necessarily say anything, just blushed. They both ate in silence for a moment.

'He said Damian Sweeney is an artist,' Jack said at last.

'Is he the one you had the fight with?'

'Yes.'

She laughed.

'I remember that. Blood is so bright. I don't remember why or anything like that, just the bright blood on your shirt when you came to the door. Someone told me he was mixed up in something.'

She pulled a cigarette out of a box on the table and tapped the end of it with her thumb, then for some reason or other she put it back in the box again.

'Oh,' was all he said.

'He's a Socialist or something.'

'Fairly harmless, mother. I'm a Socialist.'

'There are Socialists and Socialists.'

'A profound remark.'

She looked across the table at him and smiled slightly.

'I don't pretend to understand.'

'Everyone should try. It's a duty to try.'

She shook her head.

'I feel no sense of duty.'

He wondered what she did feel, but of course he didn't ask her. There had always been some barrier between them that inhibited that sort of question.

'A member of some violent and utterly illegal organisation,' she said after a long time. 'I think that's what I was told.'

'You mean a freedom fighter?'

'We have freedom.'

This time she took the cigarette out of the box and put it in her mouth.

'You don't know what you're talking about.'

'Probably not, but then I don't think you do either. Truth gets lost so easily.'

'What on earth do you know about the truth of things? The actuality. You sit on the side of this hill and stare at the sea. Your house is warm, you have enough to eat, nobody bothers you. What have you ever known about anything – ' She just smoked her cigarette.

'It's one of the great enemies we have to fight against. Bourgeois complacency.'

'There's not much point in yelling slogans at me.'

'I'm not yelling slogans.'

'Maybe not but you're getting all worked up to it.'

'You have to yell at people who don't . . . won't listen.'

'I don't have to listen if I don't want to. That's one of the things freedom is about. Anyway, when you've something new to say . . . oh God, when anyone has something new to say I will listen . . . even here on the side of the hill. One of the few privileges of growing older is that you can choose.'

Jack laughed at that luxurious notion

She squinted her eyes together and looked at him through the cloud of her own smoke.

'You should never hold anyone in contempt,' she said quietly. 'No one ever in contempt. You can hate them . . . whatever . . . hate me if you want, but the other, no.' She moved the hand with the cigarette suddenly in an arc through the air and ash fell onto the table.

'I don't hold you in contempt,' he said rather indignantly.

She stubbed the cigarette out and continued with her food in silence.

Why do we find it so hard to speak?

He didn't want to speak to her. That is the gut of it. He didn't want her to know his secrets. He had learnt that from her. She had protected her secrets from them, Dan and himself. Quite a ruthless protector of secrets she had always been.

'He must have been very handsome when he was whole,' she said at last. 'I wonder what happened to him?'

'Who?' He was lost.

'That railway station man.'

'The war, I think.'

'Ah, yes. The war.'

'Have some more?'

'I couldn't eat another thing.'

'An orange? Have an orange.'

'I hate oranges, mother. I've always hated oranges. You ought to know that by now.'

'Yes. I always forget. I can't ever understand how anyone could hate oranges. Perhaps one day a miracle will happen. Pow, bam, you'll eat an orange.'

'Why do you never come up and visit Gran?'

'I don't visit anyone.'

'She'd like you to.'

'Mmmm.'

'Just a couple of days from time to time.'

'We were never the best of friends.'

'That's not what she says. She's terribly fond of you. She misses seeing you.'

'Your grandmother has lots of people to see. She has the three girls fussing round her like slaves . . . as well as all her friends. Not having me around doesn't make any hole in her life.'

'Dad . . .'

'Listen Jack . . . I was a dutiful wife, a dutiful daughter-in-law . . . that's all over now.'

She poured herself another glass of wine. 'There's so little time left.'

'For her.'

'For me. I don't want to be sucked back into anything again. I don't want to be mauled about.'

'You're nuts.'

'Yup.'

'What'll I say to her?'

'Nothing. Don't carry messages. Don't you remember the Greek tragedies . . . it was always the messengers had their eyes gouged, their tongues cut out. Believe you me, if your grandmother wants to see me, she'll let me know herself.'

She stretched her hand out across the table towards him.

'It's okay, pet. You and she get on. That's fine. As it should be. Your father never quite shook her off his back . . . he never wanted to. She treated him as if he were some sort of superior being. He found that irresistible. I see no reason why you shouldn't find it irresistible also, only I don't have to be involved this time.'

He stood up.

'I'm going to bed.'

She nodded.

'I'll just have another cigarette and then I'll go.'

'How many do you smoke a day?'

'Too many.'

He left her to it.

✳   ✳   ✳

It must have been the day after that that she found the old wind-up gramophone. Jack had gone out some time in the middle of the morning. Rain had been pecking at the glass roof of the shed and she heard him crash the gears of the car as he turned out of the gate and drove up the road away from the village. Her head was filled with jaded thoughts. There are those times when lethargy seems to embrace you so closely you feel the weight of it physically with each step, each gesture of the hand. Even to pick up a cigarette becomes a major operation.

Nothing fresh pushes its way into your mind. Such days, weeks, sometimes even months, she found it hard to move out of bed in the morning. A day without hope is better spent in bed. She was convalescing after such a bout and had just started to look somewhat gingerly at her work. The excuse to leave the small shed for an hour or two of burrowing through Jack's rubbish was too good to miss.

The side of the room in which he lived was neat. His bed was carefully made, the notebooks and papers on his desk in ordered piles. A small portable typewriter was covered with a blue cloth. That desire for visible order he had inherited from his father. She had never cared for neatness. Along the wall at the other end of the room were stacked two trunks and several teachests all protected from the dust by a couple of pairs of old curtains. She opened the first trunk. Two old blazers, some distorted shoes, a tennis racquet, a Maxply, grip unwinding: Jack had played quite well, probably still did, a good strong forehand drive and an accurate service, also inherited from his father. Posters, rolled neatly and pushed down the back of the trunk. The usual Che Guevara, Mick Jagger, Monroe, Chaplin and a copy of the Proclamation. A box of snapshots that he had taken himself with the Kodak Instamatic that she had given him for his tenth birthday. They showed no great signs of originality. A few books, none of them interesting, Alistair Maclean, Agatha Christie, the rest had gone to Dublin; a few more books that had been hers when she was a child, *Alice*, the *Crimson Fairy* book, *Just So Stories*, her name carefully written on the first page in large unjoined letters, *Treasure Island*, *The Black Arrow*, Kingsley's *The Heroes*. She gathered them into a pile and brought them out and put them on the kitchen table. The pages of the *Crimson Fairy* book had golden edges. The cat had been eating the butter and crouched beside the empty dish daring her to hit him. She took away the smeared dish and washed it and lit the gas under the remains of Jack's breakfast coffee.

'Bloody awful cat,' she said. 'If you dare get sick in the house I will hit you.' He flicked her words away from around his ears and went asleep.

It's strange how one person's words sound so loud in an empty room. They resound, unlike a conversation which seems to become absorbed by the surrounding objects.

She liked from time to time to confront herself with the sound of her own voice. Oral images can be as exciting, as mind-stirring as visual ones. The spoken words echo, flicker with their own resonances in your head.

The coffee was disgusting. She left it after two sips and went back to Jack's room.

The gramophone was in the second trunk, underneath a carefully padded and packed pile of old shellac records. It was awkward to lift and quite heavy. She got it onto the desk and gave the lid a rub with the sleeve of her jersey. A large mahogany box with little shutters in the front. Her father had given it to her for her birthday one year . . . it must have been round about the end of the war. She turned the knob at the side and the shutters opened. She lifted the lid. The handle was slotted into its place and there was even a box of needles. She took the handle out and fitted it into the hole in the side and turned it. It creaked slightly as it turned. It had always done that right from the first day she got it. She recognised the sound, and the slight resistance as she pushed the handle round. Having wound it up fully, she carefully began to unpack the records.

✿   ✿   ✿

At the far end of the hedge a gate led through onto the platform just beside the signal box. Someone was whistling; no formal tune, just a high rather breathless sound. Jack walked towards the gate. The base of the signal box was red brick, about eight feet high. A flight of wooden steps went up from the end of the platform to the glass door of the box itself. Damian was crouched sandpapering the newel post at the bottom of the hand rail. One hand moved round and round scouring, the other followed feeling the wood for lumps and harshnesses. A fine dust scattered in the slight breeze. He whistled. He wore a black knitted hat pulled well down over his ears. Jack stood just outside the gate and watched for a few moments. Damian scoured and whistled. The whistling might almost have been a scouring of his head.

'Damian.' He pushed the gate open and went onto the platform. Tufts of grass and groundsel grew up through cracks in the surface.

Where once the tracks had been was now a mess of brambles and scrub.

Damian stopped work and after a moment stopped whistling as he looked up at Jack. One hand marginally moved the position of the black hat.

'Ah yes,' he said. 'We don't see much of you about, these days.'

'Work. Exams. You know the way it is.'

'Oh, aye.'

He turned away. He ran his left hand over the top of the newel post and then down the length of it, feeling the smoothness, then he began his scouring once more.

'Ever heard tell of Manus Dempsey?' Jack asked at last.

'Uh huh.'

His hand never stopped moving round and round. Tiny particles of dust flew from under his fingers and floated to the ground.

Jack walked right over to him.

'Manus said he thought we ought to get acquainted.'

The hand slowed down. Damian looked up and smiled slightly.

'Haven't we been acquainted for years. Did you not tell Manus Dempsey that?' He laughed.

'Did you not tell Manus Dempsey I gave you a bloody nose?'

'It didn't seem very relevant.'

'Anyway I don't care very much for the same fella. A bit big for his boots. A Dublin swank. Maybe you're a bit of a Dublin swank yourself?'

'No. I don't think so.'

'Good. Otherwise I might have to give you another bloody nose.'

'You haven't changed much.'

'Nobody changes much. From the cradle to the grave. You learn to walk and talk and fight your corner. That's about it.'

'He says you're a real craftsman.'

Damian started to rub vigorously once more.

'Manus Dempsey wouldn't know a craftsman from an undertaker.'

Jack laughed. 'Not Manus. Him. The Englishman, Hawthorne or whatever his name is.'

Damian looked pleased. 'Did he say that?'

'Yup. A real craftsman.'

Damian put the sandpaper down on one of the steps and ran his hands down the full length of the post. Gently he did it, as if he were touching a human being. 'Feel that,' he said.

Jack moved over beside him and touched the wood. It was smooth all right.

'Like a baby's bottom,' said Damian. 'A few coats of paint now and they'll be first-class.'

A bit of wood was always just a bit of wood to Jack, but the whole job certainly looked most professional. 'It's a pity you have to paint it. It looks great like that.'

Damian fished a cigarette packet out of the pocket of his overall.

'First-class,' Jack said encouragingly.

Damian held the packet out towards him without a word.

'No thanks. I don't.'

'The first today.' He took a cigarette out of the packet and stuck it in his mouth. 'I don't know why I do it really. I'm not wild about them. I could give it up tomorrow.'

'That's what everybody says.'

'I mean it. That's the difference between me and everybody else. I mean what I say.'

'Everybody says that too.'

Damian took the cigarette out of his mouth and threw it away into the brambles on the railway line. Then he took the packet out of his pocket and threw it after the cigarette. He took a box of matches out of the same pocket and looked at it for a moment. He put it back into his pocket again. 'I'll keep that,' he said. 'In case I want to set fire to you.'

He sat down on the bottom step and took off his hat. His hair was quite long. Soft red-brown curls, rather like a girl. He wiped his face with his hat and then put it down on the step beside him.

'What do you want?'

'I only came to say hello.'

'Manus sent you all the way from Dublin to say hello?'

'Something like that.'

He stared past Jack over the hedge, over the sloping fields towards the sea. 'Want to see the box?' he asked after a long silence. He jerked his head as he spoke, upwards towards the door.

'Okay.'

'I'll call him.'

'Couldn't you . . . ?'

'It's his box.'

'What on earth are you doing working for a loony like him? He is a loony, isn't he?'

'He's okay,' said Damian. 'I like him. He pays well.' He laughed. 'I like him even and he is a Brit. There's something about him that I like. He knows when a person does something well. That's good. There aren't too many people round who care if you do things well. They want you to do them fast. That's what matters. Get on with it. Get fucking on with it and cut the crap.'

Jack didn't say a word, just stood and looked at Damian sitting there staring out at the sea. Play it by ear, Manus had said, he may need re-activation.

'I want to build a boat one day.'

'Oh.'

'I have her in my mind's eye. A beautiful wooden hull. A sailing boat.'

'A sailing boat?'

'Yeah. I've spent too much of my life on those dirty, noisy fishing boats. Engines, oil, fumes. I want to be able to go out there on my own, with the silence. Ever seen a hooker?'

'Yes.'

'That's a beautiful boat. Something like a hooker. Smaller of course. Down round Achill they make this . . . oh, about a twenty-footer. A yawl, one big sail. I've thought it might be more practical, but I prefer the hooker. So.' He looked up at Jack suddenly and grinned.

'We'll get this station into working order. And then we'll start on my boat. We have it worked out. A gleoiteog. That more or less is the same shape as the hooker, only small.'

'You mean . . . ?'

'You see the goods shed up at the far end of the platform. He says we can build it there. There'll never be any goods for storing here. It's ideal. We'll be able to run the station between us and build the boat. No problems.'

'You've gone loony too. It must be infectious.'

'Where's the harm? I thought about it for a while when he asked me to work for him. I thought then . . . I have to believe in him. I turned it over in my mind for several days. Where's the harm in believing? That's what I thought. I like him.'

Jack laughed.

Damian put his hat on and stood up.

'You can laugh all you want,' he said. 'I'll go and get him. He can show you the box.'

He strolled away from Jack along the platform.

He may need re-activation, Jack heard Manus's voice in his ear. Re-activation . . . hell. He needed dumping.

He sat down on the step to wait. The warm smell of the sawdust tickled in his nose.

What would Manus do?

His methods were quite direct. That was one of the things Jack admired about him. I suffer from some kind of middle-class furtiveness, he thought, scratching his nose. The groundwork has been done there, sonny Jim, Manus had said. All you have to do is re-activate . . .

'Ah shit,' Jack said aloud.

Those Donegal guys are a bunch of lazy bums. They'll do what they're told but they have no drive. You have to keep behind them the whole time. Nag. Get up there, Jack old son, and nag.

What he hadn't figured on though was the loony factor. 'Shit,' he said again.

Damian came out of the house and walked towards him.

'He's not up to it.'

Jack stood up. 'What's the matter with him?'

Damian shook his head.

'Sometimes he just lays there with his eyes shut. Tell him to go away and come back another time, he said. He doesn't mean any harm. He'll maybe at himself again in an hour, ten minutes, tomorrow. Come back tomorrow . . . and bring your mother.'

'My mother?'

'Yeah. He said bring your mother.'

Jack laughed. 'Like hell I will.'

'Suit yourself. I'm just telling you what he said.'

'Listen here, Damian, you know damn well I didn't come here to see him or his signal box. Manus said to contact you.'

Damian looked at him without speaking. After a moment or two he pulled his hat off again. The wind moved his hair.

'I'm going to make him a cup of coffee,' he said. 'I'll see you round.' He turned back towards the house.

'What sort of a boat was it you said you were going to build?'

He kept walking. 'A gleoiteog.'

He reached the door into the house before he spoke again. 'I'll be in Kelly's Bar at eight.' He waved his hat at Jack and went into the house.

* * *

When Jack got back to the house, Helen was standing in the yard, outside the kitchen door winding up the old gramophone. He knew she must have been messing around in his room.

'Hello,' she said as he came in the gate.

The handle creaked as she turned it.

'What are you doing with that old thing?'

'Mary Heron rang about an hour ago to remind me that I'm supposed to be helping her with the white elephant stall at the ICA jumble sale next week. I had forgotten. Oh God, I forget so much. Even if I write things down, I forget to look. I'd forgotten all about this until I found it in your room.'

'Well that's a white elephant all right. No one's going to buy that.'

'Someone without electricity might love it.'

'Don't be daft, mother. Everyone's got electricity.'

She took a record out of a cardboard box on the table beside the machine and put it on the turntable. She pushed a switch and slowly the black disc began to revolve. Carefully she placed the needle in its shiny metal pickup on the edge of the record. For a moment there was a whining and then, slightly harsh but rhythmic, the sound of a dance band. She stood quite still and listened.

Why do you whisper green grass — gravel voice — *why tell the trees* —

'Someone will buy it. You'll see. Lots of records and two boxes of needles. I wonder if you can buy those needles nowadays.'

What ain't so —

— 'Look.' She twiddled a knob on the side of the machine. 'Those little shutters make it louder and softer. Listen.'

Whispering grass — the sound rose — *the trees don't* — and fell — *need to know.*

'I used to spend all my pocket money on records. They broke very easily. It's amazing there are so many left really.'

The gravelly voice battered around the yard. Quite incongruous.

'We could dance.' She did a little experimental twirl. 'Oh God, your father was a terrible dancer. He used to get all embarrassed when he danced and sort of seize up. The Ink Spots they were called. I suppose they must have been black. They sound black don't they?'

She twiddled the shutters again. The singer was talking now in a very black voice.

'Charlie Kennedy was the great dancer. It was such fun dancing with him. He could do anything. He used to practise steps that he saw on the films. The others stood on your toes or counted to themselves. He was great though. I wonder what ever happened to Charlie?'

'He changed his name and became Gene Kelly.'

'He was a divinity student, I think. Yes. He's probably a bishop by now. A dancing bishop.'

Suddenly she leaned forward and took the needle off the record. The black disc whirled round in silence.

'A dancing bishop in Matabeleland. Beautiful black girls with naked breasts and men beating drums. In the middle of them all Bishop Charlie Kennedy dancing away in his surplice.'

'Matabeleland doesn't exist any more.'

She made a slight face and then pushed the switch on the gramophone. With a sigh the turntable slowed down and then stopped. She took the record off and put it back into the box. She closed down the lid of the machine.

'How strange,' she said, 'that I never played it down all those years. It's amazing really that it works after such neglect. Put it in the porch for me like an angel so it's ready and waiting for Mary when she comes to collect it. Don't drop it. I cherish it. I really cherish it.'

He did as he was told. There was a pile of his old clothes on the floor of the porch. He put down the gramophone and picked up his old school blazer which lay neatly folded on top of the pile. He ran back through the house and out into the yard. She was leaning against the low wall staring at the distant sea.

'Look here,' he said, waving the blazer at her. 'You can't give my blazer to a jumble sale.'

She looked round at him.

'Why ever not?'

'It's my school blazer.'

She laughed.

'You can't let anyone go wandering round in an old St Columba's blazer.'

'I wouldn't have thought that a thing like that would have worried you.'

'Well it does.'

'They can always cut the pocket off. It's hardly worn. Remember you did a terrible spurt of growing just after I bought it and I had to get you another one practically immediately.'

She put out a hand and touched the sleeve.

'It's very good material. The moths'll eat it if we just leave it lying around.'

'I'd rather you didn't sell my blazer.'

She shrugged. 'Okay. Okay. Take it away. Feed it to the moths. Do what you like with it. I'm going to go and have a swim. My head is full of unresolved thoughts and I smell of your old musty clothes. Come and have a swim.'

He shook his head.

'Do you good.'

'Dashing in and out of icy water never did me good. It's some sort of fantasy notion of yours that it does.'

'I'll bike,' she said, not listening to him. 'If you're not coming I might as well bike. Then I'll be so healthy I'll be able to shut myself in the shed for days and days without thinking about exercise or fresh air or anything like that.'

'What do you do over there for days and days?'

'Paint.'

'But why, mother?'

'Why not? After all, a long long time ago I thought for a time that the one thing I wanted to be was a great painter.' She smiled. 'That was a long time ago. I must have been about fifteen. Another fantasy notion.'

'Why didn't you? What stopped you?'

'I just didn't have the gumption. I didn't feel like suffering.'

She scraped at a piece of moss on the wall with her finger.

'Why would you have had to suffer?'

'I'd have had to uproot, learn how to be alone, wrestle with devils. So . . .' She looked at him. The phrase 'wrestle with devils' had annoyed him, she could see that. He looked so like Dan at certain times, his mouth slightly pursed with displeasure.

'So . . .' she continued. 'Here I am. Here you are. Here we both are.'

✲ ✲ ✲

It was downhill all the way to the shore, cutting across the village street between Harkin's Bar and Doherty's Spar shop. A hundred yards or so beyond the village the road became a track, pitted and hollowed by the wheels of cars and caravans. A gate in the high hedge of thorn and fuchsia led into one end of the caravan park, but the track itself meandered on between the hedges until it widened into a flat patch where day trippers parked their cars in the summer. The sea was hidden by hills of sand and only the low roar told you what to expect when you climbed through the bent and the neat piles of rabbit droppings to the top of the dunes.

The beach was long and straight, offering no shelter from the west wind that blew in from the ocean, whipping the sand into little eddies that scurried along above the ground stinging your legs and even sometimes whirling up into your eyes.

There was no one about. Wheel marks showed where a tractor had been down earlier in the day moving sand up to someone's farm. Criss-cross bird tracks patterned the sand near the water's edge. The sun behind a streak of cloud was moving at speed towards the rim of the horizon and, strangely, the moon, like a pale shadow of the sun, floated also in the sky. Helen had never been able to grasp the movements of the moon, but she felt quite honoured to be there alone on the beach with the pair of them. She gave a little wave.

'Here I am. Here you are. Here we all are.'

What a damn silly thing to have said to Jack.

How damn silly at the age of fifty or whatever to feel evasive, protective about the inside of your head.

She kicked her espadrilles off onto the sand. It had been so hot at times in the summer that to stand barefoot had been almost impossible; each grain of sand had seemed to scorch its way into the soles of your feet . . . Now the sand was cool and slightly damp. She unfastened her jeans and pulled them off. Jack's indifference was slightly less friendly than Dan's had been. There was that element of contempt that prickled her. She dropped her jeans beside her shoes and began to walk towards the sea. Goddammit, the disease of parenthood was terminal. No way out round it, no hope of re-assessment.

'Nuts,' she said.

Five years before, five or six children had been drowned off this stretch of the beach. City children they had been, camping in the sand dunes. Sucked away into the innocent-looking sea by vicious undertow. She remembered the helpless sorrow they had all felt as each young body had been recovered. The county council had put notices along the beach after that, warning people of the danger, but now they had become weathered, illegible, vandalised. She unbuttoned her shirt and let it fall onto the wrinkled sand.

'Why do you whisper green grass?'

The waves curled round her ankles. Not cold. For a few moments a million tiny stones, driven by the waves, beat into her legs and then the water became deep. You could feel the current pulling you as you lay upon the water. It wanted you to go towards the rocks at the southern end of the beach and then if you weren't careful away out into the ocean. The bodies had been washed in again about three miles down the coast, at the outermost point of the wide bay.

'Why tell the trees what ain't so?'

She lay on her back and allowed herself to drift. She knew for how long she could indulge herself in that pleasure before turning over and swimming strongly back into the safety of the breaking waves.

'Whispering grass, the trees don't need to know.'

The sun was quite indifferent as she sang, the moon as usual smiled.

'Why tell them all your secrets . . . deedeedee long ago?'

She was half-way to the rocks. A seagull floated above her, quite relaxed on a current of air.

'Whispering grass . . . oh no no no. The seagulls don't need to know.'

She turned over and swam back against the roll of the sea. After a couple of hundred yards she turned on her back once more and let the waves roll her in towards the shore.

'Oh no no no. Whispering grass . . .'

Her bottom hit the sand.

She had judged it correctly, her shirt lay only a few yards away. She put it on and squeezed the water out of her hair.

'Whispering grass, the trees don't need to know.'

* * *

Kelly's Bar was dark and smelt of beer and a century's cigarette smoke. As Jack came in through the door he was wrapped in the smell, it crept into his pockets and up his sleeves, a total embrace. He got the notion as he stood at the bar and peered through the darkness that if the building were to fall apart at that moment, a solid block of undispersable smell would remain by the street-side. In the darkest corner Damian sat alone at a small round table. He raised his hand. Jack nodded briefly and ordered a pint of Guinness. He took the drink and carried it over to the table, pulled up a chair and sat down.

'I haven't had a smoke since I saw you last,' said Damian.

'Big deal.'

'Even my mother noticed. What's up with you, she said. No fag hanging out of your face.'

He laughed.

'She'll give me a medal, she says, if I keep it up for twelve months. I suggested she should make it hard cash. What would I do with your medal I asked her . . . knowing the kind she always has in her mind, smiling Jesus pinned to my vest. Aren't medals for to assist in the saving of souls? What do I care about damnation? She gets so mad at me when I say things like that. Upset. I shouldn't do it. She thinks I'm the walking personification of the ten deadly sins. Praying for me occupies a large part of her time.'

'Seven,' said Jack. 'There are only seven.'

'A Protestant point of view maybe . . .'

'Ten commandments, seven deadly sins. Quite multi-denominational, I assure you.' Jack's voice was filled with humourless reproof.

Damian laughed again.

'There you are. I am an ignorant renegade. A bastún. She's right. Why is it that mothers are always right?'

One finger flicked away some Guinness froth that had been clinging to the gingery moustache that drooped over his upper lip. His eyes were amused as he looked across the table at Jack.

'I haven't noticed it,' said Jack.

'You don't live at home. When you live at home you find out these things. Mothers are always right. The truth becomes irrelevant when mother is around. Keep your head down and say nothing, that's what I've learnt. The odd leg pull and the rest of the time say nothing. Ah, she could be worse. I've seen worse. I've seen your mother down on the beach drawing pictures. I wouldn't have thought there was much to draw, but she crouches down on the sand like . . .' he paused for a moment '. . . some sort of a mad creature. Lost to the world. If you were standing next to her she wouldn't notice you.'

'She has bad eyes. Problems with her eyes.'

'It's not that. Lost is the word you'd use.'

Jack shrugged slightly.

'You don't say much do you?'

'You don't give anyone much chance.'

Damian stood up grinning. He picked up his empty glass and nodded towards the bar.

'I'm having another. Will I get you one? It'll maybe loosen your tongue.'

'I'm okay.'

'Live dangerously.'

Jack watched as he walked across the room and stood, his two hands flat on the bar, leaning towards the barman. Neat in his gestures, economical with his physical movements. Unlike his gabble. Over-fond of the sound of his own voice. Look at him there now, gabbling again as the black liquid crept into the tilted glass. The boy behind the bar laughed at something he had said, mopped the bar around the glass with a white cloth and laughed again. A bit of an opinion of himself.

I wonder why is he involved? Family background? Never heard that. Conviction? Boredom? No, no, no. Not this one. Hate? He doesn't look the hating type. He looks to me like someone who drifted in and hasn't bothered to drift out again. Dangerous. They are the dangerous ones. No blinding commitment.

'There you are.'

Damian put the pint glass down on the table in front of Jack.

'Bloody bastards fleece you now for the harmless pint.'

'Thanks,' said Jack.

'Slap another tax on pleasure every time the country gets a bit low in funds. Drinks, smokes, books, the pictures, football. Squeeze another few dollars out of the buggers. Squeeze.' He laughed. 'There's one thing they forgot though.'

'What's that?'

Damian drooped one of his eyes and said nothing.

Jack thought for a moment.

'Oh. That.'

'Aye, that. It's a good thought that no matter how hard they try neither Church nor State can stop people doing that.'

'They do their best.'

'I reckon if they put their minds to it they could come up with some system. A computer implanted under the skin of every growing boy. Monitoring bad thoughts, sinful acts. At the end of the year you get a bill from Dublin. Five pence for a bad thought. A pound for self-abuse and a couple of quid every time you go the whole way. The country would be solvent in five years. I don't really amuse you, do I?'

Jack looked down at the table.

'Never mind,' said Damian, 'I amuse myself. You can't do better than that. Be amused by your own codology.'

'Manus . . .' began Jack.

Damian put his glass down on the table and frowned.

'What of Manus? The great God Manus. I can see you're dazzled by his very name.'

'You haven't a notion . . .'

'And keep your voice down. Do you want everyone for miles round to know your business?'

Jack felt his face going red.

'I'm sorry,' said Damian. 'I speak a bit too quick at times. You shouldn't pay any heed. What's on the bugger's mind?'

'Well . . .'

'Well . . .' Damian mimicked.

'He's not too keen on the way things are going up here. There's a sort of . . . ah . . . casual attitude to things. I think he's not too happy about.'

Damian smiled.

'He said to tell you he'd be up. He'd have to come up.'

'Aye,' said Damian. 'Let him come up. That would be best. No messengers.' He groped in his pocket for a moment looking for his cigarettes and then remembered. 'Anything else?'

'We need a staging post here. Somewhere stuff can be stored, adjacent to the border. Somewhere secure. It'll only be for a few weeks at the most. You're to find us somewhere secure. Quite quickly. No messing about.'

Damian nodded.

'How much space?'

'Quite a bit of space.'

Damian rubbed his finger up the side of his glass.

'About,' suggested Jack, 'the size of a goods shed.'

'Bugger off,' said Damian.

He lifted the glass and took a long drink.

'Think about it. You said yourself that no one uses it. Manus only wants it for a couple of weeks. You can see that the Englishman isn't around when we're moving stuff. You'll be there to keep an eye on things. Think about it.'

Damian put the glass down carefully on the table and wiped his mouth with the palm of his right hand. He didn't speak.

'What the hell are you doing in the Movement anyway?' asked Jack after a long silence.

'I'm not in it. I'm sort of alongside it. I'm not cut out to be a soldier.' He laughed. 'My mother's old man was a Connaught Ranger.'

He took another drink and wiped his mouth again with his hand. 'There was soldiers. He caught a shark when he was sixty-eight. Out one day in a half-decker between here and Tory Sound. I remember that.'

'That's . . .'

'Listen. Will you listen. You don't speak anything but crap and you don't listen either . . . except perhaps to Manus. He lived with us for six years after my gran died. All the way up from Connemara he came. He found it hard to settle. She thought the world of him. She'd do more for your grandaddy than she'd ever do for me, my father used to say. She has all the books of old brown photographs . . . and his medals. He went to Dublin a couple of times, I mind, for reunions or something. My father used to take him to the train in Sligo. He'd bring his medals in a little black box. He always came back a new man . . . not just an old fogey telling his stories to the kids, because no one else had the time for him. You wouldn't remember his shark?'

'I heard the story. I didn't know it was your grandfather caught it.'

'Yes. Swan song.'

'But none of this is . . .'

'Yes. Inside my head it is . . . relevant I suppose you were going to say . . . something like that. He used to talk. Maybe that's where I get my clacking tongue. Sit outside the kitchen door on summer evenings or by the fire in the winter and talk about the wars he'd seen, his old friends, the travelling, the great times they'd had together. India, terrible tragedies, happy days . . . all together like some kind of fairy story, only it was true. He would just sit there and let the brightness of his past catch up with him. I had all the time in the world to listen. And he'd talk about Ireland. You'll have to shoot them out, he used to say. They'll never go any other way. If you want them out you'll have to shoot them out. They simply don't understand the need that people have for freedom. People would rather be poor and suffer and be free. The English . . . he always talked about the English . . . don't understand a stupid thing like that. So you'll have to shoot them out, lad, and the quicker the better.'

'Well? Wasn't he right?'

'He didn't think it was right. He thought it was inevitable . . . like an operation without an anaesthetic, painful and possibly maiming. To be born Irish is a bitter birth, lad, he said to me. So many times he said that.' He picked up his glass and drained it. He held it out, the inside patterned with froth, towards Jack.

'Are you buying?'

Jack stood up. He took the glass from Damian's fingers.

'Manus doesn't like messers.'

'I don't like Manus.' Spiky orange lashes framed his hostile eyes. Jack shrugged slightly and went over to the bar. Guinness was written on the round mats placed at intervals along the bar. Three men played cards in the corner by the bar and from the carpeted saloon he could hear the sound of a girl laughing.

'A pint,' he said, pushing the glass across the counter to the barman.

'Only the one?'

'Only the one.'

There didn't seem to be any point in having the rest of Damian's life spilled out across the table at him. He had delivered his message. No point in wasting time.

'I talk too much,' said Damian, as Jack sat down across from him. 'Aren't you having one yourself?'

Jack shook his head. 'My mother is waiting.'

'Ah.'

'We eat at odd hours.'

'I like my meals at regular four-hourly intervals.'

'What'll I say to Manus?'

'How soon does he want this place?'

'Within the month.'

'I'll be in touch with him. You can give him that message.'

'Secure.'

'You said that before. One of the few words you have said.'

'I suppose we should try and like each other.'

'Remember the bloody nose I gave you?'

Jack nodded. 'I gave you one too.'

'You loosened one of my teeth.'

'Did I? I never knew that.' He felt obscurely pleased.

'It fell out six months later. Look.'

He rolled up his lip and Jack saw that a right-hand front molar was missing.

'I'm sorry,' Jack lied.

'No hard feelings,' said Damian. 'The girls like a fellow to be battle-scarred.'

'A sabre scar would be more glamorous.'

'True.'

They both laughed. Anyone coming into the bar at that moment might have thought they were good friends.

'I must go.' Jack stood up abruptly.

'Suit yourself. Thanks for the drink. I'll see you around.' Damian picked up his drink and sauntered over to the corner where the men were playing cards. He pulled up a chair and sat down beside them.

*   *   *

Helen looked at the four small watercolours on the table in front of her. They were unframed, but neatly mounted on dark cardboard mounts. Scenes of sky and sea and bare hills. Light spilled from the sky, down into the deep blocks of shadows, lonely hollows, through the branches of the trees to become absorbed into the unkempt fleece of sheep searching for shelter behind a thorn hedge. Energy drained down, down all the time. The light troubled every object that it touched.

She ran her fingers nervously along the edge of the table. This may be the most ludicrous thing to do, she thought, but I must move now, somehow announce my presence.

A large canvas lay on the floor in the centre of the room. She painted that way, crouching down beside the canvas, leaning and stretching, the light coming above her head through the glass panes with which she had re-roofed the shed after she had moved into the cottage. Makeshift.

Exposure.

I have to have exposure now or become some sort of a mad woman locked into an ivory tower, pointlessly punishing myself for so many years of sloth. I must see them now in the hands of other people, see their eyes consider, explore, reject. Note the interest or indifference. Is it possible that for a moment they will recognise my existence?

Exposure.

She lit herself a cigarette. The tips of the fingers of her right hand were stained brown by nicotine.

'I want someone to buy you, even for ten pence off a jumble stall, and hang you on a wall. Another wall. Any other wall.'

She picked a black plastic sack off the floor and one by one she put the pictures into it. She folded the plastic into a neat bundle, her fingers in the end caressing the shiny surface of the bag as if it contained some dear and loving creature. Then she stood and stared at the bundle, hunching her shoulders up to her ears and letting them fall slowly again. She thrust the fingers of her left hand into the crevices between her collar bone and her right shoulder blade, probing to find the source of the stiffness that made sudden movement painful.

Decrepitude, she thought, creeping decrepitude. How stupid, how typical to leave exploration so late that decrepitude is setting in. She crushed the remains of the cigarette out in a saucer already filled with dead butts.

My whole life is makeshift.

'Mother,' Jack's voice called across the yard.

She hadn't heard the car.

'Coming.'

She picked up the black bag.

'Mother.'

'Coming, coming, coming.'

✻ ✻ ✻

Dismal rain spread down from lethargic clouds.

'Where are the Cornflakes?'

'Darling, you said the other day that you didn't like Cornflakes. You threw them out. You said no more Cornflakes.'

'A passing phase. Today, I need Cornflakes.'

'They're in the press.'

He didn't move from behind the *Irish Times*. She sighed and went and got the packet from the press and put it down in front of him.

'There.'

'Mmmm.'

The cat, bedraggled from the rain and a night of entertainment, licked with vigour at his fur. When he was quite dry he would take himself to Helen's bed to sleep for a couple of hours.

She sat down at the table.

'Season of mists and mellow fruitfulness, how are you!'

The paper was a wall between them.

'Mists, yes . . . maybe it's mellowly fruitful in England.'

He turned a page, refolded, neatly, the paper. Newsprint in the country edition always greyed the fingers.

'Keats can't ever have visited the west of Ireland.'

Silence.

'Or was it Shelley?'

She stretched out her hand for the cigarettes.

'I always get them mixed up.'

Matches.

'A symptom of my crass ignorance. I regret . . . I really do regret that I didn't bother to learn anything at school.'

She struck the match sharply on the box.

'Everything seemed so irrelevant. Virgil's Aeneid and the isosceles triangle. Both equally . . .'

She lit the cigarette and took a deep pull.

' . . . irrelevant. Litmus paper. What the hell about litmus paper?'

Smoke trickled from her nose and mouth.

'I did an exam question once on the Diet of Worms. I wonder what I said?'

Silence.

'Shakespeare, Yeats and Synge were as irrelevant to other people as litmus paper was to me. I noticed that much.'

The cat yawned exquisitely, exposing the pink roof tree of his mouth and the arc of pointed teeth.

'Any more tea?' Jack pushed his cup across the table.

'Do you think,' she asked as she poured, 'that Cézanne knew about Archimedes' Principle?'

'For God's sake, what does it matter?'

'I just have this feeling that everything should link up somehow. Form a pattern.'

'Do you always talk so much at breakfast.'

She poured the tea.

'I usually read the paper.'

She handed him a cup.

'It's a strange thing about men. They all feel they have this God-given right to read the paper first. Your father was the same. Untouched, unbreathed upon, unscrumpled. A male prerogative. Of course he paid for it . . . I suppose that made a difference. Sometimes he'd read me little bits from it . . . like throwing scraps to the waiting dog.'

Jack stirred some sugar into his tea.

'Father also said that talking to yourself was one of the first signs of madness.'

He went back behind the paper.

She smiled slightly, remembering Dan's voice as he had spoken the words, half-joke, half-serious to her so many times. A headline caught her eye and she leaned forwards across the table, screwing up her eyes to catch the small print.

'Oh dear.'

The cat jumped down from the draining board and walked out of the room.

'They've shot another man in Fermanagh.'

There was no reaction from the other side of the paper.

'Sixty-eight,' she read. 'A retired policeman. Letting the cows out into the field after milking.'

She put her cigarette down in her saucer and peered more closely.

'His wife was still in bed when she heard the shots. She got out of bed and looked out of the window. She saw him lying in the lane. Are you listening, Jack? I'm throwing you a scrap.'

He didn't answer.

'She threw a coat over her shoulders and ran out to him. He had been shot in the head and chest. She called for help. It was twenty minutes before anyone came. She put the coat over him and sat beside him and watched him die. She called and called. She didn't want to leave him on his own. Are you listening, Jack?'

'I read about it.'

'She must have been cold sitting there without her coat. Mustn't she?'

'If you would think mother. From time to time, just think.'

'Two men drove off in a yellow Ford Cortina which was later found by the side of the road two miles away.'

Abruptly he folded the paper and handed it to her.

'There's your thirty pence-worth of liberal rubbish. I will now read the Cornflakes packet. It is just about as illuminating.'

He shook some Cornflakes into a bowl and poured milk on them. She watched. A sprinkling of sugar.

'I don't ask you questions,' she said.

He put a spoonful into his mouth. After a moment he grimaced.

'They're stale,' he said at last. 'That's what's wrong. Yuk. Stale.' He pushed the plate away.

'Probably.'

'I am grown-up, mother. I don't have to answer to anyone. I am an autonomous person.'

She smiled slightly.

'Brutus is an honourable man.'

'Father couldn't talk to you either.'

'We just talked about different things, that was all. You are very like him.'

'I . . .'

'Oh I know you wouldn't agree with me. He believed in the hierarchy of power. He believed that it was possible to impose, to keep peace by the use of violence . . . He wouldn't have called it violence though. He didn't believe in God.'

'He went to church . . . every Sunday off we trekked.'

'He acknowledged God in a sort of social way. He didn't believe in Him though. He preferred symbols to the truth.'

'I suppose you said all those things to him?' His voice was sarcastic.

She shook her head. 'Oh no. I didn't begin to understand him until after his death. I certainly never recognised his fear.'

Jack didn't seem to hear that word.

'He told me once that he sometimes thought you were a little simple.' She laughed.

'Anyway I'm not like that. Not remotely.'

'Let's wait and see, shall we?'

They sat in silence. She put out her hand and took the lid off the pot and peered inside.

'The tea is cold. Would you like some more? I'll make some more.'

'Don't bother. I'll be off in a few minutes.'

'Off?'

'I'm going back to Dublin.'

'Oh, I didn't realise . . . I hope it isn't because of . . .'

'No. Bag packed and all. I have things to do this afternoon.'

'Do you want sandwiches? A thermos? Anything like that? Hard-boiled eggs?'

'No. No need. I'll stop on the way if I feel like it.'

'Some fruit. I have some bananas. Easy to eat and then throw the skins out of the window. Bio-degradable banana skins.'

'Stop being motherly for God's sake.'

She got up and took her cup and saucer over to the sink.

'That's what I am,' she said. 'That's how I know I exist. I'm a mother.'

'Yoohoo.'

A voice shouted from the front door.

'Oh God,' said Helen. 'It's Mary and I'm not dressed or ready or anything . . . Halloo. Halloo. Kitchen.'

The door opened and a small woman in an anorak walked into the room.

'I'm not dresssed or anything, Mary.'

'I can see that. Morning, Jack. I didn't know you were home.'

'Just a fleeting visit.' Jack stood up.

'Cup of tea, Mary?' asked Helen.

'No time to stand beneath the bough, dear. I've got loads of stuff to collect. ICA sale, Jack dear. We've the white elephant as usual. Why I said I'd collect you first, Helen, I can't imagine. I should have known you wouldn't be ready. How long are you here for?'

'I'm off this morning actually . . .'

'Lovely to be young again. No cares. Here today and gone . . .'

'I have the stuff packed and ready in the porch, Mary. Why don't you take it with you in the car and I'll come down later on the bike?'

'My dear it's simply lashing.'

'A little drop of rain won't do me any harm.'

'If you really don't mind. Then you could take your time. See Jack off the premises. Dilly and dally. I have no doubt you'll dilly and dally. Won't she, Jack?'

'Darling, would you pack those things in the porch into the back of Mary's car for me? Sure you won't have a quick cup?'

Jack nodded and left the room.

'No tea, dear. I had the most enormous breakfast only a few minutes ago. I'm sure we won't have time for any lunch. He's looking well. So grown-up these days. Didn't he have a moustache when he was last here? I get so confused about moustaches. If you really don't mind about the bike, dear, I think that would be best. Do keep covered up though. You wouldn't want to stand round all day in wet clothes. I'll fly away then. Must be there to marshal the troops. Don't be too long, dear.'

'I promise. I'll just see Jack off the premises and then I'll be right down.'

'Righty ho.'

She marched towards the door as Jack came in from the hall.

'Sorry you're off so soon, Jack. See you at Christmas, I suppose. Don't keep your mother hanging around for too long. I'll be needing her below. Bon voyage. Tooraloo, dears.'

She was gone. The hall door banged behind her. They stood in the silence for a moment looking at each other. He moved across the room towards her and put out a hand and touched her shoulder.

'Tooraloo, Mum. See you at Christmas.'

* * *

The rain stopped in the early afternoon. The sun came out and a small cold wind began to dry the village street and tease the leaves that lay in sodden heaps in the gutters. Liam the road man was supposed to sweep them up as they fell and take them away in his little cart, but nature's persistence always seemed too much for him and the leaves remained until the winter storms did Liam's work for him.

The hall was warm, quite stark, but cheerful. Mary Heron always refused to allow time to be wasted on paper chains and hanging decorations. On the platform at one end of the hall a dozen small tables had been set up and covered with coloured cloths and a number of women were sitting drinking tea and eating their way through plates stacked with sandwiches and home-made cakes. Helen was behind the white elephant stall.

Mary and I, she thought, are the true white elephants here. No one will buy us though. Neither useful nor decorative. That's not quite fair on Mary. She has her uses. She has drive, for what it's worth. This damn operation for instance, all these people pushing and buying cakes and useless objects they don't want, and arguing over second-hand cardigans, if Mary hadn't tooralooed and tallyhooed at them down all the years they'd all be safely at home watching an afternoon soap opera or darning their husband's socks. Would they have been happier? We all spend our lives waiting for something to happen . . . and I suppose in the end of all we're probably quite relieved when nothing does happen. Oh God, I remember when I left the College of Art to marry Dan I was so sure that some magical explosion of love would occur, would shake me to the very marrow of my bones. I hoped then to be rattled into life and I was too damn lazy even to feel unhappy when it didn't work out like that.

'Wake up, wake up.'

Mary's voice poked into her head.

'You're asleep, Helen. Mrs O'Meara's been waving that tea cosy under your nose for ages.'

'I'm so sorry, Mrs O'Meara. How terribly rude of me.'

Mrs O'Meara waved the tea cosy again.

'Emmm . . . how . . . emmm?' She was shy and quite newly married and didn't really need a tea cosy.

'What about fifty pence? It's quite pretty. It looks as if someone made it by hand.'

'Fifty pence my eye,' said Mary. 'It's hand-made all right. Victorian. A real piece of Victoriana that. Beautiful work. A pound. What would you say to a pound, Mrs O'Meara? After all it's in a good cause, isn't it? You've all come here today to spend some money, haven't you? A pound.'

Mrs O'Meara, as if hypnotised, opened her bag and took out a pound which she handed across the trestle.

'Marvellous. Thank you so much. You won't regret it. You've bought a lovely little piece of the past. It might end up in a museum one day.'

Mrs O'Meara melted into the crowd, the lovely little piece of the past tucked under her arm.

'You are terrible,' said Helen, laughing.

'She can well afford it. That shop of her husband's is . . . what do they call it nowadays . . . a rip-off.'

'You're not too bad at ripping-off yourself.'

'Freddie always used to say I could get blood out of a stone.'

'I'd give anything for something else out of a stone at the moment.'

The old woman leaned down and pulled out a box from under the trestle. In it was a large thermos flask and several plastic mugs.

She picked up the thermos and unscrewed the top.

'A mug, a mug. Quick, get a move on. I see Father Quinlan heading in our direction.'

Helen held out two mugs and Mary filled the mug with what looked like effervescent water.

'I'm afraid it's vodka, not gin,' she said, screwing the top back on the flask again. 'Doesn't smell. It's cold . . . and strong.' She pushed the box out of sight with her foot. 'Down the hatch. Whoops.'

'Whoops,' said Helen.

'I thought our spirits might flag as the day wore on. Good afternoon, Father Quinlan. What can we persuade you to buy?'

'My house is filled with white elephants, Mrs Heron. Good afternoon to you, Helen.'

'Good afternoon, Father Quinlan.'

'I have strict instructions from Katy . . . just stick to the useful articles, she said, as I was leaving the house. So this year, Mrs Heron, I have to spend my money wisely. Jam, pickles, home-made biscuits. Katy will praise me when I get home, not scold. You wouldn't have Katy scolding me, would you?'

'Dear Father Quinlan, Katy will scold the Lord God Himself when she gets to heaven, so you'll be in good company.'

He smiled.

When he smiled he showed an expanse of rather yellowing teeth and his tired eyes gleamed for a moment. He was a gardener, and his fingernails were more times filled with earth and his finger tips rough and pitted with grubbing in the soil. In spite of Katy's most strenuous efforts he was frequently seen with the knees of his trousers seamed with mud.

'I spend most of my life on my knees,' he would smile and his eyes would gleam and his fingers would brush without much enthusiasm at the stains. His eyes wandered over the stall and rested for a moment on one of Helen's watercolours propped up against a tarnished brass jug. He put out a hand towards it. Helen turned away. She groped for the plastic mug and took a large gulp. Then she turned slightly so that she could see what was happening out of the side of her eye. She saw his black nails.

'Framed up and it would be a nice little picture. Who did that now?'

'I haven't the faintest idea,' said Mary. 'Do you know, Helen? There's another couple somewhere.'

'No . . . well . . . No.'

'Framed up,' said the priest, holding the picture at arm's length. 'A bit of glass and a nice narrow frame. What do you think, Helen?'

'Yes,' said Helen foolishly.

'I don't see that Katy could make too much of a fuss about a nice wee picture of sheep and shadows.' He laughed suddenly. 'I'm sure I can find some suitable soothing text to calm her. And all that admirable jam.' He turned the picture over and peered down to find a signature.

'A modest artist,' he murmured. 'How much . . . ah . . . Mrs Heron, would you want me to be forking out for this charming picture?'

'There are two more, if you wait a moment . . .'

He shook his head quite firmly.

'No. I am very happy with the one I have. If you produce two more I will have to make decisions, judgments. Also, Mrs Heron, confidentially with that little bit of sun, I want to get back to the garden. There is so much tidying-up to do before the winter sets in.'

'Five, father. Five. It's all in a good cause and as you said yourself it's a nice little picture.'

He took his wallet out of his pocket and handed her over a five-pound note.

'When it comes to raising funds, Mrs Heron, there's no one to beat you.'

'Get back to your garden quick now, Father Quinlan, and God bless you.'

He tucked the picture under his left arm, made a little bow towards the two of them and turned and walked quickly towards the door.

Mary put the note into the cash box.

'Where the hell did I put the other two? Do you think we can do that again? Ah, here they are. I doubt it.' She pulled the pictures out from under a pile of discoloured lace and propped them up against a couple of jugs. 'Freddie liked him. Did you paint them dear? Quite nice, quite nice. Perhaps I should have asked him for more. I like him. He used to come up and play chess with Freddie when he was dying. He'd chat about trees and things . . . fishing . . . all the things that Freddie liked you know. Of course you never knew Freddie did you? He had more time for him than old Canon Fergusson. That was in the days when we had a Rector . . . old Canon Fergusson. He didn't know a bishop from a castle. He played bridge quite well though. He used to want to talk to Freddie about God. I suppose he felt it was his duty or something like that. Freddie hated that. Silly old bugger he used to say . . . just because he wears his collar back to front doesn't mean he knows any more about God than I do. Poor old Canon Fergusson. He was a little dim. Could you call that blasphemy? I don't suppose so really, just a bit of arrogance perhaps. I don't suppose God held it against him. Do you?'

She took her plastic mug from the window sill and drained it. 'Bottoms up.'

'Does that gramophone work?

Helen turned, startled by the strange voice.

'I'm sorry . . .'

'The gramophone.'

He pointed with his only arm at the gramophone which was sitting on an upturned box beside the trestle table.

'Oh, Mr Haythorne . . . yes . . . it does . . . but you have to wind it up.'

He smiled. His mouth twisted up to the left and seemed to get caught in the scar that ran down his face from the eyepatch to the chin.

'Yes,' he said gently. 'I presumed you had to do that.'

'It is Haythorne, isn't it?'

'Hawthorne. Roger Hawthorne. I don't mind winding it up. In fact

I'd quite enjoy it. Hawthorne.' He repeated a little sternly. He looked at her for a moment.

'I think perhaps I was a little rude to you the other day. Brusque . . . I . . .'

'It's all right,' she said. 'It doesn't matter.'

'Of course I'd need some records if I were to buy it. Wouldn't I?'

'There are some. Not classical, I'm afraid. Look.'

She hoisted up the box of records from the floor and balanced it on the trestle.

'They're terribly old. My father gave me the machine when I passed my school certificate. 1947. Isn't that a ghastly thought. I did have some decent records, but they all seem to have disappeared. I suppose I must have thrown them out at some stage. Do have a look through these and see if there are any you'd like. There are several boxes of needles too. Every modern convenience.'

'Introduce me to your friend.'

Mary had the thermos flask in her hand.

'Oh yes. This is Mr Hawthorne. Mrs Heron.'

He bowed formally and held out his hand. Mary took it. 'Cold hand, warm heart. How do you do?'

'How do you do, Mrs Heron? I'm afraid it's merely bad circulation in my case. They say my heart is equally cold.'

She bent and picked a mug from the box. She filled it up from the thermos. 'A heart-warmer.' She offered it to him and then filled up her own mug and Helen's. He looked rather nervously at the liquid.

'It's not Eno's Fruit Salts,' she said. 'Down the hatch, man. Unless of course you're TT.'

Helen laughed. 'It's vodka and tonic. It's only recommendation being that it doesn't smell. So no one knows the sin that goes on behind the white elephant stall.'

'Thank you.'

'Personally,' said Mary, 'I'm a whiskey drinker. But there are times . . . Mud in your eye.'

He smiled.

'Mud.'

'And if you're interested in the gramophone it'll be five pounds and the records two pence each.'

'Really, Mary . . .'

'Take it or leave it.' She put her mug down and turned to deal with a woman who looked as if she might be about to buy a small oriental gong on a black lacquer stand.

'So, now you know,' said Helen.

He put the mug down carefully on the table and took a record out of the box. 'Spring will be a little late this year. Worth every bit of two pence, I'd have thought.'

'I think the records should be thrown in. After all . . .'

'Embrace me, you sweet embraceable you. On the sunny side of the street. Deeda deedadeeda.'

He looked weird, she thought.

'This is a lovely way to spend an evening. The tune is in my head but the words escape me. Go back, Mrs . . . go back to your selling and leave me to wallow in vodka and nostalgia.'

'If you're . . .'

'I am. Quite, quite all right.'

He was brusque again, very dismissive.

Odious, unpleasant man, she thought. How I dislike you. She moved up to the other end of the trestle, putting Mary between herself and the man. Let her extort what she can from you.

Bong.

Mary had just struck the gong with its padded beater.

'A fine mellifluous note. Much, much too cheap at a pound.'

A note changed hands.

Bong.

The new owner struck it again before picking it up and heading for home, to a better life now that she owned a gong.

Cakes and Biscuits were packing up, shaking and folding the white cloths with which the card tables had been covered. Home Produce and Flowers were counting money into a black tin box. Teas were still going strong. The rain was banging on the corrugated roof once more, bursting and racing down the roof and over the gutters and into the street. Women struggled into macintoshes and put up umbrellas in the porch and children were pulled roughly in off the street to the shelter of the hall again.

'Would it be all right if I were to check that the machine is in full working order?'

His voice was polite again.

'Of course.'

He lifted the domed lid and examined the turntable. He twiddled the knob that worked the shutters.

'Nice piece of mahogany,' he said.

'Things were made to last in those days,' said Mary. 'They hadn't cottoned on to the idea of consumerism.'

Beside Helen some children were dropping coins into a bucket of water. The handle squeaked as he turned it.

'What are we going to do with all this junk now, Mary? I don't think anyone is going to buy anything else.'

'We'll pack it all up, dear. I'll bring the lot home and put them in the cellar and roll them out again next time round. My dear, there are objects here have been on this stall for ten years.'

Helen picked up her two unsold pictures.

'I'll just . . .'

'Take anything you like, dear.'

Track forty-nine . . . Swelling fortissimo as he opened the shutters.

The children by the bucket looked round, startled.

It's the Chattanooga choochoo —

'Heavens.'

Mary clapped her hands over her ears.

All aboard

Wooohooo —

The children looked rather pleased.

It's the Chattanooga choochoo.

'Shall we dance?' He held out his hand to her.

'I . . .' She propped the pictures up on the window. 'Why not?'

You leave the Pennsylvania station at a quarter to four —

A totally forgotten shiver happened in her stomach as she put her hand in his. Fright and then relief that you weren't going to be left alone smiling into space while the whole world danced around you. Foolish Helen –

Dinner in the diner –

He let go of her fingers and put his hand firmly on the small of her back.

Nothing could be finer –

Tentatively she took hold of both of his shoulders. Was that the right thing to do?

Than to have your ham and eggs in Carolina.

'Ca-ha-rol-ina.' He tilted his head away from her and sang.

Woohoo.

Everyone was watching.

He twirled her into the middle of the floor. It was sticky, she thought, her feet wouldn't slide, damp patches on the floor and Coke bottle tops, crisp packets. Not quite the Metropole ballroom or the Gresham Hotel. 'Whirl,' he whispered in her ear. 'Let's whirl. Let's show them something.' They whirled in spite of the sticky floor. It was fun, she thought. Such long-ago fun. It's amazing he dances so well with his . . . disabilities. Rhythm. That was always the important thing. Rhythm. He must have been good when he was . . . when he was . . . I suppose at some time he was whole. People's pink faces smiled.

Won't you choochoo me home.

'Thank you,' he said and bowed quite formally.

Several people clapped.

'Avanti, avanti,' shouted Mary from beside the gramophone. She put another record on the turntable and gently lowered the needle.

Plinky plonky plinky plonky –

'Mmmm,' said the man, taking hold of her back again. His eye smiled at her.

Why do you whisper green grass?

'Why indeed,' he said.

Why tell the trees what ain't so? Some of the children began to dance as well, swaying slowly on their own.

Whispering grass –

'I know this one,' shouted Mrs Walsh, sweeping the floor by Home

Produce. 'This brings me back. The trees don't need to know,' she shouted.

Oh no.

'Remember the Ink Spots.'

'Mr Hawthorne . . .'

'Why tell them all your secrets? Call me Roger.'

'I haven't got any secrets.'

He smiled. 'I don't believe that. You have the most secretive face I have ever seen. Cool, private. Hiding things.'

'You dance well.'

Then she blushed. What a cow-like thing to say. His hand pressed her back for a moment.

'I used to dance a lot.'

Don't tell it to the trees or they will tell the birds and bees and everyone will know because you told the babbling —

'1944.'

He laughed.

Tree . . . ee . . . eeoooeeooee — slower — *and oooeeooee* —

'Oooeeooooeee,' crooned one of the children and the record stopped turning.

He let go of Helen and turned away. He walked quickly to the white elephant stall, just leaving her there standing in the middle of the hall.

'I'll have it,' he said to Mary. He pulled a wallet out of his pocket and produced two five-pound notes. He handed her the money.

'Here. That's what I'll give you.'

'Too much,' she said surprisingly. 'Give me seven.'

'Take it.' He pushed the money into her hand. 'I'll go and get my car. It's down by the hotel. If someone could . . .'

'That's all right. One of the boys will carry it out for you. Wait a while though till the rain eases off. You'll drown in that.'

He shook his head and walked away towards the door.

'Fifty-seven pounds twenty-six pence.'

She put the money into the cash box.

She repeated the figure to Helen as she arrived beside her.

'Great.'

'It must be a record. It just shows the quality of our white elephants.'

'Or perhaps that our customers have more money than sense.'

Mary laughed.

'Vodka all gone. Let's clear up as quickly as we can and get home. Hot bath. Feet up. Here you, Kevin . . . it is Kevin, isn't it . . . ? Carry that machine out to Mr Hawthorne. He's gone to get his car. And the records. Don't drop it for heaven's sake . . . and don't let those records get wet.'

Helen took the folded plastic bag out of the coat pocket and carefully put the two pictures back into it.

'Mad as a hatter,' said Mary.

'Who?'

'That railway station man.'

'A grumpy bear, I'd have said. Mother had one of these. I always thought they were lovely.' She was folding a green velvet bridge cloth with gold tassels at each corner. 'I stole it once and wore it to a fancy-dress party. Wrapped round me like a cloak. I felt so rich. I spilled something on it, lemonade . . . something like that. There were ructions.'

She put it into the box they were filling.

'I suppose people don't play bridge with such formality any longer.'

'In and out of hospitals for years. Reggie and Anne know his people. He's been a thorn in their flesh for years. He buys railway stations.'

'A fairly harmless thing to do, I'd have thought.'

'One thing leads to another.'

Helen laughed. 'Don't be silly, Mary. He's a harmless bad-tempered crank. You're making him sound as if he were a homicidal maniac.'

'You just never know, dear, with the deranged when something terrible may bubble up to the surface. His family consider him to be deranged. Norfolk or somewhere like that they come from. There, I think we've done enough, dear. The others can cope with the final clearing-up. Just let me dispose of the cash and I'll drive you home.'

'I have the bike, thanks.'

'You'll get wet.'

'No matter.'

'Rain never hurt anyone.'

'So they say.'

'Run along then, dear, and thank you. See you soon. Tooraloo.'

'See you soon.'

* * *

Helen tied a scarf around her head in the doorway before stepping out into the rain. Dismal chiaroscuro street disfigured by prosperity. What a dismal thing to think. What nobility is there in the picturesque hovel? A horn hooted as she stepped into the road. Patience, she muttered. Her bike was leaning against a concrete lamp standard. Should I get a flashy new one? Gears? Thin wheels? All that sort of thing? Keep up with the times. Or keep old faithful for ever.

Old faithful, we'll roam the range together.

The horn hooted again.

Old faithful, in every kind of weather.

Old faithful never knew about the North West of Ireland, that was for sure.

Damn! Hole in a sole and water seeping . . . now that was one of the world's most unpleasant sensations. Water seeping across the sole of the foot, clammy tights, cold, squelch.

'Squelch.'

'I've been blowing the horn at you for two minutes and all you say is squelch.'

He leaned over awkwardly and opened the door of the car. 'Get in.'

'I . . .'

'It's too wet to argue, just get in.'

'My bike . . .'

He gestured impatiently with his hand. 'In, woman. In, in, in.'

Goodbye, old faithful.

She got in and closed the door.

'That's better,' he said. 'I thought we might go for a drive and then I'll leave you home.'

'It's not a very nice day for a drive.'

'If you want to drive any day will do.'

He did things with his feet and the car moved off.

'Perhaps you have other plans?'

'Perhaps I have.'

'I won't eat you,' he said gently.

'I feel I'm being kidnapped.'

'That's right. Only temporarily though. You don't need to be nervous. I handle a car very well.'

She felt her face going red.

'I'm not nervous.'

'This car cost a lot of money. If I were to pass out at any moment it could drive itself home and put itself in the garage.'

She laughed.

At the end of the village he took the right fork. This was onto a road that wound out through the rocky hills of a small peninsula. Water was spinning everywhere, blown by the wind. Wet trees squatted by wet stone walls, burnt slashes where the whins had been, glittered in the rain. No one lived any longer on this inhospitable headland. Sheep grazed among the rocks and the tumbled gables.

'The last time I danced was in 1944,' he said eventually. 'Thirty-five years ago, or thereabouts.'

'You dance one hell of a lot better than some I know who've been on the floor regularly for the last thirty-five years.'

'September the tenth.'

Oh God, she thought, he's going to tell me the story of his life.

'Do you mind if I smoke?'

He shook his head.

'Some people mind. They hate their cars reeking of stale smoke. I can't say I blame them.'

She felt in her pocket for the packet.

'They say nowadays that we . . . the smokers of the world are slowly poisoning all the rest. It's a dismal thought really. I suppose it's true too. I have tried to give up . . . oh ages ago, that was. My husband . . . late . . . my late husband gave it up just like that.' She clicked her fingers. 'I tried . . . but . . . He encouraged me in every way . . . but . . . as you see I'm still at it. My character is woefully weak.' There was silence. She clicked her fingers again to disperse the silence, but it remained. She put a cigarette in her mouth and lit it. The road had become very narrow, almost a track. Wet branches from the hedges scraped the sides of the car.

'I'm sorry,' she said, after a long time. 'I interrupted you.'

He nodded, but didn't say anything.

Maybe he is a homicidal maniac, she thought. But how efficient can you be with only one arm? One eye? Superhuman strength in his wrist, kicking, trampling feet? A rapist perhaps? I'd rather be raped than dead. No question. She looked cautiously at his face. She could only see the Picasso profile, the travesty.

How young he must have been on September the tenth, 1944.

'I was fourteen,' she said.

There was a gate in front of them. He stopped the car. He reached into the back of the car and handed her his anorak.

'Put this on,' he said. 'There's something I'd like to show you. I hope you don't mind getting a bit wet.'

'But you . . .'

'I don't mind.'

He opened the door and got out of the car.

'It's only a couple of minutes' walk. You see when the wind is coming from the west like this . . . strongly from the west.' He moved towards the gate, where he fumbled with the bolt. 'Well . . . you'll see . . .'

She put the anorak over her shoulders and got out. The rain and the west wind battered at her. The left sleeve of the anorak was tucked neatly into the pocket. She pulled it out and shoved her hands into the sleeves. He bumped the gate open across the grassy track. She walked beside him in silence. She knew where they were going. She knew the track like the back of her hand. Round to the right, down into the slight hollow where three thorn trees tangled their branches together. The wet oozing in through the soles of her leaking shoes as she walked. I will have pneumonia tomorrow, or at least chilblains. Up a steep short hill and out through a hedge of whin bushes onto the headland.

When they reached the edge of the grey plateau of rock he stopped walking. Without saying a word he pointed to a spot half-way between where they stood and the edge which hung out over the sea. They each stood in their own silence and waited. Grey is a most dismal colour, she thought. Dismal veils of rain. Dismal wind. I could be at home in a hot bath. She shivered with sudden delight at the thought of that pleasure ahead of her. Suddenly, like fireworks erupting, a great spray of water shot high in the air from a fissure in the rock.

'Ah,' she said with satisfaction.

'It only happens,' he said, 'when there is a strong west wind blowing. The water is thrust into an opening in the rocks below with such force that the only way out is up through that hole there.'

'Yes.'

He turned and looked at her.

'You've seen it before?'

She smiled.

'I've lived here quite a long time, you know. Six, seven years.'

'I'm sorry.'

'I didn't mean to sound rude. I thinks it's amazing . . . and it's ages since I've been here. Thank you for bringing me.'

He nodded abruptly.

'Jack and I used to bike along here when he was . . . younger . . . a kid. It's a good place for picnics. No sand to get in the sandwiches . . . and a marvellous view. You need a good day. Sometimes you feel if you screw your eyes up into slits you could see America.'

Great bars of rain moved in towards them, no America today.

'A good day,' he repeated.

'Perhaps you'd bring me back on a good day. We could have a picnic too. I haven't been on a picnic for ages.'

The column of water spouted again. Twenty feet straight up into the air, and then melted into the rain.

'Yes.'

He turned and set off back the way they had come at an odd jogging run. It looked as if it was quite hard for him to keep his balance. By the time Helen reached the car he was sitting inside it mopping at his face and hair with a handkerchief. She took off the dripping anorak and threw it into the back.

'They used to tell me when I was a child that rain would make your hair curl.' She slammed the door and wriggled her shoulders to keep the stiffness temporarily at bay. 'It never did me any good.'

He laughed. 'Nor me.'

He began to manoeuvre the car around. 'After all,' he said. 'Curly hair is a disease. A well-known fact.'

'You can't mean that all those millions of Africans are diseased.'

'Every one of them. The American blacks; all those Greeks and

Italians with hair like corrugated paper, all, all diseased.'

'That just leaves you and me and Hitler.'

'Absolutely correct.'

The car was pointing in the right direction at last.

'That was what the last war was all about. The survival of the straight-haired. No kinks, waves, bends left on the face of the earth. Even the criminals, the perverts, the loonys, the murderers and the child rapists are to have straight hair. That's why I'm alive. I'm a straight-haired loony.'

The back wheels of the car were spinning in a puddle.

'It's just my luck to be caught in the bloody pouring rain, miles from home with a one-eyed, one-armed, straight-haired loony in charge of a lethal weapon.'

He began to laugh. He did something with his feet and the car moved more sedately forward.

Helen blushed and then she too began to laugh.

'I have passed a test . . . many tests . . . you know . . . and the machine has been adapted . . . at enormous expense. I'm really very safe in my machine.'

'It just slipped out.'

'My dear Mrs Cuffe, if I were in your position, I'm sure I'd feel the same.'

'Please call me Helen.'

He nodded. 'It's more helpful really when people acknowledge the disabilities of others. Mutilations, colour, madness, religion . . . whatever it may be. I have spent the largest part of my life among the mutilated. That for me is normal. I find the real world . . . I had an aunt called Helen.'

'Oh.'

'My father's sister. I didn't like her much. She too was crippled . . . by her own sanctity.'

He swung the car out onto the road.

'Madam doormat, my father used to call her. Oh God, here comes Madam doormat, and the temperature of the house would sink several degrees. He wiped his own feet on her when it suited him and despised her at the same time. So the name Helen . . .'

'Doesn't appeal to you.'

'It has unpleasant connections. A long way back. We shouldn't allow ourselves to be influenced by such memories.'

'I think the rain is easing.'

'I thought perhaps I had discovered something new . . . a place no one had ever seen before.'

'That would be quite a triumph nowadays.'

'Yes.'

'It was really nice of you to bring me to see it.'

It was strange, she thought, how between one word and another the strange face could become a mask. It was like a grotesque sleight of hand; suddenly the magician removed all life from the puppet.

'Tobar na Diabhal it's called.'

He probably wasn't listening.

'The Devil's Well.'

There was silence between them for a long time.

'If you'd given me notice of your kidnap I'd have worn my gumboots. These shoes let in.'

'I never really know these things in advance. I tend to work on impulse. Anyway, here you are at home. Soon, you can be comfortable again.'

'Will you come in and have a cup of tea . . . a drink?'

He stopped the car by her gate.

'No thank you. I would rather get on home.'

He turned his head and stared at her.

She opened the door and began to heave herself out.

Ten years ago, five even, I would have been able to skip skedaddle, now I heave and creak, like some ancient sailing vessel. Heave, creak.

'Are you sure . . . ?'

He still stared at her.

'I'm quite sure.'

'Will you be able to manage the gramophone on your own . . . to get it out of the car?'

'Yes. Thank you.'

It's like a drill, she thought, that eye, painfully penetrating. I'm so cold, drowned cold.

He nodded. He did things with his feet. She slammed the door.
'Thank you,' she called.

The car moved off and as it turned the corner she realised that she had left the plastic bag with the pictures in it on the floor by the front seat.

'Shit,' she shivered.

*   *   *

The door scraped.

Helen looked round from where she stood at the Aga, just taking the coffee off the heat.

Must mend that bloody door. Automatic, eternal thought. Useless thought. Roger stood there, the plastic bag tucked neatly under his arm.

'Excuse me for . . . I saw you through the window. It seemed silly to go to the front door.'

'Oh, hello.'

She still looked quite scrubbed after her bath. Her hair straight and very clean spread out from her head as she moved. Some nights after she had washed her hair it would be filled with static electricity and crackle and spark when she brushed it.

'Do come in. You're just in time for a cup of coffee.'

'You've washed your hair.'

'I had a boiling bath. You have to push that door quite hard to shut it. One day . . .' She fetched another mug from the dresser and put it on the table, pushing the debris of plates, dishes and a few books up to the far end. 'Sit down. It's good coffee. Bewleys. A major extravagance. Instant makes me feel sick.'

Before sitting down, Roger put the bag carefully on the table. 'I thought you might be worried about your pictures.' He sat down. 'Yes . . . I'd love some coffee. I hope I'm not disturbing you.'

'Black or white?'

'Black, please.'

His hand lay quite still and heavy on the plastic bag, as if he were protecting it against some surprise attack.

'Sugar?'

She put the cup down in front of him.

He shook his head. 'I used to take sugar, but too many people wanted to help me . . . I don't know why . . . scoop it in, stir, take away the spoon just in case I dropped it on the floor, look at me with sympathy and concern. One day I just gave up sugar. Life seemed easier after that.'

Helen burst out laughing.

'How unkind of you.'

'Hardly that . . . self-protective.'

'Would you like a glass of whiskey? Or some red wine? That's all I've got. Do have a whiskey. I'd love one myself.'

'That would be very nice. You're very cosy here.'

He watched her move to the cupboard, the sink.

'Everything at hand.'

Then back to the table with glasses, the bottle, water in a jug.

'Shipshape.'

She laughed. 'I wouldn't say that. I am famous for my lack of organisation. They wouldn't have me on a ship. Do you take water? Help yourself if you do.'

'A little water.'

She sat down opposite him and lit a cigarette. She flicked the match into a saucer already filled with butts and dead matches. 'How's your house coming on?'

Her fingers fiddled nervously with the cigarette. A thin string of smoke was caught in the light.

'The essentials for living are there. Your health.' He lifted the glass. 'Sláinte.'

'Damian has the box in working order. It won't be too long before we're ready. Then it will be up to CIE. I think we'll have to operate the level-crossing gates manually to begin with, but I hope that after a while we will be able to tie them in to the box.'

'It was very good of you to bring that back for me. It was so stupid of me to leave it behind. The rain . . .'

'I hope you don't mind, I took the liberty of looking . . . I hope that doesn't annoy you . . . your private parcel . . . ?'

'No . . . of course not.'

'Your work?'

She nodded.

'You didn't tell me you were a painter.'

'We haven't really had that sort of conversation . . . anyway I'm . . .'

'You're a painter.'

She stretched her hand out across the table for the bag. But he replaced his hand, heavily, where it had been before.

'I would like to buy them.'

'Don't be silly.'

'After all, you were prepared to sell them at that terrible jumble sale. Why not to me?'

'It wasn't a jumble sale.'

'Next best thing. Why not to me?'

She shook her head.

'My walls are as good as the next man's. Better perhaps. Bare white walls crying out for pictures.'

'I would like you to give them back to me. I'd like to consider. You've taken me by surprise. I don't like that.'

'I took the precaution of writing a cheque before I came here.' He pulled the bag over to his side of the table and felt in his pocket. He took out the folded piece of paper and pushed it over the table towards her. 'I hope you'll forgive me and I hope you'll accept it.'

She stared down at it.

'Please.' His voice was very gentle.

She picked up the cheque.

'Why?'

'As I said this afternoon, I work on impulse. I like your watercolours. I want to hang them on my walls. For me that is quite simple.'

She unfolded the cheque and looked at it.

'A hundred pounds. I can't accept this. You're out of your mind.'

'So they tell me.'

He pulled the bag off the table onto his knee.

'I didn't mean . . . you can't possibly give me a hundred pounds.'

'I'm buying your pictures. That I believe is a reasonable assessment of their worth. I also believe that you don't know whether it is or not.'

She shook her head. 'I may of course be wrong. It's not very likely though.'

He took a gulp of coffee.

'There's no need to look so darn miserable.'

'I'm not miserable. I'm delighted. I really am.' She held the cheque out at arm's length and stared at it. 'I'll frame it.'

'I'd cash it first if I were you. I'll give it back to you when I get it from the bank. You can frame it then.'

'Yes. I don't know what to say. Have another drink?' She pushed the bottle towards him. 'Some more coffee? A slice of cold roast beef? Do have something.'

'No.'

He stood up. 'I'm going home. I find night driving a bit hairy. May I come back sometime?'

'I'm always here. Somewhere about.'

'I'll find you.'

'Yes.'

'I'd like to see what you're doing. Would you allow me . . . ?'

'Yes.'

He gave the door a sharp pull and the cat walked in, weaving through his legs.

'A cat. Your cat?'

She nodded.

'Well . . . really I'm his human being. You know what cats are like.'

'I'm glad you have a cat. I have very good relationships with cats.'

'Come or go,' she said. 'I mean . . . well . . . don't just stand there with the door open. The heat . . .' She waved her hands. 'Come back in. We could talk a while.'

'No. Not tonight. I want to go home and play all those records and see how I feel. See what they bring back.'

'Masochism.'

'Possibly. Goodnight, Helen.'

'Goodnight. I hope you won't be found drowned in a pool of melancholic tears.'

'Unlikely.'

'And thank you. Thank you so much.'

The door bumped, scraped, screeched a little and was shut.

She listened to his steps across the yard. She poured herself some cold coffee. A freak?

In 1944 I was fourteen.

He clicked the gate shut behind him.

September the tenth, just coming to the end of the summer holidays. Time for dentists, shopping for new school clothes, warm vests, those terrible green knickers that matched the gym tunics. Time for squeezing your feet again into sensible lace-up shoes, feet spread by summer freedom.

The car started . . .

He couldn't have been all that much older. Eighteen? Nineteen?

Drove away. The sound twisted along the road.

Only the wind then bruising the white walls.

In my whole life I have made two decisions. One was to marry Dan. I suppose that was a decision. I suppose at some stage I said yes. Pondered. Did I ponder? Or was I grasping at straws? I think for the record I will have to call it a decision. The second, of course, was coming here to this place, buying this house, throwing away all the detritus of the past.

I must be some sort of freak too.

She stabbed at one of the butts in the saucer with a match, impaling it finally like a cocktail sausage on a stick, then started on another.

The de-insulation programme has to begin.

The cat jumped up onto the table.

'Do you hear me, cat? Hear. Understand? I have to say it aloud. I am making a decision. Get that into your yellow head, through your yellow eyes.'

The giant step.

What was that game we used to play?

Forget it. Just get on with this decision-making moment.

The cold coffee was foul.

I could leave the issue untouched. I could continue to dabble in paint. Express myself to myself or whatever crudity of that sort is in my mind. I could sell the odd picture, get that satisfaction. It could be for ever a pastime. Pass time. If I could stop time, hold it here in this room. You may not pass on, old time, until I give you leave.

Oh for God's sake, even if I were to give up smoking and live to be a hundred that only gives me fifty years of rapidly passing time.

She stood up and remembering the game for a moment took a giant step across the centre of the room.

Cynical yellow eyes drooped.

Forty-nine years. Forty-eight.

I will become.

She went upstairs to bed.

When she woke up the next morning and looked at the moving shadows on the ceiling, she was filled with a joy that she had never experienced before, and likely never would again. Everything seemed so simple, so right. She lay and looked at the shadows and understood the meaning of ecstasy. Quite, quite abnormal for a person who had never allowed herself to be shaken radically in any way by emotion. For a while, five minutes, an hour, a whole morning, it was impossible to remember later, she felt liberated from doubt, from her own special wriggling worm of fear. Of course it all drained away, nothing could stop that happening, and she was left the same as she had been before.

☆   ☆   ☆

No rain on Wednesday. A fine sharp breeze blew the clouds across the sky. Like a race, she thought as she crossed the yard, a mug of tea in one hand, the cigarettes and matches safely clutched in the pocket of her dressing gown. Boats, spinnakers full of wind racing across the sea-blue sky. I will go to Dublin and buy myself a whole load of beautiful brushes. I won't blinking well stint myself on brushes ever again. I'll keep them clean, healthy. Build racks for them on the wall. Each one its allotted place. Fantasy of course. That sort of neatness was not in her nature. Anyway, she thought as she opened the door of the shed, the sky isn't sea-blue, so it isn't.

She had been working for about half an hour when the door opened. She looked up from the floor, startled.

'Excuse me,' said Roger, as he came into the shed. 'You said I could come and see your paintings. Forgive me if I take you by surprise.'

'You certainly do. I haven't even combed my hair. I . . . I'm not . . .'

'I can see you're not dressed.'

'I'm not even in my right mind yet.'

He smiled slightly.

'I thought if I came early I'd be sure to catch you in.'

'I'm always in.'

They stared at each other in silence. She struggled up from the floor, straightening the creaking knees.

'I'll go away if you prefer?'

'No. That's all right. I'm sorry if I was rude. You're the first visitor I've ever had in here.'

'Jack?'

'Oh God no. He never comes over here. I think he's frightened he'll despise my work and won't know how to cope with that.' She rubbed at the paint on her right forefinger with the forefinger of her other hand. 'He has his own way of looking at things you know . . . not a bit like mine at all.' She turned away and looked out of the small window at the end of the shed. In the distance a fishing boat moved against the rhythm of the sea, no smooth flow like the clouds, it butted against the sea and wind. Aggressive. Almost like I feel, she thought.

'He doesn't have to be involved. I would hate dutiful respect from him. I think I've probably hurt him quite a lot. He never wanted to come here. I think he felt quite orphaned as he was growing up.'

'It's impossible to protect other people all the time.'

She sighed and then she laughed suddenly.

'I spend a lot of my time over here in my dressing gown. I'll have to change my ways if I'm going to have a constant stream of visitors.'

'Why don't you go and organise yourself and I'll just stay here and . . .' He gestured around the room with his hand. 'You wouldn't mind if I did that, would you?'

'I suppose not.'

She walked over to the door.

'I won't be long.'

'Don't rush. I'll be quite happy poking around here. By the way, I told the boy he could sit in the kitchen. I hope you don't mind.'

'What boy?'

'Damian Sweeney. I didn't feel like driving this morning, so he brought me over. I've taught him to use the pedals in my car. Sometimes

I feel lazy, disinclined. I left him in the kitchen.'

'You do make yourself at home, don't you?'

He bowed.

She hadn't cleared the breakfast dishes, nor indeed the remains of her last night's supper. Time enough for all that when the light was gone, when her energy was low. Damian was sitting at the table with the cat on his knee.

'Good morning, Mrs Cuffe.' He stood up politely as she came into the kitchen. The cat, at his first movement, stepped off his knee and onto the table.

'Bloody cat, get off the table,' said Helen crossly. 'Good morning. He eats the butter.'

'I think he's eaten the butter.'

Damian pointed to an empty saucer that might once have had butter in it.

'Bloody cat,' shouted Helen, clapping her hands. The cat jumped off the table and walked across the room past Helen and out into the hall.

'You probably don't remember me . . .'

'Yes, I remember you.' Her voice was brusque. 'This place is in a mess . . .'

'Yes,' he said. 'What of it? What's a bit of a mess for God's sake? You couldn't remember me. We've never met. I've seen you round the place, riding the bike and that, but we've never met.'

'You hit Jack.'

'That was years ago. We were only kids.'

'He came home in a terrible mess It wasn't long after we came here and I thought, oh God, what have I let us in for. He was all covered in blood. Noses bleed such a lot. What a little bully that Damian Sweeney must be. A brat.'

'My mother felt much the same way about Jack. I'll say I'm sorry now. Better late than never.'

He held out a hand towards her.

She nodded and touched his hand briefly, then she plunged her hand into her pocket and took out the cigarettes. She opened the box and held it out towards him.

'Smoke?'

He was tempted. She could see that. He shook his head.

'I'm giving them up. Trying to, anyway.'

'Saint?'

She plucked one out of the packet and put it in her mouth.

'No. It just suddenly seemed a silly way to kill yourself. I think I'd rather drink myself to death, it's more fun.'

She lit the cigarette and took a deep pull. 'Do you see Jack at all? I never know who his friends are these days. He doesn't bring them home.'

'I had a jar with him in the pub the other night.'

'I hope . . .' she began and then stopped.

He waited for a moment. 'You hope what?'

She made a hopeless gesture with her hands.

'Would you make some tea? Can you make tea?'

'I can make tea.'

'I must get dressed. I really must. If you'd . . .'

'Sure.'

'Will you be able to find everything?'

'Sure. Sure. Run along. I've been making tea since the age of five. I can open tins and fry eggs and gut fish and knit . . . I was ill once for quite a long time and Mammy taught me to knit. I knitted a navy scarf.' He laughed. 'I used to hide it under the pillow when the others came home from school so they wouldn't see it. She was the only one knew . . .'

She paused by the door. 'What did you do with it?'

'I have it yet. I wear it in the winter. It's long.'

He wound an imaginary scarf several times around his neck. 'You go on and put your clothes on. I'll make a great cup of tea. Three great cups of tea.'

She nodded and left him to it.

* * *

It was strange, she thought as she scrubbed her teeth, backwards and forwards, she had never been able to come to grips with the up and down strokes recommended by the dentist, to hear other people, total strangers when you came to think of it, taking control in your house. Down the short flight of stairs Damian clattered domestically. She bared her teeth, grimaced into the glass. Yellow horse's teeth. If I stopped smoking perhaps? Across the yard Roger poked around through her entire private life, her being. She bared them again. Sparkling Doris Day? Too late. Yellow horse's teeth were more suitable to her age and station. He would be really shocked at the state of her brushes. Oh God, those awful half-drunk cups of tea, the old milk shining on the surface. At least they're my own, she thought, for the time being. One day maybe, I will have a mouth full of shiny Doris Day choppers. Keep them in a glass of gin beside the bed. But, after all, Mother didn't have a false tooth in her head, buried with her own smile. Runs in the family that sort of thing. Fingers crossed. She gave an extra scrub for luck.

Rinsed water round her mouth and spat.

Damian ran water into the sink, pumped in mild green Fairy Liquid and began to wash the dishes.

He looks nice. I wonder if he's mixed up in all that business. I suppose you shouldn't believe everything you hear. Nicer looking than Jack . . . not so buttoned up, sullen. Would sullen be the word for Jack's face? If Dan were still alive I wonder . . . I wonder? My eyes were always too pale to sparkle. Washed blue stones. Jack's eyes too, unreceptive. Are you receiving me? One two three testing. Are you receiving me, son? Silence on the air waves. A clatter of sound from downstairs. What the hell is he doing?

She picked up her comb and began to pull the night's tangles out of her hair. Damian turned on the radio. He really was making himself at home. Tchaikovsky's little cygnets heavy-footed in the kitchen.

'The tea's wet,' his voice called up the stairs.

'Thanks. I'll be down in a minute.'

She heard him open the back door and call across the yard to Roger.

The cat liked to sleep like a human being, tucked into the bed with his head on the pillow. He lay there, yellow eyes half-closed, as she tucked the clothes around him.

'If you sick up a quarter of a pound of butter on my bed . . .' she threatened. He wasn't receiving her either.

Damian had put cups and saucers on the table, milk in a jug, the fruit bowl centred neatly. No sign of debris.

'You'll make someone a good husband,' she said.

'My mother says no one will have me, so I may as well learn to look after myself.'

She sat down at the table.

'I'm not just a pretty face,' he said.

'So I see.'

She took a loose cigarette from her pocket and tapped it on the table for a while. The young man switched off the cygnets and stood looking at her in silence. Finally as if she had come to some immense decision she put the cigarette in her mouth and struck a match.

'It was really Jack made me give it up.'

'Jack?'

She wondered what he was talking about.

He nodded towards the cigarette.

She shook the flame dead and threw the matchstick into one of the saucers.

'He's never done anything so constructive for me.'

'I don't think he intended to be constructive. He just annoyed me.'

She sighed.

'I've seen you painting.'

'Oh yes.' She sounded vague.

'Up on the cliffs and along the shore. I sat and watched you once for nearly an hour. I wanted to come and have a look . . . but I didn't think you'd be pleased. It looked private.'

'Don't you have a job?'

'On and off. I'm working for him at the minute.'

'What . . . actually are you doing there? I mean you hear such mad rumours.'

'I have the signal box in working order now. Beautiful it is. Single-line token block. Beautiful. You should have seen it before. It had to be re-floored, new handles for the levers, new steps, completely new wiring, bells replaced. It's a gem now.'

'But listen . . .'

'The token machines . . .'

'Why?'

'What do you mean, why?'

'What on earth is the point of doing up an old signal box like that?'

'Station. The whole station. Soon we'll be able to work trains through the system again.'

'Don't be ridiculous, Damian. There are no tracks. There are no trains any longer. What are you talking about? Have you gone mad too?'

'He's not mad.'

'I suppose you could turn it into a museum. A railway museum. Tourists, schools, that sort of thing.'

'Will I pour you a cup of tea?'

'We'd better wait for . . .'

Damian leaned across the table towards her and spoke, almost in a whisper.

'Don't you go saying things like that to him. Do you hear me?'

'I . . .'

'Just believe him, that's all I ask. After all, where's the harm?'

He sat back again and looked at her. She put the cigarette down on the table, standing like a little pillar on its butt end. She stared at the thread of smoke, at the neat crown of ash. Oh hell, she thought, there has to be disaster, unhappiness somewhere in all this. She heard his footsteps in the yard. She picked up the cigarette and knocked the ash into the saucer. Briefly she nodded at Damian. He looked relieved.

'You may pour the tea out now,' she said.

'How lucky you are.' Roger came across the room and put his hand on her shoulder, leaned his weight for a moment on her and then sat down.

'Good tea. No other brew in the world quite tastes like Irish tea. I see signs over there that you are beginning to work . . . to find your voice.' He smiled slightly. 'Your silent voice.'

'Why do you say that I'm lucky?'

'Because you have eyes to see and the courage to want to use them. Maybe I should have said that you are unlucky. But I don't think you are a person who is looking for peace of mind. I knew a man once . . . a boy, I should say, whose parents called him Dieudonné. Imagine that. Imagine landing your poor child with a name like that. We just called him Don.'

'What happened to him? I mean how did such a stylishly named man deal with his life? With equal style I hope?'

'He died young. God regretted his gift and took it back. Arnhem, seventeenth of September 1944. Poor Don had the misfortune to come in on a glider that crashed. He missed the chance of becoming a hero. Very good tea, Damian.'

'I told her ... Mrs ...'

'Helen. Please call me Helen.'

'I told her she should come and see the signal box.'

'Yes. You must do that. Come along any time.'

'Was that a parable? Was I meant to learn something from it?'

'A purely fortuitous reminiscence, I assure you. I haven't thought of the poor chap for years. It was just the name Godgiven ... slipped ... into ... my mind.'

'Did you become a hero?'

He laughed.

'Alas. By the evening of the eighteenth of September I was just one of a rather large number of embarrassing reminders that God is not necessarily on the side of the British. We were all so convinced that He was. I'm not loving and forgiving, you know. I hate quite a lot of people ... and I mourn the needless dead. You see, you haven't acquired a very cheerful neighbour.' Damian got up and went round the table. Gently he put a hand on Roger's shoulder.

'I think it's time we went home. We have all the down platform to clear. Remember? We said we'd do that today if the weather was good. Remember?'

'Good man, quite right.' He stood up and bowed formally to Helen. 'We burst upon you ...' he said. 'I do apologise.'

'I just take a long time to get myself together ... well, socially ... in the morning. I'm glad you came.'

He moved slowly towards the door. A nerve twitched in the left-hand hollow of his neck. She could see it struggling from where she sat.

'All the needless dead.' He gave a helpless tug at the door. Damian stepped past him and pulled it open. He bent down to examine the bottom of the door.

'That's some big task you've taken on,' said Helen. 'Hating the living and mourning the dead. I don't know when you're going to have time to play all those gramophone records.'

Damian stood up. 'I'll come round one day and take a piece off the bottom of that door for you.'

'Oh, I . . .'

'Dead easy job. No bother. Slán.' As he stepped outside he called back, 'Helen.' Just trying it for size.

'I didn't mean to be rude,' she said to Roger.

'I am aware of that. I think you should get together a portfolio of your work and bring it up to Dublin. If I could be of any help . . .'

'Thank you.'

'You'll come and see the box? Soon. Come and visit us soon.'

He went out.

✢   ✻   ✢

The days drifted past. The storms blew themselves out and the trees and the hedges glowed in the autumnal air. The evenings had a frosty sharpness and the glitter of the sun was tarnished by blue streaks of mist. After the hours of euphoria Helen felt a little bleak, insecure. The weather called her out of the house and she pedalled several times to the Devil's Well. It took almost an hour each way . . . Soon, she thought, without too much hope. I will be fit and svelte.

She made sketches of the flat pre-historic rocks and the reflecting pools. Neolithic is such a good word, she thought, probably quite incorrectly nudging its way into my mind. It gives that feeling of grey unproductive rocks, existing eternally in spite of their unproductivity. The pools, large puddles really, quite still only reflect the glitter of the sky . . . Lethargic birds stand, also still, waiting for a moment of lifting air, caring neither whether they stand or drift.

The house stank of size. She had to heat it in the kitchen and in spite of open doors and windows the smell was everywhere. She stretched and painted the canvas and cried with the smell and the reeking in her eyes. The canvas was beautiful. She stood looking at it, a delight of anticipation filling her. Then she went and had a bath and washed her hair, scrubbed the smell from every centimetre of her body.

She poured herself a glass of wine and went out to the porch to watch the last gasp of the sun. She rubbed at a geranium leaf and the smell burst out from between her fingers The sea had that enamelled look she loved. How can anyone bear to live facing to the East? Miss every evening this . . . in one shape or another . . . dramatic death.

The telephone rang.

Blinking miracles of modern science.

'Mum . . . mother.'

'Darling, hello.'

'Hello there.'

'Is everything all right?

He rang so seldom.

'Fine. How are things with you?'

'Just the same as ever. Beautiful weather. No news at all really.'

'I thought I might come down again for a couple of days. End of next week, perhaps. If that suited you.'

'Darling, of course it suits me. It would be lovely.'

'I have a friend I might . . . could he have a bed for a couple of nights? There's that old camp bed in my room. Would you mind? He's never seen . . .' Crackle of some sort got mixed in with his words.

'Lovely,' she shouted. 'What's his name?'

'I'll be in touch before then. Let you know whether it will be Friday or Saturday.'

'Perhaps he doesn't have a name.'

Oh hell, she thought, why can't you keep your mouth shut. He'll hate that.

'Don't go to any trouble. We'll be out most of the time. He wants to see . . . We'll amuse ourselves. Sure that's okay? Thanks a lot, mother. See you.' He was gone and by the time she got back to the porch the sun had set.

✻   ✻   ✻

She got up with the light and worked for a couple of hours before becoming restless. She walked around the shed, avoiding looking at the canvas that lay on the floor. She had painted a layer of white into it with a short stubby brush then scrubbed at the wet paint with a cloth, dragging it across the canvas, clothing the bareness with a ragged substance. But, now, to her the white space was no longer inviting, she longed again for the naked canvas. She lit a cigarette and wandered across the room to look at her sketches pinned on the wall. She opened the end window to let in some air. She put the cigarette in a saucer and crouched down again by the canvas. She picked up the cloth and began to rub, harder and harder until in places the canvas began to show through the paint, faintly transformed in colour, but yet its own textured self.

'That is more like it.'

The sound of her own voice almost made her jump in the silence of the room. The cigarette had smouldered out. She lit another one.

'The first sign of madness.'

Again the voice startled her.

That was what she had always been told as a child. Talking to yourself again, Helen? The first sign of . . . you know . . . knowing wagging finger.

Helen loves the sound of her own voice.

If you can't think of anything interesting to say, Helen, it's better not to say anything at all.

My voice is too loud in this room. Keep the words internal.

Inspiration is a bugger.

Rising with the light was a rotten idea. Here I am, mind a blank and it's only ten o'clock in the morning.

Air.

My mind is blank, bleak like the scrubbed canvas.

How the hell do other, perhaps more mature people, manage to pin down the elusive bugger inspiration? Dan always said I was undisciplined.

Dan was always right.

She stubbed out the new cigarette.

God, how I hate the taste of them.

'One day . . . one day . . . one day . . .'

She went out into the air.

In the house fat Mrs O'Sullivan was running the hoover over the sitting-room floor. She wore old tennis shoes without laces as she worked, to ease the pressure on her bunions. Helen put her head round the door.

'I'm just going out for a while, Mrs O'Sullivan,' she shouted

The woman switched off the machine. It whined into silence.

'I feel like some fresh air.'

'It'll likely rain.'

'I don't think so. It looks gorgeous.'

'You should bring your mac. The man on the wireless said it was going to rain. Rain spreading from the west was what he said. I took my mac with me. No point in getting soaked through. Our Mary said I was foolish to take the mac on a day like this. Cloudless. A cloudless day. I said to her you never can tell and did you not hear what the man on the wireless is after saying? After all he's paid to know. Isn't he?'

'He's not always right though.'

'That's what our Mary said. Better safe than sorry was what I thought. I suppose you'll be taking the bike? They say that a regular spin on the bike is good for the muscles.' She switched on the hoover again. No point in carrying on fruitless conversation when there was work to be done.

Helen cycled along the upper road towards the old station.

The wheels snapped and crackled over scattered twigs.

Bones dem dry bones, she sang in her head.

Soon the furnishings of the earth would be gone, leaving only dry bones and stones, no clutter.

Hear de word of de Lord.

Someone had swept the dead leaves into a pile to the right of the station house. Smoke drifted casually up from the pile and there was a sharp smell of burning. She propped the bike beside the door and went into the hall. She walked over to the window of the booking office and looked into the room beyond. He was kneeling at a tapestry prie-dieu in the centre of the room, his head bent over his loosely clenched hand. She drew back quickly from the window, embarrassed to find him at such private practice. She moved as quietly as she could back across the hall to the door. A mist of smoke now gave the air substance. She hadn't really thought of him as a man who might pray. She had in fact never known anyone who had prayed with conviction. Prayer had always seemed polite acknowledgment of God's existence, quite formal. How do you do . . . goodbye . . . thank you so much for a lovely evening . . . see you next week. She moved out into the smoke and then, caught by its bitterness, she sneezed.

'Hello? Who's there? Is someone there?' his voice called.

'I'm sorry.' She went back into the hall again. 'It's only . . .'

He appeared at the door that led out onto the platform.

'I'm sorry. I didn't . . .'

'That's all right. Come on in. I was just praying.'

He said the words quite unselfconsciously and held out his hand towards her. 'You are most welcome.'

'I felt I needed a change of scene . . . so I came up to talk to . . .'

'That's nice.'

'Have a chat. I had to get out.'

'That's good. I'm pleased you came. Come in, come in. We'll have a cup of coffee.'

'I don't want anything.'

She passed him and went into the room.

'A drink?'

'Oh no thank you.'

'You must have something. I might get offended if you didn't have something.'

'Very well. Coffee would be lovely . . . at least . . . I'm not fussy, whatever's easiest.'

He moved the prie-dieu from the centre of the room, pulling it awkwardly across the floor to stand against the wall by the window.

'It was my mother's,' he explained. 'I'll just put on the kettle.'

He left the room and she could hear him moving in what she supposed to be the kitchen. Each sound came to her as if through an echoing cave. He struck a match. She wondered how he managed to do a simple thing like that. The gas popped. Water ran into a kettle, for a moment musical and then just broad splashing. He had hung her pictures on the wall. One above the fireplace, the other above a small Victorian desk piled with papers. They both looked new and unexpected to her in their somewhat prim wooden frames. His feet shuffled on the stone floor. The tin lid scraped on the kettle. She moved closer to the picture over the fireplace, to rediscover it in its new condition.

'You see,' he said behind her. 'They're good. I told you they were good. One day I'll bring them up to Dublin and have them properly mounted and framed. Damian made those frames.'

'Damian?'

'He has a great way with his hands.'

'I like them. I think you should leave them like that.'

He put two mugs and a bowl of sugar lumps on the table.

'It came as quite a shock seeing them there. I had resigned myself to never seeing them again. I don't quite know why.'

He opened a drawer in the table and took out two silver teaspoons. He put each one down carefully and exactly beside each mug. An obsession with symmetry was also one of the symptoms of madness.

'I have only instant coffee, I find. Would you rather have tea?'

'No. That's all right.'

He went back into the kitchen. She crossed the room towards the other picture. The wet weight of the sheep's fleece seemed to burden it into the earth. It's okay, she thought. I thought it might just turn out like an illustration, but it does have an identity of its own. A little substance.

'Black or white?' he called from the kitchen.

'Black, please.'

She moved away from the picture feeling slightly guilty. 'Did your mother do the tapestry on the prie-dieu? It's beautiful.'

Old muted greens and blues. A unicorn gaily pranced through spring flowers. A girl sat under a formal oak tree plaiting her long golden hair.

He came back into the room with a jug and poured coffee into both the mugs. 'No, no. It's very old. It was her grandmother's, but it goes back a long way. French. She always had it in her room. I remember it all my life. It stood right in the middle of the room . . . bravely somehow. She believed greatly in prayer. Help yourself to sugar.'

She pulled a chair up to the table and sat down. She picked two lumps of sugar from the bowl and dropped them into her cup.

'She used to talk to God.'

'Do you do that?'

He was looking down at his coffee with a certain distaste. She thought he wasn't going to answer.

'No,' he said at last. 'I can't do that. She believed in miracles.' He laughed. He took a drink of his coffee. 'Oh, God, I hate that stuff. We should have had tea. She truly believed that I lived because she prayed. I'm glad to say she died before she . . . well . . .' He waved his hand towards himself. 'She died. Maybe that was the miracle. You can never tell with God. He has his own way of doing things.'

'Why do you pray then? I mean, if you're not talking to God . . . ? What? What are you asking him for?'

He pulled for a moment at the patch over his eye.

'I used to pray that I would die. I learnt however after a long time that I wasn't going to be given that . . . gift. My gift was going to be life. So . . . now . . . I ask for strength . . . grace . . .' He locked across the table at her. 'Comfort. I pray a lot for comfort. It's no dialogue though. I batter his ears.' He laughed. 'You look quite bewildered. You shouldn't ask people such questions.'

She clasped her hands and looked up at the ceiling.

'From ghoulies and ghosties and long-leggedy beasties and things that go bump in the night, good Lord deliver us. Amen. A very important prayer.'

'I went to Sunday school and all that, but I think we were politely informed that all lines of communication to God were through them . . . you know . . . the authorities. Be good and we'll see you through. Don't bother God, he has a lot on his mind. Later . . . I suppose about fourteen I became sceptical about the whole thing and then indifferent. I go to church from time to time, for a sort of silly reason perhaps. I think the poor old Church of Ireland is a bit beleaguered at the moment. I don't suppose my occasional presence helps them much. I must say I prefer empty churches to full ones . . . silence is more appealing to me than hymns. What happened to your mother?'

'She was killed. Just at the end of the war. She had been to visit me in the hospital and a buzz bomb just came out of the sky.' He snapped his fingers. 'Like that. Somewhere near Victoria station. She was dead. Straight away. They didn't tell me for months. I couldn't understand why she wasn't coming to visit me. All the silly excuses they made. I knew they were lies, you know. Then when I was being shifted to the skin-graft unit my father came in and told me. Very casually . . . one of those joke English scenes. By the way, your mother was killed six months ago, by a buzz bomb.'

He picked up his spoon and tapped it three times against the side of his mug. Three sort of exorcising taps.

'I laughed.'

'You shouldn't have done that.'

'What else was there to do but laugh? In another age I would have been able to cry. Now I would be able to cry, but then, I wouldn't have been allowed. It wouldn't have done.'

'Presumably your father was trying to save you pain.'

'Pain.'

He threw back his head and laughed heartily.

'I'm sorry,' she said. 'I'm not very well acquainted with pain. My life has been filled with minor complications and confusions, but very little pain. I think that might make me a little insensitive.'

'When your husband . . . ?'

She shook her head most vigorously, but didn't say anything. He looked at her for a moment or two.

'I hope you are going to paint.'

'Yes.'

'Not just mess about.'

'Yes. I intend to take a portfolio to Dublin and see what happens then. There's so little time left. I've no one but myself to blame for that.'

He stretched across the table and put his hand for a moment over hers. He wore a gold signet ring on his little finger and the weight of it pressed painfully into her flesh. When he took his hand away she saw that he had left a red mark on her skin.

'Drink up your disgusting coffee,' he pushed back his chair and stood up, 'and come and see my signal box.'

'Have you a cigarette? I've left mine at home.'

'No cigarettes. You smoke too much.'

She drank some of the coffee. He was right, it was disgusting.

'Everyone says that to me.'

'You should stop.' His voice had a faintly schoolmasterly tone. He moved towards the door as he spoke.

'That's easy to say. I say it to myself all the time . . . when I wake up in the morning and feel like hell . . . when I look at the brown stains on my fingers . . . each time I cough. I'll stop on Monday I say . . . and then next Monday . . . after Christmas . . . I gave it up for Lent once, but I thought I was going to die after about a week so I started again. I have very little strength of purpose.'

He laughed. 'So I see.'

They walked along the platform. Most of the grass and weeds that had pushed their way up between the flagstones had been removed. The broken panes in the windows of the station buildings had been replaced and the doors and window frames had been painted green. Between the platform and the white wooden fence that ran down towards the signal box a newly dug flower-bed was waiting for the spring. A new sign on the fence was neatly lettered in black, Knappogue Road. 'We're going to plant bulbs in there. Just for a start. Red and yellow dwarf tulips. They'll flower quite late in the spring. We'll have to work out what to do after that. I like a station to have bedding plants, but it's an awful lot of work. Damian's digging another bed up by the level crossing. I've always loved those stations that had their names written in flowers. That's probably a bit too flamboyant for us. I expect we'll end up with something like heaths . . . perhaps even dwarf conifers. What do you think?'

'I don't know a thing about gardens. Dan never let me near the flower-beds because he said I pulled up the plants and left the weeds. I was relegated to cutting the grass and burning the rubbish. I must say you have it all looking very nice.'

'Yes. It's coming along nicely. We should be ready for traffic in the New Year.'

She didn't say anything. She gave him a false bright smile and for a moment was afraid of his sharp eye.

'I'll go up first.'

They had reached the steps leading up to the box.

She climbed up after him. He pushed open the door and went in. She stood for a moment on the platform and looked towards the village roofs below them. Beyond the dunes a huge front of cloud was boiling up into the sky. Tremors of wind were starting to shake the empty branches of the trees.

'Everything is spick and span. First-rate,' she heard him say. She followed him into the box. There was a smell of new paint and brass polish.

'Have you ever been in a signal box before?'

She shook her head.

'This works on the electric token-block system. There is only a single line here, as you presumably know, so the important thing is to stop there being more than one train in the section at any time.'

He looked at her to see if she understood.

She nodded. So far so good.

'The driver of each train has to carry a token . . . in some cases it's a staff. That's the most common . . . You've probably come across them. But in this line it's a small metal disc. Look, it fits into this box.'

He showed her the slot in the polished box on the wall.

'When I put the token into that box it locks the section that the train is just leaving. No other train can go into that section without having that token. Then, this box, here, holds the token for the next section . . . understand?'

'Mmm.'

'When I take it out of the box, the signal levers for the next section are unlocked. Then I check with the next station that the line is clear. The bell . . . There is a whole series of signals and replies. Listen.'

He pressed the bell twice. The two beats sounded quite clearly. She looked startled.

'It works.'

He ignored her comment.

'Train entering section,' he said. He moved to the signal handles. 'This one comes off danger now and then this. After she has moved into the new section, you put the signals back to danger again. It's absolutely foolproof. Of course, we have the level crossing here on the up side. That will have to be hand-operated, I'm afraid. We're a little behind the times here. Basic . . . but very simple to operate.'

'You might forget all these signals.'

'It's all written down very carefully in the rule book and I have the bell signals up on the wall there. If you are in any doubt at all you just refer to the book. Anyone could do it you know. There are never too many crises in a station of this size. The odd cow on the line, only minor problems like that. It's a good life. My station in Scotland was very similar.'

'You had a station in Scotland?'

'Yes, for four years.'

'Why did you . . . ? What happened?'

'I had family problems.' He laughed abruptly. 'They wanted me to go and live in a home of some sort. Put quite a lot of pressure on me. They are strongly convinced that I can't look after myself.' He smiled. 'It's all to do with money really. I've never bothered them, you know. Tried to keep out of their hair. We haven't much in common. I'd been there about four years . . . yes . . . and they all descended one day without warning. A whole regiment of them. Brothers, sisters, their appendages, lawyers, doctors, all rabbit's friends and relations. They wanted me to sign things . . . to come quietly.'

He looked out of the window towards the distant sea.

'I never did them any harm.'

'What happened?'

'Well . . . I played them along for a bit and then did a bunk. I came over here. Out of the jurisdiction so to speak. It's much more difficult for them to get hold of me over here. I'm not really as much of a fool as they think. My lawyer's an old pal. School . . . all that . . . army rubbish. A good chap. He keeps them at bay. It took me over a year to find this place. It's good. I like it here. This is where I'll stay. They'll never dig me out of this place.' He turned towards her. His eye stared into her face.

'I never did them any harm.'

'I'm sure you didn't.'

'My mother left me a lot of money. That's the crux of it all. It enables me to live the way I want. After all that's why she left it to me. She changed her will shortly after . . . She didn't know how things would work out for me. She told me that. She wanted me to be able to make my own decisions. It upsets them a lot. I do have to say that I get a certain amount of amusement out of upsetting them. Know what I mean?'

Sometimes his eye shone a brilliant blue, she noticed, sometimes it faded almost as you watched to a pale, tired grey.

'They can have it when I die. What's left of it. I think they're afraid I'll leave it to some absurd charity. Do you think I'm mad?'

'We all have a right to live the way we want.'

'That wasn't what I asked you.'

'I don't know the answer,' she said after a long pause. 'I mean, I don't think you are a person to be afraid of in any way . . . but, beyond that . . . I have to admit, I'm not sure where the boundaries are between sanity and madness. I mean anywhere . . . not just you. There is such a fine line between people who can accept the formalised madness of the world and those who can't. In Russia, after all, they put poets in lunatic asylums.'

'Here we leave them outside but don't bother to read what they have to say. There's madness for you.'

She laughed. No more tension. His eye lost its dazzle, softened in colour.

'You like the box?'

He gestured with his hand, embraced with the gesture the brass and shining polished wood, the boxes and handles, the telephone high on the wall in its cradle, the high-standing desk with grooves for pens, the inkwell sunk in one corner and also, outside where the line had once curved away from the station, the curve slightly falling with the slope of the hill, the hedge that had been neatly clipped beyond which she could see the first signal standing at danger.

'It's beautiful. It looks just . . .'

'Just?'

'Well, ready for use.'

He nodded and opened the door.

'It's the boy. Damian. He likes things to be perfect.'

He jerked his head towards the door, commanding that she leave the box.

'I've wasted a lot of your time.'

'Oh no.' She moved out on to the top of the steps. Leaves scurried along the platform. They descended the steps in silence. He grunted slightly each time his right foot thudded down on to the wood. They walked along the platform.

'I'm glad you said that,' he said.

Blue smoke twisted up from the chimney of the house. She could hear the sound of Damian digging at the other end of the platform, the rhythmic crunch of the spade entering the earth, the occasional clatter as he threw an unwanted stone out of his way.

'Said what?'

'About my not being a person to be afraid of. I wouldn't like you to be afraid of me.'

'I must get home, back to my cigarettes.'

'You'd better say hello to Damian before you go. Just a quick word.'

The tiny waiting room, she could see as they walked past, had a bench running round the wall and a polished table in the middle of the floor.

'A visitor, Damian,' said Roger.

Damian straightened up and stuck his spade in the earth. He wiped his right hand on the seat of his trousers and held it out towards Helen.

'How are you doing?'

She shook his hand.

'You're working hard.'

'There's no let-up around here. The boss there would have had the pyramids built in half the time.' He winked.

'He's a slave driver is he?'

'Ah no,' said Roger behind her. 'Sweet reason is more my style.'

'Jack is coming up next week and bringing a friend. Perhaps you'll come up to the house and see them. Have a drink or something?'

Damian pulled the spade out of the ground and began to dig once more.

'I'm sure he'd be pleased.'

He pressed his foot down on the spade and it sliced deep into the earth. 'If Jack wants to see me, he knows where to find me.'

'Yes,' she said and turned away from him. 'Yes, of course. I'm sorry.' She walked quickly back along the platform, feeling a fool. Roger followed her. She walked through the hallway, past the window of the ticket office and out the door. She picked up her bicycle.

'He was rude,' said Roger, 'but then you were pretty silly.'

'I know. Fulsome, motherish, interfering daft. We can't all be perfect.' She got onto the bike and sat, one toe on the ground looking at him. 'People say he's a Provo.'

'People say stupid things. Invent things.'

'In a small community like this, they usually know what they're talking about.'

'He never talks politics. I never talk politics. I have no politics in my head to talk. If he's a Provo it's his own affair.'

'They kill people.'

'Yes,' was all he said.

'Innocent people, children. Blow people's arms and legs off.' She thought for a fleeting moment of Dan. How surprised he must have been when those bullets hit him. No time for pain or anger, perhaps not even time for surprise.

'Before the British dropped us fools on Arnhem, they bombed a lunatic asylum. They were told that was what it was. They were told there were no Germans there, but they bombed it just the same. Better sure than sorry, I suppose some top brass hat said. The woods were full of poor mad creatures . . . just wandering, crying some of them. Lost. They were dressed in white sort of pyjama things. We all kill when we think it is expedient.'

'Is that true . . . about the lunatic asylum?'

'Oh yes, absolutely true. I only found out about it years later. I always presumed that those poor white creatures were part of my dementia. Sometimes I was conscious, then I suppose I was unconscious, but I always saw those white figures. Floating. They seemed to me to be floating. *Il Purgatorio*. You don't know how privileged you are never to have suffered.'

She blushed and kicked at the pedal of her bicycle. 'How do you know whether I've suffered or not?'

'Don't be angry with me. After all you said yourself you were not very well acquainted with pain.'

'I'm not angry . . . It's just that so many people seem to believe that unless you have been through some sort of . . . oh God, what word can I use . . . hell, torment, anguish, you're not a whole person . . . you lack a whole dimension to your life. That's a form of arrogance I can't accept.'

His face was delighted.

'You are angry. You have such an untroubled face I thought perhaps you might never get angry. Anger is a very healthy emotion.'

She pushed off with her foot and left him standing there, idiotic grin dragging at his mouth. At the corner she turned and saw him still standing there grinning. She flapped a hand at him.

'Goodbyeee,' he called. 'Goodbyeee.'

✳   ✳   ✳

Mrs O'Sullivan was mopping round the kitchen sink when she arrived home.

'My floor is only washed.' She looked with suspicion at Helen's feet. The veins on the backs of her hands bulged as she squeezed and bent the cloth. Helen sometimes had visions of her wringing the necks of chickens, rabbits, unwanted puppies even, her deep brown eyes quite calm as the hands moved. It wasn't that she was unkind, savage in any way, she just had all this power inside her, was unaware of her own strength.

'You're all red. It doesn't do to get overheated.'

It was the wind as much as anything else, blowing in my face.'

'I've just made the tea. Will you have a cup?'

'Lovely. Thank you.'

'There's nothing like a cup of tea when you have everything red up.' She flapped the cloth out in front of her and hung it on the rail in front of the Aga. She picked the teapot off the range and brought it over to the table.

'Sit you down and rest yourself a minute. Let yourself cool off. Biking is for young ones. Not,' she plonked two mugs on the table, 'that young ones would give you two pence for a bicycle these days. It's cars they want.' Mrs O'Sullivan's huge hand fished in the pocket of her overall for her cigarette. She always seemed to have a partially smoked one in there with a box of matches. She would have a few puffs and then carefully pinch it out and put it back in her pocket again, waiting for the next cup of tea. Then out it would come again.

'I was over at the station.'

Mrs O'Sullivan gave a deep and somewhat bronchial laugh.

'Now in the name of God what did you want to go over there for? Isn't that cowboy half-mad? You want to mind yourself with people like that.'

'I just thought I'd like to go and see what he was doing.'

'Curiosity killed the cat,' she said cheerfully.

'It's amazing. He and Damian Sweeney have done a great job. It really looks as if trains could start moving through it at any moment. All fixed up.'

'Now what sort of a person would want to do a thing like that at all? Half-mad is right . . . or whole mad. More money than sense.' She took a great swig of tea and swished it round inside her mouth before swallowing it. 'I mind well the time you could go all the way to Dublin in the train. You had to change of course in Letterkenny and Strabane. All the way to Dublin. I had cousins in Omagh. God when I think of the gas we used to have on them ould trains. The buses were never the same at all. And expensive. Holy God!'

Another little swish of tea.

'My uncle Eoin, that was my father's brother, he was signalman up there for near on thirty-two years. His heart was broke after they closed down the line. That's what they said anyway. He was too old then for a job on the buses. Some of them got jobs on the buses but he was too old to learn the new ways. You know what I mean? He lived for the trains. Loved the trains. Six months was all he lasted after that. I remember the very day he died. We had the Emergency then and nothing would do but my auntie Bridie had to pack her bags and away over to Glasgow to live with her daughter Alice. Emergency or no Emergency, said she couldn't face it here without Eoin. My mother and father begged her not to go. Sure as eggs is eggs, they said, you'll be killed by the bombs. She wouldn't pay them a blind bit of heed. She took a new lease of life over there, lived to be seventy-eight. Ah, sure you wouldn't remember them days.'

'Well, I do a bit you know.'

Mrs O'Sullivan crimped the end of her cigarette carefully between her finger and thumb.

'Maybe he's a spy.'

She dropped the butt into her pocket.

'Who?' asked Helen, surprised by the turn of things.

'Your man above.'

Helen exploded into laughter.

'What on earth would . . . ?'

'I'm just telling you what they say. I'm not saying he is a spy. He could be a spy.'

'There's not much spying anyone could do here.'

'You find them everywhere these days. Tell me why else would he be here . . . ? Messing around with that old station? Where would he get the money to do a thing like that?'

'I think he's quite rich and he likes trains. That's all. Obviously loves trains . . . like your uncle did. He's nice I think.'

'So they say. A gentleman, even an' he's had half his brains blown out.' She dipped a ginger biscuit in her tea and nibbled at the damp edge. 'Mind you what he wants to go getting mixed up with that Damian Sweeney for, I can't think. He's a bad lot if ever there was one.'

'He works hard.'

'He works when it suits him. He's all mixed up with . . . you know.' She looked sternly at Helen, defying her to say a word.

'He keeps secrets from his mother. Now, the one thing I have to say about my lot is, they never keep secrets from me. Never did and never will. Open.'

'How do you know?'

'I rared them, didn't I? I brought them up in the fear of God and not one of them has ever set foot outside the marks; that's the truth. Mrs Sweeney gave those kids too much liberty and look at them now. Two in America doing God knows what, and Damian. Never puts his head inside the church from one end of the year to the next. I said it to her, so I did, face to face, so I'm not speaking out of turn. Cissie, I said, you made your own bed, now you must lie on it. Too soft she was with them altogether. You know yourself.'

She gave Helen an accusing look.

'Oh dear,' said Helen.

'You know yourself.' Mrs O'Sullivan repeated the words triumphantly.

'Well . . .'

'It's all in the raring.'

That seemed the end of the conversation. Helen filled up her cup with hot tea and retreated across the yard to the safety of her shed.

* * *

Next morning she walked to the northern tip of the beach. No one ever came here at all. Rocks grew up through the sand, grey lumps of granite. The odd cow wandered down from time to time from the unfenced fields on the hill. Sea birds lazed and strutted, hardly concerned by her presence. In the winter storms the sea lashed right up to the edge of the sloping dunes, but now the sand was still dry and bright with a tiny powdering of shells. She spread her towel beside a rock and sat down. She unwrapped her sketch book and began to draw, examining for her own edification the objects she saw around her: the strands of acid-green weed clinging to a broken razor shell, piles of discarded sand thrust up by some burrowing worms, the angle of a beak probing for food, the tight, delicate mechanism of a poised leg, the curve of rolling swell and the exact moment the spray burst. Page after page she filled. Behind her the rock still held the remains of summer warmth. She remembered having seen some notebooks of Leonardo, the explicit studies of a hand, fingers crooked, ridges of muscles running into the wrist; a bent leg full of power, the angles between jaw and neck, the tensions created even in stillness. After a long time her eyes were hurting, the fingers of her right hand felt as if someone had held them in a vice. She put the book and pencils down by the towel.

She stood up and pulled off her jersey and shirt and then her jeans and her pants and ran across the sand into the sea. She waded out over the breaking line of waves and then, falling forward onto the water, she swam straight out to sea, something that she normally wouldn't dream of doing, fear always keeping her within scrabbling distance of the land. She swam for a good six or seven minutes, thinking of nothing but the movement of her body through the water, the soft cleaving of arm after arm, the rhythm of her stretched legs beating, then suddenly frightened by her own courage she turned and swam back towards the shore. The rhythm was lost and her limbs felt the strain. She faltered, splashed, gulped mouthfuls of water. She moved from her kind of crawl to a more staid breast stroke. She turned over on her back and lay resting for a few moments, her eyes closed, her feet moving only enough to keep her steadily afloat. Having got back her nerve she began to swim again, feeling rather foolish. The tide was with her and she found she was moving quickly and calmly towards the beach. Once she found herself inside the arm of the bay she relaxed and began to enjoy again the motion of swimming, the weightlessness. What a life mermaids must lead, she thought. She shook the water from her face and eyes and looked towards the shore. A tall figure was standing beside her clothes. A hand went up to greet her. It was Damian Sweeney.

Bugger.

Oh God, she whispered a quick prayer up to the sky where he might or might not be watching over her well-being . . . don't let there be any hassle. No demoralising happening . . . Please God, I promise I'll buy some bathing togs. I promise I'll wear them, if that's what you really want . . . but oh bugger . . . Dear God, why isn't he digging flower-beds or turning table legs. The ground was under her feet now. She stood and began to walk slowly through the breaking sea. He bent down and picked up her towel from the sand. He shook it, both hands cracking it into the breeze, then he walked down to the water's edge to meet her. She stopped when the water was about knee-high and, catching her hair in her hands, twisted it into a rope, wringing the wetness out of it.

'It looks freezing,' he shouted to her.

She shook her head.

'I thought you were never going to come back. You don't swim well enough to go away out there. Were you not frightened?'

'A bit.'

She stepped onto the dry sand and took the towel from his hand. She wrapped it tightly round herself. It was cold now. She rubbed at her running nose with the back of her hand.

'It's lovely,' she said. 'You ought to try it yourself.'

'I've more sense.'

She sniffed and laughed.

'I've no sense. It's a well-known fact.'

She picked up her shirt and jumper and pulled them, still attached, together over her head. She rubbed at her legs with the towel, thumping at herself with her fists to keep the circulation speeding. She turned round towards him. He was jogging naked towards the edge of the sea.

I hope to God he doesn't catch pneumonia, she thought. I bet he hasn't been in there for years.

Scrawny.

She dropped down on her knees and picked up her sketch book. Stringy. Jack wasn't like that.

He loitered on the edge of the water, his energy dissipated by the cold. His shoulders were hunched, his arms wrapped round his chest.

Jack was well covered, no sign of the framework.

He stepped cautiously like one of the wading birds across the first ripple of the waves.

Jack was pale. He took a sudden plunge across the waves and was down under the water. His arms worked for a few moments and then he stood up again and began to move back towards the shore. Suddenly in a great explosion of energy he rolled into the foam and leapt up into the air again. He twirled round, his arms high above his head and then down he went again, rolling again. Up he came and ran through the shallow water kicking great sparkling fountains up ahead of him as he ran. He ran towards her, shaking the water from his body as a dog does after a swim.

'Can I have a borrow of your towel, missus?' He put on a whiny child's voice.

She handed it up to him. 'You're all covered in sand. You should go in and wash it off.'

'Do you want to kill me?' He walked back to where his clothes lay, rubbing at himself savagely. She continued to draw as he dressed himself, as he rubbed hopelessly at the sand clinging to his legs and arms. He turned his back to her and stood on one leg and then the other, pulling on his pants and then his trousers. When he was dressed save for his shoes and socks he came back and dropped the towel beside her.

'What are you drawing?'

'You.'

He blushed suddenly and ran his fingers through his hair. He looked away from her out towards the horizon.

'Me?'

'Yes. Here, do you want to look?'

He squatted down beside her and she handed him the book.

'They're only sketches, but you can look if you want to.'

He looked carefully at each page. The trials and errors, scorings, shadings, heavy lines, light, almost invisible, wisps of grey. Stones, sand, wings, claws, beaks, sea, an arm, a leg, movement, stillness. After he had finished he handed her back the book.

'It looks like you're trying to teach yourself something. It's like a school book.'

She nodded.

'Do I look like that?'

'More or less. I haven't drawn a human figure for years. It was great to have you there miraculously . . . when I was in the mood.'

'I was up there.' He pointed up towards the hill. 'I couldn't think what you were drawing. There didn't seem to be anything to draw. I watched you for a long time.'

'You must have.'

'When you went in to swim I thought I'd better come down. I felt . . .' he blushed again '. . . if I'd stayed up there, it would have been like spying on you. So I came down.'

She smiled.

'Thank you for coming down.'

'What will you do with those now?' He nodded towards the book.

'I have a plan in my head for a series of shorescapes. It's just an idea at the moment . . . a wriggling germ, but I hope it will grow when I start to paint. I know it will.'

'Will you put me in it?'

'You'll have to wait and see. I'll have to wait and see.'

He leaned forward and began to draw on the sand with his finger. He made deep grooves in the sand and then swept away the scattered grains as they got in his way. A small high-bowed boat, plain, heavy-looking, sitting squatly down into the sea. A long bowsprit and one mast. His finger drew tiny waves and a mainsail filling with wind.

'Do you know what that is?'

'It looks a bit like a hooker. I'm not much good on boats, but they're very recognisable.'

'You're next best to right. A gleoiteog. That's what I'm going to build myself. I have a model made at home. Sails and all. To scale you know. I'll bring it round to show you some time.' He scrubbed the picture out with his hand. 'If you're interested, that is. You mightn't be interested. About this size.' He held his hands up to show her. 'A perfect model. I just thought you might . . .'

'Yes. I'd like to see it very much.'

'I was rude yesterday.'

'Oh no, that's all right. I was a bit silly. Motherish. I forget sometimes that everyone grows up. That sort of thing can become so boring.'

'My mother's boring,' he said. 'But I wouldn't have thought you were.'

'Jack thinks I am.'

'She's nice, mind you. I didn't mean anything like that . . . but boring. She knits for the sweater people. The sweated-labour people, I tell her she should call them. Sometimes I want to throw something at those clicking needles. I restrain myself. Jack's coming home, you said?'

'Yes. Next weekend.'

'Bringing a friend?'

'So he said. I thought at first it might be a girl. I got all motherly and excited again.'

'But it's not a girl.'

'No.'

'I suppose he does that quite a lot? Brings down friends?'

'No. I think he likes to protect his friends from me.'

He looked away out to sea. He looked, she thought, as if he were trying to see America.

'Did he say who he was bringing down?'

'I asked him, but I don't think he heard me. Why?' She gathered together the book and her pencils, the wet sandy towel.

'I just wondered. I thought maybe it was someone I knew.'

'Oh hardly . . . I mean . . . well . . . hardly.'

'Yes. Hardly. I'd better be getting back to my work.'

'You're mitching today.'

'I work my own hours. He's very reasonable like that.'

She stood up.

'I hope I didn't bother you.'

'Of course not. I hope you won't suffer any ill effects from your swim.'

'Not a bit of it. Sometimes he's not well at all. It's quite hard then for the both of us. He gets these moods, like. You have to understand.'

'Do you think he'd like it if I asked him over for dinner one evening?'

'Aye. I think he'd like it. Goodbye then.' He took a few steps. 'Helen.'

'Goodbye, Damian. See you soon.'

He walked away up the beach, his shoes and socks dangling from his right hand, leaving deep footmarks in the sand.

✳   ✳   ✳

For the next two days she lived in the shed, making short trips across the yard from time to time to make herself a cup of tea, boil an egg, feed the cat, who took quite unkindly to what he considered to be desertion. Bananas were useful, she thought. In Africa native tribes had existed for thousands of years on bananas; now, presumably, the glories of the sliced loaf and instant coffee had reached them. Monkeys too, very healthy, very energetic. A lot could be said in favour of the banana. Elephants even ate them with the peels on. She didn't bother to sit down to eat, just moved restlessly around the kitchen, watched by the disapproving eyes of the cat. The cups had brown stains inside them, a sign of true sordidness, she thought.

She remembered a moment with Dan. She blotted at the toast crumbs with a damp cloth as he sat watching, also, like a cat, disapproving.

'The really dreadful, debilitating thing about housework, domesticity, whatever you like to call it, is that over and over again you're doing the same bloody thing. He hated that word. She only used it when she really wanted to annoy him. 'Bloody,' she repeated. 'You clear the table.' She threw the cloth across the room towards the sink. The cloth landed on the floor. 'You lay the table again. You wash the bloody saucepans and then you dirty them again. You wash them specifically to dirty them. You lay and unlay. Make beds in order to get into them and crumple them. On and on and on for ever until you die . . . or end up in the local bin, gaga, incontinent and unloved.'

'Your problem is that you're a slut.'

'No,' she said sharply. 'I wish I were. If I were a slut I wouldn't care.

231

I'm just a boring woman with a boring sense of duty. I feel my whole life is rushing down that bloody sink with the Fairy Liquid bubbles.'

'I do wish you wouldn't use that word.'

'Bloody,' she said just to show that she wasn't intimidated by him.

She laughed at the memory of it and went out into the yard, closing the door on the banana skins and the brown-stained cups and the crumbs on the table and the cat.

The first painting was growing. The canvas had become a magnet drawing out of her head an implacable coherence that she had never felt before. Each stroke had its purpose, its truth. The gaunt bones of the young man became a great stalk growing up through the centre of the canvas, from its own black shadow on the sand. She painted fast, the fear always in her mind that if she faltered, looked back even for a moment over her shoulder, Orpheus-like, she would lose her vision. She spoke words to herself as she worked, meaningless jumbles of sound, and sang snatches of songs that had become embedded in her head for no reason. Over and over again the same phrase would burst out of her into the room, until sometimes she would put down her brush and give a sharp slap to the side of her face to try and dislodge the irritation.

'What day is it?' she asked aloud.

No one answered.

She put down her brush and stood up. She stretched her arms up above her head. Stiff. Every bone, joint, muscle, whatever they all were, seemed to be locked hopelessly together. Grey cloud pushed down on the glass roof.

'Thursday,' she answered herself.

She bent down and, carefully lifting the canvas, she carried it across the room and propped it against the wall. She stood for a moment or two staring at it.

'Thursday it is.'

No one disagreed.

She looked around.

'Bloody pigsty.'

She went over and opened the window. She emptied the ashtrays into a plastic bag and then threw in some tissues that were lying on the floor. Stiff back as she bent. Some dirty rags, and then some rolled-up used tubes of paint. Marginally less like a pigsty.

She went out into the yard and put the plastic bag in the bin, then she got her bicycle out of its shed and set off for the station. It wasn't raining, but the west wind was damp and squally. She had to struggle quite hard to keep the bike on the left-hand side of the road.

She didn't hear the car until it passed her coming round a corner. Roger put his hand on the horn in greeting and then stopped. She got off the bike and crossed the road.

'Hello.'

'Good morning . . . perhaps it's afternoon, I'm not sure. I was just going to call on you.'

'Snap,' he said.

He looked tired. The scars on his face were bunched together and shiny . . . somewhat grotesque. She felt suddenly guilty at thinking such a thing. She put her hand through the window of the car and touched his shoulder briefly.

'Go on ahead,' she said. 'I'll follow you back. I've finished a picture and I'd like to show it to you . . . well . . . to someone. I just suddenly thought I'd like to show it to someone. You seemed to be . . .'

He nodded. The car gave a slight shudder and then moved slowly down the road. She turned the bike round and pedalled after him.

She brought him in through the little glass porch. Several of the geraniums still flowered bravely and the air was sweet. They walked across the hall and out into the yard.

'I've just been down looking for Damian,' he said. 'There was no sign of him this morning so I thought I'd go down and find out what was up. I thought he might be ill. He is usually so meticulous about everything he does.'

'I hope nothing's the matter with him.'

'No. His mother says he's gone away for a few days. Just took off last night. Odd he didn't say.'

'Yes. Odd.'

She opened the door of the shed as the first raindrops pattered around them.

'Rain,' she said.

She crossed the room and closed the window.

'I also wanted to see you,' he said.

The rain thickened suddenly, almost startlingly, rattling off the roof, splashing down into the yard. Everything in sight changed its colour.

'Gosh, we were only in in time.'

'For several days, I've wanted to come and see you. I don't quite know why I didn't come. Some kind of reticence prevented me.'

'This place is a pigsty. I'm sorry. Dan always said that I was a slut. He must have been right. I argued with him at the time, but . . .'

'Are you going to show me this picture, or have you changed your mind?'

'Shut your eyes.' Oh God, she groaned. 'Eye. Shut . . . listen to that awful rain.' She looked at him. He stood by the door, his eye obediently shut. She walked over to the painting and lifted it up carefully.

'I wanted to see you,' he repeated.

'That's nice.'

She carried it across the room and put it standing up on the only chair. 'You can look now.'

She heard the telephone ringing from across the yard. She considered the possibility of leaving it to ring itself out, but decided against it. She pulled open the door and dashed across the yard. Curiosity killed the cat, Dan would have said coolly. The telephone had held no magic for him at all.

'Hello.' Puffed.

Crackle.

'Mother.'

Crackle.

'Hello.'

'Hello.'

Crackle.

Miracles of modern science how are ya.

'Mother, can you hear me?'

'Yes. Just,' she yelled.

There was a long crackling silence.

'Jack. Hello. Are you still there?'

She caught the sound of his voice again. A voice drowning in crackles. As it went down for the third time she heard the words, 'tomorrow evening.'

'Tomorrow evening?' she shouted back. 'Is that what you said? You're coming tomorrow evening?'

There was total silence.

'Hey. Yoohoo. Anyone there?'

It sounded as if someone sighed.

'Bugger the Minister for Posts and Telegraphs,' she said into the mouthpiece and hung up.

An old respectable umbrella of Dan's stood in a corner of the hall, ready for emergencies. His name was written on a thin gold band around the handle, in neat looping letters. He had always kept it immaculately rolled.

'Hopeless, hopeless,' she muttered to herself as she picked it up.

Roger was standing looking at the painting.

'Hopeless,' she repeated to his back. 'Do you know that the people are leaving this country in thousands because they can't communicate with each other. Thousands. What the hell is the point of paying to have one of those odious little black gadgets in your house, if it doesn't work?'

'I think it's a very remarkable painting,' Roger said.

She crossed the room and picked up several brushes that were lying on the floor.

She poured some turpentine into a cup and began to clean them.

'Why do you live alone?'

She rubbed at the handle of one of the brushes with a cloth.

'I'm not unhappy.'

Blue paint stained two of her fingers.

'That wasn't what I asked.'

'I like to be alone. It's funny how long it takes you to learn these things about yourself.'

She put the brush into an enamel jug where several others were standing and picked up another.

'I didn't discover that truth about myself until after Dan was killed. Up until that moment I saw nothing but my own inadequacies.'

She twirled the brush for a moment in the turpentine.

'I'm not lonely you know,' she said quite firmly, 'just alone. I like to live on the edge of things.' She sighed. 'Dan . . . he was very sane and well balanced. I suppose that was why I married him, I saw the lack of balance in myself. He . . .' she hesitated.

'Go on.'

She put the next brush in the jug with the others and turned round to look at him. He was still staring at the painting.

'He would have considered me to be irresponsible. He believed in structures and hierarchies, responsible involvement.'

She patted the pockets of her overall for a moment, feeling to see if her cigarettes were there. Having found that they were, she didn't need one any longer.

'Sanity. He believed in sanity.'

'I'll buy it,' he said.

'Buy what?'

'The picture.'

She burst out laughing.

'Don't be a damn fool.'

'I'm not. I want to buy it.'

'Well, I don't want to sell it. I intend to do a series . . . sequence . . . call it what you like. I see four in my mind. Then I'll take them up to Dublin. If I finish them I'll feel I really have something to show people. I'll be ready then. So . . .'

'So?'

'No more talk of buying. I don't want . . .'

He smiled slightly as he waited for her to finish the sentence.

' . . . don't get me wrong . . . kindness, charitable offerings. I don't mean to be rude.'

He nodded. He plucked at his eye-patch and she thought that he was going to pull it off. She didn't want to see an empty socket, or perhaps the eye was still there, threaded with red veins like the blind man who used to tap his way down the street where she had lived as a child. She wouldn't want to see that either.

'Of course you're right. Absolutely right. Look here, I feel like a drink. How about coming down to the village with me and we'll have a drink?'

'We could have one here.'

'No, no, no. Let's get out of here. Mr Kelly's insalubrious bar . . . or the hotel? Take your pick. A celebration. Both are equally dismal. We could go further afield if you preferred.'

'The hotel.'

'Right. The hotel it is. Come along then.'

'I'm not really fit to be seen.' She laughed nervously. 'I don't think I've even combed my hair today.'

'You'll do.' He turned abruptly and walked towards the door. 'It's not the Ritz. Not even the Shelbourne Hotel, Dublin.'

He opened the door. It was still pouring.

'Hold on,' she said. 'I have the umbrella.' He was striding across the yard, impatient to be off on this jaunt.

'I must wash the paint off my hands.'

'Don't fuss. You'll do the way you are. Women always fuss so. Prink, pat, fiddle.'

'I am not going to prink, pat nor fiddle. I'm going to wash the paint off my hands. If that upsets you in any way, you can go to hell.'

She marched past him into the kitchen and turned on both taps with ferocity. He didn't follow her. He walked on down the narrow hall and when she came out of the kitchen he was standing in the porch among the geraniums.

'Did you have this built?' he asked.

She nodded.

'I've always had a vision of myself as an old lady sitting wrapped in shawls watching the sun set, in a porch filled with geraniums. The building of the porch was phase one.'

'Knitting?' he asked.

'Heavens no. Not doing anything useful at all. I don't see that my personality will change with old age. Staring into space.'

'A rocking chair?' he suggested.

'Perhaps.'

They scuttled out to the car through the rain.

'You don't like women much, do you?' she asked as she settled herself into her seat.

'I have observed their manipulations from a healthy distance. They tell lies.'

'Everyone tells lies when it suits them. Dan, who was the soul of honesty, did. Mind you, he pretended he didn't, but he did. And you do too.'

'I don't tell lies.'

He slammed the car door and began to fiddle around with the keys.

'Of course you do. What's all this railway nonsense then? Trains? There hasn't been a train here since 1947 or some time like that. Over thirty years. There are no lines. No hope of trains. No more trains. Never.' He didn't say a word. He turned the car very carefully round and they drove in silence down the hill. She took her cigarettes from her pocket and put one in her mouth. He leaned slightly forward as he drove, peering with care through the triangle cleared by the windscreen wiper. She lit the cigarette and took a deep pull.

'I'm sorry,' she said, as they reached the first house in the long street. 'I shouldn't have said any of that. I feel dishevelled, mentally as well as physically. I hope you'll forgive me.'

'There isn't anything to forgive. You have your right like everyone else to your point of view. I see my station working. Trains running through it. Goods. Not many passengers I admit. Most people have cars these days. Moving extensions of their homes; the same sweet papers on the floor, the same music, your old coat on the back seat, your own smell. Trains are different. Trains will run through my station again . . . That's not a lie, Helen.'

He stopped the car outside the hotel. Macnamara's Hotel was written in black letters over the pillared door. Licensed Bar in smaller letters. Prop. Geo. Hasson, very small indeed. She got out of the car and followed him into the dark hall. The bar was empty. The eight plastic stools waited hopefully, the fire smouldered.

Beer and smoke and a smell of fried fish.

'Stool or table?' he asked her.

'Over by the fire, I think.'

He rang the bell on the counter and a voice called something from another room.

'I met your son here one evening . . . Jack?'

'Yes. He mentioned that.'

'He seemed a nice boy.'

'I don't think I know him very well.'

Mr Hasson came in, in his shirt sleeves. 'Well, well,' he said. 'Sir and madam. How's Mrs Cuffe? Well I hope.'

'Fine thank you Mr Hasson.'

'Weather changeable, wouldn't you say?'

'That's autumn for you. Unreliable.'

'And you, sir. All well? I hear the station's coming along nicely. What can I get you?'

'Helen? What would you like?'

'The young fella away back to college, is he? We don't get to see very much of him these days. Of course you can't expect young people to stick themselves away in a place like this. Back of beyond.'

'I think a glass of wine would be nice. If it's possible.'

'Now I wouldn't hold that view myself mind you. No better place to my way of thinking. Born and reared here . . . Mr-ah-sir and my mother and father before me. Out of the soil you might say and back into it again one day. The young people dont feel like that at all.'

'Have you any wine, Mr Hasson? I think we'd like a bottle if you have one.'

'Away to Dublin they go the minute their ears are dry. I have a son in Saudia Araby. Making a pile. A pile. He'll be able to buy me and sell me when he comes back. Mrs Hasson doesn't take it well at all. Isn't she terrified he'll marry a black girl and come back and make a show of us all? Red or white?'

Roger looked at Helen.

'Red.'

'God made us all, I said to her, but she's a hard woman to convince. I had a word with that new young Father Mulcahy about it. Her nerves were getting real bad over the whole thing. Shocking. Wine. I have a few bottles. I always like to keep a few bottles in the place. You never know the moment when someone won't pop in for a meal and ask for a bottle of wine. I have red all right . . .'

He turned and gazed along the rows of bottles standing on shelves behind the bar.

'What did Father Mulcahy say?' Helen hated a story to be left in mid-air.

'Ah, what would he say? She suffers from the exeema you know. The doctor can't do a thing about it. When her nerves get bad it breaks out all over her.'

'How awful.'

'Spanish there is. Rio . . . ja three quid the bottle. Or French. That's more expensive. Four-eighty. The French white is cheaper. We'll cross that river when we come to it, Mrs Hasson. That was what Father Mulcahy said. Standing out there in the hall. I mean what more could he say? Just don't be worrying your head about it, he said that to her.'

'What more indeed,' murmured Helen.

'I think we'll have the French red please, Mr Hasson.'

'Right you be, sir.'

He took down a bottle from the shelf, watching himself all the time in the mirror that duplicated the bottles. He watched Roger and Helen watching him. All tidily duplicated. He wiped the dust from the bottle with a cloth and turned it round and placed it on the counter. He reached under the bar for two glasses which he placed neatly beside the bottle.

'Never suffered from exeema?' he asked Helen.

She shook her head.

The corkscrew already had a cork impaled on it which he twisted off with his fingers and then threw behind him onto the floor.

'You were spared.'

He belonged to the old school of those who put the bottle between their knees and withdrew the cork with a certain amount of effort. Helen wondered how Roger managed about things like corks.

'Not much call for wine.' The word much puffed out of him as he pulled. 'Take them glasses over to the fire, Mrs Cuffe, and I'll give the gentleman the bottle.' He gave another pull and the cork came away this time. 'There's a bit of smoke from the fire today. It's the wind in the west. Mrs Hasson always wants to install the electric fires, but there's nothing like the open fire I always think and you don't notice the smoke all that much. There's pleasure in sitting by the open fire.'

Roger followed her over to the fire and put the bottle on the table. He picked up the poker and approached the dismal smoking fire.

'That's right,' called Mr Hasson across the room. 'Give it an old wallop with the poker, a good dunt.'

Roger pushed the poker into the sad heart of the fire and tried to raise the sods; ash whirled in the air for a moment with the smoke.

'I'm not cold anyway,' said Helen.

'It's the gloom of it,' whispered Roger. 'Would you rather . . . ?'

'I'll leave you to your peace.' Mr Hasson retreated from behind the bar back into the hotel again.

'Never mind the gloom, Roger. Let's try the Léoville Barton 1969.' He laughed and put the poker back in the grate. He poured two glasses of wine and sat down beside her.

'Cheers.'

'Cheers.'

The wine was acid.

They grinned almost childishly across the glasses at each other.

'What's fact or fantasy?' he said. 'Madness or sanity? We all live our lives in our own way. It's only when we become confused, disturbed in our own mind about things, that we should start to worry. I am neither confused nor disturbed.'

'I envy your conviction. I've flitted for so long from one half-thought out truth to another, I've had no convictions worth bothering anyone about. I'm not even sure why I started to paint again. It certainly wasn't a desire to say something important to the world.'

There was a long silence. Somewhere outside someone switched on a radio, something country and western plucked and moaned.

'I don't have anything to say anyway . . . that isn't pitifully thin.'

'Perhaps you're not the best judge.'

She ignored him.

'It would be so much easier if I wanted to paint charming landscapes for tourists. You see them all round the place in gift shops. Fifty pounds a crack. Something to remind you of your holiday in dear old Donegal. Blue mountains, thatched cottages, a donkey or two. Efficient. All bloody efficient. Dan tried to persuade me to do that years ago.' She smiled. 'We had quite a row about it. He simply could not understand why I wouldn't do it. We both said quite a lot of silly things to each other.'

Roger rattled his fingers on the table. Rhythmic beats.

'We usually said nothing to each other.'

He stopped drumming for a moment and touched her hand. She didn't seem to notice.

'I think I was a sore disappointment to him. I wonder why nobody ever tells us the truth?'

He was rattling again. The wine in their glasses trembled.

'Truth? My dear girl, if they started to tell us the truth we'd all jump back into the womb again and refuse to come out . . . Anyway people need those lies to keep themselves going. The more often you repeat something the more likely it is to become true. I was meant for you . . .' he sang the words softly '. . . and you were meant for me . . .' The fingers beat out the rhythm after his voice had stopped.

'Slow foxtrot,' he said. 'Remember the slow foxtrot?'

'There's one thing.' Her voice was low. He had to lean across the table to catch the words. He kept his fingers quiet. 'For such a long time I've wanted to say this to someone . . . but the right person never seemed to be around. I have never had either a priest or a psychiatrist . . . or perhaps a friend. You know Dan was shot?' She looked across the table towards him. He nodded. 'That in itself was terrible. That brutality. Unforgivable, really. I found it unforgivable. I still feel that, each time I read about another . . . snatching of a life . . . I feel that same unforgiveness rising inside me. I don't mean I want vengeance or anything like that. I just feel I'd like the . . . well, perpetrator to know that I will never forgive him. Or her.' She smiled slightly. 'I don't suppose anyone would be too worried by the awfulness of that threat. It's terribly un-Christian though.'

She reached into her pocket and brought out the box of cigarettes. She stood the box on the table in front of her.

'That's not really what I wanted to say. After the shock, the disbelief, the confusion I felt happy. I mean I never mourned his leaving my life, never missed him. I never cried in the night because he wasn't there any more. I felt happy. I haven't dared to say those words to anyone before.' She opened the box and snatched a cigarette and put it in her mouth. She sat there staring at him, with the cigarette dangling from the corner of her lips. He put his hand out again and touched hers. He ran his fingers over the bumps of her knuckles and the wrinkling skin. He traced the blue veins with his finger.

'How do you feel now?' he asked.

She pondered for a moment.

'Much the same as I did ten minutes ago.'

'So much for confession.'

He took his hand away from hers and plucked the cigarette out of her mouth and put it back in the box.

'We'll abandon the goat's piss,' he said. 'Lets go to McFaddens in Gortahork and have a real bottle of wine and some food. A night out. Hey?'

'I . . .' She looked down at her overall. 'I . . .'

'Yes or no? No rumbling and mumbling about clothes or washing. Yes or . . . ?'

She laughed.

'Yes.'

*   *   *

It was late, the sky alive with stars and a hard bright moon hanging just out of hand's reach. He stopped the car outside her door. The glass porch glittered and reflected moon and night brightness. She opened the car door and got out. Politely he did the same, or, she wondered, did he have some ulterior motive.

She looked up at the sky.

'What is the stars, Joxer? What is the stars?'

'I had a telescope once. Oh . . . a long time ago. I rather fancied myself as a star gazer when I was about fifteen. I used to spend hours wrapped in a blanket on the roof, searching for something new. A comet or something that no one had ever seen before. Hawthorne's Comet.'

'No luck?'

'No luck.'

'It's been a lovely evening. Thank you.'

She moved round towards the gate.

'I hope you didn't find the drive home too much of a strain.'

'I never worried for a moment. That's drink for you. Had I been sober I would have been in a state of nerves the whole way home.

Thank you, Helen.' He held his hand out towards her. She put her hand in his and he bent and kissed it. Then he stood quite formally by the gate as she took the six steps along the little path to the door. She turned the handle. She felt the warmth of the house touch her as the door opened.

'Goodnight,' she said. 'Come and have a meal on Saturday evening . . . and protect me from Jack and his friend.'

'Yes. I'd like that. Goodnight.'

She moved into the porch.

'Helen,' he called.

She turned back towards him. From where she stood she could only see the whole side of his face. Silver sculpture. He looks quite Roman, she thought, a bit grim, like Romans always seemed to look.

'Yes?'

'I've had women you know. I'm not . . .'

'You don't have to tell me things like that,' she shouted at him. 'I can't bear people who tell me things like that.'

He nodded. He reached into the car and took the keys from the dashboard. He shut the door carefully and walked off along the road towards the station. She watched him as far as the corner, body stiff and slightly stooped. Man in the moon, not a Roman, she thought. She closed the door quietly so as not to disturb his walking silence.

When she got up the next morning and looked out of the window the car had gone.

✻ ✻ ✻

It was a long drive. Boring afternoon, boring dusk, boring darkness across the entire flatness of the country.

Jack remembered as they passed through Boyle that he hadn't telephoned to Helen to say they would be late. She'll be rabid, he thought, and rude.

What the hell?

Boring.

Manus had been asleep since they had left Dublin, or had seemed to be asleep. Not anyway wanting conversation. His head lolled down towards his chest, his hands clasped loosely on his knee as if he were, in fact, at prayer. Even asleep his face looked quite composed, his clothes as well as his face remained uncrumpled. Two pens and the metal-framed glasses tucked into the top pocket of his grey suit gave him the respectable air of a minor official . . . on the way up of course, definitely on the way up.

As they approached Sligo town Jack spoke.

'Will we stop for a drink? I could do with a drink. How about you?'

There was no reply from Manus.

'Manus?'

'Uhhuh?'

One of his hands moved slightly.

'Will we stop for a drink?'

'Where are we?'

He didn't bother to open his eyes.

'Sligo.'

'To hell with Sligo.'

That sounded like no drink.

Jack sighed.

It was a long time before either of them spoke.

'Under bare Ben Bulben's head

In Drumcliffe churchyard Yeats is laid.'

Manus stirred beside him. Raised a hand and rubbed at the side of his nose.

'An ancestor was rector there

Long years ago, a church stands near.

By the road an ancient cross.'

'To hell with Yeats.'

'Cast a cold eye . . .'

'All poets.'

On life, on death. Horseman . . .'

'The Russians have it right.'

' . . . pass by.'

'Prison is the place for poets.'

'That's the only piece of poetry I remember after all those years wasted at school, learning, learning.'

'I don't mean the moon in June types. Let them rant on and on about love and cypress trees and sunsets as long as they like. There's nothing like a good piece of patriotic verse. Workers arise and shake off your chains. Highly commendable. It's when they step out of line. Interfere with the inside of people's heads. Prison.'

'No one reads them. I mean for God's sake, who reads poetry? A few students and a handful of highfalutin' intellectuals.'

'The most insidious form of subversion. The artist's role should be to enhance, encourage, not undermine. The people must speak with one voice. I believe it is possible to achieve the perfect society. Perhaps the artists may have to be sacrificed.'

'I never know when you're pulling my leg.'

'You have an easy leg to pull. Where are we?'

'Bare Ben Bulben's head is on our right.'

'I may have heard of Yeats, but I never learnt any geography. How much longer dismal driving?'

'You've been asleep.'

'On and off.'

'Why did you never take up driving?'

'I couldn't be bothered. There's always someone around to give you a lift. No point in heaping that sort of hard work on yourself.' He paused for a long time. 'The old eyes aren't great, if you want the truth. No need to spread it round.'

'About an hour,' said Jack. 'A bit more perhaps. My mother may be angry. Don't mind her.'

'No. I don't suppose I will.'

He closed his sore eyes and appeared to sleep again.

'Horseman pass by,' said Jack with resignation.

It was after half past eleven when they arrived in the village. Three street lamps and the odd glow from behind tightly pulled private curtains, no dogs or even drunks were about. As Jack turned the corner and began the uphill drive Manus opened his eyes. His head turned slightly to the left, his eyes glistened for a moment in the light from one of the lamps.

'I can't stand the country. I feel my life falling apart further out of town than the Phoenix Park, for God's sake. Are we nearly there?'

'Two minutes.'

'I hate silence. And darkness. And bloody culchies picking their noses.'

'You're going to have a very painful couple of days.'

'All for Ireland.'

They both laughed for a moment, and then the cottage was there, a light shining in the porch.

'That's it,' said Jack. He pulled over to the side of the road and stopped the car.

Manus got out and stretched his arms above his head, wriggled his stiff shoulders, took the cottage into his eyes.

'I've always been told that Protestants didn't live in cottages.'

Jack laughed. He opened the back door of the car and took out their bags.

'It just shows how misinformed you've been all these years. Here.' He held Manus's bag out towards him. Manus took it. Jack opened the gate and they walked the few steps to the hall door.

'Breathe that air,' said Jack. 'That's great air.'

'Give me petrol fumes and the smell of the gas works.'

Helen was in the sitting room watching the advertisements on the television.

She was in her dressing gown and bare feet with her hair still damp hanging down around her shoulders. Like as though she was still young, thought Jack. Not fifty, getting on.

She stood up when they came into the room and switched off the set.

'Have you never heard of a telephone?' she said.

'I'm sorry, mother.'

'I was just about to have a last cigarette and go to bed. Waiting . . . waiting is so tiring.' She looked past Jack at Manus. 'Hello.'

'This is Manus.'

'Hello, Manus.'

Manus nodded his head and mumbled something.

She went over to Jack and kissed him.

'You're forgiven. I saw a tangled heap of metal on the road some-where. I'm like that.'

'All the telephones we tried were vandalised,' lied Jack.

She laughed. 'Don't bother with that rubbish,' she said.

Manus spoke. 'It was my fault, Mrs Cuffe, I held him up leaving Dublin. Slap me if you like.' He held his hand out towards her. She ignored the playful gesture.

'You must be exhausted. Go and put your things in your room and I'll get you both a drink. I've put up the camp bed in your room, Jack, you can both argue about who sleeps where. I've only the two bedrooms,' she explained sideways to Manus.

Another myth shattered, thought Jack.

When they went into the kitchen, ten minutes later, she was stirring something in a saucepan on the stove.

'Help yourselves to a drink. There's just soup and scrambled eggs. I hope that's okay?'

'That's fine.'

Jack poured out two glasses of whisky and shoved the water jug towards Manus.

'You? Mother?'

'No thanks. I'm going to bed quite soon. I'm getting up early to work these days.'

Manus put a drop of water into his whisky and drank the lot in one large gulp. 'God, I needed that.' He looked meaningfully at the bottle. Jack poured him another measure.

'Thanks.' He clasped both hands around the glass as if he were afraid that someone might try to take it from him.

'Are you in college with Jack?' asked Helen.

Manus laughed.

She turned from the scrambled egg to stare at him.

'No,' said Jack.

'I have been educated in the university of life,' said Manus, still laughing.

'Ah.'

She continued with the stirring.

'The Brothers slung me out at fifteen and said never darken our doors again. It was their loss.'

'He's a joker,' said Jack.

'So I gather. Will you have some soup, Manus? Jack, deal with the soup will you?'

'What sort of soup?' asked Manus.

'Well . . . vegetable mainly.'

'No thanks. I only like tomato soup. Heinz.'

'Oh! Do you want some, Jack?'

'Ah . . . no thanks, mother. I'll just have eggs. Just eggs. We'll both just have eggs.'

'Dear me,' she said.

She bent down and took two plates from the oven and scooped scrambled eggs on to both of them.

'There you are. There's toast on the table. I'll leave you to yourselves. Have you plans for tomorrow?'

'Don't worry about us, we'll . . .'

'Yes,' said Manus. 'We've plans.'

'Roger Hawthorne is coming to supper.'

'Is that the man with the station?' Manus asked.

'Yes.'

'I've always had a great interest in the railways. Isn't that so, Jack?'

'Absolutely.'

'Ebsolutely,' mimicked Manus, somewhat unkindly.

Helen ran water into the scrambled-egg saucepan.

'I'm going to bed. Just help yourselves to anything you want.'

'Steam engines were before my time. I never cease to regret that fact. Before your time too, Jack. Isn't that a very regrettable fact?'

'Eat your scrambled eggs and shut up.'

As Helen passed Jack on her way to the door, she put her hand on the top of his head. The corrugated texture of his hair reminded her for a startling moment of Don. She thrust her hand into her pocket and moved to the door. 'If you want me in the morning I'll be in the shed. Otherwise just do whatever you want yourselves. Goodnight.'

Manus bowed politely towards her.

'Goodnight, mother,' said Jack.

✻   ✻   ✻

Jack was awakened the next morning by Manus moving round the room, the electric shaver in his hand, buzzing away at his face. His left hand followed the shaver down the contours of his face feeling for stubble.

'Up, up,' he said as Jack turned over and looked at him. 'No fucking mirror.'

'You seem to be managing very well without one.'

'Up. There's only one way to get out of bed painlessly . . . open the eyes and out. If you stop to think about it at all, you might stay there all day.' He took his finger off the starter and the buzzing stopped. He rubbed at his chin vigorously with his left hand.

'Baby's bottom,' he said. He began to shave the other side of his face. Jack got out of bed and put on his slippers.

'Breakfast,' he said.

'Yeah,' said Manus. 'Let's have a good breakfast. A slap-up feed . . . save us having lunch. Sense?'

'Sense,' agreed Jack and went into the kitchen.

No mother.

Of course no mother.

Jack sighed and opened the fridge. He took out bacon and eggs and tomatoes. Manus came into the room, fully dressed and a slight touch of aftershave.

'Does your man know we're coming?'

'No.'

'I hope we have no trouble with him. There's a cat wanting in the window.'

'Let it in.'

'I get asthma from cats.'

'I've never known you to have asthma.'

'Hay fever, eczema, spots. Let's make it quite clear we won't take any trouble from him.'

Jack was spooning fat over the eggs, watching the yolks turning from yellow to pale pink. The white frilled round the edges.

'What do you mean by trouble?'

'Watch those eggs. I hate mine burnt. Turn down that heat a little.'

'It's a range.'

'Well whatever it is, don't burn my fucking egg.'

Jack moved the pan to the edge of the ring.

'Argument, prevarication, codology of any sort. I like it hard but not turned.'

'Sit down and pour yourself a cup of tea for God's sake, you're making me nervous.'

Manus moved away.

'Mother not cook breakfast?'

'I think she must be across the yard working.'

'Oh yes, you said she painted.'

He pulled out a chair and sat down. The cat stared unblinkingly through the glass at him.

'Any good? Any money in it?'

'I don't know. I've never seen any of her stuff. It's probably awful. She only took it up a couple of years ago. She studied art before she was married. I presume this is some sort of menopausal madness.'

Jack took a quick look at Manus as he said this. Manus always hated that sort of remark. He pursed his lips slightly in disapproval. Jack smiled internally.

'Egg,' said Manus.

Jack scooped one of the eggs off the pan and onto a plate. Two slices of bacon, a tomato cut in quarters and a piece of fried bread. He put the feast down in front of Manus and then took his egg off the pan.

'Do cats really give you all those things, or can I let him in?'

'Let him in if you insist.'

As Jack went over to the window the cat jumped from the sill and walked away across the yard.

'He seems to have some objection to you too,' said Jack. 'I hope your egg's okay.'

'We can manage without him. If he argues at all, that might be best. It'll be best not to tell him too much to begin with. He might not be secure.'

'I doubt that.'

Manus cut himself a slice off the pan.

'He might try to be clever.'

'He wouldn't split. Maybe he won't co-operate, but he wouldn't split.'

'We haven't the right to take chances. You mustn't let your bourgeois liberal attitudes colour your judgments.'

'I don't have bourgeois liberal attitudes.'

Manus laughed and began to wipe the white bread round and round his plate, mopping up all the remaining juices and flavours.

'If you could catch sight of yourself,' he said, shoving the bread into his mouth.

'You'd win an Olympic Gold for speedy eating,' said Jack.

'No point in letting good food get cold on your plate.' He stretched across the table for a piece of toast. 'My mother always said feed the inner man.'

Butter.

'I don't think that's got anything to do with eating,' said Jack.

Marmalade.

'Sure it has. To her at any rate. The inner man is all those coils of intestines, seventeen miles of intestines. Did you know that we have seventeen miles of intestines?'

'No,' said Jack.

'Something like that anyway. That's what she means. It takes a lot of food to keep all that in full working order. A woman is never done cooking, she says . . . feeding the inner man.'

'And woman?' suggested Jack.

'That's good marmalade.' Manus took his first ever bite of Cooper's Oxford. 'Better than Little Chip.'

Jack sighed. He preferred to think of Manus as a leader, a plan-maker, his mind and energy geared towards action, not the eternal talk that went on and on with all the rest. Reminders of his reality always unnerved Jack.

'There's Doherty, Sweeney and Fehily in Dungloe.'

He pushed a corner of toast into his mouth as he spoke.

'And Clancy. Where's Clancy?'

Jack shook his head. It was a rhetorical question. He wasn't supposed to know where Clancy was.

Manus stood up suddenly. His plate was polished clean, his cup was empty, a few scattered crumbs on the table and a drift of tea leaves up the side of his cup were the only evidence that someone had recently eaten.

'We'll go and take a look at her pictures and then we'll have a quick look for your man. We won't waste too much time on him.'

'I . . .' Jack wondered about his mother for a moment.

'Come on,' said Manus impatiently.

They crossed the yard and opened the door of the shed. She was crouched on the floor dragging paint across a canvas with a rag. She was in her dressing gown and her hair was pulled tightly back from her eyes into an elastic band. The room smelt of turpentine and cigarette smoke.

Good heavens, thought Jack, she really does paint.

She seemed to drag her head up and around to look at them as they came in. Her eyes and mind took some time to focus on them.

'Good Lord,' she said. 'I'm sorry . . .'

Manus interrupted Jack.

'I thought I'd like to see your pictures.' He walked over to where she was crouching. 'He told me you made pictures.'

She put the rag down on the floor and then rubbed her fingers on the front of her dressing gown. She stood up slowly, stiffly. She smiled slightly as she moved and Jack thought for a moment she was going to make some awful joke. She didn't.

'Yes, I make pictures. You're welcome to look at them.'

He frowned down at the canvas on the floor.

'And you too, Jackson . . . you are also welcome.'

Irony in her voice.

'Why do you paint on the floor? I thought . . . ?'

Manus made a gesture in the air, indicating an easel.

'I thought I'd better not get an easel before I knew whether I could paint or not. That would have seemed to be tempting providence. Now, I've got used to the floor. Mind you . . . I do get stiff, so perhaps I'll have to get an easel after all. An admission of old age and decrepitude rather than anything else. I'm only starting on that one. Laying down a sort of background.'

'Don't you use a brush?'

'Yes, but you don't have to only use brushes. It depends on the effect you want to get.'

'I see.' His voice was polite but fairly uninterested.

She waved her arm.

'Have a look. Be my guest.' She stooped and picked up the cat who was about to step onto the canvas. 'I'm weeding out the sheep from the goats at the moment. I'm trying to put together enough paintings to bring up to Dublin. I hope perhaps that someone will take me on. Let me show you some of these little water colours. I need a framer badly. I thought that maybe . . .' she stopped abruptly and spread four of the watercolours out on the table . . . 'I think I'll have to bring them to Dublin to be framed. It costs a lot you know to get a picture ready for sale.'

Manus nodded.

For a short while none of them moved. The cat rubbed his head against her shoulder.

Jack was staring at the man on the beach. The shadow lay long on the furrowed sand. God, he thought, it was right what I said to Manus . . . menopausal madness. Sad to think of your fifty-year-old mother fantasising about naked young men. The sun hung white and very cold above the young man's head. A searchlight, he thought.

'They're nice so they are,' said Manus.

'I'm working more with oil at the moment.'

Jack moved away from the painting, over to look at the watercolours on the table. Nicely painted, he had to give her that. Sheep, trees, safe pastoral subjects. I must ask her for a couple for my rooms in college, he thought, and then looked across the room once more at the man on the beach. For a moment it became Damian Sweeney. The shock of that gripped him inside his body. He felt himself blushing and turned quickly away. Jesus, he thought. Jesus. He looked again and saw only a lank figure, feet in a wisp of sea, black shadow marks.

'We should be off,' he said.

'I'm working on a series.' She pointed towards the painting. ' "Man on a Beach".' She giggled. 'Not what you might call a very original title. I'm working on number two at the moment.'

Manus stared in silence at the painting.

'Who's the fella?' he asked at last.

'No one in particular. Purely a figment.'

'Not Jack?'

She burst out laughing.

'Not Jack. I haven't seen Jack naked since he was about ten and I used to rush into the bathroom and scrub his filthy neck from time to time.

He has always been the very essence of modesty . . . at least as far as I am concerned.'

Manus smiled.

'The very essence of modesty,' he repeated. 'I like that. That's good.'

'We should be getting on.'

'Now, who would buy a thing like that?' Manus nodded his head towards the painting.

'Perhaps nobody,' she answered.

'And yet you paint it . . . on spec so to speak.'

'Yes.'

'Would you say it was art?'

'That's really for someone else to say, not me.'

He nodded.

'Manus . . .' said Jack. 'We should be getting on.'

'Right you be. He's going to show me a bit of the countryside, Mrs Cuffe.'

'If you're not back by half past eight we'll eat without you, and I'll be raging, Jack, really raging.'

'Don't fuss,' said Jack.

*　*　*

'No,' said Mrs Sweeney. She'd no idea at all where Damian was. Hadn't seen neither hide nor hair of him for the last two days. Never said a word nor left a message.

'No,' she said. How could you tell when he'd be back if he hadn't even said he was going? It could be Galway. There was an uncle in Galway he visited from time to time. Didn't he work for the Englishman above at the station and wouldn't he likely be back on Monday morning?

'Yes.' She'd say they'd called looking for him. That would be the sum total of the help she'd be able to give them.

Two red-haired children stood by her side, nodding as she spoke.

A silent dog ran beside the car for the best part of half a mile as Jack drove away.

Neither of them spoke.

In the few weeks Jack had been away the leaves had been blown from the hedges. Thorns and fuchsias were now bare. The first gap in the hedge was the track through the caravan park and up onto the dunes above the beach. Jack turned through it and they bumped across the grass and up the hill until they could go no further. Below them stretched the wide beach and the sea.

'Is this where your mother paints naked fellas?' Manus's voice was sour.

Jack didn't say a word.

Manus pulled a bar of Fruit and Nut from his pocket and unwrapped it. He opened the window a crack and let the blue and silver papers scatter away with the wind. He then proceeded to eat the chocolate.

'Fucking culchies.'

He stared in hatred at the sea as he chewed.

'I wouldn't stand there with my feet in the sea and let any woman paint me.'

'She said it was a figment of her imagination.'

Manus laughed.

'Figment my backside. Fig leaf.' He laughed again at his own joke. 'Fig leaf.'

He took a handkerchief from the pocket and wiped the chocolate from his fingers.

'I've said it again and again and you're my witness, there's no use expecting anything from the fools around the country. Fucking slíbhíns. Full of hot air. Words, talk, but try to get them to do anything and they disappear to Galway or down a rabbit hole. Doherty, Sweeney, Fehily.' He shook his head. 'We'll not engage anyone further in this. It's only a staging post we need. You know the lay of the land.'

'Yes,' said Jack.

Below them the wind caught the top layer of the sand and blew it along the length of the beach. Jack remembered how his bare legs used to sting as the grey and golden grit was blown against them.

'We'll take a look at this railway shed that you were talking about. That shouldn't be any problem. This guy . . . the owner . . . sounds like a bit of a nutter.'

'A war hero,' said Jack, his eyes still on the racing sand. 'Blown apart in World War Two and then sewn together again.'

Manus smiled slightly.

'I can't get over the thought of that fella standing down there and letting your mother draw pictures of him in his skin. Ballybofey.'

Jack turned on the engine.

'War hero.' Manus smiled again. 'I have a man to see in Ballybofey. You can have a drink or go for a walk.'

He was like that. Never let his right hand know what his left hand was up to. Jack backed away from the edge of the dune and then turned carefully in the caravan park. On a line at the back of one of the vans a forgotten dish cloth flapped forlornly in the wind. They bumped over the grass and out onto the road.

'Ballybofey,' said Manus.

Jack turned left. Manus leaned forward and pressed the button of the radio. They drove, each one thinking his own thoughts, Radio Two pulping past their ears.

* * *

For some reason Helen had taken the six candlesticks out of the kitchen cupboard and unwrapped them from the yellow dusters in which they had lain comfortably for so long. She had even cleaned them and hated the way the skin on her fingers had stiffened and smelt with the ingrained pink polish. Handsome Georgian silver, not too many curlicues. Might get a few bob for them one day if the need ever arose. Candles are nice, she thought. People look so gold and secret. All faces divide quite in half, black shadows make caves and the gold is soft, malleable. Faces look medieval; that is too romantic a thought. Jack's friend has eyes like sharp bright stones.

'What are you thinking? You've disappeared from us.'

Roger's voice.

She turned to him.

'I'm sorry. I was just thinking how beautiful we all look by candle-light. Our warts are eliminated.'

He looked around the table.

'I wouldn't say they were eliminated, made mysterious perhaps. You and I . . . our . . . I won't say old . . . our used, experienced faces are mysteriously beautiful . . . The two young men with smooth untouched faces merely look boring.'

'I object,' said Jack.

'Objection overruled,' Helen laughed. 'For once let the young be at a disadvantage.'

'Don't you find your mother mysterious?' asked Roger.

'No.'

'Oh dear. I always found my mother mysterious. Perhaps that was because she was killed before I was old enough to have looked at her realistically. And you . . .'

He turned to Manus, who was twiddling his glass round and round in his fingers. Candle flames danced in the wine. 'Do you have a mother?'

'Of course I have a mother . . . just a straightforward run-of-the-mill mother. No mysteries.' He looked across the table at Helen almost accusingly.

'I don't believe in mysteries. There are conjuring tricks, but no magic, as far as I'm concerned.'

'Ghosts?' asked Helen.

'In people's heads. Too many bloody ghosts in people's heads.'

'Don't you find it boring to have an explanation for everything?'

'On the contrary, I have never felt bored in my life. Boredom is quite a disease of the middle classes you know. I know what I'm doing and why and I get on and do it.'

'May we ask?' Roger pulled at his eye-patch for a moment as he spoke.

'Ask what you like. I don't have to answer any questions that I don't want to. This isn't Castlereagh.'

Helen balanced her cigarette on its end on her plate and watched the smoke rise thin and straight into the darkness above them.

'I hate cross-examinations,' she said. 'I think there are so many things inside each of us that we don't want to say, and that other people don't want to hear. We could become quite unfriendly . . .' Her voice trailed away like the smoke.

'How do you mean, mother?'

'Well . . . political perhaps . . . I'd rather not . . . be forced to make judgments.'

Jack laughed sharply.

'One day, mother, your ivory tower will fall down. Then where will you be? Then you'll have to ask questions . . . answer questions . . . draw conclusions.'

'If my ivory tower, as you call it, falls down, I'll build another one.' She got up and began to move the plates from the table. 'And I'll always prefer my mysteries to your conclusions. There's chocolate mousse. Who wants some chocolate mousse?'

They all wanted chocolate mousse.

She took it out of the fridge and put it in the middle of the table. That was for Jack anyway, she thought, as she handed each of them a plate. Chocolate mousse for Jack.

'And miracles.' She sat down again. 'Help yourselves.' She picked up the smoking cigarette and crushed it out onto the plate. 'I believe in miracles. Not the bleeding heart kind.'

'What would you consider to be a miracle, Mrs Cuffe?' Manus's voice was curious.

'Well . . . I suppose the intervention of something quite outside your own experience into your . . . Something perhaps that permits a revelation of yourself. I think the intervention permits the miracle rather than is the miracle itself. I seem to gather thoughts, ideas in my head that I can't express in coherent words. Perhaps that's why I paint. I have to expose some truth.'

She muttered the last words to herself.

'Give us an example,' said Jack. 'Tell us about one of your own private and personal miracles.'

She shook her head.

'One thing is clear to me . . .' Roger broke into the silence . . . 'this chocolate mousse is a miracle. That's for certain sure.'

She laughed.

'No, no, no. It's the only thing I can cook with complete conviction that it is going to turn out all right. Correct, Jack?'

'Pretty well correct. Even Gran . . .'

'Your grandmother couldn't make a chocolate mousse like mine if she lit a million candles to the patron saint of cooks or crawled seven times round the Black Church on her hands and knees. It was my single personal triumph over your grandmother.'

'Helen tells me that you are interested in trains.'

'That's right. My granda was a fireman in the old GNR. He has never done telling us stories. He made you believe that nothing in the world was ever like the Dublin–Belfast run.'

Jack looked towards him with admiration.

'Steam. Of course I don't remember the steam myself . . . only his stories.'

'No,' said Roger. 'You wouldn't remember the steam. That would have been before your time.'

'Every Sunday afternoon until just before he died he'd step off to the marshalling yards beyond Amiens Street . . . that's what he always called it . . . Amiens Street. He and several other old guys, have a bit of a rabbit about the way things used to be. It's funny the way old people always think that things are worse now instead of better. He used to rave about things when he got home, carelessness, dirt, incompetence.'

Perhaps he's talking the truth, thought Jack. I know so little about him.

'I used to go with him sometimes. There was a lot of old stock in the sheds there never saw the light of day. I enjoyed it when I was a kid. But then . . . well you've heard all the old stories a thousand times, and you find you've better things to do than listening to old footplatemen trying to pretend they haven't one foot in the grave.'

'I'd be delighted to show you the station. Delighted. When can you come over?'

'Tomorrow. We'll be free all day until the evening. We have to set off back then. That's right isn't it, Jack . . . we could manage tomorrow morning?'

'Splendid. I'll expect you then . . . about ten-thirty. Helen, will you come with them?'

She shook her head.

'I think not, thank you. Have some more chocolate mousse.'

✻   ✻   ✻

'I must say, you've done a great job. I'd like the granda to have seen that box. He wasn't into this narrow-gauge stuff being a city man, but he'd have really appreciated that box.'

'Thank you,' said Roger. He looked as if he hadn't slept all night. His eye was fretful, his face pale and without much life.

'What are you working on at the moment?'

'The crossing gates. Damian is replacing a lot of the timbers. They were badly rotted. That shouldn't take too long. They'll have to remain manual for a while, but we hope to automate them before too long. It's a nuisance that, in bad weather, but it can't be helped.'

'How about the track?'

Manus walked along the edge of the platform and looked down at the weeds.

'We'll clear that. All that mess will die back when the winter comes. Until I see the state of the track I can't say how long that will take. I may have to call in some outside help if we need to re-lay any sleepers.'

'What's that shed over there?'

'I think this was mainly a goods stop. Stuff must have been stored there for local farmers to come and collect. I have been surprised myself at its size. I don't use it. It's quite a decent piece of railway architecture though, I'd hate to pull it down. No doubt we'll find a use for it some day.'

'No doubt. Mind if I go and have a look?'

'By all means. Excuse me if I don't come with you. Sometimes I feel quite unwell.'

'Is there anything we can do?' asked Jack. 'I could run over to the doctor for you.'

'No. I just like to be left alone. There isn't anything anyone can do . . .' He turned away from them and walked towards the house slowly. At the door he stopped. 'Go ahead,' he said. 'It's not locked . . . just the bolt.'

Without even saying goodbye he went into the house.

They walked in silence to the end of the platform and then across the tracks. The shed had a wooden door in surprisingly good condition, held closed by a large iron bolt. It had been oiled at some stage and slid back without fuss. Inside, dust, cobwebs and dead flies veiling the small windows and a large empty space.

'It's one of your mother's miracles,' said Manus.

Jack pushed the door shut behind them and looked around.

'I think it's a crazy idea.'

'Why?' Manus's voice was shrill. 'What's crazy about it? They don't use it . . . don't touch it. There's no one else for miles around. No nosey kids even.'

'You wouldn't know what he'd do, for God's sake . . . or Damian. How will you get the stuff in and out of here without him finding out?'

'Leave it to me, why don't you? You just do what you're told. Have I ever let anyone down? Answer me that. Have I bungled? Hey? Have I?'

'No. But . . .'

'But fucking nothing.'

'I think you're as mad as he is.'

Manus ignored that. He stared around the shed, his eyes glittering with excitement. He put his hand into his coat pocket and pulled out a bar of chocolate. He unwrapped it and shoved the paper back into his pocket.

'The trouble is,' he began to munch at the bar, 'with people like yourself, you've no imagination.'

'As far as the set-up is concerned, I've too much imagination.'

'Always picking. I don't know why I'm lumbered with you.'

'You know well why you're lumbered with me . . . you sent me down to talk to Damian. You needed to use my car. That's why. You have a marginal, menial use for me.'

'That's right. Now that you have it clear in your mind can we drop the subject?'

He finished the chocolate in silence.

'I simply feel,' said Jack, 'that I could be used in some more constructive way. I am, after all . . .'

'You're not an active-service guy.'

'I . . .'

'You're not. You can take it from me. You are most usefully employed in helping to produce a back-up service.'

'I . . .'

'People like you faint at the sight of blood.'

'You haven't the faintest idea whether I faint at the sight of blood or not. You've never given me the chance to find out.'

'I know what I'm talking about. If you want to stay with us . . . be useful . . . very useful. For God's sake what do you want . . . the whole organisation to fall apart without you? Be your age. If you want to be useful then do what you're told. Okay.'

Jack nodded.

'We'll win you know. Then you'll probably be quite glad I didn't allow you to get up to anything . . . You can never tell when the bourgeois conscience will begin to prick. There aren't really too many of us who have the clear eye.' He laughed. 'And a steady hand.'

He took out his handkerchief and wiped the chocolate from round his mouth.

'I need you.'

He folded the handkerchief so that the chocolate stains were inside and then put it back in his pocket.

'You need the clear eye. Only the vision counts. Some people find that hard to take.'

'I suppose you're right.'

'That's the ticket. Come on . . . we've seen all there is to see here. We'll get back to Dublin as soon as possible after lunch.'

He opened the door and they went out into the sunshine.

'I presume your mother'll be giving us lunch?'

'I imagine so, yes.'

They crossed the line and went out into the road through a little wicket gate by the level crossing and walked round to the front of the station where the car was waiting.

'I'd say she had a clear eye,' said Manus.

'Who?'

'Your old lady.'

Jack laughed.

'Tell me,' he asked as they got into the car. 'Was your grandfather really a railwayman?'

'Sure thing. He'd have loved that station. A really great job that Englishman has done.'

'And Damian.'

Jack started the engine.

'Bugger Damian.'

＊　＊　＊

On Wednesday at about half past eleven Damian opened the door without knocking and walked into the kitchen. Mrs O'Sullivan was washing cloths at the sink.

'Look what the cat brought in.'

She wrung black water out of a duster.

'That floor is clean.'

He shuffled his feet on the mat.

'Have you lost your tongue?'

She pulled out the plug and the dirty foamy water circled out through the hole.

'I'm just surprised to find you here, that's all.'

'It just shows how little you know about what goes on. I've been keeping this place in order for the past five year. If you're coming in, come in and close that door behind you.'

He pushed the door shut, remembering as he did so that he'd said he would take a piece off the bottom of it.

She turned on the hot tap.

'Well?'

'Is she about?'

'Who's she? The cat's granny.'

'Mrs Cuffe.'

She threw the cloths into the basin again and agitated them around.

'What do you want with her? She's working.'

'I have a message.'

'She doesn't like to be disturbed when she's working.'

She wrung the duster out again and then cracked it in the air above the basin. His mother went through the same rigmarole, he thought.

'It's a private message.'

She walked across the kitchen to the Aga and hung the cloth on the metal rail above the ovens.

'Is your mother keeping well?'

'She's grand, thanks.'

'I've tea made.' She picked the teapot from the top of the Aga. 'You can take her over a cup and save me the walk across the yard. That's a wind would kill you.'

She took down three mugs from the dresser and carefully filled them with tea, and a few drops of milk, pursing her lips as she poured, disapproving of Damian's presence.

'And yourself.' She nodded towards the mugs. 'Sugar?'

He shook his head.

'Away on. You and your message.'

Helen was startled and pleased by Damian's appearance. She got up from the floor and took the mug of tea from his hand.

'Thanks. What a nice surprise. Sit down. When did you get back?'

There was only one chair and that had a canvas standing on it.

'Or rather I should ask . . . where have you been?' She lifted the picture from the chair and stood it against the wall. 'You did a disappearing act.'

'Is that me?'

He put his mug on the table and moved over the floor towards the painting of the man on the beach.

'Well . . . yes and no.'

He peered closely at the picture, straining his eyes to recognise himself.

'I'm not that thin. Am I?'

'If it looked like you it would be a portrait. It's just a man on a beach. Any man on any beach.'

'I was happy that morning.'

She smiled.

'It was funny being naked in the daytime.'

'Yes,' she said.

'You haven't made it a very happy picture.'

She didn't say anything.

'Why?' he asked after a long silence.

'I just do what I'm told.'

He looked at her.

'I paint. My hands mix and paint and scrub and scrape and squeeze the tubes empty. Light the cigarettes. I move. Down there on the floor.' She pointed to the canvas on the floor. He moved over towards it and stared down at it. A man ran through the unfolding water, light exploded above and behind him in the sky and his huge shadow filled the foreground of the canvas.

'Is that me too?'

'Yes and no.'

'What do you mean you do what you're told?'

He crouched down beside the picture in the position she used for painting.

'There is a voice . . . quite a clear voice. It's always been there, but when I was young it frightened me, so I didn't listen and it went away. If I kept quite still, moved with extreme caution it didn't bother me. I just have to thank God I didn't kill it with my inattention.'

'He hears voices too. I hear him sometimes quarrelling, raging against them.'

'Ghosts,' she said. 'He lives with ghosts.'

Damian stood up. Helen noticed with a certain satisfaction that his knees also cracked.

'Will someone buy them?'

'I hope so.'

'How . . . I mean . . . how?'

'I'm not really too sure what I'll do. But, I think . . . when I've finished this series . . . I have four in my mind . . . then I'll pack them up somehow and a selection of the others and take them up to Dublin. See if I can find a gallery to exhibit them. It probably isn't just as easy as that. I haven't worked that end of things out yet. I will. When this is finished then I'll have time to think about that sort of thing.'

'They're big for packing.'

'Umm.'

'I could maybe make you a box . . . a sort of case out of timber. We've lots of timber above . . . If only his trains were running, we'd have no transport problem. We can work something out between us.'

'You're very kind.'

'You wouldn't want them damaged. It might have to be padded inside. I'll start thinking up something for you.' He looked at the two canvases, measuring, judging with his eyes. 'Easy as winking,' he said.

She handed him his mug of tea.

'Drink this up before it gets cold. It'll be some time yet before I'm ready to pack them.'

'I can be sorting out the wood I need . . . and the others, the smaller ones, if I can get to measure them up, I can make another box for them too.'

'Where were you?' she asked.

He took a drink from the mug.

'Why did you go away like that without telling anyone?'

'I just felt like a trip to Galway. I take a run down there from time to time.'

He took another drink.

'About once every couple of months or so. I have cousins, uncles, aunts. My mother's people are from down there. Don't tell me you were worrying after me?'

She looked around for her cigarettes. He saw the box before she did and bent to pick it off the floor.

'Thank you.'

She didn't open the box, just held it in her hand.

'I just wondered if it was anything to do with Jack, that's all. I know it's none of my business.'

'Jack's your business.'

'Not really. Not any longer.'

He drank again, looking straight into her face over the edge of the mug.

'What gives you that idea anyway?'

'Oh . . . I don't know . . . you were angry last week . . .'

'Oh, that.' He remembered.

She took a cigarette from the box and put it in her mouth. She dropped the box onto the floor.

'I don't like Manus.' He put his hand into his pocket and miraculously took out a box of matches.

'I wasn't mad about him either,' she said.

He put the mug on the table and struck a match. He held it out towards her. She leaned forward and lit the cigarette.

'Thanks. Where did you meet him?'

'Around.' He smiled slightly. 'I'm twenty-four you know, I've been around. Next question?'

'People say things about you.'

'Aye. People say things about anyone who doesn't quite toe the line. That's not a question.'

'I just wondered if they were true.'

'I thought we were talking about Jack.'

'We are. You know as well as I do what I'm talking about. You know right well the question I'm trying to ask.'

He turned away from her and walked over to the window. A huge front of cloud was building up on the horizon.

'The wind is getting up,' he said. 'Helen,' he felt quite brave as he spoke her name. 'Ask me the question. What are you afraid of?'

'Are you in the Provos?'

'No.' He laughed. 'You asked the wrong question.'

'I hate being messed about, confused. I've screwed myself up to hear some sort of truth, I wish you'd get on and tell it to me.'

'What's truth? Manus's truth and my truth wouldn't come within a mile of each other. Perhaps I'll have a cigarette after all.' He held his hand out towards her.

'No. If you've stopped, you've stopped.' But she picked the box off the floor and threw it across the room to him just the same.

'At eighteen, seventeen, sixteen, whenever it is you stop thinking like a child, well to put it a bit differently, start to be your own man. Right?'

She nodded.

'I thought . . . well there has to be more to the whole damn thing than just kick the Brits out and then wham . . . paradise. I thought a bit about how I felt people should be able to live. I talked around a bit. Listened. Read the papers. You've a lot of time to pass when you don't have a regular job. I did odd jobs, here and there. I've never wanted to be a layabout. But I'd time to spare. I joined the Sticks . . . you know . . . ?'

'Yes. The Official IR . . .'

He held his hand up.

Not a word. Excuse me, missus, the Workers' Party. We've gone straight, political. Fight elections, members in Dail Eireann. You must know . . .'

He pointed the cigarette at her, like an accusing finger.

'I read the papers.'

'I used to run messages for them. Do odd jobs . . .'

'Quite the little odd-job man you seem to be.' Her voice was angry.

'That was before they . . . modernised . . . saw things in a new light. Shut down . . . that side of things. That was a democratic decision, but . . .'

'There's always a but, isn't there?'

'There's always a few who like to do things their own way. I did the . . .'

'Odd jobs again?'

'Aye. A few. Not for a while though I haven't. Not for . . . I lost the heart for that sort of thing.' He laughed suddenly. 'Must be growing old. I don't see much point in killing people. Maybe I'm just wet.'

He put the cigarette in his mouth and then took it out and held it out towards her. 'I thought I was a great guy once upon a time. A God-save-Ireland hero.' He moved slowly towards her, the cigarette in his outstretched hand. She took it from him and dropped it on the floor.

'You asked the question,' he said after a long silence. He let his hand fall slowly to his side.

'And Manus?'

'Manus doesn't believe in democracy. Manus likes to run things his way. He still believes that the gun is mightier than the word.'

'Why doesn't he join the Provos then?'

Damian laughed.

'The Provos have a structure, an army, rules. They wouldn't look at Manus, only to shoot him.'

She walked over to the chair and sat down. Her shoulders were very stiff.

She needed a spell in a deep hot bath. She needed . . . she needed . . . 'Jack?'

What the hell about Jack, she thought. Jackson Cuffe. What the hell about him?

'I shouldn't worry too much about Jack. He'll be okay.'

'What do you mean don't worry? Don't be damn silly. He's my son. He's . . . he's . . .'

He thought she was going to cry. Don't let her cry. He crossed his fingers for luck as he used to do as a child.

'Jack's only in on the edge of this. I mean I think he quite admires Manus . . . that sort of thing. I'm not saying his political motives aren't quite pure. I'm sure they are. He's just running messages too, like I was. You don't have to worry. He won't get any further than that. It's quite exciting you know. You feel alive, relevant. Manus knows that. Manus is no dozer.'

She shook her head.

'Well, it is. But Jack hasn't the balls to use a gun. I don't think he could even light a fuse. Like me. I like to think I backed my way out of all that because I thought about it and came to conclusions, but I think I probably didn't have any balls either.'

She lifted her hand and rubbed at the left side of her neck.

'What should I do?' she asked.

'Nothing. Leave him alone. Paint your pictures.'

He put a hand on her shoulder.

'Now you know why I went to Galway. It seemed the easiest thing to do.'

'What did they want you for?'

He shrugged.

'No idea.'

'And you wouldn't tell me if you had.'

'That's right.'

She gave a sudden little burst of laughter.

'Oh God, if his grandmother knew.' That bitchy thought makes me feel a little better. 'Will we go and have a drink?'

'Another time. I must get back. I've stayed too long as it is. I just came around to tell you that he's bad the last couple of days.'

'Bad?'

'He just sits there. I mean it's happened before, but I thought that perhaps you . . . He likes you. He just sits there. I hate to see him like that.'

'All right, Damian. I'll go over this evening. I'll bring some food . . . supper . . . If you think . . .'

'I'd be pleased if you'd do that.'

He moved towards the door.

'I'm sorry.'

'That's all right. I'm glad you told me.'

He nodded and opened the door. As he stepped out into the windy morning she said after him: 'Don't stay away, Damian. We can be friends now.'

He shut the door and went across the yard and out of the gate onto the road. It wasn't until she heard the gate click that she allowed the tears to slide from her eyes.

×   ☆   ☆

The wind blew up. By four o'clock in the afternoon it was tearing in from the north-west, ripping branches from the startled trees and scattering the remaining leaves from the hedges. The waves frothed like egg whites on the dull surface of the sea. More and more clouds piled up behind the horizon. Gulls, seemingly blown backwards, looked spectral against the grey sky. Everything was grey: the fields, the frenzied trees, the hedges, the distant roofs. Only the birds and the waves startled the eye.

Helen's storm had subsided. By four o'clock in the afternoon the house was filled with the safe smells of cooking and steamy bath water and she sat on the floor in front of the sitting-room fire drying the tangled wet hair that lay stretched across her shoulders. The cat, who always took a personal exception to high winds, was curled, eyes shut, but not asleep, on an armchair.

'Why?' she said directly to the cat. Her hair steamed.

'Wise cat. Answer no silly questions.'

The cat's ears flicked away her words.

Do I have to have a role in this, she wondered? Can't I just paint? Unravel my own mysteries?

She shook her head ferociously and drops of water sizzled into the fire.

If the poor little nameless girl had lived would things have been different? Would I have in some way been forced to face my responsibilities?

Useless now to speculate.

All he learnt from watching me was an obvious distaste for non-involvement. Perhaps that's a mark in his favour.

I thought he loved his father. I relied in a way on that mutual love to keep me guiltless.

What is the point in hashing and re-hashing tired thoughts?

No point.

Perhaps Jack really cares? That too would be a point in his favour. I doubt it somehow. There is so little caring.

A cigarette.

My death-defying gesture.

And live a coward?

A craven coward.

The tune rocked into her mind.

And live a cow . . . and all my days.

God damn you, Jack, for throwing this rock into the pool of my isolation.

☆   ☆   ☆

It was just dark when she set out to walk to the station, an old-fashioned basket, into which she had tucked a hot pie and fat baked potatoes, over her arm. She was afraid that the wind might blow her and her bicycle into the ditch. She was wearing a long woollen skirt which the wind slammed back against her legs and then pulled and plucked it behind her and her hair and her coat that she held right across her breast with one clutching hand. I'm quite mad to be doing this, she thought as she closed the gate behind her so that the wind wouldn't blow it off its hinges. The cat sat in the window and watched her go, exasperated by her foolishness. He might just send me home again. Might rant, rage at her presumption, or just sit silently until she left again, defeated.

Even from here she could hear the roar of the sea as it crashed on the beach and was sucked out again dragging sand, stones, wrack, only to hurl them once again onto the shore. She thought she should join in the noise with a song, but found that with the strength of the wind in her face she was unable to open her mouth. So she sang in her head instead. Oh Thou that tellest good tidings to Zion, good striding music. She imagined herself blessed with a rich contralto voice. Oh Thou that

tellest good tidings to Zion diddleiddleiddle diddle diddle, Get thee
up into the high mountain, from which you would be blown away into
outer space this moment, Oh thou that tellest good tidings to Jerusalem
diddleiddleiddle Arise, shine, for thy Light is come. Handel's walking
in the wind music. Arise. Shine . . . There was no sign of light in the
station house as she turned the corner and she thought rather crossly
of being pushed and twirled back down the road by the wind. Undignified it would be. The cat would laugh to see her reappear, a pile of
refuse in the power of the north-westerly. As she approached the house
she saw the flicker of firelight from the window of the sitting room.
She pushed open the station door and went across the hallway. At the
door to the room she paused for a moment, suddenly realising how
wild she must look, but she turned the handle and opened the door.
He was sitting in a deep chair by the fire. He wasn't asleep, she could
see the firelight flicker in his eye.

'May I turn on the light?' she asked.

'Who?' His voice was a murmur.

'Helen.'

She reached out her hand and groped along the wall for the light
switch.

They both blinked in the sudden glare.

'Helen.' He pushed himself up out of the chair. 'My dear Helen. I
thought you were a ghost. Do come in.'

'It's a night for ghosts. I do hope you don't mind me intruding on
you like this.' She closed the door firmly behind her and then walked
over and put the basket down on the table. 'I didn't feel like eating alone
so I brought some food over here for both of us. Is that all right?'

'I'm not very good company.'

'Neither am I. We can be gloomy together.'

They stood looking at each other in silence for a long time. Then he
laughed.

'You are the most wind-blown thing I've ever seen. Here, come over
to the fire. I'll just put some more wood on it. Let me take your coat.'
He stood quite still, unable to think what to do first. She picked the
basket up from the table and headed for the kitchen door.

'Before I do anything else, I'm going to put these things in the oven.

I'll be right back.' She left him to recover his equilibrium.

By the time she came back he had combed his hair, put on his tweed jacket and done something miraculous to the fire. The overhead light had been switched off and two lamps lit instead. The room looked mellow.

'Metamorphosis,' she said as she looked around.

'It's more welcoming. I'm sorry I was a bit dazed when you arrived. I have whisky or wine. Which would you like?'

'Oh . . . I . . .'

'Whisky first anyway. Sit down.'

She sat down by the fire and watched him move around the room. He was amazingly deft, she thought, neat controlled movements, no fumbling.

'I've been a bit off colour these last couple of days, so things are in a bit of a mess. I haven't been keeping things up to the mark. Here.' He handed her a glass of whisky. 'It's good that. Scottish malt. Doesn't need water. Unless you . . . ?'

She shook her head.

She sipped. Smoky, potent.

'It's lovely . . .'

'I suppose Damian told you I wasn't well. Ran around and laid that burden on you.'

She felt her face go red.

'I . . .'

'He fusses like an old hen. I just get days of . . . I don't know what you'd call it . . . melancholy perhaps. Depression is what they call it now, I think. I prefer the word melancholy. It has a poetic ring about it.' He sat down and raised his glass towards her.

'Sláinte.'

'Sláinte. Life is butter melon cauliflower,' she said and giggled.

'Butter melon, butter melon,' he sang, to her surprise.

'Melon cauliflower.' She joined in.

'Cauliflower.' Neither of them would have won a prize for singing.

'Why didn't you stay in England and become a managing director or a barrister or something like that?'

'Because I'm mad. Haven't I explained that to you before? I am poor mad Roger. I didn't want to be a managing director. I didn't even want to be a chairman. I didn't want anything that they expected me to want. I have been under constraint you know . . . in the nicest possible private homes. Shadowed night and day. Just in case I did myself some harm . . . I don't think even they thought I would harm anyone else. Just myself.'

'Did you . . . would you . . . ?'

'I don't think so . . . not even then. Now . . . to spite them I'd like to live to be a hundred. A pauper of a hundred. All that money gone, dissipated. I'd like them to have to pay for my funeral.' He grinned at her. 'You see, melancholy is followed by spleen. Soon, I will be normal again.'

'Do they know where you are?'

He shrugged.

'Probably. I imagine they'll leave me alone for a while though, unless I provoke them in some way. I have no desire to do that at the moment. Have another drink?'

'Are we going to get drunk?'

He got up and came over and took the glass from her hand.

'No. Perhaps we are going to be happy.' He poured some more whisky into both their glasses. 'I'm hungry. Do you know I haven't really eaten since Sunday. Just picked. Poor Damian tried to tempt me with food, but he got eaten instead. I will apologise to him tomorrow.'

'What did you think of Jack's friend?'

He grimaced. He put the glass into her hand and went and got his own.

'Not much. It's hard to tell just like that. Not much. Why?'

'I just wondered.'

'He knows quite a bit about the railways. That was quite nice. Not too many people have that enthusiasm any longer.'

'I suppose not. He's . . . Damian says . . . he's mixed up in . . . involved . . . in violent activity of some sort.'

'Well?'

'And Jack.'

'Ah, yes. Jack.'

His face was quite non-committal.

The fire crackled and she suddenly was reminded of the evening she had been writing the Christmas cards. The fire at her back had crackled.

Fires in the streets.

'You're upset? You're surprised?'

'Yes. Yes, of course. Wouldn't you be?'

'No. At the same age, in the same situation I might well have done the same thing.' He laughed. 'How foolish of me . . . I did . . . only I had no choice. Come come, Helen. Suppose it was the thirties and Jack had gone off to fight in the International Brigade. You'd have felt frightened for him, but a little bit proud. Wouldn't you?'

'I don't know. Sitting here with things the way they are I can't put myself in that position. There has to be some other way.'

He was silent. The fire glowed in his eye.

She thought quite irrelevantly of the Wandering Aengus.

A fire was in my head

I went out to the hazel wood

Because . . .

          ✻   ✻   ✻

'Very few people have ever had the courage or the love or the commitment to lead the other way,' he smiled. 'Only two spring to my uneducated mind. Jesus Christ and Gandhi. Look where it got them. Others have talked, preached, moved, yes a bit they've moved but they've been crushed. Viciously crushed. The crushers are always ready. Only in art, Helen, is there any approach to perfection achieved. In living there is none. There never can be. I sometimes think the man with the gun sees things more clearly than we, poor tired creatures of good will.'

'If things had been different . . .'

'You feel if you had filled him full of moral outrage, picked and plucked at his mind all through his growing years? Rubbish, Helen, rid yourself of that sort of guilt. For God's sake he might have become a chartered accountant.'

They both burst out laughing.

'Finish up your drink,' he said. 'We must go and eat whatever delicacy you have out there in the oven for us. What is it, by the way, so that I can open an appropriate bottle of wine?'

He held out his hand towards her and pulled her gently to her feet.

'A raised chicken pie.'

'My dear Helen, how scrumptious. I haven't had a raised pie since I was a boy. Come along, come along. Happiness is just around the corner.'

✳ ✳ ✳

They asked me how I knew
My true love was true.
I, of course, replied,
Something here inside
Cannot be denied.

Sweet tenor voice turned and turned.

They said some day you'll find
All who love are blind.
When your heart's on fire
You must realise
Smoke gets in your eyes.

They moved together in the middle of the room.

Walking shoes, she thought, are not quite the thing. I should have brought my dancing shoes, like children's parties, over my arm in a cotton bag.

'Will we play the remembering game?' he asked close to her ear.

'No.'

His arm held her very close. His hand was spread warm across her back.

'I never really enjoyed those times. I was always so full of expectation.'

So I chaffed them and I gaily laughed to think they could doubt my love
And yet today my love has flown away

Turning and turning. A slight sigh as the needle gathers up the sound from so long ago.

I am without my love.

'I never quite knew what it was I expected . . . but it never happened anyway.'

'Kisses in the dark?'

'Even that seemed . . . well so run-of-the-mill . . .' she laughed. 'Inept too, only you never liked to admit it.'

'I was never much good at the slow foxtrot.'

'I think we're doing very well, all things considered.'

So I smile and say

When a lovely flame dies

Smoke gets in your eyes.

He moved his cheek against hers and the sudden scratch of stubble made her heart thud. Oh no God, please God, don't let anything stupid happen.

The music stopped.

'A bit before your time, that one, I'd have thought,' he said.

'It was my absolute favourite when I was about fourteen. I think I must have stolen it from my parents.'

He held her still. She moved her head and looked at him.

'What'll we have next?' he asked.

The warm hand moved from her back.

'I'll wind, you choose,' she said.

'Slow, slow or quick, quick?' he asked.

'Anything except a tango. I never mastered the tango. I always used to start laughing when you had to do those little rushes. This is fun.' The handle creaked as she turned it. 'Isn't it?'

He nodded.

'Glen Miller, Tommy Dorsey, Spike Jones and his City Slickers.' He handed her a record. She looked at the title before putting it on the turntable. *This is a Lovely Way to Spend an Evening.* She smiled.

'Sinatra, Crosby. I hated Crosby. The nurses used to play Crosby until I wanted to scream. Maybe I did scream. Maybe that's why they thought I was mad. Do you know I still think about those poor lunatics in the woods at Arnhem. Imagine being shut up for years and then suddenly finding that the walls had fallen down and that you were free. Free to wander in such a nightmare wood. If I could have painted, those would have been my pictures. I'm glad you don't have such pictures in your head.'

She pushed the switch and the record whirled. She put the needle gently down on the edge of the record. After a moment the music began.

'Shall we dance?' he asked.

She turned towards him.

'Yes.'

'We weren't going to play the remembering game.'

'No.'

'I'm sorry.'

'If it helps . . .'

'It doesn't.'

They danced in silence. After a while she raised the hand that had been holding his empty shoulder and touched the destroyed face.

She thought it was going to alarm her, the feel of the dry cobbled skin, but to her fingers' surprise it was almost like running them over a canvas, grainy stretched parts and then densely textured paint, but warm like flesh should be, not canvas-cool.

The music stopped. The needle whirled and no sound came any longer to them as they stood close together in the middle of the room, her fingers gently touching his face.

'Please,' he said suddenly to her. 'Please, oh Helen, please.' His head drooped down onto her shoulder and he spoke the words into the angle of her neck.

'Helen. Please. Please. Helen.'

She moved her fingers to cover his smooth lips.

'Sssh. Yes,' she whispered.

He kissed her. Held her tight with his hand on her back so that she could feel his hardness. The stubble scratched, oh God, she thought again, where are You now? Why didn't You do something before it was too late?

It was half past eleven. Ten minutes later neither of them upstairs in his bedroom heard the lorry stop above the bend in the road, nor the steps of the two men from Ballybofey as they walked down the hill to the old level-crossing gates. Quietly they opened the door of the goods shed. They shone the torch around the inside, into the corners, up to the roof and down again, round through the cobwebs and the dead flies the beams ranged. They didn't speak. They stepped out into the wind again and bolted the door behind them. They walked back up the hill and got into the lorry and drove away.

*　　*　　*

The sky was streaked with blue when she woke up the next morning. After a moment of puzzlement she remembered where she was and why she was there. His warm body was quite still beside her. She turned her head. His eye, a deeper, more constant blue than the sky, was looking at her.

'I must go.' She whispered the words as if the house were full of listening ears.

She scrambled out of the bed and began to pick up her clothes from the floor. He just lay there.

'Are you angry with me?' he asked at last, as she fumbled with the buttons on her skirt.

'No.'

He sighed.

'Why are you running away?'

'I'm not. I have to go. I mean, there's the cat, and I have to work, and the Aga needs filling and . . . and . . . oh no I'm not a bit angry.'

She moved round to his side of the bed and bent and kissed him gently on the cheek.

'I just have to hurry home.'

She went over to the door.

'You are a funny woman,' he said after her. 'I love you.'

She turned back and smiled at him.

'Thank you,' she said.

She hurried home.

The wind had almost calmed itself and the morning was silent. She could smell the sea tang and the drift of turf smoke from the village. She ran along the road, not running away, but running to her work.

The cat walked angrily past her when she opened the door.

'Silly cat,' she shouted after him.

She rattled out the Aga and filled it with anthracite, put the kettle on and went upstairs to change into her jeans. She looked at herself in the glass as she undressed.

'I must diet,' she said.

It was a passing thought rather than a decision.

She worked until the light began to drain away. She got up and turned on the light, rolled her head round and round, dislodging stiffness, stretched her arms. Hunger moved inside her. Carefully she lifted the canvas from the floor and propped it up beside the first one.

'Yes.'

She cleaned her brushes and stood them into the white enamel jug. She threw the dirty pieces of cloth into a box under the table. She emptied ash from the saucers and butts and broken matchsticks. Finally she laid a new canvas on the floor. Then she turned out the light and went across the yard to the house.

The kettle was sighing on the Aga.

The sound penetrated her mind after a few moments.

The cat was curled in the middle of the table.

That fact too became, after a moment, a puzzle.

The cat jumped onto the floor and rubbed its body round and round her ankles. 'Cat,' she said. She bent down and scratched his head. 'How on earth did you get in?' She listened to the kettle.

'Hello,' she called out. 'Who's here?'

Steps in the hall and Roger appeared in the doorway.

'I didn't want to disturb you.' he said.

She stared at him.

'I'm sorry,' she said after quite a long silence. 'I don't want to see anyone at the moment. My head is full of work . . . full of other things, not . . .' she gestured round the room. 'Not . . .'

'My head is full of you.'

'Please, Roger, go away.'

'I'll make you a cup of tea. I'll put the kettle on. You're tired.'

'Yes, I'm tired. I don't want a cup of tea.'

That was a lie.

'A drink?'

She shook her head.

'Just . . . I don't want to see anyone. Anyone. I don't want to talk, explain, argue.'

'Helen . . .'

'I want you to understand.'

He turned and went out into the hall. One of his shoes creaked.

'I'm sorry,' she shouted after him, rather half-heartedly.

He walked out into the porch and opened the hall door. A little wind rustled along the hall floor.

'No umbrage, Roger. No . . .'

He closed the door.

She didn't move until she heard his car starting. Behind her the lid of the kettle tapped and water spat out onto the stove.

Why can't I be the right person at the right time? The bubble is broken.

She heard the shattering glass in her head.

She poured some water into the teapot and swirled it round as she walked over to the sink. The warmth penetrated through the earthenware to her hands.

His hand's warmth on her back.

He stirred my sleeping guts.

She tipped the water into the sink.

Yes.

She walked back to the Aga and took the tea caddy down from the shelf. Two spoonfuls, make it three. Make it strong enough to stand a spoon in. Was what happened last night love? Desperation? Alcohol?

Yes, really. Yes to all three.

Such pleasure . . . rich uncomplicated pleasure. Unsearched for, that was one of the good things.

Why the hell did he have to come round and burst my bubble?

She tipped the kettle forward and a stream of water flowed into the teapot.

I don't want to love anybody. I don't want the burden of other people's pain. My own is enough.

Dear God, why did you give us eyes to see so much pain?

She put the lid on the teapot and closed down the Aga.

Forget I ever said that, God, I'm just feeling neurotic. She smiled. As if the Old Bugger didn't know.

She took down a mug from the dresser and put it on the table.

Why do you whisper green grass?

We didn't dance to that tune.

Why tell the trees what ain't so?

Whispering grass.

The trees don't need to know.

I am a bitch. That's really all there is to tell the trees.

OhOhOh.

Whispering grass . . .

The tea was dark brown. She knew before she even tasted it that it was going to be quite, quite disgusting.

It is possible to enjoy loving.

Tannic acid, she had always been told, stripped the lining from your stomach.

'Hello,' said Roger, from the doorway. 'I came back.'

In silence she got another mug from the dresser.

'Have some unbelievably disgusting tea.'

'I'm sorry,' he said. 'I came back to say that. That's all.'

'Is it possible to enjoy loving?' she asked, as if he'd been in the room with her all the time.

'Yes,' he said. 'I think it is.' He moved silently back out through the door again. She heard no sound of steps, no door close, no car. She wondered after a few minutes if he had been there at all.

⁂ ✻ ✻

The man was moving out into the centre of the sea. His arms, like bird's wings poised now for swimming. Above in the sky, a gull, his echo, coasted. She worked quickly, hardly taking daylight time off for air or cups of tea. She didn't even smoke much, lit the odd cigarette, puffed, left it on a plate to burn itself out. Expensive, she thought once as she caught sight of the cylinders of ash lying side by side on the white china. A terror drove her on, the thought always in the back of her mind that she might not get the pictures finished. It was almost as if she herself might disintegrate, in half an hour, tomorrow, leaving nothing behind but an unfinished thought.

She slept restlessly, just waiting really for the light to come again, thinking or dreaming, she never knew which, of the mad people at Arnhem, lost among the trees and the young men falling from the sky. The sun and moon together watched as the young men fell. The cat, unperturbed by dreams, slept comfortably in the angle between her neck and shoulder. She tried to keep out of the dream, to keep her eyes open, to be aware of the cat's warm reality against her. But the trees, burdened yet with their dusty summer leaves crowded the room, their scarred limbs split, echoed men, limbs also split, silent, disturbing images. The demented moved with care through the trees, their ironic freedom full of danger.

'I actually don't have to put up with this,' she said. She sat up, pushing away the cat and the warm bedclothes, feeling on the floor with her feet for her slippers. To her surprise there was daylight coming through the window. The sun before seven touching the chairs and dressing table, the snap of Dan smiling in a silver frame. She wondered each time she caught sight of it why she didn't get rid of it. She didn't have to have him keeping an eye on her like this. It was probably the thought of having to explain his disappearance to Mrs O'Sullivan, who cleaned the silver frame once a week, that prevented her from disposing of the picture. Mrs O'Sullivan might consider any act of that kind to be akin to murder.

The cat yawned. One day I must get the elegant structure of that yawn onto paper. She tied her dressing gown around her and went downstairs.

*   *   *

That evening she went over to the house to find Damian re-hanging the kitchen door.

'Good heavens,' she said. 'What are you doing? Life is full of surprises.'

'I took about a quarter of an inch off the bottom of that for you. You'll find it works easier now. Don't mind the mess. I'll clear it up in a tick. Here, could you just steady this a minute till I get the pins into the hinges.'

'This is really very kind of you. I'm sure you have other things you should be doing.'

'We have the first gate finished and hung. It looks great. I just have to give it a couple of coats of paint. We've been really hard at it the last couple of days. Otherwise I'd have been over to do this before. That's okay. You can let go now. See.'

He opened and shut the door a couple of times.

'I've given the hinges a taste of oil too.'

'Thank you, Damian. I . . . Can I get you a drink?'

'Aye. That'd be great. Let you tell me where is the dustpan and I'll clear this mess and you go up and get dressed.'

She suddenly realised that she was still in her dressing gown.

'Oh God,' she said.

'He might come round. He said to ask you if that would be all right.'

'Yes. I've finished. I think I've finished the paintings. You'll have to come and see them. Yes. I'm glad he's coming. We can have a party. We can celebrate.'

'Why don't you go up and get dressed?'

'Yes.' She moved towards the stairs. 'Will you go and tell him?'

'No. He'll arrive.'

'I was so cross with him the other evening . . .'

'Where's the dustpan?'

'Oh . . . in the cupboard . . . are you sure . . . ?'

'Will you go and get dressed, woman. You look terrible. He'll be here otherwise.'

She rushed upstairs.

When she came down about half an hour later he was sitting at the table, looking at the paper. He grinned as she came into the room.

'That's better. You're a sight for sore eyes now.'

'I have sore eyes. I feel they're going to fall out of my head. A week in the Bahamas is what I'd like now. Just a long empty beach and warm sea. No bothers on me.'

'The beach would be packed. I've seen the crowds on the telly. Sharks would be waiting to bite your feet off. You're better off where you are.'

'Don't you believe it. Drinks by the pool served by handsome black men with shiny teeth. No newspapers. How the other half lives. Champagne for breakfast. I have wine or whisky, which would you prefer?'

'What are you having?'

'I think I'll have a glass of wine, but you don't have to have the same.'

He hesitated.

'Whisky,' she said for him.

'Okay.'

'Come into the other room. I see no reason why we should confine ourselves to the kitchen. Put some water in a jug, I'll just put a match to the fire.' When he followed her into the sitting room she was kneeling on the floor beside the fire. Early flames flickered through the sticks and coal. Smoke was just beginning to be drawn up into the chimney. She waved her hand towards a table in the corner of the room.

'Help yourself, and me please. I'll have a glass of red wine. And a gasper.' She felt in the pocket of her skirt. 'It's days since I had a proper smoke. Are you still saintly?'

'Yes.'

There was a burst of energy in the fire and the sticks began to crackle.

'You seem a very solitary sort of person,' she said. 'Don't you have friends? Don't you do things with friends? Brothers? I never see you around with people of your own age.'

'I do what pleases me.'

He crossed the room and handed her a glass of wine.

'Thank you. Sit down. The room'll warm up quickly.'

He sat in an armchair by the fire looking down at her, his glass held awkwardly out in front of him.

'Well,' she said. 'Here's health.' She held up her glass and smiled. 'Mud in your eye.' They both drank.

'No girl friend?'

'Girls come and go.'

'Lots of young men of your age are married.'

'Aye. The most of my friends. I don't feel like settling you know. I want to make my boat. You've no peace with a wife and kids.'

'Love, comfort, companionship? What about those sort of things?'

'I've never come across a girl yet I've felt I'd like to spend fifty years with. It's the settling worries me. There's all the time in the world for that. Later. My mother'd like to see me married. Get me off her hands.'

'Most people rush into it too quickly. I did myself. It's hard to rush out again if it doesn't work.'

'Another couple of weeks now and we'll start on the boat. I have enough money put by for the timber. We're going to take the electricity over to the goods shed and we can work there during the winter. Then in the spring, when the weather starts to get better we're going to lay the tracks . . .'

'How do you lay tracks? You and Roger can't lay tracks. It takes a whole gang of men to lay tracks.'

'In the spring we're going to lay the tracks,' he repeated.

She sighed.

'I think perhaps that was when he got into trouble last time,' said Damian.

'How do you mean?'

'In Scotland, or wherever it was. He started to have rows then with the railway people and his family got roped into it all. It was bad trouble. I don't know why people won't just leave him alone.'

'I suppose he annoys them.'

'You wouldn't want to see him harmed, would you?'

'No.'

He smiled at her.

'I didn't think you would.'

She leaned over and put some wood on the fire.

'Do you want to come and see the pictures?'

'Yes. My fame.'

'Come on then.' She pushed herself up from the floor and led him out across the yard.

The four canvases were standing against the wall. In the fourth painting the beach and the sea were empty expanses. A seagull moved across the glare of the sun and footprints displaced the sand, leading from a pile of clothes to the edge of the sea. The clothes were the only colourful objects in the four paintings. A red jersey thrown on top of faded blue jeans, a blue shirt, red and white striped runners, grey woollen socks to one side of the pile.

'Where am I?' he asked. 'What have you done with me?' His voice sounded slightly panic-stricken, as if she had disposed of his reality in some way.

'You've gone.'

'But why? Why did I have to go? Couldn't I come back again?'

She laughed.

He examined the clothes closely, stooping down to study them.

'They're mine all right,' he said. 'I must be going to come back. God, Helen, that's a creepy thing to do to someone. Make them disappear like that.'

He clicked his fingers.

'Well,' she said. 'Not quite like that. You can see from the beginning that he's going to disappear.'

'He?'

'You, if you like.'

He looked at each one in turn again.

'Yes, I suppose you can.'

'You just have to forget that it's you, Damian. If it upsets you.'

He nodded.

'What are you going to call them?'

'Rather boring really. "Man on a Beach".'

'That's all?'

'1, 2, 3, 4.'

'Helen.'

Roger's voice called across the yard.

'Here,' she called back.

'Man on a Beach, Man in the Sea, Man Swimming and A Pile of Lonely Clothes would be better names,' suggested Damian.

Roger's lurching steps crossed the yard.

'Man on a Beach. Like it or lump it,' said Helen.

The door opened and Roger came in.

'I've finished.'

'The Short Story of Disappearing Damian.'

'Pay no attention to him,' said Helen.

Roger looked at the pictures in silence. Helen watched his face for a while and then turned away and began to tidy up things on the table. Pencils, brushes, into neat rows, smallest to the left. She scraped at the clotted paint on the blade of a knife with her finger nail.

'Yes,' he said at last. 'It's finished.'

She put the knife down on the table.

'I . . . well . . . what do you think?'

'I think you are a most remarkable woman.'

'The painting . . .'

'To have held all that inside you for so long, without driving yourself into some state of insanity. Looking at that, one would think you'd been painting for years.'

'I have. In my head.'

He took her hand and kissed it.

'Hey,' said Damian. 'She's made me disappear and you kiss her hand. That's my fame there and look what she does to me.'

She linked her arm through his.

'I'll paint you building your boat. How will that be?'

'No more disappearing?'

'No. Solid as a rock.'

'Okay.'

'Let's go. Let's have a happy time.'

They crossed the yard to the house, linked together not merely with their arms, but by an exuberant peacefulness.

Three people are happy, she thought, as she pulled the curtains tight almost as if to keep out the world's unhappiness. That's a crazy senti-mental thought if there ever was one. She wondered if she could have ever felt this way with Dan and Jack. There had been too much judging. How strange. I was happy when I started to pull the curtains and now here I am, as I finish that act, melancholy once more. A passing melancholy, that's all I intend it to be.

'What's the cat's name?'

'Sorry.'

She turned from the curtains and looked towards them. Damian was leaning over the back of the sofa scratching the cat's stretched orange stomach.

'I've brought some champagne,' said Roger. 'But it's the one thing I can't manage. It's in the kitchen. I'll just . . .' He went out of the room.

'He doesn't have a name.'

'Why not? I've never heard of a pet before without a name.'

'Dogs, yes. A dog without a name would be a lost soul, but cats are different. "I am the cat who walked by myself and all places are alike to me." I think you diminish a cat by calling it Tommy or Smudge or something . . . anyway they come if you call puss, puss, so why bend your mind any further than that. He's puss puss at meal times and bloody cat when I'm angry with him.' The cat twitched his ears at the familiar words.

'You win,' said Damian. 'I'll never call a cat Tommy or Smudge.'

Roger came back with one bottle in his hand and another tucked awkwardly under his arm.

'Oh what a beautiful sight,' said Helen. 'I don't think I have the right glasses. I hope you don't mind.'

'I've never tasted champagne,' said Damian.

'The great cure-all. Here.' Roger put one bottle on the table and handed Damian the other one. 'The doctors' surgeries would be empty if only more people were aware of its magic qualities. Glasses at the ready, Helen? Lesson number one. Take off the paper and then unscrew the wire. Right. Hold it carefully and then with both thumbs ease the cork. The right hand over the top. That's it. Feel it coming?'

Damian nodded.

'Glass, Helen. It shouldn't pop too hard. A well-pulled champagne cork should just jump quietly into your hand. That's it. Great.'

Helen caught the bubbles as the cork came away. Damian filled three glasses.

'Man on a Beach.' Roger raised his glass.

'Man on a Beach.'

'Me,' said Damian.

They drank.

'That's lovely. You didn't get that down in Mr Hasson's hotel.'

'I did not. What do you think, Damian? As good as a pint of Smithwicks?'

'I think I could learn to love it, given a bit of practise.'

'That's good. Mind you, you can get ghastly stuff. Sweet, like sparkling eau de cologne. Knappogue Road.' He drank again.

'Knappogue Road,' said Helen. Might as well, she thought, it's his champagne.

'Aye,' said Damian. 'The station.'

*   *   *

'I suppose we should eat,' said Helen about an hour later. 'I think I may only have eggs.'

290

'I love eggs,' said Roger.

Damian stood up.

'I'd better be going.'

'Don't be silly. Why would you go? Sit down, Damian. We're all going to eat eggs . . .'

'My mother'll have saved my tea.'

'It will be disgusting now.'

'I think . . .'

'If you really want to.'

'Yes.'

Roger groped in his pocket and took out his keys. He held them out to Damian.

'Here. Take the car. I'm going to be in no fit state to drive. Just mind it. Mind yourself.'

Damian took the keys.

'Thank you. Yes. Thank you.'

He did a little bow to each of them in turn.

'Tomorrow.'

He went out jingling the keys in his hand.

'Well,' said Helen after a moment.

'Well what?'

'A trifle high-handed perhaps?'

'Not at all. I simply thought I didn't want to give the postman, nice as he is, the fun of seeing my car outside your door at eight o'clock in the morning.'

'You're making assumptions . . . Anyhow I never get any post.'

'Am I?'

'Omelettes,' she said, standing up. 'Scrambled, poached, boiled . . .'

'Am I, Helen?'

'Fried, coddled . . .'

'Helen.'

'Take your pick. Yes. You're making assumptions . . . but they're correct. I expected you to stay the night. Even if you hadn't brought the champagne I'd have expected you to stay the night. I'll even go so far as to say that I want you to stay the night.'

He smiled.

'What's a coddled egg? That's a new one on me.'

He got up and followed her into the kitchen.

'Good heavens, did you never have coddled eggs when you were a child?' She took a bowl of eggs from the top of the refrigerator and put them on the table.

'Almost hard-boiled and then broken into a cup and sort of mushed around with lots of butter and pepper and salt. Then you eat it with fingers of toast. Maybe it wouldn't be nice now. Oh dear, that's a really nostalgic memory. Nursery tea, and our pyjamas warming on the guard in front of the fire. How peaceful and safe it seemed.'

'I don't think we'll have our eggs coddled. Apart from the fact that you would obviously drown in sentimentality, I've brought a nice bottle of claret. An omelette would be the most suitable dish on offer.'

'You seem to have a bottomless well of wine up there.'

'I see no reason to deprive myself of the good things of life, just because I choose to live separately.'

She took a bowl from the dresser and began to crack eggs into it.

'What would you have done, Roger, if... if... things had been different? If Arnhem hadn't happened?'

'I think the Bar and then perhaps politics was what they had in mind for me.'

'What did you have in mind for yourself?'

'I did not have time to find out. Those last couple of years at school I actually didn't care who won as long as the war ended before I had to get out there and fight. My head was full of such patriotic thoughts,' he laughed. 'I remember saying that to my father one night. I thought he was going to kill me on the spot. After that I kept my nasty thoughts to myself and just used to pray that I would be killed quickly. So you see I didn't have much time to work out what I wanted to do with my life.'

'To be serious ...'

She mixed the eggs together with a knife, tilting the bowl sideways as she worked.

'Oh I suppose I'd have liked to have been a writer, a painter, a poet, but I didn't have the gift. Nothing else ever seemed worthwhile to me. That's serious, Helen. I have left no footmark on the world. Three railway stations and a whole lot of angry relations . . . a great legacy.'

'Lay the table for me. You're starting to sound sorry for yourself.'

'No. I promise you, not that. I have enjoyed my railway stations and I'm embarrassed to say I've also enjoyed teasing my family . . . and I look forward to death. So . . . no sorrow. No happiness either. Just equilibrium.'

'You'll get knives and forks in the drawer behind you. I don't know what you're talking about at all. You've got less equilibrium than anyone I've ever met. Do you like herbs in your omelette?'

'Of course. Do you love me?'

She burst out laughing. She threw the knife across the room, clattering it into the metal sink. She picked up the bowl and walked with it in her hand over to the Aga. She stood there a moment with her back to him, before reaching to the cupboard for a small black iron pan.

'I don't know,' she said at last.

'I suppose that's not too bad an answer.'

He was meticulously spacing the knives and forks, the round rush mats, the wine glasses.

'Why do you wear your shirt in bed?' she asked.

'I would have thought the answer to that was obvious.'

'I'm not exactly a thing of beauty. Aren't those things forgettable?'

'Mutilation is an indignity. I like to preserve what dignity I can. It's pride, I'm afraid, Helen. Will you allow me that?'

'Yes. I'll allow you pride. Do you like your omelette runny in the middle?'

'No. Eggs should be hard.'

He poured them each a glass of wine.

*   *   *

It was the cat who woke Helen in the morning. Having jumped on to the bed, as was his custom, fairly early every morning, and found his pillow space to be occupied, he sat himself on Helen's chest and proceeded to stare morosely down at her face. After a few minutes she opened her eyes and stared back into the yellow ones that were staring at her. Beyond his head she could see blue sky through the window, the white frame reflected the hard glitter of the sun and a million dusty

particles seemed caught in the morning light. Amazing, she thought
how that one shaft of sun creates reality and mystery at the same time.
Hard-edge solidity at the window, then diffused, nothing defined any
more, objects almost shimmering further into the room. Everywhere
pools of dark. The cat bent forward and rubbed his head on her face.
She disentangled a hand from the bedclothes and scratched at the top
of his head.

'I suppose breakfast is in your mind, crude cat,' she said.

'Breakfast is in my mind too,' said Roger's voice from beside her.

She was startled.

'Had you forgotten about me?' he asked. 'So soon? *La donna è mobile.*'

She laughed.

'No, no, no. I hope you haven't been awake for long thinking about
breakfast.'

'Just a few minutes. The cat and I have had a small confrontation. I
don't think he likes me.'

'He's just confused. He's a creature of habit. You're in his space.
What time is it anyway?'

She looked at his watch.

'Eight.'

'Late. I'm usually up long before this. I've usually had two cigarettes
by eight.'

'Well, I've at least saved you from that.'

'True. But on the other hand, the Aga may have gone out. It's also a
creature of habit. It likes to breakfast at half past seven . . .'

She began to hustle herself out of bed. He put his hand on her
shoulder, holding her.

'Don't go.'

'I must.'

'Rubbish. Let the bloody Aga go out. Stay here with me. After all . . .'

She shrugged his hand off her shoulder and got out of the bed.

'No.' Her voice was faintly exasperated.

The cat jumped down from the bed and rubbed himself around her
bare legs.

'Even for Paul Newman I wouldn't let the Aga go out.'

She took her dressing gown from the back of the door and put it on.

The cat dashed out onto the small landing and waited at the top of the stairs for her to follow. She hunted round on the floor for something to put on her feet. The rope soles were under the bed. She bent down to pull them out. His fingers grappled into her hair.

'You're being very unromantic,' he said.

'I'm too old to be romantic.'

She shuffled her feet into the shoes and stood up.

He lay there already looking abandoned.

'There's too little time,' she said. 'Far too little time.'

She almost ran out of the room and tripped over the cat outside the door and they both fell several steps before she grabbed the bannister and landed angry and undignified half-way down the stairs. The cat fled round the corner and into the kitchen.

'Bloody cat,' she yelled after it.

'Are you all right?' Roger called from the bedroom.

'No bones broken. Dignity impaired. Suffering from mild shock. Blood pressure going crazy. Otherwise everything all right.'

'It's a judgment on you for being unromantic. What's so great about Paul Newman anyway?'

He stood in the doorway looking down at her, the bedspread draped around him. She stood up slowly, creaking and crackling like a pair of cheap shoes.

'Just the glorious unattainable.' She began to laugh. 'You look like a Roman senator. Heroic and noble.'

'And crumbling. One half of the face removed by the worms of time and weather. I like the idea.'

One of her shoes was at the bottom of the stairs. She hobbled down and put her foot into it.

'Do you want a bath?'

'Roman senators spent their time having baths.'

'You'll find towels in the press in the bathroom. There'll be breakfast in about half an hour. Ave atque vale.'

'Miaow,' screeched the hungry cat.

Aga revived, the cat content and asleep on the chair in the porch, they sat, almost accustomed to each other at the kitchen table, eating toast. He was amazingly adept, she thought. He seemed to be able to cope more neatly with his one hand than she had ever managed to with two.

'Did you never think to have an attachment of some sort . . . a false arm . . . you know?'

'I tried. Yes. Years ago. When I was still in hospital. They all thought it would make life much easier for me. I found it a bit repulsive though. Things might be different now, but then, what they offered me was quite crude and . . . well . . . repulsive is the best word I can think of. A lot of straps and things.' He smiled. 'I was allowed out one weekend to stay with my father and I went off for a walk and dropped the damn thing in the river. They were quite cross really. All of them. Yes. Quite cross. They considered I was ungrateful. I thought that was funny. There was a lot of trouble round about then.'

'What sort of trouble?'

'Trouble.' He looked vague. 'Prison and that sort of thing.'

'Prison? You've never been in prison, Roger. What on earth are you talking about?'

'It was prison all right. I wanted to go to Oxford. I had it all set up. They made allowances in those days for chaps like . . . injured . . . you know . . . allowances.'

He looked past her out of the window, his eye, reflective, had lost its blue energy.

'I could have managed.'

'I'm sure you could.'

'I wanted to be shown how to start my head working. I knew I had to do that before I could do anything else. No, they said. Damn it all, I'd passed those exams at school. Place all ready waiting when you come back from the war, they said. I could have managed.'

She was making a ring of cigarettes on the table, each one standing upright like a soldier, on its filter end.

'No, they said. You're not fit yet. Not fit to look after yourself. Not fit. When you're fit we'll reconsider. So, it was prison.'

'Not prison,' she said, keeping her eyes on the cigarettes. 'You told me yourself, a nursing home.'

'Genteel bars at my window, so that I couldn't throw myself out. A shadow always there, always walking behind me, watching me read, eat, sleep. I wasn't even allowed to lock the bathroom door. The degrees of comfort are irrelevant, the disciplines are irrelevant. A prison is always a prison.'

'What had you done to them?'

'I hadn't done anything. They just wanted me to be normal. Fit. Fit to be taken about in polite society. Our hero son. Polite, hero, son. Heroes should be grateful for the passing admiration in the eyes of others. Grateful for a pension. Grateful for the small attentions we throw to them. Grateful to be alive. I didn't want to fit in or to be fit. So they thought it was best to shut me up somewhere. They used to tell me how much money they were spending on me.'

He smiled again. The scar beneath his eye-patch puckered with the strain.

She saw it suddenly in terms of textures, painful colours mixed on the palette. A line of light ran from the black patch down to the jaw.

'It was my money. They had nothing to complain about.'

'That's over, a long time ago,' she said gently.

'No. Now at this moment perhaps I'm free from the ghosts. But any moment, without any warning, Helen, they take over my mind . . . and my body. Pain and ghosts. I become imprisoned again.'

'Those are all images of the past. I'm inept at this sort of conversation. It's all over now. Stop conjuring up nightmares. Leave the past alone. That will be your freedom.'

He said nothing for a long time. Little pulses beat beside his eye and in his throat.

'Why are you doing that with the cigarettes?' he asked at last, his voice normal.

She flipped her hand and the standing cigarettes fell down. She began to put them back into the box.

'I get quite nervous,' she said. 'When people talk. I talk so seldom to other people. I feel disadvantaged. It wasn't inattention, I assure you.' She laughed. 'Like Mrs Hasson, I suffer from nerves. Luckily no exeema, just straightforward nerves.'

He stood up suddenly, the tension gone miraculously from his face. 'Up, up, woman. Go and dress yourself. I'm going back to the station to collect the car and have a word with Damian and then we'll go and have our picnic at the Devil's Well. Tobar na . . . whatever you call it.'

*　*　*

There was no strong west wind blowing. The flat rocks were dry, the reflections in the narrow pools were without movement. Through the mirrored sky you could see clearly the sloping sides covered with barnacles and wisps of weed. Limpets clung just below the surface of the water and a discarded claw from some tiny crab lay among the pebbles on the bottom of one pool. She wondered how she could translate to canvas the opaque mystery of reflection imposed on the reality of granite, weed and shell. Odd, she thought, I've always looked through the reflection in the past, disregarded that dimension. Such blindness. Untrained eyes.

He took her arm and they walked to the edge of the blowing hole and looked down. Far below them, in the darkness, water plocked, glittered for a moment and was still, plocked again.

'When Damian's boat is finished,' said Roger, 'we'll get him to bring us close in, to see the entrance to the cave. It must be very low down, totally covered, I'd say, at high tide. I wonder why they called it the Devil's Well? It's not a well at all.'

'It looks like one from here. Those smooth sides look almost man-made. It's not till you see it in action that you realise what it is. A spout. The Devil's Spout would have been a better name. Wouldn't it?'

She bent down and picked up a small stone and wondered whether to drop it into the hole. She decided against that traditional gesture and instead turned away from Roger and walked to the edge of the rocks. She threw the stone out into the sea and watched while it dropped out of her sight. A gull, interested for a moment, changed course, floated down almost to the water and then without any apparent effort rose back to its original flight path once more.

'I get vertigo,' shouted Roger. 'I always have the terrible temptation to jump from heights.'

She moved back from the edge towards him.

'It would be such an exciting way to die. They say you become unconscious quite quickly, so you wouldn't feel the nasty bit at the end. You'd just fly out of life. That appeals to me.'

'Too nice a day for morbid thoughts,' Helen said. She stared down at the flat rocks.

'Do you think these rocks are neolithic?'

'I haven't the faintest idea what they might be.'

' "Of or belonging to the later stone age." That's what the dictionary says. Not much help. I did some paintings of them and wondered whether I could call them neolithic or not. The OED is usually more helpful than that.'

'That's probably helpful enough if you know the difference between the later stone age, the early stone age, the bronze age, the ice age. I'd use the word neolithic if it pleases you, if it seems right.'

'I'd better not. Some elderly geologist would be bound to complain.' She bent down and stirred in a shallow pool with her hand.

'Will you marry me, Helen?'

Oh damn, she thought, straightening up, shaking the drops from her fingers. The tiny stains dried almost at once, leaving the rocks unblemished.

'Helen.'

He was just behind her.

She was suddenly conscious of a lark's song spiralling above her and she stared up into the sky, trying to catch sight of the moving bird. Roger spoke her name again, a foreground to the distant warbling.

'No,' she said.

'Did you hear what I asked you?'

'Yes.'

She turned round and looked at him.

'Thank you. Yes, I heard. Thank you very much, but no.'

'Why not?'

She laughed a little.

'Men always ask why not.'

'I mean, is it because of the way I am . . . physically? Is that it?'

'No.'

'I love you, Helen. I never thought I'd find myself in this position. I never thought I'd find anyone that . . . I never thought I could love anyone. Perhaps we could be happy, Helen.'

He picked up her left hand and held it to the whole side of his face. It felt almost feverish, she thought.

How unkind of God to dangle the prospect of happiness in front of me at this moment in my life.

They stood in silence for a moment. The lark continued to sing.

'You don't love me,' he said at last.

'I do. I promise you I do.' She took a step forward and leaned her head on his chest.

'Why, then?'

'I want to own myself.'

'Darling, it won't be like that. I swear. I don't want to take anything away from you. I only want to give you whatever you want. Everything.'

'I only want one thing, you know.'

'I know what you're going to say . . . freedom. Isn't that right? I'll give you freedom.'

'I don't want you to give me anything. I want my own space. A little bit of time. I don't want anyone to give me anything. All that kindness, all that giving that you talk about, offer me, it could be like a prison. Couldn't it? I'd rather love you outside that. I haven't the energy for another marriage, Roger. Please try to understand.'

She rubbed at his cheek with her fingers. She smiled.

'I'd say the same thing to Paul Newman.'

He pulled himself away from her and walked across the rocks back towards the lane where the car was parked.

'Bloody man,' she shouted after him, as if he were the cat. 'Why don't you understand? I thought at least that you would understand. That's one reason I love you. Because . . . you should . . . you . . .'

He walked away.

Tears filled her head.

The lark was quite unperturbed.

The sea, the rocks, crumpled and splintered with the tears in her eyes.

I will not cry, she said. Not cry after any person who doesn't understand.

'Hail to thee blithe spirit,' she shouted into the splintering sky.

'Bird thou never wert

That from heaven or near it – '

The danger receded. The world came once more into her own peculiar focus. The bird flickered in the light, remained in her eye's sight.

'Pourest thy full heart in profuse strains of unpremeditated art.'

Flick, flick.

'That's what comes of sleeping through all those years of expensive education. You can't get beyond the fourth line of one of the world's classics.'

Bastún. Ignoramus. Layabout.

She sat on the edge of a rock and felt in her pockets for the cigarettes.

Or was it perhaps the fifth line?

She heard his step on the rocks.

'I've forgotten the rest,' she said.

He carried the thermos flask under his arm and in his hand her cigarettes. 'There's a bit about harmonious madness. I never liked Shelley.'

She looked alarmed.

'Keats. Surely. "Ode to the Skylark" is Keats, isn't it?'

He sat down beside her with a heavy graceless thump.

'Shelley. Nightingale Keats, skylark Shelley. I'm sorry, Helen. I didn't mean to be insensitive. Here. I've brought your poison . . . and the coffee.'

She took the box and the matches from him and put them in her pocket.

He put the flask between his knees and unscrewed the top. He handed the top to her and then filled it with coffee. Her hand was shaking and the liquid swirled up to the edge and back to the centre again. She ducked her head down towards her hand and sucked some coffee into her mouth. It was black, sweet, laced with whisky.

'Oh, that's good.'

She drank some more and handed him the cup.

'A loving cup,' she said.

He took a drink and put the cup down on the rock beside him. He picked up her hand and kissed it.

'I only thought that perhaps we could push a bit of loneliness away. Yours as well as mine.'

His mouth moved against her fingers.

The lark had now moved so far away that she could barely hear it.

'No,' she said. 'Time. Perhaps if we'd been young there would have been time for everything. I don't think so. You think that all time is there before you. Lovely empty time. If you're not very careful your past is empty time too and you have nothing to recognise yourself by. That nearly happened to me. Only a cruel accident stopped it happening to me. A cruel miracle maybe.'

The sky was now silent.

'I have so many questions to ask, Roger. Ask and ask and ask.'

He passed her the cup of coffee.

'Thanks.'

She took a drink, and then another and then handed the cup to him.

'That's all,' she said. 'That's the only reason. It's to do with me, not you.'

He looked silently at the cup in his hand. Tiny freckles patterned his wrist. She wondered how she had never noticed them before.

'Marriage isn't a cure for loneliness anyway. Sometimes it makes it more painful. I suppose some sort of close relationship with God is the only real answer to that. How absurd we are on such a day to be so melancholy.'

'Yes.'

'We can enjoy what we have, you know. There's nothing to stop us doing that. Darling Roger, thank you so much for your generosity. I'm just sorry I can't be equally generous in return. But let's enjoy what we've got.'

She was wearing those damn shoes again and dampness was seeping through to her feet. Will you never learn sense? Dan had always been so right in the things he said to her.

'Will you let me take you away somewhere . . . just a couple of weeks . . . a holiday . . . that sort of thing?'

'Yes. I'd love that. As soon as I get my pictures up to Dublin, weather that storm. Yes.'

He smiled at last. He finished the coffee in the cup and poured some more into it from the flask.

'It struck me the other day,' he said, handing her the coffee. 'That we

302

should go to Florence. You shouldn't spend the rest of your life here painting neolithic rocks without having been to Florence. It would give me great, great pleasure to be with you in that particular city.'

'Oh, yes. Such a beautiful prospect. Let's go home and light the fire and make plans. I love making plans.'

She stood up and held out a hand to him.

'And make love?'

'Of course.'

She pulled him up.

'My feet are wet. Cold. Think of all the lovely Italian shoes I can buy. I'll be able to throw all my clompers away.'

He laughed.

She bent down and picked up the flask and the top.

'Loving cup again.'

She took a long drink and handed it to him. He finished it. She screwed it onto the top of the flask.

'Are you sure about Shelley?' she asked.

'Quite sure.'

* * *

The miles drove by under their wheels.

As before, Manus didn't speak, though this time he was awake, his eyes open staring out through the windscreen of the car.

It was the old situation of the right hand not letting the left hand know what it was doing. Presumably Manus had been organising the thing for days. If I followed in my mother's footsteps, I'd now be devouring the cigarettes, stick after stick. From time to time Manus broke a piece of chocolate from a bar in his pocket and put it into his mouth. Never offered it around. He must have had about a dozen bars softening away in there. Amazing he didn't ever feel the need to puke.

He'd been standing outside the Arts block when Jack had come out of his last lecture and had followed him across Front Square to his rooms.

'Right,' he said, as Jack put his papers down on the table. 'We're off.'

'Off where?'

'Donegal. Come on. I've been hanging around for the last hour waiting for you.'

'I'm supposed to be going to my grandmother tonight.'

'Ring her,' said Manus. 'And get a move on. The lads are waiting beyond Maynooth with the stuff in a truck.'

'You mean . . . ?'

'Don't ask any questions, because I'm not answering them. Here's money for petrol.'

He took six fivers from his pocket and handed them to Jack. 'Now ring your fucking granny and let's go.'

Half an hour later on the road heading out of Dublin, Jack spoke.

'What am I supposed to do?'

'Drive.'

'Don't be damn silly. When we get there? What then?'

'We'll see when we get there. There may be no call for you to do anything but sit in the car and drive me home again.'

'It all seems a bit undefined to me.'

'What does that mean?'

That was when he took the first bar from his pocket, Cadbury's Fruit and Nut, a meal in itself. He snapped a row off the bar and dropped the paper on the floor between his feet.

'Casual. Unplanned. Liable to fall apart at the seams.'

'When I want your opinion I'll ask for it. Just drive.'

He shoved the chocolate angrily into his mouth.

Jack drove.

Kilcock, Mullingar, Langford, Carrick on Shannon, Boyle, interminable flat miles.

From time to time Manus turned his head and stared out the back window, checking that the lorry was still behind them. Outside Killucan, Jack had drawn into a petrol station and he had watched the lorry drive past them, two men in the cab. He wondered what their load consisted of. Manus ate more chocolate. Through the town and the lorry pulled off the verge and fell in behind them again.

As it began to get dark, Manus spoke.

'Don't drive too fast. Don't make it hard for them. We don't want the buggers getting lost.'

Silence.

I wonder why I do this. I get no satisfaction no glory . . . just an aching bum. What am I trying to do? Right some ancient wrong? Come, come, surely not that. Cancel out in some way the labels they hand on me . . . West Brit, shoneen, bourgeois? Show them . . . whoever they may be, that my heart is in the right place? He drove a car for fifty thousand miles for Ireland. Got blisters on his arse for Ireland and a first-class degree to please his grandmother . . . with a bit of luck. Some curriculum vitae that. Menial tasks for Ireland. What about the dead? The sad? The suffering? You can't make an omelette without, ha ha, breaking eggs. I have my own dead.

My mother sat alone all those evenings. She never held my hand. I could run this whole damn outfit a million times better than Manus, with his devious ways and his bars of chocolate. This operation for instance. No plans . . . just a vague hope of muddling through. We'll see what happens when the moment comes. Apart from the Englishman and my mad mother there's Damian to contend with. Maybe I just conjure up difficulties. Have too much imagination, like Manus said. Officers should only see what will happen, not what might happen. Stick to driving cars, Jackson Cuffe, certainly until you have your motives sorted out.

'Easy. Slow down. Easy through Sligo. Who do you think you are? Stirling Moss?'

Motives.

Could we look at the possibility of creating a situation where the blabbing mouths of the political posturers were silenced once and for all? That, as Shakespeare said, is a consummation devoutly to be wished. Worth getting blisters on your backside for.

But. Oh but, but, but, is it worth, ha ha, breaking eggs for? I often wonder to myself why I don't use that brisk word . . . kill. It makes me feel uneasy, that's why. Manus has a gun on his person. Manus has no scruples. Does he really have a dream, or merely no scruples?

I would think that I am probably driving across Ireland with a chrysalis beside me. One day, he too, like so many others with no scruples, will emerge, blossom from his chrysalis state into a free-flying political posturer. For that it is not worth getting blisters on your . . .

Do I really have to do this to prove my identity?

Or am I just too lazy to do it any other way?

Why was I born with a silly name like Jackson Cuffe around my neck?

If my father hadn't been shot and I hadn't been the recipient of a considerable sum of compensation, I wouldn't have a car in which to drive Manus interminably silent miles. What then? What other menial task would they have entrusted to me?

I depress myself at times.

'Pull up here, for a minute or two. I want to piss and have a couple of words with the lads.'

Jack drew in to the side of the road and stopped. The lorry stopped about twenty yards behind them. Manus got out of the car and walked back along the road.

Jack opened the door of the car and got out to stamp the stiffness from his bones. It was very cold and starry bright. The huge flint-sprinkled sky hung silent above him. His hands were silver, the road, the low thorn hedge and the hills, quite silver, naked, nowhere to hide. He could smell the sea, hear though no sound, only the low voices of the three men talking secrets.

He got back in the car and banged the door closed to dispel the unease that came to him sometimes with night silence. The inside of the car smelt disagreeable. He rolled down the window and waited until he heard Manus's footsteps returning along the road, then he put out his hand and started the engine.

Manus settled himself into his seat and groped for chocolate.

'That's okay,' he said. 'Want a piece?' He offered a bar of Kit-Kat in Jack's direction.

'No thanks.'

'I've told them to give us twenty minutes. That's in case your man is around.'

'If he is?'

Manus dropped the paper on the floor and began to eat the chocolate. 'That's your problem. You'll think up something to get him out of the way. If that happens, if we're seen . . . or rather if you're seen, you'll have to spend a couple of days with your mother. I'll go back to Dublin with the boys in the lorry.'

'What'll I say to her? She'll be extremely amazed to see me.'

'You'll think of something. Move it.'

'Sure they won't get lost?' asked Jack, jerking his head backwards towards the lorry.

'If they get lost, I'll have their balls.'

There was no light, no movement at the station. Jack stopped the car and Manus got out.

'It's a bugger of a night. You could hear the grass growing and see it too.'

Jack nodded.

'Get on down anyway and see if he's at the house. If he is we're elected.' He looked at his watch. 'Give us half an hour minimum. That's fifteen minutes . . . and half an hour . . . keep him occupied till ten-thirty. I'll see you back in Dublin.'

'If he's not there?'

'Don't go in. Come back up here and park the car outside the door. If he comes back it'll be up to you to occupy his mind. I'd say he'd be at the house below.'

He closed the car door quietly and pointed down the hill. Jack nodded and drove off.

They lay on the sofa in front of the fire, half-drunk with love and wine. The flickering light from the fire made their bodies seem to writhe, but they were in fact quite still, quite peaceful. They heard nothing but the sound of their own breathing, the pumping of two hearts. They heard no car, no latch click, no steps in the hall. The first moment they were aware of Jack's presence was when he opened the sitting-room door and switched on the light.

'Mother . . . oh Jesus God!'

Helen stared, confused across the back of the sofa for what seemed like a long time before she gathered into her mind what was happening.

'Jack.'

She stood up, fastening the buttons down the front of her shirt.

'You never told me you were coming down.'

She bent and picked her skirt from the floor and stepped into it.

Roger sat up, rubbing at his eye as if it were paining him.

'Hello, Jack.' His voice was composed.

Helen picked up his trousers and dropped them on top of him.

'You should have let me know you were coming. I think we've probably eaten all the food.'

'I don't need food. I tried to phone but I couldn't get through,' he lied.

She nodded, not believing him.

'I think I'll just . . .' He backed out of the room into the hall . . . 'just, bathroom.'

He disappeared and they heard him running up the stairs. Roger got up from the sofa and pulled his trousers on.

'I suppose we've shocked him,' said Helen. 'Oh dear . . . I hope we haven't appalled him.' She giggled. 'His face was appalled. I hope he doesn't do anything awful up there.'

'Don't be silly, Helen, he'll just recover his equilibrium and then he'll come down. You'd better give him a large drink.'

Helen was punching at the cushions on the sofa.

'Is this sordid?' she asked, suddenly anxious, 'or really a bit funny? It's not very dignified.'

'It would have been one hell of a lot less dignified if he'd arrived ten minutes earlier. A whisky? I'm having a whisky. To induce the correct light-hearted approach.'

'I'll stick to wine.'

Jack came into the room.

'Whisky?' asked Roger. Jack nodded abruptly and walked over to Helen who was standing with her back to the fire.

'What's all this anyway?'

'What's all what?'

'This . . . this . . .' He pointed towards the sofa.

'Have your drink, Jack dear. There's no need for you to get all worked up.'

'I'm not worked up.'

Roger came across the room and put a glass of whisky into his hand.

'I'm embarrassed. I'm ashamed. For God's sake, I might have had someone with me.'

'But you didn't,' said Helen. 'And anyway if you'd said you were coming down we would have behaved in a more appropriate way.'

'Would you mind very much opening this bottle of wine for your mother? I can't use this corkscrew.'

'Yes, I do mind. My mother's had enough to drink already. I can see that by looking at her.'

'You're being a bit grotesque,' said Helen, coldly.

'Grotesque. I'm being grotesque. That's good. Do you know how grotesque you're being? Nauseatingly grotesque.'

'Jack . . .' She put out a hand and touched his shoulder. He shuddered her hand away.

'Don't you touch me.'

Roger took Helen's hand in his.

'You'll have to get over your nausea, young man, because your mother and I love each other and . . .'

'Love . . . what do you mean love?'

'I'm sorry that you don't know the meaning of the word yourself.'

'She didn't love my father. How can she love someone like you? You're both making fools of yourselves.'

Helen uncoupled her hand from Roger's.

'You go home, darling. Jack will pull himself together and then we'll talk about all this. Just Jack and I will talk about it.' She smiled at him and nodded her head.

'Are you sure?'

'Quite sure.'

She put her arms around his neck and kissed his mouth.

'I love you.'

He held her for a moment.

'Yes,' he said.

As he moved across the room, Jack suddenly became aware of what was happening.

'No. Don't go.' He made a move to follow Roger, but Helen took hold of his arm.

'I'm sorry,' he said. He pulled at her fingers. 'I'm sorry. Stay. Let's talk.' Roger, in the doorway, raised his hand and smiled at Helen.

'Courage,' was all he said.

'Roger,' called out Jack.

Helen took hold of his shoulders and pushed him down into a chair.

'Call him back, Mother. I'm sorry. I was stupid. Please . . .'

'Don't be silly, Jack. If you want to have a vile conversation, have it with me. I don't want him hurt.'

Jack gave her a push that sent her sprawling onto the floor. He jumped out of the chair and was away out of the room.

'Roger.'

She heard his voice in the hall.

'Roger.'

She heard him almost wail outside in the road.

Roger's car drove off and then after a moment Jack followed. For some inexplicable reason he had his hand on the horn and she heard the blaring twist away along the road.

She got up from the floor.

How absurd we are, she thought. How easily we become affected by panic. I will be calm, domestic. I will clear away the signs of our panic. I will open the wine, bang the cushions, set straight the rugs, polish the glasses. They will be back soon and there will be no more panic.

Then there was the first explosion. The house shivered and the glass in the window cracked from the top down to the bottom, and shards, slivers, splinters, slid scattered across the floor.

I didn't think that anything else mattered.

As in a fugue the shattering glass recurs and recurs, punctuates the rhythm of my life. New endings, new beginnings occur. Each shattering unveils the eye. Damian pointed out to me, though, that there was one fact about which only he and I were aware.

Neither the police, nor the coroner, judges, lawyers, nor the news men, nor the casual devourers of news, no one at all in fact was aware of the presence of Manus at the station on the night of the explosion. There was no trace, no inkling of his presence, though we knew that he must have been there. He must have started running when he heard the blaring of Jack's horn. Up behind the station, onto the hill he must have run, off the roads and up among the whins and the grazing sheep.

After they had gathered together the bits and pieces, the sad human detritus from the hedges and the surrounding fields, after identifications, investigations, and enquiries, it was officially stated that four men had died. Two, young men, whose names I have forgotten, who had been in the lorry when the accident happened; poor Roger, half-drunk with wine and love; and Jack whose hand was still on the horn as he ran into the back of Roger's car.

Needless was Roger's word.

I mourn the needless dead.

The recollections that I keep in my head are part of my private being.

On canvas, I belong to the world. I record for those who wish to look, the pain and joy and loneliness and fear that I see with my inward and my outward eye.

All those questions.

God-given.

And no answers.

In moments of viciousness, I quite like to think of Manus running up over the bare hills. Cold hills with little shelter. I like to think of him alone, frightened, exposed under the bright moon, the flinty stars, running.

Running.

Running.

Fool's
Sanctuary

There are no new days ahead of me.

Is this what they meant by limbo?

Waiting time, floating time, time for snatching at the comfortable and uncomfortable moments of the past.

Why do I die is not the question. All fools know the answer to that one.

But how?

How has my life led me to this moment?

There is no day, no night, here.

The river is wide and slow.

They pluck from time to time at the remains of my body with their kind, warm hands.

Their voices flow, a counter-stream across me.

As yet, I hear no voice from God.

I do pray from time to time that when, or should I say if, there is some revelation of heaven, it won't be like living eternally through *Songs of Praise*.

I don't want to meet all my loved ones again, their faces burnished with soulfulness and goodwill; if I have to come across them, I want them to be as they were, undiminished by the eternal joys of heaven.

I can still laugh at myself.

Deo gratias.

Paradise holds out no charms for me.

I said to Cathal once . . . yes, to Cathal . . . only to him would I have said such a romantic thing, that I would be a ghost here, along with all the others. He laughed. I remember the sound of his laugh. I remember the evening sun hurling its light across the water. The memory hurts my eyes.

The ghosts here have always been so solitary, no carousals or laughter; distant doors close, steps move past you on the stairs, someone will sigh. Well ordered, you might call them, but not unhappy. Perhaps they are all content to pass eternity here at Termon, their sanctuary.

I have wondered from time to time over the last few years, what will become of this house; this white elephant.

Thirty years ago it would have been bought by the nuns, but they're selling the convents now.

A country house hotel maybe? I suppose it could have a worse fate.

If anyone were to ask me I would say that I would rather it were just left to fall down. Isn't that terrible of me? How everyone would disapprove. Feckless, thoughtless, typical of Miranda, they would say.

A romantic ruin full of ghosts. The children and young people from the village and roundabout would make daring trips, hoping against hope to see or hear something that would set their hearts racing with fear and excitement. Stories upon stories would be told, truths and half-truths argued over. That would be the most acceptable solution for the ghosts. Then the house would truly become their sanctuary.

I am not nostalgic for old times.

Things are different now, better perhaps in some ways. Yes, yes of course better.

People have freedom. That was what everyone wanted.

I think it was. That was the word they used.

I used it too.

I talked wildly about freedom.

I felt briefly at one time a longing to fight for freedom, but I merely cried for freedom; an inadequate contribution to the struggles of a nation.

I am laughing.

Can't you hear me laughing?

Their hands adjust the covers, smooth my hair.

They cannot hear me laughing.

They would be upset if they could hear me.

They would be sure to consider it a manifestation of physical pain and they would in their kindness inject me with drugs. A stinging in the wrist or my backside and I would be relieved. My head, even, is lost to me when they do that in their kindness. I can no longer see or hear the images of the past. Then, I am lonely, afraid. So I try not to upset them in any way.

I can call them all to my side now, as I was never able to through my living years.

Father.

Andrew.

Nanny.

Harry.

Cathal.

The cast of my play. The play that is in my head, always in my head. Mother?

Mother, whose lingering presence was so strong for the others, was, and still is for me, merely a series of sharply recollected sounds in my head; the swish of a dress in my nursery bedroom as she crossed the floor to kiss me goodnight, the tapping of her shoes on the flagstones of the hall; the sound of the piano playing, always playing, summer and winter, afternoon and evening, music always, always drifting through the air.

> Au clair de la lune,
> Mon ami Pierrot,
> Prête-moi ta plume
> Pour ecrire un mot.
> Ma chandelle est morte;
> Je n'ai plus de feu.
> Ouvre-moi ta porte,
> Pour l'amour de Dieu.

I didn't know what the words meant, but I sang them obediently for her each evening, before climbing the stairs with Nanny to my room.

Nanny didn't know what the words meant either.

'Don't always be asking questions. It's a song that's what it is.'

She herself would sing me songs, in Irish as well as English.

Songs that grew inside my bones and head; incomprehensible, sorrowful words.

ImBeal Atha na Gár atá an stáid bhrea mhóduil . . . No, this is not the time for Nanny's song.

'Don't always be asking questions. You're a holy terror for asking questions.'

No.

Mother is not among my cast.

Of course, if Mother had been alive, had been with us that weekend nothing would have been the same. I would not have been the same Miranda, nor Cathal the same Cathal. Idiotic really to muse on such things. We are faced all the time with the indelible reality of the past. Even if we dare to shut our eyes to the truth, it is still there waiting to outface us when we open them again; if we open them again, perhaps I should have said.

Maybe I should have married after all; raised a great brood of children, if only to keep this place alive and kicking, save it from the gombeen men; or the nuns, or the country house hotel crowd.

But I didn't allow myself that freedom.

There were times when I cursed myself and God and even Nanny for the position in which I had landed myself, times of real loneliness and pain; so often I longed to do a bunk, like Andrew, get away, like any sane person might have done.

Yes, get away.

But here I am still and it's all over now.

When Father died in 1939 the little church was full.

Luckily it was a warm spring day and our Catholic friends and neighbours and tenants stood outside in the sun waiting for the service to end. The church smelt of the dust that had heated and cooled with the years on the central heating pipes, of Brasso and of all the funeral flowers heaped along the altar steps. Andrew and I stood in the front pew, he sleek and upright, his face like the face of a ghost.

> The day Thou gavest Lord is ended,
> The darkness falls at Thy behest;
> To Thee our morning hymns ascended,

Thy praise shall hallow now our rest.

So lonely, he looked, so pale. Pale ghost, I see you now.

> The sun that bids us rest is waking
> Our brethren neath the western sky,
> And hour by hour fresh lips are making
> Thy wondrous doings heard on high.

'Sing loud,' I said. 'Please Andrew, sing loud.'

He opened his mouth and for the first time in our lives did something that I had asked him to do.

> So be it Lord, Thy throne shall never
> Like earth's proud empires, pass away.

I could hear the people outside the church singing also.

I remember hoping briefly that they wouldn't be excommunicated.

> But stand and rule and grow forever,
> Till all Thy creatures own Thy sway.

When he kissed me goodbye his lips were cold and his eyes burned like the windows of the house in the evening sun.

'Are you all right?' I asked.

He held me tight against him for a moment.

'I don't want to come back. Ever, Miranda. Don't make things hard for me.'

I laughed.

So unkind.

We laugh in this country for such strange reasons.

I didn't understand his pain until it was too late.

I suppose I was the only one who might have persuaded him to come back, but I didn't realise that until it was too late either.

It takes so long to learn.

It's the fumbling I have hated; painful groping through grey light, the only certainty being that you will arrive at this gate.

In a hundred years from now no one here will remember my name, nor Father's.

His trees will have been cut down by then. His reclaimed land will still be farmed, rich fertile land, but no one will remember that once it was sand and bent grass, beautiful desolation. Maybe even the little church will have become a supermarket or a craft shop; that sort of transformation is happening all over the place these days. Perhaps some lovers of the curious will have collected Father's pamphlets on reafforestation and land reclamation; his meticulous maps of these townlands, his notes like black ants crawling on the margins. Perhaps they will become collector's items. He would have been amused by such a thought.

Henry Augustus Martin, collector's item.

I won't even leave that mark.

I walked like King Wenceslas's page, in his footsteps leaving no trace of my own.

It was so easy to do that.

I lost my taste for danger when they killed Cathal. After that I chose my road. At the time it seemed the right thing to do, creep in Father's warmth; avoid confrontation with the world. Of course, looking back from here, I see how wrong I was.

I should have battered at their doors.

Gutless.

As gutless as the men who took Cathal away that night and shot him in the head.

I looked for heroes then.

Those men were the heroes that I got.

Better keep quiet.

Better not think such thoughts.

Better not waste what little energy I have on bitterness.

They move again. I hear their whispers and the soft rustling of their clothes.

They are ready. The tears are waiting behind their eyes. I will be washed from their lives. Soon. Kind lives. Kind hands. Kind murmuring voices.

I am almost ready.

Just one more time I must assemble the cast. I must search for the clue. Maybe there is no clue. Maybe the truth is anarchy. Maybe there is no truth. Maybe there is only pain.

No.

They move away now. They are the ghosts now. Their arms rise and fall. Their voices rustle. They fade into the darkness beyond my knowing.

I am alone.

It is time to begin.

Father

Andrew

Nanny

Harry

and Cathal.

*　*　*

Still, golden afternoon.

The sun leaning towards evening, casting long evening shadows. The leaves already changing colour. No more green among the branches.

That which gives an Indian Summer its memorable quality is the warmth of the colours as well as the unexpected warmth of the air.

The cycle is for a short while disrupted; even time seems to pause. Seems to pause.

The clocks cease to tick.

We live for a few days, a week even, through an unearned respite.

Through the stillness sliced the whistle of the train, its energy startling the peace.

This perfection is an accident, an aberration. Termor belongs to the world. The cycle will re-commence, has, in fact already begun to do so.

Miranda heard the whistle and put the top on her fountain pen.

Though the office was on the wrong side of the house to get the evening sun it was still warm, stuffy, full of dust. The maids were never allowed in here to clean, so, thought Miranda, even the dust was antique. From time to time Mr Dillon took a broom to the place and swept the mouse droppings and decayed spiders' webs out into the yard, stirring the lazy dust as he did so which then settled again on the books and papers and on the big mahogany desk.

I hate figures, she thought, as she screwed the top of the ink bottle. I hate adding and totting and multiplying. It gives me a headache and inky fingers. I hate writing boring figures down into these account books, lines and lines of boring figures and boring words, and boring, boring facts.

I wonder will Cathal like my hair, or be angry. Father hasn't noticed. He hasn't said he's noticed. That probably means he doesn't like it. Cathal will notice.

She rubbed at the ink on one of her fingers.

If he comes.

He'll come. He has to come.

My head feels light, not just from losing a weight of hair, but from the weight of figures. A paradox.

Is that what you'd call a paradox?

I am such an ignoramus.

'Miranda.'

It was Nanny calling.

Amazing how her old voice had so much carrying power.

She has heard the train too. Old hawk ears. That's why she's calling me; to let me know she knows my innermost thoughts.

Old hawk brain.

She'll shake her finger in my eye, that's what she'll do.

'Miranda.'

The yard was warm and smelling sweetly of horses.

Not a breath of wind stirred her shingled hair or the golden leaves on the chestnut trees outside the gate.

'Miranda.'

She never has to be told anything. She knows everything that goes on in the whole world. She knows bad thoughts, good thoughts, nothing escapes her hawk eyes.

'Coming.'

She ran across the lawn below the house.

'Coming, coming, coming.'

The old woman was sitting on her usual summer seat under an oak tree by the path that ran down to the beach. When the sun was shining it was warmer there than in the house, she always said, and now she had need of all the warmth she could get. From her seat she could keep her hawk eyes on the movements of the maids opening and closing the windows to let warm fresh air into the house, the boy weeding the long border on one side of the lawn and the kitchen yard, where in her opinion the cook wasted too much time talking to the gardener when he brought the vegetables up to the door . . . and of course the comings and goings of Miranda. Her knitting bag was beside her on the seat, her fingers twitched fretfully in her lap. Her fingers had once been deft, but had become in the last few years arthritic, painful and clumsy. She no longer had control over the needles and fine soft wool. To her anger and slight shame, she now had to fumble with the largest needles and thick strands of wool.

'Blankets and shawls are all I'm fit for now,' she would mutter, as if reproaching herself for her own inabilities.

'I called you,' she said, as Miranda appeared beside her. 'I called and called.'

'I heard you. I answered you. I came.'

'I like people to jump when I call them.'

'I jumped. Don't I always jump? You have me very well trained.'

'Ttttt.'

'What did you call me for, anyway?'

'I'm out of wool. I need another skein wound. Sit down there now and hold it for me.'

'Nanny . . .'

'It's in the bag. The blue. Stop hopping around like a cat on a brick and do what you're told.'

'Can't I do it later, Nan . . . or get you one of the girls? I was just going down to the beach.'

'Sit down there, child. The beach won't run away. Don't think I don't know what's in your mind. I can't see with the lamp to knit, so I need it now before the light goes on me.'

Miranda sighed and sat down.

'You're a bully.'

'Yes. But where would you all be without me here giving you the odd little push? Dootherers.'

'I'd be down on the beach.'

'Hold that wool still, till I find the end of it. Giving cheek will win you no prizes.'

She began to wind the wool round two fingers. Her hand moving slowly backwards and forwards as she wound. Old comforting routine, thought Miranda, twitching her thumbs as the wool ran round them.

'Do you like my hair? Father didn't notice.'

'He notices nothing these days. The house could fall down and he wouldn't notice. Schemes. That's all is in his head. Schemes and dreams. And his old trees. Your mother had lovely hair, God rest her.'

'It's my hair I'm asking you about, Nanny. My modern hair. Do you hate it or love it? You didn't say a word when I came home yesterday.'

'I can't see why you wanted to get it cut. A woman's hair is her crowning glory.'

'Everyone's getting their hair cut. No more silly fiddling with those awful hairpins. I like it anyway. I looked at myself in the glass this morning and I thought I was someone else. Someone old.'

Nanny tweaked at the wool.

'Someone sophisticated. Do you think I look sophisticated?'

'Hold your hands out like a good girl. You're letting the wool slip.'

'I'd love to look about twenty-five.'

'People of twenty-five have a little sense.'

'I am sensible. I've spent all afternoon being sensible and dusty. Look, my fingers are all covered with ink. If I didn't do those boring accounts, who would? Answer me that.'

'Your mother was twenty-five when she came to this house.'

'We could go bankrupt, for all Father cares.'

'If she could see the state of things now she'd turn in her grave. You're as bad as the master. I don't know what the pair of you would do if old Nan wasn't here to keep things up to the mark.'

'My head is full of dust and boring figures. I want a swim, some evening air . . .'

'Your mother had skin that was white like a lily. She didn't go rushing in and out of the sea at all hours of the night and day.'

'You're always on about the past. On and on and on.'

'Isn't it all I have now, child of grace, the memories that crowd in my head. The dead.' She sighed. 'The dead.'

Miranda put out a hand and touched the old woman's knee.

'There's Father and me . . . You have us, and you're right, what would we do without you . . . and there's Andrew. I know something you don't know about Andrew. The only thing in the whole world that you don't know.'

'Hands. Andrew? What about Andrew? He's not getting married? He wouldn't get married over there to someone we don't know.'

'He's over here. His regiment's been sent to Dublin. There's that old job done. Now can I go?'

She held the last wisp of the wool up and Nanny pulled it gently from her fingers.

'Glory be . . . wouldn't that be a great thing. Andrew coming home. After all these years. I must see to his room. I wonder if that chimney needs cleaning? Little Andrew. A great thing. I hope there isn't a smell of damp in that room of his. I tell the girls to open the window once a week, but you can't keep an eye on them all the time. Glory! Andrew.'

Miranda stood up and shook the creases from her skirt.

'I think it's terrible. Horrible.'

Nanny's hands were shaking as she pushed her needles and the wool into her bag, groped then with her right hand for the stick she had to use now when she left the house.

'Don't worry about him, pet. Didn't he come through that dreadful war? If he managed that he'll be safe as houses here.'

'He shouldn't have come. He should have refused point blank. That's what I'd have done. No, I'd have said no.'

She drew herself up into what she thought to be some military stance and said no, to a general covered in gold braid.

Nanny fiddled and fussed and talked on.

'Such nonsense you talk. Isn't he a soldier and don't soldiers have to do what they're told? Hunh? Go where they're told? Orders is orders in the army and there's no arguing agin them. It's a pity a bit of discipline didn't come your way . . . and a few others I could mention and I'll name no names.'

The bell of the village church, half a mile away across the fields as the crow flies, chimed out the angelus. Nanny laid her stick against the seat for a moment and blessed herself.

'Six o'clock. Oh Nanny, how awful of you to keep me so long. There'll be no sun left on the beach if I don't fly.'

'Have a weenchy bit of sense.' Nanny hauled herself to her feet and clutching her bag to her chest she moved slowly over the grass towards the house. 'A weenchy bit. It's all I ask.'

There was no one there to hear her, or to answer back.

* * *

I suppose I was happy; filled with such expectations. I suppose everyone of eighteen or thereabouts is filled with expectations. No one understands then, the illusory nature of happiness. We have the same attitude to it as we do to a good job, a house, enough to eat; it is one of our rights, not the shadowy dodging thing that escapes when we need it most and then at the most unexpected moments manifests itself again for a short while. Father always seemed happy, at least when he was working among his books and maps, or discussing planting with Mr Dillon. He was cocooned from the world by his own dreams. Like someone in a fairy tale he was hedged around by his own trees, his theories and, as Andrew would have less romantically said, his drainage schemes. He saw nothing else with the clarity he preserved for these things.

* * *

A bank of cloud was building out on the horizon, threatening the sun.

Miranda ran down the last steep slope onto the beach. The tide was curling in over the sand. The detritus of an earlier storm lay marooned quite high on the beach; bleached driftwood, tassels of brown weed and everywhere the colourless pads of dead jelly fish. Bird footmarks crossed and re-crossed near the water's edge. The oyster-catchers had been catching oysters. She laughed at her thought.

'Bonsoir, Maman.'

She pulled off her shoes and walked with the decorum that her mother might have liked down to the water's edge.

'Regardez comme la mer est bleue. Regardez comme la mer est calme.'

The water that rustled round her feet was still warm.

'C'est une très belle soirée, Maman, et je vais . . . umm . . . umm . . . vous chanter une petite chanson pour vous donner plaisir au Paradis.'

She stepped from the water onto a small barnacled rock and threw her hands out in front of her, in a dramatic gesture, towards the sun.

> Au clair de la lune,
> Mon ami Pierrot.
> Prête-moi ta plume,
> Pour écrire un mot.
> Ma chandelle est morte.
> Je n'ai plus de feu.
> Ouvre-moi ta porte,
> Pour l'amour de dieu.

'Bonsoir, chère Maman, et dormez bien au Paradis.'

'Have you gone mad or something?'

She hadn't heard Cathal's footsteps. She almost jumped out of her skin and her heart pounded inside her ribs.

'Oh golly, you frightened me. Don't do that. Out of my wits you frightened me.'

She splashed off the rock and frolicked towards him, like a young puppy.

'Hey,' he said. 'Don't wet me. Hey . . . hey . . . Mind. I'm in my Dublin shoes.'

'I thought you weren't coming. I'd given you up. I heard the train such ages ago.'

'Nothing would stop me from coming.'

He threw his case on the sand and his hat and he stretched his arms towards her. She stood there quite still, staring into his face, as if she had forgotten the pale city skin, the blue eyes, sparking now with the pleasure of seeing her. 'You know that. Don't you?'

She moved almost cautiously towards him.

'You must have walked so slowly. Crawled.'

'Give me a kiss and then tell me what you were doing.'

She stood for a moment on her toes and rubbed his stubbly cheek with her soft one.

'That's not a kiss . . .'

'I was talking to ghosts. This place is full of ghosts. You have to talk to them from time to time.'

'A French ghost?'

'No. Silly. Not a French ghost.'

She kissed his mouth.

'There! What kept you? Why didn't you run?'

'I ran all the way. I dropped in to see your father for a moment. I thought I should do that.'

She moved away from him, back into the trailing edge of the sea.

'I think you love him more than you love me.'

He sighed.

'No. Sometimes he looks so tired, but this evening he looked all up in the air . . . young, somehow . . . something . . .'

She bent down and scooped up some water in her hands and splashed it over her face. She turned and looked at him. Drops sparkled on her face.

'Horrid journey?'

'Yes.'

The hem of her dress was wet, and clung to her bare legs. She stirred at the sea with her foot for a moment and then came back towards him. She put her arm through his and they walked together up onto the dry soft sand.

'I never know what to say when I see you first,' she said as they walked. 'I feel like a stranger, someone quite new to you. It doesn't mean . . .'

He squeezed her arm tight against his side.

'I know.'

'Let's sit upon the ground and tell sad stories of the death of kings . . . unless you'd rather swim, or walk or something.'

She sat down with her back to a rock and patted the ground beside her.

He took off his coat and, folding it carefully, he slipped it between her back and the sloping stone. As he sat down he opened the wrist buttons of his shirt and with great neatness rolled the sleeves up as far as the elbows. She waited, watching the meticulous movements of his hands, until he was settled beside her, then she spoke again.

'Nothing ever happens here. The days just pass, so you begin. Tell me about Dublin.'

He wriggled his body down until he was lying stretched on the warm sand.

'You'll get sand in your hair,' she said.

'I've been trying so hard to get some work done. The exams are in two weeks. I shouldn't be here. I read all the way down in the train. I feel my eyes are going to pop out of my head.'

'You don't have to worry. You'll sail through.'

'I worry. All the time, bloody nagging worry. I want to do well for him as well as for myself.'

He put his hand over hers and let it lie, warm and light.

'You've no idea how hard it is to work up there at the moment. The atmosphere is electric. Living here you couldn't even begin to imagine what it's like ... it's like sparks are coming out of people's heads. Everything looks normal, but when you breathe in ...'

Miranda pulled her hand out from under his and began to dig a hole in the sand.

'Sea weed, warm salty stones, that's what I breathe. The wind has changed. I can smell the real ocean. I haven't been able to do that for days, and look at the clouds. I think our Indian summer is going to end very soon.'

'It's not like that in Dublin. There's real anger and fear ... even in the bloody library you can feel it. My shoulders are all stiff. It's fear. It's from staring out of the eye in the back of my head the whole time.'

Her fingers burrowed under the surface of the sand; her face was quite still, almost like stone. Above them a gull drifted on the changing wind, without any apparent purpose.

'They've lifted a lot of the boys in the last few days. They seem to be getting a lot of information from somewhere. From who? That's what we all want to know. From who?'

'Whom.' She whispered the word.

The digging continued.

'You find yourself looking sideways at your friends. You feel all the time they're looking sideways at you.'

'Cathal.' Her voice was careful. 'Can't you drop it? I don't mean forever . . . just . . .'

She started on a second hole, carefully scraping the sand out and patting it into a neat wall.

'. . . till your exams are over. Give yourself a chance. Can't you?'

'You know I can't do that. I couldn't back out now. I don't want to back out.'

'Not back out. I wouldn't want you to do that either . . . but . . . well . . . give yourself a chance.'

'No. I've thought about it. Holing myself up somewhere. But I couldn't do that. I haven't the right just to look out for myself . . . not at the moment. Your father'd see that, even if you don't.'

'Father's not a fighter. He doesn't understand about fighting. He'd just want you to get on and do what you have to do.' She looked up from her digging, out across the path of the sun.

'I don't think he'd want anything to happen to you. You know what I mean.'

'Two of our lads were shot yesterday. Dead. Just walking down the road. Near the canal, minding their own business. The Tans. Bastards.'

He laughed suddenly.

'What's funny?' she asked.

'My father would say it was no more than they deserved. Dear Mam would pray for their immortal souls and for their poor bereaved mothers, but she does that for the other lot too. Her brother was killed on the Somme. She can't see that bloody uniform as a threat. It doesn't leave much room for heroics. Does it?'

'Can't you just forget it all while you're here? Can't you think of the sun, the sea, home, us? Can't you? A few days of forgetting.'

'No.'

'I've made a tunnel. You put your hand in that side.'

He rolled over towards her and squeezed his hand into the hole. The sand was cold and damp down there and stuck to his skin. His fingers met hers.

She laughed like a delighted child who had just made a tunnel in the sand for the first time.

'Your father taught me everything. You know that; everything he would have wanted to teach Andrew.'

She looked at him for a moment when he mentioned her brother's name, but didn't say a word.

He didn't seem to notice her glance.

'We have to drive them out. They'll hang on here until we do that. They simply don't understand. I hate the thought of people being hurt too. I promise you that. I don't fight for any reason except for freedom. You understand that, don't you. You always seemed to understand. It has to be that way. It has to be war.' He pressed her fingers into the sand. 'I wish I knew how to . . . oh Miranda . . . you don't live in the real world.'

She pulled her fingers away from his, scattering the packed sand as she took her hand from the tunnel.

'There are so many different worlds. How can you say that one is more real than the other? Anyway, if you don't believe in the reality of this world, why did you come back? Why didn't you stay in Dublin?'

'You know right well why I came back. To be near you, even for a couple of days. To breathe the same unreal air as you.'

He shook the damp sand off his hand and pulled her over towards him. She lay beside him in the comfort of his arms.

'Look how white your arms are,' she whispered. 'Look, compared to mine. You've become a real city boy. Will you ever come back, Cathal?'

He kissed her. It seemed to be the only answer that he could give. 'Blow me.'

She pushed him away as she spoke and sat up.

'You're as bad as Father. You haven't noticed my hair.'

She shook her light head in his direction.

'Indeed I did notice. You look like a city girl.'

She threw a handful of sand at him.

'A real city girl.'

'Is that good or bad? Nanny's been a bit beasty about it and Father hasn't noticed. It cost me a fortune. Do I look old?'

'As old as the Hag of Beare, but prettier.'

'I hate you.'

He put up his hand and stroked the back of her neck.

'I like that. I love that. A very beautiful thing has been revealed to the world.'

She laughed.

'I suppose you say that to the city girls too.'

'Every hour of the day.'

He scrambled to his feet and pulled her up after him.

'Let's walk a little. For days I've dreamed about walking along the beach with you. It would have been just my luck if the weather had changed before I got here.'

'We could have walked in the rain.'

'It's not the same thing at all.'

Arm in arm they set off for the end of the beach. She stretched her legs to keep pace with him. The gull flapped lazily down and took its place on the rock they had borrowed from him.

*   *   *

If I could be there again.

If I could change time around, I could have said, Run Cathal. Run back over the footsteps in the sand, run, run, run, because though we love you, Father and I, we won't save you. You will save us and all we'll be able to do will be to remember that fact forever.

I held his warm arm close to my side and we walked to the end of the beach and as we turned to come back, the clouds were blowing up into the sky, a shivering little wind made our bare arms cold and goose pimpled. Above us, at that moment, as we turned, as my arms felt the cold wind, I saw two men on the top of the hill above us, but thought nothing of it.

'It's getting cold. When the sun starts to go these days, you really know it's autumn. How long can you stay?'

'Just the two days. I must get back to the library.'

'It's lonely when you're away. I get afraid sometimes.'

'There's nothing you should be afraid of.'

'No. You misunderstand. I get afraid for you . . . not so much that something will happen to you, but that you will do something that you'll regret forever. Something that'll change you . . . make you different, scar you in some awful way. I'd love us just to stay the way we are now, at this moment, for ever and ever.'

He stopped walking and put both his arms around her, pulled her so tight against him that she felt almost part of him. 'Silly, silly, silly child . . .'

'I'm not a child.'

'Yes you are. A child with a woman's hair style.'

She laughed happily.

'What'll happen when you grow up, dear child? You can't stay here forever, you know.'

'I have to. You know that. There's no one else. Andrew will never come back and live here. I couldn't abandon Termon, throw it out of my life. It's been so many hundreds of years . . . Anyway I want to live here . . . grow here. I wouldn't know what to do with myself anywhere else. This is my sanctuary. Surrounded by my ghosts. Ho ghosts! Hey ghosts! Hey, hey.'

She let go of him and ran down to the edge of the sea then, turning, embraced the bay, the world with her outspread arms. The two young men on the path turned the corner up above them and started walking down the long slope to the sand. 'I love my ghosts,' she shouted to Cathal. 'One day I'll be a ghost here too.'

He moved cautiously towards her, taking great care not to wet his Dublin shoes.

'What about me? What will happen to me? To us? Have you given any thought to that?'

'One day . . . one day we'll talk about that. When all the killing and pain is over. When we have time and freedom to think. Then we'll talk, make decisions. There'll be so much time then.'

'Miranda.'

She stood still for a moment, her head tilted to one side, listening like a bird he thought, just about to be disturbed.

She smiled at him.

'Then . . .' she repeated and the voice called again.

'Miranda.'

She laughed.

'Oh golly, more ghosts.'

She began to run along the edge of the sea, foam ruffling round her feet as she ran.

'Such an evening for ghosts.'

The words floated back to Cathal.

Two soldiers were coming down the path; he became aware of them for the first time; officers they were, their shadows trailing behind them on the pale stones of the path. Men and shadows moved down towards the beach; one of them raised his hand in the air, the shadow imitated the master.

'Miranda.'

She cut up across the sand, heading for them, running and skipping, almost dancing like a child.

Cathal stood still where he was and watched her dancing away from him. As she approached the two young men, they took their caps off and stood waiting somewhat awkwardly by the rock where not so long before he and Miranda had been sitting. His coat lay there on the sand, neatly folded. The seagull had recommenced its circling. The taller of the two young men took a step towards Miranda.

'Miranda.' He held his arms out towards her and she whirled into them.

'Andrew. Brother Andrew! Oh what a superb surprise.'

'Let me look at you. Oh God, I didn't realise I'd been away so long. You've grown up. I was expecting a little girl with long, long pigtails. About so high.' He held his hand out in front of him, very close to the ground. 'Why did no one let me know? You are Miranda, aren't you? Where are your pigtails and those big silk bows? Grown up lady, where is Miranda?'

'I had my hair off yesterday. Imagine that! If you'd come twenty-four hours earlier, you'd have seen the long long pigtails. Do I really look grown up? You should have told us you were coming today. Nanny'll have your life.'

He laughed.

'She already has. We dropped our gear in the hall and she found us there. After she'd recovered from the shock I got a serious lecture about manners, but I think she was really pleased to see us. But we fled. We haven't even found Father yet. I was afraid if we stayed in the house another second she'd have us making beds, cleaning chimneys, all sorts of things like that. She said we'd find you down here. She said you were to fly up at once to her. Oh do forgive me, this is my friend Harry. Let me introduce you. Harry Harrington. Harry, this is my sister Miranda.'

Miranda let go of Andrew and stretched her hand out towards Harry.

'How do you do, Harry Harrington.'

She laughed as she spoke.

'H-how do you do.' He gave a little bow and his face went pink as he took her hand.

'Excuse me for laughing, but what a funny name you have.'

Andrew frowned at his sister.

'Y-yes. I suppose so. Wh-when you hear it first, it is possibly a little humorous. I think people get used to it quite quickly. I did.' He smiled.

'Were you called after your father?'

'L-luckily I was spared that. His names are Cosmo Archibald.'

She didn't say anything for a moment, but peered at his face, her head slightly forward, then she laughed.

'I don't believe you. I think you're a joker. You're more than welcome anyway, whatever your father's name may be.'

She took hold of Andrew's arm again and rubbed her face against his sleeve.

'Mind you, I do wish you weren't wearing those awful uniforms. Couldn't you have come dressed as human beings?'

'Manners, sister. Remember, the plaits have gone now. You have to behave.'

His eyes wandered from her towards Cathal, who had forgotten that the tide was coming in and whose Dublin shoes had suddenly and disagreeably been filled with water.

'Won't you introduce us to your friend? Is he someone I know?'

'Silly Andrew. Cathal,' she called. 'Andrew doesn't remember you. Come and be recognised.'

Cathal, wretched about his wet feet, wondered whether to take off his shoes and his socks, and decided it was probably easier in the long run to leave them on. He squelched towards the waiting trio.

'Cathal? I don't know anyone . . . Don't tease, Miranda . . . ?'

'Cathal,' she repeated as Cathal arrived beside them. 'Look at your shoes.'

'I'm sorry,' said Andrew. 'I've been away such a long time, I'm afraid . . .'

Cathal held out his hand.

'I wouldn't have recognised you either. Charlie Dillon. We've all changed a bit, not just Miranda. . . . It's good to see you home again. Welcome back.'

He stood with his hand outstretched.

'Good Lord, old Charlie Dillon. So it is.'

Andrew looked from Cathal to Miranda, then took Cathal's hand briefly.

'Yes. This brings me back a few years all right. Still shooting, old man?'

Cathal shifted his wet feet and turned to look out to sea. Andrew addressed Harry in an explicatory way.

'Charlie and I used to play together when we were children. Mess around, you know. His father taught us both to shoot. Yes. This is my friend Captain Harrington, by the way, Charlie.'

'How do you do, Ch-charlie?'

Harry took a step towards him and held out his hand.

Cathal smiled briefly and continued to look out to sea.

'How do you do . . . sir?'

Harry put his hand in his pocket.

'And fishing. He taught us fishing too. Long time ago. I hope your father's keeping well these days?'

'He's very well, thank you.'

'And Mrs Dillon? She used to make splendid gingerbread. I hope she's well. In the trenches I used to remember your mother's gingerbread. You could tell her that.'

'I'll pass the message along. I hope you'll have time to come and visit her.'

'Do you like swimming?' Miranda took Harry by the arm and turned him around to face the sea. The sun was drowning now in the silver plucking waves.

'Oh . . . ah . . . y-y-yes. You're not still swimming, are you? It never occurred to me to bring my swimming gear with me.'

'The water here is amazingly warm. I swim right up to the end of October, sometimes even later. When the tide is right in, it's lovely. You can dive from the rocks over there.'

'I-I'd like to do that.'

'We can find you some togs tomorrow, if you like. But I think the weather's going to change. Look at those clouds. We haven't seen a cloud for ten days.'

'Yes,' Andrew's voice could be heard, after a long silence. 'I must make a strenuous effort to get down to see your parents. This is a pretty brief visit, but tell them I'll make a strenuous effort.'

'Soon those clouds will cover the sun and we won't see it again for weeks or months . . . or perhaps ever.'

'That's perfectly horrible of you . . . just as I was all worked up about h-having a swim.'

'We can swim in the rain. That's fun. Have you ever done that? Great big drops . . . er . . . dropping on you.' She raised her voice. 'Have you ever bathed naked in the rain?'

Harry laughed. Miranda laughed cautiously.

'Miranda!'

Cathal's voice was angry.

'Cathal always gets cross when I say things like that. He thinks I'm silly. I haven't persuaded him to do it yet. He doesn't like getting into the sea at the best of times. Do you, Cathal? Except in his shoes.'

'I have to go, Miranda, my mother will be wondering what's happened to me.'

'Your shoes will be ruined. Salt water makes them go all hard.'

He bent down and picked up his coat. He shook it and little particles of sand flew around among the four of them. 'My mother'll see to them.' His voice was surly. He rolled his sleeves down and carefully fastened the buttons at the wrists before putting on his coat. Andrew stared at the sea. Miranda watched Cathal's hands again as she had watched them earlier.

'Come back tomorrow, won't you, Cathal? Come to lunch. Yes. We'll have such fun tomorrow.'

'I don't think I can manage . . .'

She put a hand on his arm.

'Please.'

He nodded.

'All right. I'll do that so.'

He moved away from them towards the rock at the bottom of the path where his hat and his bag lay. As he passed Harry, he nodded.

'Good evening, sir.'

'G-good . . .'

'Good evening, Andrew.'

Andrew didn't look round. ''Evening Charlie.'

His wet shoes left heavy indentations in the sand. He picked up his hat and for some reason looked for a few moments at the inside of it before putting it on his head.

'Goodbye Cathal, see you tomorrow,' called Miranda.

He nodded again and started the long walk up the steep path.

There was a brief silence. They could hear the scrunching of the stones under his heavy feet.

'You didn't have to do that.'

Andrew hadn't moved. He still stared out to sea.

'Do what?'

'Invite the chap to lunch. After all, Miranda, we're only here for a . . .'

'The first person you always asked for when you came back from school. Where's Charlie, you used to shout as you came in the door. I want to see Charlie. Why can't I go and play with Charlie? Father and I mightn't have existed, for all you cared about us.'

He kicked at the sand for a moment and then turned towards her.

'That was years ago. We were children. You were only a little brat then.'

'You were like brothers.'

'More than ten years. Everything's changed since then.'

'Not here.'

He sighed impatiently.

'You changed when you went to Winchester. I remember. You became a blinking snob.'

'I-I . . .' attempted Harry.

'I began to grow up. That was all. After that we just had different interests, he and I. Less common ground.'

'He used to bring horrid friends home to stay,' said Miranda to Harry. He smiled.

'Like me?'

'They were not horrid.' Andrew's voice was angry. 'You were a bloody little pest.'

'You want to watch out. I still am.'

'I can see that.'

'I th-think you're right about the weather changing.'

'I just get the feeling that Charlie Dillon's got too big for his boots.'

'He's grown up too. That's all. I was wrong when I said that things haven't changed here, of course they have. People like Cathal have some sort of future now. That's good. Isn't that good? Isn't it good that people have some sort of hope now?'

He didn't answer.

'I-I think it's g-good,' said Harry to no one in particular.

'Good heavens, sister, don't tell me you've become a Socialist. They keep popping up these days in all sorts of unexpected places. Tell you one thing, Mother must be turning in her grave at the thought of Charlie Dillon clomping round the house in his wet shoes. I bet he doesn't know what to do with a knife and fork.'

She took a step towards him and Harry thought for a moment that she was going to hit him.

'You need to take care what you say, Andrew. Father likes him. Remember that.'

'And you?'

There was a moment's pause.

'Yes. I like him.'

'I didn't have to ask that question. I could see it with my eyes. Making a damn fool of yourself.'

'Little b-birds in their nests should agree.'

'People like you and Father do more harm than good. Let's be nice to the natives. Let's invite them to lunch. Now, look what's happening in the country. They think they can take over. They think they know how to run the damn place; they think they can win this silly affair by shooting people who don't agree with them. If you're not careful you'll have another Russian revolution here and people like you and Father will be to blame . . . and they won't thank you for your help and encouragement, just you wait and see . . .'

'Shut up, Andrew. God, I wish you hadn't come back. You must try and understand what's happening here, and if you can't, just keep your mouth shut.'

Her eyes were starry with tears.

Harry found himself blushing again.

She took Andrew's hand and held it against her warm face.

'I'm sorry. I didn't mean to say that. I'm delighted you're home, honestly I am. Just please try and not upset Father.'

'If I thought that Father was mixed up in . . .'

'Sssh. Don't fight with him. He's been so excited, like a little boy at the thought that you might be coming home. He'll be so happy to see you. Don't spoil it. Let's all be happy and polite to each other for a couple of days . . . like we were fourteen years ago. Please.'

She stood on her toes and kissed his cheek.

'I'll go and tell him you're here. Get him to brush his hair for a visitor. Poor Harry . . . how rude we've been. I hope you won't take the last few minutes to heart.'

Harry shook his head and watched her run across the sand. At the bottom of the path she turned and raised her hand. He raised his.

I shouldn't have come, thought Andrew. I should have had sense and listened to the voices in my head. Steer clear of Termon. The voices of sense. Stay away. Forget, forget. The common sense voices. Oh God, I thought by now I'd have been able to cope with my own emotions. His voice also in my head. Such a gentle voice he has. Son, son, son. That makes me laugh. He never said that. Fantasy voice, that one is. Son! The turbulence, the war in my brain. The moment I stepped inside the hall door I could feel the turbulence. Bloody damn house. Where is my strength?

'I s-say . . .'

She's right. Two days. I have to play a game for two days. Then I can go. Get back to reality. Become myself, my tutored self. The self I want to be.

'Andrew?'

He heard his friend's voice.

'I'm sorry, Harry. I . . . well you know . . . I'm sorry. Not much of a welcome for you . . . a family row . . . hey?'

'Do you believe in love at first sight?'

Andrew laughed, a delighted, vigorous laugh. 'Do you believe in ghosts or fairies or life after death?'

'N-no. But . . . the most extraordinary thing has happened . . . Maybe it's an illusion of some sort . . . This place opens you up to i-i-ill . . . maybe we were too long in the train.' He stopped and looked almost apologetically at Andrew. 'I hope you don't mind, I think I have fallen in love with your sister.'

'Yes. An illusion.'

He laughed again and pushed his friend towards the path. 'I'm suffering from illusions too. It must be the weather. The Indian summer of illusions.'

'Miranda s-says the weather is going to change.'

'That's all right then. We can hold on to that. Only two days and then reality once more. Let's go and find ourselves some strong drink. We can survive two days of illusion if we have lots of strong drink.'

*　*　*

I remember that hat of Cathal's so well. It was a palish grey with a darker grey band around it; truly a city hat. He wore it dipping slightly over his right eye. I remember also, laughing the first time I saw him wearing it; he had always worn a soft brown country cap until then and I didn't think the change suited his country face at all. I got used to it though, like he would have got used to my short hair; if he'd been given the time.

*　*　*

In spite of the Indian summer, the evenings grew very cold, so fires had been lit.

In the hall the light flickered on the gilt picture frames, on the crossed swords, the pikes, the ornate tassels; the silver chasing on duelling pistols glittered alongside the medals in their glass-topped cases. The logs were not totally dry and an aromatic greenish smoke drifted up into the chimney. Sometimes with a crack sparks flew out and scattered burning debris that lay, bright for a moment and then dimmed, leaving tiny brown freckles on the faded patterns of the old Persian rugs.

The drawing room was bright with the light from seven or eight lamps, placed on the tables among the flowers and china and on the tall brass lampstands. The fire crackled cheerfully, but its flickering made no impression on the brightness of the room.

Miranda sat at the grand piano playing 'La Fille au Cheveux de Lin', and waiting for the gentlemen to finish their port and join her.

They sat at one end of the dining-room table, and the fire and the candles made their faces gold and soft, and the men in the gilt frames crowding the walls stared in arrogance down at them.

'What a b-bloodthirsty lot you must have been,' said Harry, indicating with a flick of his head the portraits and the paraphernalia of war that cluttered the walls.

Mr Martin laughed.

Andrew pulled the decanter over and took the stopper out.

'Father was the first Martin for three hundred years not to serve King and country. Or someone. Sometimes their loyalty was a bit dubious. Wasn't it, Father?'

'I am a farmer.' Mr Martin's voice was almost apologetic as he spoke the words in Harry's direction. 'I never had any desire for glory of that kind. I . . . ah . . . experiment a bit in land reclamation . . . that sort of thing . . . trees . . . you know . . . planting trees. I don't suppose it's very . . . Pass your friend . . . Captain Harrington . . . the port, Andrew.'

'Oh no thanks, sir, no port for me. It gives me a head actually. I hate to have to admit it. Jolly interesting, trees and all that.'

He caught Andrew's scowling eye on him across the table.

'Not, of course, that I know much about it . . . my p-people are very citified, I'm afraid.'

The sound of the piano reached them through the open door.

'There's so much to show you, Andrew. New land you'll never have seen before . . . reclaimed . . . a couple of hundred acres. Not just from the sea.' He turned politely to Harry. 'You must understand that one of our great problems here is wind. The hills are very desolate. You'll see tomorrow. I found that by planting thick shelter belts I was able to protect the land from the wind and gradually . . .'

'Father . . .'

'Yes, my boy?'

'We met Charlie Dillon on the beach.'

'Charlie . . . ah yes. A good lad. Bright. He's a great help to me in a lot of ways. I'm trying to get out a series of papers for publication . . . helps . . . yes . . . in many ways . . . sometimes as a sounding board . . .'

'Father.'

Mr Martin looked at him for a moment.

'A good lad,' he repeated. He sighed, and then thinking better of the sigh, he turned and smiled briefly in Harry's direction. 'We don't want to bore you with . . . with domesticities, but if you're interested I can take you tomorrow and show you some of my schemes . . . and your friend of course.'

'I-I'd . . .'

'I am a schemer. Haha. I like to think of myself as a schemer. If the weather holds. Captain . . . ah . . .'

'Please call me Harry, sir. I'd like to see what y-you've been up to, sir. I'd be very interested, really I would. A total ignoramus of course.'

The music washed round the table like the creeping tide.

'Do have a drink? A glass of brandy perhaps, if you won't have port? That's good old stuff though, laid down by my father. Old. Haha. Antique you might say. It shouldn't do you any harm. It's not like the brash new stuff some people drink today.'

Harry pushed his chair back and stood up.

'If you don't mind, sir, I'll . . . If you'll excuse me. I think . . .' He blushed again, but in the flickering darkness no one could see. 'I'm very partial to Debussy.' Somewhat gauchely he gestured towards the door.

'Tra la lala.' Andrew, almost under his breath, sang the Wedding March.

'Run along, my boy . . . Harry. Run along. Keep the girl company. She doesn't have much company. We'll follow along in a few minutes.'

They listened in silence to the sound of Harry's steps crossing the hall.

'Seems a nice chap,' said Mr Martin at last. 'There was a Harrington up at Cambridge with me. Jesus. Wonder if he's any relation?'

Between them there was only the sound of the music and the departing footsteps. Andrew twirled his glass in his fingers and frowned.

'Yes,' Mr Martin spoke at last. 'Tomorrow we'll ride out. You have no idea how exciting it is to see new land thriving. Thriving. I think even you will feel something. Such prospects open up for . . . well for . . .'

'Miranda's grown up.'

'Oh . . . ah . . . yes. Of course. You don't notice so much when you're living all the time with someone. She's become quite a sensible young woman. She's had her hair cut.' He laughed for a moment. 'She doesn't think that I have noticed, but I have. Indeed I have. She had hair like her mother. But you wouldn't remember. Long, wavy hair. Your mother used to be able to sit on her hair when it was down. You never would have seen that.'

'The last time I was here she had a plait right down to her waist, tied with a big bow, like a butterfly. A great big yellow butterfly. Of course I remember Mother's hair. I remember . . .'

'You don't notice the time flying past and all of a sudden your children are grown up and you have difficulty bending down and picking things off the floor. Yes. She's a good girl.'

Andrew poured some more port into his glass.

'Why don't you think about sending her over to London for a while? Aunt Helen would be delighted to have her. Six months or so.'

'I never could stand Helen. Even your mother would never ask her to stay.'

'She's not as bad as you always made her out to be.'

'A dreadful woman. Plain too. I always thought it strange that your mother could have such a plain sister. Maybe she's improved with age. Some women mellow.'

'I know she'd love to have Miranda.'

'I don't think Miranda would want to go.'

'Well, I think she should . . . if you want my opinion. She's at the age she should be meeting people.'

'She does meet people.'

'Father, you know what I mean.'

'You might as well finish up that port while you're at it. It will have lost its bloom tomorrow. It's a pity your friend doesn't drink it. I opened it specially for you both. Ask her if you want to, my boy, but I don't think she'll want to go.'

'If you were to insist.'

'Come now, why should I insist?' One of the candles began to flicker wildly and he leant across the table and snuffed it with his finger and thumb.

'For her own good. If Mother were alive . . .'

Mr Martin sighed.

'I think we should spare Miranda all those things that your mother would have thought important. I can't see . . .'

'You've always been so hopeless. Can't you look into the future? What's the future going to be here for a girl like Miranda? She should at least see a bit of the world before she becomes . . .'

He took a drink and then stretched out his hand towards the decanter again.

'. . . stunted. Stifled.'

'Such strange words you use,' muttered Mr Martin. 'This country is in a state of evolution and you use the words stunted and stifled. I hardly think you are being fair or looking clearly at the situation. It would seem to me, that when your country is in a state of evolution, you should be there, living through it. Otherwise something may be lost to you forever . . . lost in you . . . if you see what I mean. Maybe I'm wrong.'

'Of course you're wrong. Apart from anything else, there are areas in the country where people like us are no longer safe.'

His father laughed.

'Come come, my boy. I am no threat. Whom do I threaten? I can see a future . . .'

'Oh God! Nothing here ever changes. You can't see beyond the end of your nose and you talk about the future. You may find the future is going to be something you didn't bargain for. Mother always said . . .'

'Let's not bring your mother into this. I know what your mother would have said and done. She wanted something for her children that

I never wanted . . . and for me also. She wanted me to . . . I had to fight her off, become a schemer. Now it's my life. I have my own visions, my own freedoms. This is where I belong, no matter what may happen in the next few years, and I believe Miranda thinks the same. My roots are long and deep into this earth.'

'Romantic rubbish.'

'So are yours, my son. You should bear that in your mind.'

*　*　*

Stunted. He used that word. Father told me all that he had said after the whole thing was over.

Perhaps he was right.

Perhaps I have never become a whole person.

What is a whole person?

I don't remember what I saw in front of myself. I have no recollection of any sense of purpose; no search for a pattern. I was of course very young, very immature. Perhaps my problem was that I never reached maturity. I never allowed myself that luxury.

What a strange state to approach death; virgo intacta in so many ways.

Children.

I would have liked to have had children; to talk to about my dreams if nothing else.

Of course they wouldn't have listened. Children never do; but they remember later.

I remembered later. I understood my father's dream later. I saw how much closer he was to sanity than we gave him credit for.

For years after Cathal's death he and Mr Dillon drove round the countryside giving lectures, talking at public meetings; they haunted the Department of Agriculture and the various Ministers. They never let up. All through the Civil War, out and about all the time; such crazy energy they seemed to have. I used to get so frightened here on my own, worrying about the pair of them driving in the dark, blind like fools to what was happening around them.

Mr Dillon always wore the black band on his sleeve. Even after his death just before the second war. They put the band between his fingers like some people put rosary beads. I cried when I saw it there.

My father died not long after that. He was old of course, but I think he felt the loss of his one true friend. Servant, some people would have said; master and servant. But it never seemed like that to me.

They never called each other by their Christian names, that is true; nor ate formally in each other's houses. But their lives were so bound together, their dreams were the same dreams, their tragedies the same tragedies, they spoke a language to each other that none of the rest of us really understood.

Isn't that what love is, the discovery of a mutual language? They are lighting the lamps now. Their shadowy figures grow in the lamplight. They touch the coverings. Their hands smooth my hair. I had hair like my mother's until I had it cut off that day in Cork. Such freedom that was, such pleasurable freedom.

✵ ✵ ✵

Harry paused just inside the drawing-room door and looked across the room towards Miranda. It was a while before she became aware of his presence and then, in a certain confusion, she took her hands from the keys and stood up.

'Please don't stop,' he said. 'I heard you from the dining room. I didn't think you'd mind if I c-came in. If I l-l . . .'

She smiled. 'No. I don't mind.'

'Go on playing then. I love Debussy.'

In spite of his words she moved away from the piano, towards the fire.

'Do you play?'

Her dress was red, just tipping red silk shoes.

He felt his body tremble as he watched her move, watched the dress tremble around her.

'A bit.'

She rubbed fiendishly at her fingers as if they might stiffen suddenly on her and never work again.

'Not nearly as well as you d-do. M-my fingers don't work any more.'

She stretched her hands out towards the fire, splaying her fingers wide.

'It's so long since I've been able to practise. His Majesty doesn't supply Steinways to the mess.'

She laughed and then gestured towards him, beckoning him to her side; or to the fireside, he wasn't sure which.

'You look so nervous there, hovering in the doorway. Come in. What are you nervous about? I won't eat you. Do I look as if I'd eat you?'

He shook his head.

'N-n-n . . .'

He moved cautiously towards her.

'I'm sure you'd like some coffee.'

She pulled the silk bell rope that hung beside the fireplace. In the distance he could hear the bell jangle.

'I didn't get it before. I didn't know how long you'd stay in the dining room.'

'I thought I should leave them to themselves. They m-must have so much to talk about. Anyw-way . . .'

There was a long pause. She wondered if he was stammering and waited politely for him to continue speaking. He didn't. He looked into the fireplace and said nothing.

'Anyway what?' she asked him eventually.

'I thought I'd like to come and listen to you playing the p-piano.'

She nodded slightly in acknowledgement of his words.

'They won't you know.'

'Won't what?'

'They won't talk to one another. Not really you know. They get afraid.'

'Oh rot. What's there to be afraid of? They haven't seen each other for years.'

'They've never had anything to say to each other. They're not really very good friends you know. I'd have thought you might have gathered that. They don't have very much in common.'

'I suppose all families are like that. I don't have m-much in common with my people n-nowadays. I . . .'

'Play. Will you play? I'd love to hear your stiff fingers.'

'I-I c-can't . . .'

'I insist.'

She took his arm and pulled him over to the piano. 'Oh do. Please do. We've lots of music. Look! What would you like?'

She opened a box beside the piano and pulled out books and books of music and carefully written manuscript sheets.

'Chopin? Will you start off with Chopin? I'm absolutely rotten at Chopin and I love him so much. I do him no justice at all. I clomp when I play Chopin. It's awful.'

He stood in silence determined to resist her demands until she turned and smiled up into his face.

'Please, Harry. You have no idea what pleasure it would give me. Just to hear some other fingers struggling, just to hear some music.'

He blushed.

'You'll laugh.'

'Cross my heart and hope to die, I won't laugh. Even my music teacher isn't coming any more. The train was held up one day and some men were taken off it. He was terrified. He's quite absurd really. I mean to say who on earth would want to harm him? He adamantly refuses to come any more. That was six months ago. So please, please.'

'Righty ho. I'll have a stab at something. S-something easy. No Chopin.'

He began to look through the music.

'And if you l-laugh or even smile I'll stop at once. I promise.' He laid a book of Schubert Lieder to one side and Chopin's Nocturnes.

'Something very romantic. I feel peculiarly romantic tonight.'

Not Brahms; three leather-covered books with gold tooling, someone must have loved Brahms. Schumann, Schubert, he put them both to one side. He heard her voice and looked up. A young girl had come into the room with the coffee.

'Put it on the table, Bridie, and I'll pour it out myself. Thank you.'

'Will I fix the fire, Miss Miranda?'

'It's all right. Don't bother hanging around for us, we can manage. I've all these men to do the work for me this evening. Isn't it lovely?'

'Nanny's going wild about Mr Andrew being home. It's like God came down from heaven. We have the uniforms all sponged and pressed for him and the other young gentleman.' She nodded in a friendly way towards Harry. 'To get the smell of the train off them. The smell of them old trains is terrible.'

'Thank you very much, Bridie. Don't let Nanny have you up all the night with her fussing. Be firm, that's what you have to be with Nanny, very, very firm.'

'It's easier said than done.'

The girl moved towards the door.

'Goodnight miss. Goodnight sir.'

'Goodnight.'

They both said the word at once and began to laugh as Bridie left their room.

'Have you chosen?'

He picked up a volume of Mozart piano concerts arranged for four hands.

'How about a d-duet?'

'That's not fair.'

'Let's have a go.'

He sat down and set the book up in front of him.

'Listen. This is about the most romantic piece I know.' After a moment of staring at his fingers and willing them to work, be began to play tentatively the first bars of the Andante from the piano concerto no. 21. His fingers fumbled and fluffed.

'Now please don't laugh.'

She came over and sat down beside him.

'I'm not laughing.'

He laughed for no apparent reason and then the sound strengthened and began to flow. After listening to him for a few moments, she rubbed her fingers together, pressing them hard each against the other, and then she too began to play.

✻ ✻ ✻

Andrew moved uneasily as the sound of the music reached him; his head was thick with wine and ghostly pressures.

'I . . .'

After the long silence his voice sounded strange in the dim room.

His father turned his head and looked towards him.

350

'My boy?'

'My mother's hair,' was all he said, his voice thick too with wine.

Mr Martin sighed.

'That was all so long ago. Over, done with. The past is better forgotten.'

The young man shook his head, the room swayed for a moment around him, and then he stretched out his hand for the decanter, the comfort of cold glass in his grip. The men on the walls smiled faintly as a log flickered; they, too, had known the room to sway.

'Are you going to get drunk?'

Mr Martin's voice was peevish.

'I may.'

'I would prefer it if you didn't.'

'I'm sure you would, Father, but, as you said yourself, it would be a pity to leave the port. You don't have to sit there and watch me though, you know that. I like my own company. I get on better with the ghosts when I am on my own.'

Mr Martin pushed back his chair and stood up.

He moved slowly towards the door. He heard the clink of the glass on glass as Andrew took the stopper from the decanter. He closed the door behind him and walked slowly across the hall towards his study, his books, his safety.

☆　☆　☆

Miranda clapped her hands with pleasure after they had played the last notes. The sound of the music settled into silence, then there was the clapping of her hands and a crackle from the fire.

He stared down at his fingers in surprise.

'I got through it. I never thought I would.'

'It was good. Lovely. Your fingers aren't rusty at all.'

He smiled.

'I can't explain that. Yes I can. It's this place. This . . . You, Miranda . . .'

'We must play more duets.' She interrupted him quickly. 'I've hardly ever played duets . . . only with Mr Slevin . . . the master . . . I told you . . . and that was work . . . no . . . no . . . It was much more fun playing with you.'

He nodded.

'I hope you can stay for ages.'

'No. Alas, not this time. This time we're . . . what's the word? I c-can't remember the word.'

'Skiving is what we call it here.'

'Skiving.' He smiled at the unknown word. 'But we'll come back . . . and I'll try and practise so when we play again we can make it sound like real music. I p-p-promise to practise.'

She jumped up from her chair.

'I'd forgotten the coffee. It will be cold. What a rotten hostess I am.'

He twirled round on the piano stool and watched her move across the room. He touched his fingers together to feel their reality. She stooped and picked up the large silver coffee pot from the tray.

'Do you take sugar? Cream? I have a whole box full of duets . . . all almost untouched by human hand.'

'Just a little sugar please.'

She came towards him with the coffee cup in one hand and a small silver bowl filled with sugar lumps in the other.

'You're honoured,' she said, handing him the cup. 'Nanny only lets us use these cups when there's quality for dinner. She's a terrible snob. These are the absolutely top-class quality coffee cups. Father'll be raging. He likes big common cups.'

He laughed.

'I'm glad I meet with Nanny's approval.'

She filled a cup for herself and pulled one of the armchairs round so that she was facing him.

'Perhaps Andrew told you . . . our mother was a pianist. That's why we have so much music round the place.'

'Andrew never talks about his mother. How old was he when she died?'

'Nine, ten, something like that. Old enough to know her. I hardly remember her at all.'

Bonsoir Maman.

The child's voice echoed for a moment in her head. She touched the top of her coffee with a sugar lump and watched the whiteness turn brown, then she popped it into her mouth.

'What happened to her?'

She crunched the lump with pleasure, the taste bursting into her mouth as her teeth closed on it.

'Am I being too inquisitive?'

'Oh . . . no . . . She died in some sort of hunting accident. She was a marvellous horsewoman, so they say. I mean I don't know. I only know what I've been told. I was only . . . Nanny could tell you everything.' She laughed. 'That's not true. Nanny knows everything, but she doesn't tell. If you ask her she'll shake her finger at you.' She shook her finger at him. 'And say curiosity killed the cat. That's Nanny all over. So much locked in her head. Locked . . . and she sits and knits and broods upon it all. Hour after hour. Broods. It must be terrible to be old.'

She picked another lump from the sugar bowl and dipped the edge of it, again in her coffee.

'I hope you don't find Father boring.'

'I-I . . .'

'I know he goes on and on and on . . . well you know . . . about his trees and that. Farming, land reclamation and all that sort of thing. It's really quite interesting when you get the drift of what he's talking about. He thinks it's terribly important. Possibly he's right. I haven't made up my mind yet. I suppose I should have by now. I like to do a lot of watching before I make my mind up about things.'

She sighed.

'I think I'm probably quite boring too. They weren't a very well suited pair.'

'Who?'

'Mother and Father. You were asking me about Mother, weren't you?'

'Y-yes. Do go on.'

'She had friends all over the country. She used to go and stay with them. Hunting and all that sort of thing. Father never liked going away from here. He hardly ever moves . . . just to give lectures . . . or do research . . . He goes abroad quite a bit, to meet other people with the same . . . well, not for sociable reasons. She was sociable. Very. Anyway it happened in County Wicklow, a fall, a bad fall, that's what I was told. I don't remember much. Father had to go and Nanny cried all over the place. I don't remember what I felt, I don't suppose I understood what had happened. Andrew came back from boarding school for the funeral. He had a black band sewed to the sleeve of his coat. Isn't it funny, the things you do remember? Have some more coffee?'

'No thanks.'

'It's cold. I'm sorry. Nanny says I have no social graces. She seems to think I'd have had some if Mother had been alive. I suppose one should have social graces. What do you think?'

'I think you're the most marvellous girl I've ever met.'

Miranda threw her head back and roared with unromantic laughter.

'D-don't laugh. Please don't laugh. I-I . . .'

'Mother. I'm telling you about Mother.' She spoke the words suddenly and quite severely. 'Mother. Andrew loved her so much. He's never been able to see Father straight because of that. I think he feels that Father made Mother very unhappy. I'm not sure he ever looked properly at them both. You must understand that I may not be right; I find I'm sometimes terribly wrong in the conclusions I come to. People are so complicated, aren't they? Even if you watch quite carefully, they're hard to understand. Father's probably right . . . it's better to stick to books and theories. It's more comfortable.'

'I don't find people complicated.'

'I don't think English people are very aware somehow.'

'Aware of what?'

'Of people's feelings, their complications. I'm not very good at explaining myself. You see I think Father gets a bit guilty at times about not having made her life particularly happy . . . for not being the sort of person she wanted him to be. She hated his reclusive ways. He has only ever really wanted to get on with his plans. I sometimes wonder why people get married. I mean . . . Have you got happy parents?'

He felt himself going pink in the face.

'I've never really thought about it. They seem quite pally.'

She frowned for a moment, more to herself than in his direction.

'Father has this notion that the land should be taken over by the government and parcelled out to the farmers in economic holdings. You take what you need from your holding and the rest goes into some sort of co-operative market.'

'But that's Bolshevism.'

She looked surprised.

'Is it? I don't know what you'd call it. I thought Bolshevism was something really dangerous. He gets stacks of papers from all over the world. His study is piled high with pamphlets and books and then there's all the stuff he writes himself. He speaks a lot at public meetings. I don't go with him much, I'm afraid. I find it all a bit boring. Mr Dillon goes. He always goes.'

'What . . .' Harry paused a moment and then continued. 'What does he th-think of this lot . . . that w-we're having trouble with?'

'He's a Republican . . . if that's what you mean, but he believes in Parliamentary democracy, not violence . . . not murder, he hates that sort of thing . . . Time, he says, patience and time and . . .'

'And you?'

She pulled the red silk of her dress into little folds across the top of her knee. Her hands looked strong, not like the pale fragile hands of the girls he was used to. 'I am only in the process of forming my thoughts.' Her voice was low, she spoke down towards her hands. 'I don't know very much yet about the world.'

Harry laughed.

'I think that like most Irish people I've ever met you just talk on and on about things you don't understand very well.'

Her fingers stopped moving.

'Thank you.'

'I didn't mean to be r-rude. But you seem as a race to have this capacity for turning feeling into fantasy, and then you all get so worked up about oh . . . ah . . . d-dreams. Always dreams. M-maybe I'm quite wrong. Maybe when I've been here a little longer I'll begin to understand what all the f-fuss is about.'

Miranda stood up and walked over to the fireplace.

'I feel I have the whole weight of this war tied round my heart like a stone. If I were to fall in the sea I might drown with the weight of it. I really feel that. I'd drown. Sometimes I feel I'm drowning already.'

She bent down and picked up a piece of wood which she threw onto the fire. Sparks chased each other up into the chimney. Harry laughed again, but with unease.

'War? This a w-war? My dear girl there's nothing for you to worry about. I d-don't blame you for being af-fraid. I'd be afraid too if I lived out in the wilds like this, but it . . .'

'You misunderstand me.'

He got up and moved towards her, longing to touch her hair, or the soft shadowy nape of her neck, or even the thin bones of her shoulder just where the red silk dress seemed to weigh on them.

'I'm not afraid. I'm not much good at explaining the way I feel.'

She turned towards him and looked almost passionately up into his face.

'I do . . . I truly believe that we . . . we . . . we, as a nation, I mean, have a future of our own. We do need freedom, even if it's only, as you and Andrew think, to make a mess of things. I don't understand why everyone can't see that. Freedom.'

She said the word as if it were some magic word, had some magic power. The very speaking of the word made her shiver and she clutched her hands to her shoulders as if to warm herself.

'There is some obscure morality inside me that stops me from going out with a gun and fighting.' She groaned and turned away from him again. 'I think I'm just a coward . . . a terrible coward . . . afraid of reality. That's what . . . That's what . . .'

She turned back and looked at him and put out a hand to touch his arm. 'I see I've shocked you. I'm sorry. The whole thing is so difficult to explain to . . .' She was searching for the word.

'The e-enemy?' he suggested.

She burst out laughing.

'Don't be an ass. You're such a nice person. The nicest person I've met for ages . . . a guest. And I'm a hopeless hostess. I give you cold coffee, I bully you into playing the piano and now I insult you. Will you forgive me? You must admit, though, you inveigled me into this conversation, didn't you?'

'I am quite confused. At home nice, well brought up girls don't go round talking about guns and freedom.'

'I don't suppose too many of them here do either.'

He scurried away from her, back to the piano and picked up his coffee cup.

'I must say I'm glad I met you and not any of the others. I-I'll have another cup of cold coffee now if I may, p-please.' As she took the cup from him he carefully avoided touching her fingers.

'Why do you . . . ?'

'Are you n-n . . . ?'

They both stopped and laughed. Miranda handed him back the cup. 'Go ahead,' she said.

'Are you never afraid here?'

'Why should we be afraid?'

He took a sip of his coffee.

'Why?' she asked again.

'You're so unprotected here. Such terrible things have happened. Anyone could just walk in . . . like Andrew and I did . . . j-just walk in.'

The cup in his hand was fine, almost translucent bone china, very old, the gold handle had no use other than decoration.

'We mustn't quarrel. That would upset Father. He holds to the very old-fashioned belief that whoever comes into the house must be treated with impeccable courtesy.'

'Even the Shinners? If they came storming in with guns?'

She sighed.

'You and Andrew have guns in your bedroom.'

'That's n-not the same, Miranda. Y-you know . . .'

'Of course it's the same. Only you didn't storm in. You came in logically and lawfully through the hall door and one of the girls carried your cases upstairs for you. Your baths were run. Your beds will have been turned down, the curtains pulled. Nanny will have filled your beds with hot jars, just you wait and see. The guns are there. We all know that. Everyone in the house knows that. Guns like dirty boots should be left out in the yard.'

'You have an answer for everything.'

'I wish I had. You play the piano better than I do.'

He laughed. She laughed. Young happy laughter filled the room as the music had done earlier.

'You are all so unrealistic and p-probably m-mad.'

As he spoke the door opened and Mr Martin came in.

'Well, well,' he said, crossing the room towards them. 'Are you throwing that word at us as a family or as a race, young man?'

'I-I . . .'

Miranda interrupted him.

'At me, Father dear, just me.'

As Mr Martin sat down by the fire Harry could see that his movements were slow and careful. Stiffness in his bones, perhaps even pain; there were signs of pain in his face.

'He thinks I'm mad, but he quite likes me in spite of it.'

She poured her father some coffee and dropped one lump of sugar into the cup.

'You've been bullying him. I can see that. My daughter, Captain . . . um, ah, has been very badly brought up. What's this, child?' He protested as she handed him the cup. 'I hate my coffee in a thimble.' He took a sip.

'Cold coffee what's more.'

'You can't expect hot coffee if you spend so long in the dining room. What have you done with Andrew?'

'He seems hell-bent on getting himself drunk, so I left him to it. So you find my daughter a little mad, young man, eh?'

He handed his cup to Miranda to be refilled.

'D-disconcerting might be a better word, sir.'

'These cups were made for the tiny fingers of elegant women.' He held the cup up between his finger and thumb and drained the coffee from it in one go. 'Ladies who sip rather than drink. Tiny white fingers. We're not like that, Miranda and I, our hands are quite unsuited to such fragility. We have too much of the peasant in us.' The white porcelain glowed pink in the light from the fire. He looked for a moment as if he might crush it in his fingers, but he handed it to Miranda instead.

'Harry plays the piano. Did you hear him?' she said.

'Miranda's mother was a very fine pianist.'

'She told me.'

'She used to shut herself up in this room for hours on end and play and play. Chopin, Beethoven, Liszt, Brahms. It was her secret life. She would never play for anyone else. Brahms. She played a lot of Brahms. The whole house used to be filled at times with the sound of her music.'

Miranda put out a hand and touched his shoulder gently.

'She used to play for me, Father. I remember.'

She crossed the room and sat down at the piano. For a moment her fingers hovered over the keys and then she began to play and sing.

'There was a man lived in the moon, in the moon, in the moon. There was a man lived in the moon,
And his name was Aiken Drum.
And he played upon a ladle . . . Do you know it, Harry?'

'Great oh . . . nursery songs . . . Yes, yes, I remember it.'

He pulled up a chair beside her and began thumping on the bass.

'. . . a ladle, a ladle.
He played upon a ladle,
And his name was Aiken Drum.'

Laughter, and in the laughter the door opened and Andrew stood on the threshold of the room.

'Um . . . ah . . . what . . .'

Laughter.

'His buttons . . .'

'Yes . . .'

'His buttons were made of . . .'

'Why are you singing that?'

Andrew's voice was loud and angry.

Mr Martin looked up and saw him standing there.

'It's a song her mother used to sing.'

'Good cream cheese, good cream cheese, good cream cheese. His buttons were made of good cream cheese. Don't you remember it?'

'Why, why, why?'

With each word he stepped further into the room.

'As you can see, your friend Harry has an aptitude for the piano.'

'And his name was Aiken Drum. You must remember, Andrew?'

Miranda spoke across her shoulder.

'He played upon a ladle, a ladle, a ladle,
He played upon a la . . . hay . . . dle,
and his name . . .'

'I must admit I don't recall it myself.'

Mr Martin spoke the words softly.

'And his name was Aiken Drum.'

'She was my mother too.'

'And then . . . what then, Harry?'

'H-h-is . . .'

'My mother.'

'. . . b-britches . . . ?'

'Yes. That's it. His britches were made of haggis bags . . .'

'I was just reminding you of the fact that she was my mother too.'

He was by the fireplace now, flushed, his eyes shining in the fire light, angry eyes, staring down at his father.

'Haggis bags, haggis bags.'

'Miranda.'

'His britches were made of haggis bags,
And his name was Aiken Drum.'

'Wasn't she?'

'Wasn't who what?' asked Miranda and Harry sang bravely on.

'He played upon a ladle, a ladle, a ladle . . .'

'She was my mother too.'

'What on earth are you talking about?'

'How would you play on a ladle?'

Harry turned round from the piano and plucked at the strings of a guitar, pizzicato plucking, his fingers pinching at the strings.

'You hardly knew her. You always say that yourself. Nor did Father know much of her, if it comes to that.' His voice was venomous. Mr Martin seemed to shrink into the shadow of his chair. Miranda continued to play. Harry, like a magician turned his guitar into a trumpet, and blew ornate sounds towards the ceiling.

'And his name was Aiken Drum.'

'For God's sake, Harry, stop playing the blithering fool.'

There was a moment's silence, then Harry laughed uneasily.

'My dear chap, it's a ladle I'm playing. I'm surprised that a m-man of y-your taste and d-discernment d-d-d . . .'

Miranda put a hand on his shoulder and stood up.

'Maybe it's you who's playing the fool.' She moved towards her brother. Her voice was low. 'Maybe you've had too much to drink. Of course she was your mother, darling. You knew and loved her. To me she's only a shadow, one of Nanny's stories.'

Harry played four sonorous chords on the piano.

'Why don't we play bridge?'

He spoke hopefully to the company, but no one paid him any heed.

Andrew was standing over his father, staring down at the figure crumpled in the chair.

'You didn't know her. You didn't try to know her. You . . .'

'B-b-bridge? I'm a whizzer at bridge. Ask Andrew.'

'. . . never bothered about me either. From the moment she died you never gave me a thought. You treated me as you had treated her.'

Mr Martin moved cautiously in his chair as if he were afraid of some physical attack from his son.

'Miranda's right . . .' he began.

'Do you play bridge, sir?'

Miranda took hold of her brother's arm and pulled gently at it, but he shook her off.

'I'm saying what I have to say, so don't paw at me, sister.'

Her eyes had become nervous with tears.

'Poker perhaps. P-p-p-p . . .'

She turned away from Andrew and stepped towards him, the red dress rustling softly as she moved. He put out a hard towards her and she smiled. Her eyes dazzled. She didn't take his hand.

'Why do you stammer?'

She whispered the question to him.

He shook his head. He had never known. No one had ever told him.

'You were polite and kind to me, just as you were to her. You never forgot my birthday . . . even in the bloody trenches your birthday greetings arrived, but if I'd fallen off a horse and broken my neck, like she did, or been blown up . . . blown up, you'd have just shrugged your shoulders and gone back to your books . . . your trees . . . your crazy dreams.'

'You speak such passionate nonsense. Wilful nonsense. You don't . . .' murmured Mr Martin.

'Who ever wanted to hear about your crazy dreams?'

'You've had too much to drink.'

'I can do card tricks.'

Miranda laughed.

'Can you really. I'll get a pack of cards. I absolutely love card tricks.'

'Give your brother some coffee.'

'I don't want coffee. Let's leave your father to his musty old papers and his bog men. That's what she used to say.'

'Here.' Angrily, Miranda poured some coffee into a cup and left it standing on the silver tray. 'Much good it will do you.'

She disappeared into the darkness across the room and began opening and shutting drawers.

'Bog talk. That was all you ever wanted. You never seemed to realise how she longed for company, a civilised life, intelligent conversation. All she ever had here was your eternal gabbling about drainage schemes and shelter belts. Little did she know what so much of your bog talk was about.' He ignored the coffee.

'Shoes and ships and sealing wax and cabbages and kings.'

'Just the idiotic sort of remark you used to make to her.'

Miranda reappeared into the light waving a pack of cards. 'No more argufying, Andrew. We're all going to watch Harry do card tricks.'

She handed Harry the pack and settled herself on the floor at his feet, the red dress spread around her.

'I've seen all his card tricks before. He only has four.'

'There's friendship for you.'

Harry shuffled and riffled the pack like a professional.

'There have been so many misunderstandings in the past. I suppose I must blame myself for . . . yes . . . indeed I must . . . son . . .'

'Sh-shuffle. You shuffle now.'

He handed the pack to Miranda. Her fingers fumbled with them.

'Do stop quibbling, you two. Father, look, pay attention. Harry's about to dazzle us with his magic.'

'You must realise how happy I was . . . when I . . . how very, very happy . . . when you and your friend . . . It seemed to me such a joyful moment. Yes. Perhaps you are right when you say these things about me . . .'

'I'm sorry, Father.'

As if to make an amend of some sort he bent down and picked the tiny cup from the tray and drained the coffee from it.

'Cold. Ugh.'

'Pick a card.'

'I just feel so battered . . . it's the only word I can use . . . battered.'

'Don't tell me, just remember it. Pop it back, right in the middle there. That's the girl.'

'I didn't mean to make her unhappy.'

'I shuffle now.'

Magician's hands, cards flying.

'No hanky panky, Harry.'

'I don't suppose you did. I don't suppose you gave it much thought.'

'Absolutely no hanky panky.'

'Battered.'

'Now, tell me a number. Any number up to fifty-two.'

'Andrew, a number. Quick. Tell him a number.'

Andrew laughed suddenly. A light and pleasant laugh.

'Don't be fooled by him, sister. He has it up his sleeve. It's why his coats always have such terrible baggy sleeves.'

'A number.'

'Baggy-sleeved Harrington, he's known as in the mess.'

'Andrew! A number.'

'Seventeen, if you insist.'

'Righty ho.' Harry started to count the cards onto the little table beside him. 'One, two, three . . .'

Why does Andrew have to say what he feels all the time, she thought. Why can't he let us be happy, just for two days? We could just sit here by the fire and laugh or sing round the piano. Why does he burn so much? It's so good when we're laughing.

'. . . seven, eight, nine . . .'

The door opened and Nanny came in slowly. She closed the door behind her with great care, her old trembling hand turning the knob, clutching at it as if she might fall down if she let it go. They watched her in silence.

'The sheets are fresh from the hot press and there are jars in the beds.'

Miranda grinned up at Harry.

The old woman turned from the door and moved slowly towards them.

'Ten, eleven, twelve . . .' Harry whispered the words, his hands moving, his eyes on the old woman.

'I wouldn't want ye to be worrying about damp.'

She looked sharply from face to face.

Hawk eyes, thought Miranda, getting the measure of us, seeing everything.

'It's well after eleven now. You shouldn't be keeping the master up so late. He's up with the lark, rain or shine and away out before breakfast looking at his old trees.'

'Fourteen . . . f-f-f-'

'He needs to get his little bit of sleep. He's not getting any younger.'

Mr Martin laughed.

'Nanny . . .'

'And it's time you were in bed, young lady.'

'Shush Nanny, shush a minute. Can't you see he's doing a trick.'

'Sixteen, seventeen. The three of clubs. Right or wrong?' He waved the card triumphantly above his head.

'It's right. Absolutely right. How clever. Isn't that clever? Father, were you paying attention? Now, you must tell me how you did it.'

'Baggy sleeves,' said Andrew.

'It was magic,' said Harry. 'Total magic.'

'I suppose,' said Nanny, fixing her eyes on Harry. 'Ye do have the electricity at home?'

'Y-yes oh yes. We do indeed.'

She sighed.

'It would be great to have the electricity. I keep telling the master he should get it. Keep up with the times. No one ever listens.'

'It's not as easy as all that, Nanny.' Mr Martin's voice was gentle as he spoke to her. 'We'll get it one day. I promise you that. Everyone in the country'll have it one day.'

'And poor old Nan'll not be here to see it.'

The hawk's eyes moved towards Andrew who cleared his throat uneasily. He took his empty glass from the mantelpiece.

'Well . . . yes . . . ah Nanny . . . yes. I'll just have one more drink and then I'll be off to bed.'

'You'll do no such thing.'

'We'll all go to bed. Won't we? A long day . . .' His voice faded.

'You've had more than is good for you, my lad. I can see it in your face. Give that glass here to me.'

She held her hand out towards him. For a moment he hesitated and then like a good as gold child he put the glass into the waiting hand.

'Thank you. You'll just come up with me now and I'll see you into your bed.'

Andrew didn't move. Miranda stared up at her great-grandfather who scowled down from the wall.

Nanny's voice rose to a slightly higher pitch.

'Come along, Andrew, when you're told and take that impudent look off your face. March.' She pointed towards the door.

'Nanny . . .'

'Not a word. March, I said.'

He began to move slowly across the room. She moved in behind him to cut off any retreat he might have been thinking of making.

'And you're not to go opening the windows, letting the night's fumes into your lungs. We don't want you taking sick on us. I've enough on my hands as it is.'

Near the door he faltered and looked back pleadingly at the three by the fire.

'March,' said Nanny.

He opened the door and they both marched out into the hall. There was an explosion of laughter as the door closed.

'Oh G-G-G-God. Oh marv-v-vellous . . .'

'I'm sorry . . .' began Mr Martin after he had stopped laughing.

'The B-British army need men like her.'

'I'm . . .'

'Don't say a word, sir. He gets a bit worse for the wear from time to time. We all d-do.'

'Cold coffee or no cold coffee, I think I'll have to have another thimbleful after that.'

He started to push himself up from the chair.

'I'll do it, Father. Harry . . . more for you?'

He shook his head.

'No thanks. No more for me. T-too much coffee keeps me awake.'

He shuffled the cards together and put them back in their box.

'That's an old wives' tale, if ever I heard one.'

She handed her father his cup of coffee as she spoke and then bent down and kissed him on the top of his head. He looked up at her surprised, and smiled.

'No, I assure you. After more than the smallest amount of coffee I suffer from p-palpitations, stomach c-cramps and the most g-ghastly insomnia. I lie there hour upon hour counting platoons, companies, b-battalions all crawling on their stomachs under the wire.'

He banged the box of cards against the arm of the chair, a drumbeat Miranda thought it sounded like.

'Some men whose faces I've never seen before and men who I . . . and m-men . . . and m-men . . . thousands of them . . . all going out.' He laughed suddenly. 'It's the coffee.'

'I recommend you to try counting sheep like everyone else. Just jumping neatly over a small hedge. That can be very soporific.' He put the box down on the table.

'Sheep.' He laughed again. 'Y-yes. I must try counting . . .'

'You look so young.'

Mr Martin handed the empty cup to his daughter.

'So untouched by anything. Of course when you get to my age, everyone under forty looks young. You do look untouched.' He stood up and took a step towards Harry, searching his face for signs of tragedy. He shook his head.

'I must take my old bones to bed, or I'll have Nanny down chivvying me as well. We all have to do as we're told in this house. So, if you'll forgive me.'

Harry got to his feet politely. Mr Martin held out his hand.

'I bid you goodnight, young man. I hope you won't have too much trouble with the companies and platoons tonight.'

Harry touched the outstretched hand for a moment.

'Not here, sir . . . Not in this place.'

'You'll see to the lamps, Miranda?'

'Don't worry, darling. Goodnight.'

They kissed, cheeks touched cheeks, like the French do, thought Harry.

Neither of the young people spoke as they watched him cross the room and open the door. He turned and bowed towards them.

'Sweet dreams,' said Miranda.

She moved around the room in silence, bending towards each lamp, her face glowing for a moment in the light and then disappearing into darkness as she blew out each flame. The red dress lost its brilliance as the light diminished. As she went towards the last lamp he moved over towards her.

'M-M-Miranda . . .'

'You see,' she said, frowning down towards the light. 'You turn this little screw and then give a little blow. Here, you try.'

He fumbled with his hands, the wick flared up.

'Mind . . .' She took control.

'I could sit and talk to you for hours.'

'Don't touch the mantel or you'll burn yourself. Goodness you people with electricity are such noodles. Here, blow now . . . blow.' Obediently, he blew and the room was in darkness save for the light from the hall that lay in a bright stripe on the floor.

She moved away from him, treading on the path of light and her dress murmured as she walked.

'Promise . . . you'll teach me your card tricks tomorrow.'

'I'll promise no such thing.'

There was one lamp left in the hall at the bottom of the stairs. The shadows of the banisters quivered on the wall. The men in their frames seemed to sleep. She bent over the lamp and her shadow engulfed the hall.

'You go on up,' she said, 'there's a lamp on the landing, you won't lose your way.'

'I'll do it. I c-can. Let me.'

Her fingers were on the screw. He felt them warm under his. Her eyes were filled with yellow light.

'Don't set the house on fire,' she said and left him. She ran up the stairs and her shadow moved too, a giant shadow. He bent and blew and the shadow disappeared. She laughed from the landing.

'Goodnight Harry. How clever you are.'

'Sweet dreams. Sweet d-d-dreams.'

*   *   *

How easy it is to forget that the world exists.

Of all of us Cathal was the only one who saw any reality at all.

He was perhaps the only one who knew how to love.

That sounds mad, but we were all so busy loving our notions of ourselves, that we had no energy left to offer love outside ourselves. Except maybe Harry, but then Harry never belonged here like we all did.

Harry was cool fresh air when someone leaves a window open on a hot summer day.

Harry was seduced by us, by Termon, by Ireland, I suppose, like so many people are. He saw us in radiant autumn light casting giant shadows. We were never plain, pain-filled people to him.

I never discovered about his stammer. He only smiled and shook his head when I asked him about it. Very English that, not wanting to disclose things. Maybe it's admirable.

I never could have married him.

For years he used to write me delightful letters, each one ending with the same proposal. After the first three or four I stopped refusing him, I just took it for granted that he knew I meant no, forever.

Forever.

That awful word.

Nothing is forever; not even the long beach and the rocks below the house; down the years they have taken on a new shape; old rocks here, now covered with sand, new shapes uncovered there. Today there is a deep rock pool near the bottom of the path that didn't exist all those years ago. In it small crabs scurry sideways, weed moves, acid-green fronds, sometimes the flash of a tiny fish can be seen through the reflected sky. Only the very highest tides reach it, wash it out.

No forever.

I loved Cathal and then he became a dream.

There is no one left who will dream of me.

My back aches.

Cathal's pale arms were spiked with black hairs to just above his elbows and above that the pale skin of his shoulders was smooth and soft, waiting for the summer, waiting to brown again when he came back to Termon, to the long beach and the curling waves, to me.

Up my back and out round my pale shoulders the burning fire of dying smoulders all the time.

Someone is there.

Someone is always there.

I don't need to be afraid, they say. I am not afraid, only disturbed by pain.

I suppose they shot him in the head.

We never knew.

Shattering his gaunt face, the rock-pool eyes in which I had seen my own reflection. I see that shattering sometimes in nightmares. That wasteful spilling.

Is it the pain that makes me think such thoughts?

If the pain would only go I could see again, hear the voices.

If I cry out?

Yes, then they come.

They come to my call, to the sound I make.

They know how to rearrange my bones.

*   *   *

In the early mornings the shadow of the hill lies dark on the beach and distorts and discolours the opaqueness of the bay with its green and grey shades and the shivering of the trees.

That morning there was still blue in the sky and clouds seemed to hang unmoving in the air. Tiny waves flickered on the horizon and white birds' wings were caught by the sun as it moved up from the east.

Cathal stood alone in the shadow of the hill; not even one bird pecked its way along the sea's edge.

Forlorn, she thought as she ran down the path.

He never turned, though he must have heard her running feet. She had to touch his shoulder before he moved.

'Statue,' she said. 'Good morning, statue.'

He turned then towards her and they threw their arms around each other and stood locked to each other, not saying a word, not kissing, not moving, each one staring into the other's reflecting eyes. Only the sea breathed and wings and waves flickered far away.

'Oh Jesus Christ, I am such a fool.'

He spoke the words after such a long time that she had almost given up hope of hearing his voice.

'A fool?'

'I thought you wouldn't come. I thought . . .'

She took his hand and squeezed it hard against her warm morning face.

'I always come.'

'They . . .'

'They have nothing to do with us.'

'That is too easy to say.'

'It's true. You mustn't make things complicated, Cathal. Nothing can ever make me change the way I feel.'

He smiled at her.

'All over the world people are saying that to each other. A million people at this moment are saying just those words.'

'What a horrible thought. I don't like it when you say things like that.'

'Are you going to swim?'

'A quick dash in and out. You?'

'No. I've got out of the habit. I'm staying on dry land until next summer now.'

She pulled off her dressing gown and handed it to him and ran quickly into the sea. The beach shelved quite quickly and she was swimming in a moment. She made a large circle in the water, disturbing the reflections and then came ashore again.

'Freezing,' she said taking the dressing gown from him. She put it on and then wriggled out of her togs clumsily. 'But healthy, very very healthy.' She shook her head like a dog. 'It's great having no hair. Run.' She stood on her toes and kissed him with her wet lips, a cold salty taste in his mouth.

'Run on home. I'll see you at lunchtime.'

'Are you sure?'

'I'm running.'

She ran back up towards the path.

'Of course, I'm sure.'

As she panted up the path she waved. He turned and walked slowly along the beach, past the grey standing rocks; alone, slowly, along the long beach, back to the world.

What black bird is like that, she wondered, as she watched him, treading with such care? What long-legged black bird, his head slightly poked as if he were looking for worms in the damp sand?

As she came up towards the house and round the corner by Nanny's tree she heard a voice declaiming.

'Awake! For morning in the bowl of light

Has flung the stone that puts the stars to flight.'

Harry stood in the open window of his bedroom and his voice carried out over the lawn.

'And lo . . .'

He bowed courteously in her direction as he spoke the word.

'L-lo the Hunter of the East has caught

The Sultan's Turret in a noose of Light. Good morning beautiful lady.'

She waved her wet togs at him. 'How poetic you are so early in the morning.'

'I was very expensively educated. A terrible waste of money really. I c-can't remember the next line.'

She laughed.

His pyjamas were pale blue silk with dark blue piping. Most unmilitary, she thought.

'Is it early?' he asked. 'I've been standing here for ages watching the old Hunter of the East catching things. I saw you running down the path . . . to the sea? Was that where you went? Sherlock Harrington deduces you have been swimming.'

She went rather red in the face.

'I . . .'

'Can that be good for you? It's October after all. Or am I being old-fashioned?'

'I go down to watch the birds. The beach in the early morning belongs to the birds. They dance.'

'And you swim. I nearly came after you but then I thought that m-maybe . . . m . . . m . . .'

He paused and looked at her. She was dusting the sand from her feet, stooping down, fingers flicking.

'You ran through the mist. Here one minute and gone the next. You might have been a ghost for all I knew . . . Do you know . . . ?'

He leaned dangerously out of the window towards her. She looked up at him and smiled.

'What?'

'I really expected to f-find myself tucked up in the barracks when I woke this morning. It was such a relief to find all this . . . and you . . . and there is this most romantic smell wafting . . . w-wafting . . .'

'Smell?'

Miranda wrinkled up her nose and sniffed.

'Bacon and eggs.'

She laughed.

'What a dreadful fraud you are. Omar Khayyam and bacon and eggs don't go together at all.'

'Alas, I have to admit to being e-e-essentially a bacon and eggs m-man.'

'You're a clown. I'm cold. I must go and get dressed. I don't usually hang about after my swim.'

She moved away, crunching over the gravel towards the side door of the house.

'It's nice to have a clown around the place. Hurry up and get dressed, clown, or Andrew'll have eaten all the bacon.'

'I'll just throw on some clothes, and then I'll be down.'

'Not your beastly uniform I hope.'

She was gone in through the door. He heard it close below him.

'C-casual tweeds,' he said to the air. 'I h-had thought of casual t-t-t . . .'

✻   ✻   ✻

Breakfast over, Mr Martin beckoned Andrew into his study. Books were scattered and piled everywhere. On three easels were large detailed maps of different parts of the estate, the new plantings carefully shaded in. Out into the bay reclaimed land and that in the process of reclamation were marked in different colours. The side of the hill between the village and the sea were well covered now by a forest of conifers. A system of dykes and drains covered the low lying fields near the sea.

Andrew looked at the maps without saying a word. Behind him at his desk Mr Martin pulled more maps from under a pile of papers and spread them out.

'I thought you'd be interested to see . . . It's been so long . . . you haven't . . . I've always been so bad at writing.'

'I don't really understand.'

His father came over and stood looking at the maps in front of them.

'Those ones are just showing the place in general . . . the whole place. You see that's the village and the home fields, here the land right down to the bay, and that one there is Old Termon and the hills. I have it all here in much more detail. If you're interested. Look, there, that red shading, that's all reclaimed land, several hundred acres. Dillon and I thought that system up ourselves. Look . . .' He almost ran back to his desk.

'See. Look here . . . if you're interested. It's a sort of cross-hatching of drains. If you're interested.'

Andrew didn't move.

'We even went to Holland. Dillon and I. Spent a week there. I'm sure I must have written and told you about that. Fascinating.'

'It must have been.'

'I racked my brains and then I thought why on earth not go to Holland. Of course we made a couple of terrible mistakes but it all worked out in the end. I've written a very interesting paper . . .'

He looked at his son in silence for a moment.

'Paper,' he repeated. 'Yes. It was published in the *Journal of Forestry and Estate Management*. Of course it is all tied in together with re-afforestation plans . . . I mean that was why they were interested. Quite a learned publication . . . I can show you . . .'

He turned towards the book shelves behind him.

'I see you haven't changed.'

'Changed? All those pamphlets there, those are mine. You must read . . . Why should I have changed?'

He looked worried for a moment.

'Should I have changed?'

'Times are changing.'

'Yes. Yes that's true indeed. I really feel now that my work is coming to a head. Soon very soon I will have something to offer. I need Charlie Dillon's help for a couple of weeks. He makes me keep my nose to the grindstone and then all my facts and findings, all those experiments, all gathered together . . . that's, you see where he comes in. He seems to be able to put some order into my chaos. I am in the middle now of getting my proposals down on paper.'

'What proposals?'

'It's a comprehensive scheme, my boy . . . I'm not just talking about this place. I have been in the privileged position of being able to carry out my experiments here, but I'm talking about Ireland.'

He looked at his son with triumph.

'Ireland. Plans for deciduous forests and huge belts of shelter, quick-growing trees for cropping, tree farming, you've heard, I'm sure, of tree farming . . . that will be part of my scheme. You know we destroyed the land when we cut down the forests.'

'Oh come, Father, isn't that a little melodramatic?'

'No. No. I'm certain of that . . . Planting combined with major drainage schemes. Thousands and thousands of acres of derelict, abandoned land can, must be given new heart. Think of what that'll mean to the people.'

'Wild mad dreams.'

'No.'

'And when you have all this stuff gathered together, what are you intending to do with it?'

'Present it of course.'

Andrew laughed.

'To whom do you intend to present your opus?'

'I . . .'

'Who the hell will care?'

'Our own government. We will have a government of our own before too long, I believe. If they care at all for the future of the country . . . the land . . .'

'God! Father, you are an old fool. Even if you do have a government of your own they won't even begin to know what you're talking about. They'll be a bunch of jumped-up gunmen. What makes you think they'll be interested in drainage schemes?'

Mr Martin sighed.

'I think we must agree to differ in our views about this country. If you had chosen to spend more time at home . . .'

'Home! This hasn't been my home since Mother died.'

'That was the way you seemed to want things to be.'

'You never asked me, did you? You never appeared to care.'

There was the sound of voices in the hall and Miranda's laughter.

'Did you?'

Mr Martin raised his hands in a helpless gesture.

'Andrew. Hey ho, hey ho hey.'

The door opened and Miranda put her head around.

'My goodness, you both look cross,' she said. 'Come on Andrew. We've even brought your nag to the door for you. It's far too nice a day to stuff inside. I bet you've been rowing with Father. I'll tell Nanny on you.'

She disappeared, and then as she crossed the hall she called back to her father.

'By the way, I've asked Cathal to lunch. You don't have to worry, I've told Cook. Do come on, Andrew. We're not going to wait all day for you.'

Andrew made no move.

'You'd better go,' said his father. 'She's right. The weather could change at any moment.'

He sat down and pulled some papers towards him, picked up his pen, bent his head, perhaps forgot his son standing there in the room.

Andrew stood for a moment watching him and then went out, closing the door quietly behind him, to join his sister.

* * *

It was strange galloping without the weight of hair around my neck.

Freedom.

I was quite sedate and they rampaged like a pair of school-children.

Freedom.

The strain left Andrew's face as we cantered along the strand.

Our faces were polished by the warm almost sultry breeze that blew from the west. We jumped low stone walls and galloped in and out of the sea making absurd patterns over the sand. We scrambled up the hillside to the ruins of Old Termon and looked back across the bay at this house, warm, secure, its chimneys streaming flags of smoke, its windows alive with sun. We skirted the edges of one of Father's new plantations, and leaving the horses munching grass we climbed across one of his dykes and walked to the sandhills facing out to the ocean.

Light and shade as the clouds moved; our faces shadowy at moments became unveiled as the sun appeared again.

Shade and light. Concealment and revelation.

Weed floated just below the surface of the sea, great acres of it, disappearing when the sun went behind a cloud and reappearing again, heavy weighted, like my hair had been just a few days before. We laughed in the light and shade, insubstantial laughter, that the wind shook away like the calling of the sea birds, forever lost.

I remember the light and shade.

* * *

They were of course late for lunch.

When they came into the dining room Mr Martin and Cathal were standing somewhat dispiritedly sipping sherry from old cut glasses.

Miranda's face was bright with pleasure and sunshine. She rushed across the room and threw her arms around her father.

'Darling Father, I'm sorry we're late. It's all my fault, I forgot about the time. We've had a marvellous ride. Cathal hello. Mea maxima culpa.'

She took two steps towards him and then stopped.

'Ttt,' muttered Mr Martin who liked his meals on time.

He moved towards the table. 'You'll have to have your sherry at the table. Cook will be in a terrible rage otherwise.'

He pulled out a chair and indicated to Harry to sit down. 'You see, young man, I am at the mercy of my servants.'

Miranda laughed.

'Don't mind him. He's a demon for punctuality. Cathal, you sit there next to Andrew.'

'Have you met Andrew's friend, Charlie . . . Captain . . . ah . . . ?'

'Who wants a glass of sherry?'

Andrew took the stopper from the decanter.

'Sister? Good morning Charlie. Sherry Harry?'

'We met yesterday on the beach. Good morning, or sh-should I say g-good afternoon. Sherry? Yes please.'

Cathal muttered something and sat down.

'Charlie hopes to have time to help me get all my papers in order. Ring the bell, Miranda, and let them know you're back. In another few weeks he'll have time to put his orderly mind to it. Yes. He has a far more orderly mind than I do. Mind you . . .'

Miranda crossed the room and pulled the rope by the fire-place. In the far distance they could hear the clatter of metal or metal.

Mr Martin leaned across the table towards his son.

'. . . mind you . . . like you he tends to be a bit sceptical.'

Andrew laughed good-humouredly as he sat down.

'I'm not a bit sceptical, Father. I'm totally sceptical.'

His father turned to Harry.

'I hope you enjoyed your ride. Where did they take you?'

'Over the hills and far away. Qu-quite b-b-b-'

'We put him on Topsy, just to see how he would manage her. He doesn't ride badly, for an Englishman.'

As she passed Cathal's chair she put her hand lightly on his shoulder for a moment. He turned and looked up at her, his eyes sombre.

'How many times have I told you not to be unkind to visitors?'

'Don't worry about me, sir,' said Harry. 'I can look out for myself. That's a terrible, bad-tempered little mare though. She n-nearly had me off several times.'

Miranda laughed. 'It's true. It was really funny, wasn't it, Andrew.'

Andrew smiled briefly.

'She nearly had him into a whin bush . . . you should have seen his face.'

Two young girls came into the room with dishes which they put on the sideboard.

Andrew turned to Cathal.

'I gather you don't work here?'

'That's right.'

One of the girls moved round the table putting a plate in front of each person.

'I presumed you did. If I remember right you always wanted to. You used to look forward to stepping, so to speak, into your father's shoes.'

'Times have changed. You've been away a very long time. Thank you,' he said as a plate landed in front of him. 'A lot of things have happened in the last few years.'

'I had noticed.' Andrew's voice was sarcastic.

'Yes,' said Cathal. His eyes flicked towards Miranda. She smiled briefly and looked down at her plate.

'So . . . if I may ask . . . what . . . ?'

Cathal took up his knife and fork and attacked the food in front of him.

'I turned out to be able to read and write . . . when I put my mind to it.'

'We went to Old Termon,' said Miranda to her father.

'Ah.'

He turned towards the guest.

'They probably explained. That was where the house originally stood. A sort of fortified farmhouse. You will have seen the shell, of course. It was built to withstand marauders, but was somewhat vulnerable to winter storms. So my great-great-great-grandfather decided that the time had come for comfortable living and he built this house. Shelter. We have a modicum of shelter here.'

'If you don't work here,' continued Andrew, 'where do you work?'

'Termon.' Mr Martin raised his voice. 'Means sanctuary. It's from the Irish you know. Tearmann. That's approximately correct, isn't it, Charlie? I crack my tongue on the Irish language, I'm afraid.'

Cathal smiled and nodded.

'Tearmann,' he repeated the word.

'Sanctuary,' repeated Mr Martin.

'A u-useful name to have in times like th-th-th-'

'How do you pass your time? Earn your living? If I may be so inquisitive.'

'Oh Andrew, don't be such a bore.' Miranda leant across the table towards her brother. 'He's at college of course.'

Andrew looked startled. 'Good Lord!'

Cathal gave a little laugh.

'It even surprises me sometimes.'

'You mean to say you're at Trinity?'

'No. The other one.'

Andrew put a piece of cauliflower into his mouth and chewed it for a moment before speaking.

'Yes. Yes of course. The National University. Yes. Your parents must be very proud of you.'

'Tell me, sir, do you have any b-bother round here?'

'Bother?'

Mr Martin looked surprised.

Cathal spoke in a low voice to Andrew, almost whispering. 'It was your father. He pushed me. He also fought a lot of battles for me. They never would have considered such a thing if he hadn't . . .'

'You do surprise me.'

'Trouble with the Shinners, that sort of thing? You know what I mean.'

'We'll be cubbing next week. Can't you stay a few days longer? Wouldn't that be fun, Father, if they could stay a few days longer?'

'Bother.' Mr Martin frowned at the word. 'No. No bother here.'

'I j-just . . .'

'I promise not to put you on Topsy again.'

'This is a very peaceful part of the world. Will you have some more cauliflower? Do help yourself if you will. We always help ourselves at lunchtime.'

'I'd love some more.' He pushed his chair back and stood up. 'I'm simply ravenous after all that fresh air. Miranda, can I get you some?'

She shook her head.

'Anyone else for c-c-?'

There was silence around the table.

'Just help yourself, my boy.'

Harry, plate in hand, went over to the sideboard.

Andrew placed his knife and fork meticulously beside each other on his plate.

'What are you reading?'

'Philosophy,' replied Cathal.

There was a moment's silence, then Andrew threw back his head and laughed.

'Philosophy!'

'I'm glad it amuses you.'

'Where do you think that'll get you? A lot of damn fool words, ideas. Who needs that sort of thing? It only confuses people. Who?'

He stared into Cathal's face, but didn't give him time to answer.

'Churchmen and scholars maybe and perhaps a handful of high-falutin writers. Are you intending to enter the Church? No. I don't suppose you are. Philosophy! Hear that, Harry?' He tilted his chair back and looked across the room at his friend. 'Hear that?'

Harry cleared his throat and put the lid back on the vegetable dish. He came back to the table and sat down. Miranda's face looked slightly fearful.

'Yes,' he said quietly. 'I h-hear.'

'Yes,' he said. Jokes, jokes, jokes he thought, that's what we need now.

'Tell me, Charlie, what do you intend to do with your philosophy? Hey?'

'I thought I might have a stab at changing the world. It's quite useful to have a clear mind if you want to do that.'

'What makes you think the world needs changing?'

'P.H.I.L.' Harry patted some cauliflower onto his fork as he spoke the letters.

'I have my eyes. You too have eyes.'

'I think . . .' said Miranda. She looked towards her father. He was staring out of the window.

'Tell me more about changing the world, Charlie. I'm interested. Are you inv . . .'

'Father . . . Father . . .'

'P.H.I.L.O.S.O.P.H.Y.'

He banged his hands on the table and the silver rattled. 'I can spell it. I was b-best in my form at spelling. Do you know . . .'

He turned to Miranda. He reached out and took her hand and held it gently in his.

'Egypt was the last word in my spelling book, don't you think that's odd? I never could understand why. I mean, after all, it isn't the most difficult word in the world to spell, is it? E.G.Y.P.T. Simple. Even the Gyppos themselves could get that one r-r-ri . . . Andrew, why didn't you tell me that you had a b-b-beautiful sister?'

Miranda wriggled her hand out from his fingers. Her face was red. 'B.E.A.U.T.I.F . . .'

Cathal stood up.

'I think, sir, if you'll excuse me.'

They all stared in silence at the tall figure, the lank hands dangling by his sides. Mr Martin sighed and then gestured with the stiff, white napkin that he had in his hand.

'Sit down, my boy. Don't be nonsensical. You must learn . . .' he thought for a moment . . . 'learn . . .' He dabbed at his mouth with the napkin. 'I want you young people to become friends.' He looked around the table, only Harry looked back into his eyes.

'Sit down, Charlie. Finish your lunch.'

Cathal didn't move.

'Cathal . . .'

Miranda gestured across the table towards his chair.

'I'm sorry, sir . . .' He spoke the words very quietly.

'What's all this Cathal business anyway? His name is Charlie. Why do you call him Cathal?'

'I prefer Cathal.' Cathal spoke before Miranda could reply. 'You can call me what you want, but just remember that I prefer Cathal.' He turned to Mr Martin and gave an awkward bow, rather grotesque. 'I am sorry, sir, but I really do have to go. I'm late as it is already for . . .'

'How w-w-would you spell Cathal?'

'An appointment. I have an appointment I have to keep.'

'Charles is Cathal,' Miranda explained to her brother.

'Charles is Cathal?'

'In Gaelic. So sir, if you'll excuse me. I really shouldn't have . . . but . . .' He glanced at Miranda. 'But . . .'

'Oh God,' said Andrew. 'I might have known.'

'Run along, my boy, if you have to. I do believe there's an excellent pudding. It'll be a pity to miss that. But . . .'

Cathal moved towards the door.

'You'll be back won't you? Before you return to Dublin? There are a lot . . .'

'C.A.H.I.L.L.'

Harry looked around for approval.

Miranda laughed.

'I'll be back as soon as I can. I'm just not sure. As soon as I can.'

'C-ca-hill?'

'C.A.T.H.A.L. If you're interested.' He was gone out of the door.

Harry looked startled. 'Now who would have thought of that.'

'Cathal!'

Miranda jumped up from her chair and ran after him.

'Wait.'

She ran across the hall and caught at his arm as he stopped to open the front door.

'Don't let Andrew upset you. Cathal . . . He's such a tease. That's all. Don't you remember? He always used to tease us. Make me cry. Don't you remember?'

He stood by the open door and the wind flickered into the house past them and stirred the rugs on the floor and even the heavy fringes on the curtains looped back in the archway between the front hall and the staircase hall.

'The wind is getting up.'

He stared out at the gathering clouds.

She pinched her fingers into his arm.

'You were able for him then.'

He smiled and touched her face gently with a finger.

'It's not Andrew. I'm able for Andrew any time. He can be so abominable, but it's not that. I shouldn't have come at all. A message came . . . but I didn't want you to think . . . and then you were so late back . . .'

'A message?'

He nodded and drew her out onto the step, into the wind, and she shivered a little.

'A message? What message?'

'I've been ordered to a meeting. There was a note waiting when I got back this morning.'

He took her hand and put it to his lips.

'What do you . . . ? Why? Cathal . . . why?'

'I don't know.'

He spoke into her fingers and his fingers that held tight onto hers were trembling.

'I hope to God they're not going to shove me into an active service unit, just now with the exams . . . I'm late as it is.' He let go her hand and they stood looking at each other. A drop of rain exploded on the step beside Miranda's feet.

'It's gone,' she said. 'Oh dear, dear Cathal.'

'What's gone?'

Another drop and then two more. The steps were becoming freckled with raindrops.

'The illusion of happiness. It was here for a moment. In spite of . . . in . . . for a moment, but it's gone. You'll take care, won't you?'

'Yes. I'll take care.'

'You'll get wet. It's going to pour.'

He moved down the steps and then stopped and looked back at her.

'That Harry . . . ?'

She laughed.

'He's good company for you, isn't he?'

'He's a joker. It's good to meet a joker from time to time. You have no cause to worry. I told you that this morning. I meant it. Go along now and please take care.'

He nodded.

She watched him down the steps and then trudging down the avenue. The wind pulled at the back of his coat and he had to keep his hand to his hat. The leaves on the chestnut trees were trembling; ready to fall at last.

✻　✻　✻

I was twenty-nine when Father died.

Yes.

It was almost evening when I came in the door. Spring cold; spring, neither day nor night. The lights were on in the room; the electricity that Nanny had pestered on and on about. The curtains were not yet pulled and the grey devouring dusk pressed on the windows.

He was sitting in his big chair by the fire, his glasses balanced comically on the end of his nose.

He had never got used to wearing glasses; never found the knack of balancing them on the bridge of his nose; they used to slip, tilt, fall askew, if he moved his head quickly in any direction.

The door creaked as I opened it and walked into the room. He looked up from the paper, his glasses as I said balanced comically on the end of his nose.

'Miranda.'

That was all.

I never knew what he was going to say to me.

Maybe he just wanted to speak my name at that last moment. We were then both surprised by death.

The paper folded neatly, as he always folded it, slithered from his hands to the floor.

I stood in the doorway, my hair wet from evening rain and watched the paper slither to the floor, listened to the sliding sound of it, listened to the echo of my name.

'It's absolutely foul out,' I said, in answer to what I thought was his greeting.

His head just nodded forward onto his chest, like an old man dropping off to sleep.

'I'll pull the curtains.'

I moved towards the window as I spoke the words into the emptiness.

'. . . keep the cold out.'

I looked over my shoulder towards him, surprised at the emptiness of the room. The paper lay on the floor beside his right foot. A flame fluttered in the fireplace and his face trembled in golden light.

'Father . . .'

I stopped halfway to the window. I changed direction and walked across the big room towards him. The standard lamp behind his chair had not been switched on. I put out my hand, still chilly from the open air, and pushed the switch and stood for a moment looking down at him. His silver hair was still thick. He had always been proud of that, one of his few personal vanities. Thick and straight it grew, like the vigorous hair of a young man.

I've heard it said that hair and nails continue to grow for quite a long time after death. I wonder if that's true.

I bent to kiss the thick hair and as I leaned towards him I realised, no, that's not quite the right word . . . I became very slowly aware that there was no longer a person there. I put out a hand and touched his shoulder.

'Yes, it's Miranda. It's Miranda.'

His head sagged sideways and the glasses tipped further again, clinging now somewhat pathetically to the side of his face.

I bent down and took the glasses from his face. I couldn't bear for him to look absurd at that moment.

What should I do?

I stood there with the glasses in my hand, with the flames from the fire casting living tremors onto his skin.

What did people do at such moments?

Scream?

He wouldn't have approved.

Cry?

My heart seemed to be thundering in my ears.

I threw the glasses down onto the nearby table; the table that held on it at that moment a green volume of *Trees and Shrubs Hardy in the British Isles*, Volume Two, carefully annotated on almost every page in his tiny neat black writing, and a brown leather folder containing a lot of his own writings and his silver fountain pen, a present from Andrew the previous Christmas. The glasses clattered down among all those things, precious belongings.

I almost ran across the room and threw up the bottom half of one of the long windows.

I knew I had to do that.

The wind rattled at the window, scattering rain drops onto the floor, struggling to enter to destroy our neat equilibrium of living. I hoped against hope it wouldn't impede the flying spirit.

People will expect me to cry. I thought that. That ought to be the natural thing to do at this moment.

Dear Father.

I thought that, like the beginning of a letter that I was never going to write.

I stood by the window and the wind buffeted me and the rain spattered the floor and my feet; my cold hands, colder than he was when I touched him, hung by my side.

I thought absurd thoughts.

I thought dear Father.

I thought how Nanny would have known what to do.

She would have cried, I thought.

She was a great one for crying at the appropriate moments, but she was practical also, she would have known who to telephone, how to face this moment.

Papers rustled on the table beside him, a wisp of smoke escaped from the chimney and curled into the room and spread into the emptiness.

I will cry tomorrow, I decided.

I am alone now forever.

I will cry when we have performed the rituals.

My tears will be my private tears.

My tears for Cathal were also private tears.

Nineteen years.

At that moment by the window as his soul flew past me, I remembered the taste and heat of those other tears.

Salty taste for weeks in my mouth.

Dolour.

That's a word we don't use much any more.

A weighty word.

I felt the weight of it gathering on my shoulders.

The wind was cold on my ankles.

'I didn't know you were back.'

My heart, expecting only silence, thumped.

I turned and saw Peggy Dillon our housekeeper standing in the doorway.

'I thought I'd better have a look at the fire.'

She began to step heavily across the room.

Her shoes, shining black, creaked as she walked.

'He'd let it out and then be complaining of the cold. Why have you that window open? Miranda?'

She spoke my name sharply.

I couldn't speak. I couldn't think of words to say. My tongue seemed to be filling my mouth, no word could possibly pass the heap of it.

'Miranda! Miss Miranda! He'll catch his death with that window open.'

I hear her rattling in the coal bucket.

Such a normal sound.

But then of course so is death normal; the most normal of all happenings and the one for which we are the least prepared. She shook a shovel of coal onto the fire.

'Miranda, are you listening to me?'

She straightened up. She had rheumatic pains in her back in the winter months and her movements were quite slow. I pushed the window down.

If his spirit hadn't flown by now, I thought, it was because it had chosen to stay where it was.

'Is something the matter with you?'

'No.'

I found the word. I spoke the word.

'Father . . .'

I pointed towards the chair in which he appeared to be sleeping.

Peggy looked down at him; the soft hair, the paper neatly folded on the floor by his right foot.

'He said Miranda when I came into the room . . . and then . . . I think he's dead.'

She looked across the room at me as if I were mad and then bent down towards him. She put one hand tentatively on his knee and then touched his face, something I don't suppose she had ever done in all the years she had been with us, caring for us. She straightened herself again, with obvious pain, and unconsciously wiped her fingers on her overall. She made the sign of the cross.

'God rest his soul.'

'Amen,' I said.

Dear Father . . . amen, amen. My letter was written.

'I'm sure he'll be all right,' I said.

Tears started springing from her eyes. Out of the pocket of her overall she pulled a large white handkerchief and held it tight to her face.

'Oh . . . oh . . . oh . . .'

I ran across the room to her, clumsily dodging as I ran the little tables covered with ornaments and photographs, glad at that moment to have something to do with myself. I put my arms around her and held her tight.

'There, there Peggy. It's all right. He'll be all right. What a great way to die. Look at it like that.'

Great heaving sobs came from her.

'I did my best for him.'

'I know you did. He knew it. We . . .'

'I never could have minded him like old Nanny, but I did my best. God forgive me if I ever said a hard word to him.'

'Don't cry, Peggy. Please . . .'

'Oh . . . oh . . . oh . . . There I was coming into the room thinking he'd have let the fire out and . . .'

She turned from my arms and looked at him.

'Poor Joe.'

She began to cry again.

I wonder for a moment who Joe could have been and then remembered that Mr Dillon's name had been Joe. The first time I had ever heard it used had been at his funeral. Peggy was Mr Dillon's youngest sister. I took hold of her shoulders and pushed her onto the sofa.

'Sit down, Peggy. I'll get you a drink. I think we should both have a drink.'

She shook her head. 'We can't sit here having drinks with him . . . with him . . . It wouldn't be . . . Ooooh.'

I went back to the window and pulled over the curtains; moving to the sound of her moaning from window to window, pulling and smoothing the long silk curtains.

'Are you not crying?' she asked me suddenly.

'Not at the moment. I'm trying to think what we should do.'

'It's the shock,' she said, her voice now more composed. 'I'll be over the shock in a minute or so. Shock takes us all in different ways.'

I nodded.

'I'll ring Mr Malcolm. I think that's the thing to do.'

'Shouldn't we get the poor man to his bed? He looks so uncomfortable like that.'

'No. I'll get the doctor first. He'll know what we should do and then I suppose I'd better ring the colonel. Yes.'

At the thought of Andrew, Peggy began to cry again.

I went over and put my hand on her shoulder. 'He's happy, Peggy. He'll be really happy now.'

'It brings it all back. Joe and . . . and the bad times, Charlie.'

She said the name almost defiantly, as if it were a name she had made her mind up never to say again.

'Yes,' I said and went out to the hall to telephone.

✳　✳　✳

The sound of their footsteps echoed around the hall.

The sound of rain beat against the long window halfway up the stairs.

The sound of the wind battered and then, as if in apology, it sighed.

The sound of Miranda playing Schubert in the drawing room.

As the lamplight trembled, the shadows trembled.

'I've never seen so m-much military paraphernalia hanging on anyone's walls before. Quite gives me the jim-j-jams.'

Mr Martin laughed.

'I have often had the inclination to remove it all. Start again, fresh empty walls, even some of the portraits might go, but then. I feel . . . well you know it's all part of the history of the place. You can't just dispose of the past by hiding things away . . . They were in their way all brave men. They all served with distinction . . .'

He paused and smiled slightly to himself.

'. . . either King or Country.'

'Most people say King and Country.'

'Not in Ireland, my boy. Not in Ireland.'

He opened the drawing-room door and they both went in. Miranda stood up from the piano and came towards them. Even through the closed rich curtains the sound of the drumming rain could be heard.

'See there.'

As Mr Martin continued to talk he waved his hand towards the gilt-framed portrait of a soldier over the fireplace. 'That chap there. Andrew de Poer Martin . . . a fine name. The name Andrew has been in the family a long time . . . tradition . . . you know the way it is. My father was Andrew . . .'

'Before you get too involved, Father, do let me give you both some coffee. Some hot coffee this time. Where's Andrew?'

Mr Martin shook his head impatiently.

'Coffee,' he said.

Harry grinned at her and pointed with this thumb back towards the door.

'De Poer is Norman of course.'

'Of c-course.'

'He raised a troop of horse from round here . . . quite a large number of men I believe and fought under Bagenal Harvey. He was hanged outside Wexford for his pains. He has that look about him don't you think . . . a sort of premonition of disaster in his face? I've always thought so anyway.'

'Probably indigestion,' said Miranda handing him his coffee.

Harry wondered whether to ask who was Bagenal Harvey, but before he could speak, Mr Martin waved his coffee cup in the direction of another picture.

'And that chap there, the one with the red face . . . he was a general in the Peninsular War. And that's my father over there. Yes. The earlier Andrew . . . or rather, I should say, one of the earlier . . . yes. He died in the Crimea. I hardly remember him. Hardly.'

'Half a league, half a league, half a league onward,' whispered Miranda. 'Into the valley of death rode the six hundred.'

'Hardly. Yes. My mother, a most remarkable woman, for her time, lived on her own here for fifty-odd years. He was always away fighting somewhere . . . then . . . well, dying.'

He swallowed the coffee from the tiny cup in one gulp.

'Yes. He died. We brought him back, of course. I think it was quite an effort. We like to take care of our dead in this country. I was the only child they ever got together long enough to make.'

He laughed and handed the cup to Miranda.

'A strong woman. She was the best landlord for miles around. Yes. I don't think you would ever meet anyone to argue with that.'

'Is there no portrait of her?'

'She hadn't the time, she always said, to sit still long enough for her portrait to be painted.'

'Theirs not to make reply,
Theirs but to do or die.
Theirs not to reason why
Someone had blundered.'

'I was the first son for five generations not to wear a uniform of some sort or to indulge in . . . all that useless sort of nonsense. Of course I mean nothing personal. You . . . I mean . . . What a sad world we live in. She made me appreciate their heroism without having to feel the need to follow in their footsteps. I don't mean of course to disparage . . . You do understand, don't you? I do find courage a very admirable attribute.'

He looked anxiously at Harry.

There was a distant rumble of thunder. Miranda shivered and clasped her hands together as if she were about to pray.

'Y-yes sir. I think I understand.'

'I used to know so much poetry. My head was full of it when I was young. I mean about fifteen or sixteen. Now it's all slipping away. I often wonder if it matters. Am I soft in the head or something? I wouldn't like to be soft in the head.

'I look for her every day. Even after all these years. Sometimes when I come down in the morning I expect to see her sitting behind the coffee pot. I have so many questions I want to ask her. I have neither her strength nor her resolution. Maybe Miranda will be filled with resolution . . . and energy of course, that's important too . . . I don't know.

'I used to sit up in my room and learn reams of poetry. I must have learnt half the poems that were ever written. That's what if felt like anyway.'

The thunder rumbled nearer and the windows rattled nervously in their frames.

Miranda gave a little gasp.

'I'm quite foolish about thunder. I do get frightened.'

She spoke the words to no one in particular.

Harry stared at her clasped hands and longed to hold them in his.

'So, you see, Andrew is conforming to the old pattern, tradition, call it what you will. The King or Country tradition.'

None of them had heard Andrew coming into the room and now he was there among them, looking down at his father in his deep armchair.

'Again? Talking about me again? What are you saying about me this time?'

He swayed slightly as he spoke.

'I was just telling your friend . . . ah . . . Harry that you are following in the family tradition. I am the odd man out.'

'Yes. You are. How true.'

'The summer's over.'

Miranda spoke in a low voice to Harry. She had unclasped her hands and they lay like white birds, he thought, on the soft red silk of her dress.

'It is O-october, after all. You must remember that.'

'October,' she repeated vaguely.

Thunder rumbled again. She pressed her fingers hard together.

He watched her hands moving.

'We don't normally have s-s-summer in O-o-o . . .'

'I've always wondered why they call it an Indian Summer. Do you know?'

He shook his head.

'You have an answer for most things. Can't you think up one for that?'

'There's no more brandy,' said Andrew loudly. 'I've looked in the sideboard. I've looked in the corner cupboard. I've sought it here, I've sought it there. There isn't any. Where do you hide the brandy, Father?'

'Don't you think you've had enough?' his father asked him mildly.

'I think I'm old enough to decide whether I want to be drunk or sober.'

Miranda jumped up from her chair and held out her hand.

'I'll get you some. Here, give me your glass.'

He bowed.

'That's a good, dear little sister.'

All three men watched her in silence as she moved from the light into the half-dark and then out into the hall, the red flickering dress, the glass held out in front of her. As she disappeared Andrew turned abruptly to his father.

'Tell me, Father . . .'

Mr Martin bent his head to listen, moving back into the darkness of the wing chair.

'Where do you stand? I've wondered for so long. Where? What are your thoughts about this . . . rabble? Will you answer, Father? No hedging, no half-truths?'

He turned away from his father and looked down into the fire. His eyes shone almost mad in the light from the flames.

'These Republicans? I suppose you support them, hey? I get the feeling that you support them. Let me tell you something: In 1916, when they stabbed us in the back, I thought of you. I wondered then what you were thinking. Constantly I thought of you. You have no idea what those trenches were like. No one ever told people like you what those trenches were like. The best kept secret of the century. We sat there day after day, month after month waiting to die. Irishmen, Father, in case you hadn't remembered. Thousands of Irishmen as well as all those others. Waiting to die. Watching our friends die; all those deaths . . . bloody savage deaths. Actually wishing, begging God even that the next time it might be you, put an end to it.'

He stopped speaking and the room was filled with heavy silence, a tumble of rain down the chimney caused the fire to spit, a raging, sizzling spit.

'And then those bastards in Dublin had to play at being heroes and I thought of you. I thought, this will give the old man pleasure. But what about me? Is he thinking of me? Of my men, my dying thousands? Did you ever think of them? Who thinks of them now?'

Mr Martin put up a hand in the flickering light, like a policeman on point duty, thought Harry, but ineffectual.

'Oh God, I used to pray, if only they'd take me away from here and put me in charge of the heavy artillery in Dublin, I'd blow the whole damn city to smithereens and all the damn traitors and half-traitors with it. Poum.'

He smacked his right fist into the palm of his left hand.

'Perhaps even you, Father.'

The thunder was almost on top of them now.

He turned to look at his father again.

'You don't speak. You never spoke. Mother always said that. You always looked eternally bruised. I want you to speak now.'

He leant down towards him, almost threatening.

Harry got to his feet.

'Andrew old ch-ch-ch . . .'

'None of this is your affair. I came here to exorcise old ghosts. I should have had the courage to come alone.'

'The ghosts are in your head, my son. That is where the exorcism must take place.'

Andrew shook his head.

'No.'

'We all have ghosts in our heads.'

'No.'

The thunder now seemed right over the room in which they stood. Harry glanced anxiously towards the door, worrying about Miranda.

'In every room I hear the sound of her step, her sigh. You probably never noticed her sighs. Did you?'

His father didn't speak. Harry moved uneasily. There was another crash of thunder and then he heard, he alone heard her cry out. He ran. Neither of the other two men were aware of anything except each other, not even the thunder sounded in their ears.

'The pain of her loneliness is everywhere. In this room, trapped in this room . . . Always. I thought that now, after so long that perhaps . . . But I knew the moment I saw the house. I remembered at that moment the way the evening sun used to burn in the windows and I knew that

I would hear the sound of her playing the piano, in here, alone. Why did you make her lead her life alone? When I saw those golden eyes I knew the ghosts would be waiting.'

His eyes were filled with tears, the tears of a drunk man, the tears of a child, the tears of a soldier who had eluded death a thousand times.

His father stood up.

Face to face they stood by the fire.

'Golden burning eyes. Oh God, I hate it here so much.'

Face to face they stood by the fire and they couldn't speak, only stare forlornly each into the other's eyes.

* * *

'I heard y-y-y-ou. Are you all . . . ?'

She crouched down gathering pieces of glass ineptly into her hand.

'It was the thunder. The lightning. Such a flash of lightning. It just . . .' She glanced nervously towards the window. 'I got such a fright. I . . . thought . . . I broke a glass. I . . .'

'Here. Let me do that. Your hands are shaking. You'll cut yourself.'

'I feel so stupid.'

She stood up and placed the fragments on the table. He knelt at her feet searching for the slivers in the carpet.

'I'm afraid I've spilled quite a bit of Father's brandy.'

He smiled up at her.

'Saved it from Andrew. I'm sure o-brandy's good for carpets. I've heard that somewhere. There. I think that's the lot. Lethal little slivers, aren't they?'

He put the tiny pieces on a plate. 'Don't want anyone to cut themselves.'

She looked very pale.

'You'd better have a drop yourself. You look a bit rattled.'

She shook her head.

'I'm all right now. Honestly.'

A great crack of lightning lit up the world outside the window for a second, silvered the striking rain against black trees, walls and the far hills; silvered for a moment the white face, the hands holding together the lapels of the coat; long black coat and pale face, the ghost by the gate, the figment, the imagining.

She cried out again and covered her face with her hands and the thunder rattled above the house, the windows stirred in their frames. He threw his arms around her and pulled her tight against him and she stood there, her face against his shoulder, her heart thudding so that he could feel it in his body and didn't know if it were his heart or hers. The thunder faded, flickered, faded again, and then there was only the sound of the rain lashing against the windows.

'It's moving away,' he whispered.

She didn't say a thing.

'You'll be safe if you stay here in my arms like this . . . quite, quite safe.'

She disentangled herself from his arms and moved slightly away from him.

'It wasn't just the lightning. I thought I saw . . . out there . . .' She glanced towards the window and quickly away again. 'Out there . . . a man. Standing out there by the gate. That was what . . . That really frightened me.'

He went over to the window and peered out at the sheeting rain.

'You can see nothing,' he said. 'N-nothing . . . No one in their right mind would be out on a night like this.'

'I thought I saw a man. A long black coat and a . . .'

'One of your ghosts?' he suggested.

She shook her head.

'A man. You pour out Andrew's brandy, just in case I drop another glass. Have some yourself.'

'Maybe just a drop.'

The thunder growled again.

'Here, give me your hand. Let me hold your hand. Then you will be a-a-bsolutely safe. I am immune to lightning.'

'Pour out the brandy and don't be silly.'

She turned her back on the window and perched herself on the table.

'M-M-M-iranda . . .'

'Pour out the brandy, Harry, please.'

He picked up the decanter and a glass and moved slowly towards her. A flicker of lightning, almost friendly, skimmed around the room.

'Such a strange thing has happened to me. I'd like you to let me tell you. Please.'

'No. I don't want you to tell me anything.'

She slipped down from the table and moved away from him, away from the windows, towards the safety of the hall.

'I'd just like us to be friends. Stay friends. I'd value that more than anything. I don't have many friends.'

'Don't go. D-d-d –'

She turned and smiled at him.

'No, Harry, I'd just love a friend . . . Can't you try and understand that?'

'I'll pour the brandy.'

She watched as he poured quite a dollop into his glass.

He held the glass up towards her.

'I'll drink to . . . h-h-hope. Will you let me drink to hope?'

'I'll let you drink to whatever you want.'

He drank.

'To hope.'

She smiled at last.

'And Ireland. I think you should drink to Ireland.'

'Your Ireland?'

'Certainly.'

She moved to his side.

'Give me a sip from your glass. I'll drink to my Ireland. I hope you will too.'

She took the glass from his hand and tasted a drop of the brandy, grimaced slightly and handed the glass back to him.

'I don't know whether I should. A-after all, why am I here?'

'You tell me why. I'd like to know that too.'

'The CO ordered me to come. It's as simple as that. I've been trained s-since the age of eight to obey orders. Like Andrew. H-h-honour the King and keep your powder dry. Don't shoot till you see the whites of their eyes. Land of h-hope and gl-gl-gl – a whole lot of things like that. Things that seemed important. Ever since I went to school. I have been

...

saturated in that kind of thinking. The nobility of war and the British way of life. I don't understand about Ireland, truly I don't, Miranda, but you'll have to believe that I think we're here to help. I don't try to understand. That's not my j-j-job. I'm a clown who obeys orders.'

She laughed.

'What a speech.'

She put the glass back into his hand.

'Then clown, drink to my Ireland. That's an order. The Ireland you don't understand. Maybe if you stay here long enough we, or someone anyway, will be able to explain it to you.'

He held the glass up in the air.

'Amen,' he said.

* * *

Andrew spoke suddenly, breaking the long silence between them. The thunder now was only a murmur somewhere in the distance.

'It's so strange.'

He moved away from his father and stood for a moment by the piano looking down as he spoke at the keyboard, then paced on around the room, unable to settle anywhere.

'I died a thousand deaths in the damn war. Each one was as fearful ... fearful.' He looked briefly towards his father as he repeated the word almost as if he thought Mr Martin might misinterpret it, '... as the first. I was exposed night and day to my own fear; a most humiliating experience I can assure you.'

His father began to speak, but Andrew held up a forbidding hand.

'Cowardice I suppose you could call it; that terror of dying, of pain, a feeling of disintegration inside my own head. To begin with I felt shamed by my own fear, but finally as the years went by I became hardened by it. I became a good soldier. I came through alive. I am alive. But here ... this place ... I am unnerved all over again. I feel the disintegration very close at hand. The ghosts, Father.'

His fingers plucked at the silk tassel hanging from the curtain's edge, pulled at the soft strands.

'I don't want to be like you.'

His father laughed.

'I long to keep my energy intact. Where the hell is Miranda? Drink keeps things quiet inside you. You don't speak?'

'What is there to say? I don't have to excuse myself to you, defend my character in any way. I have my dreams. They have never been reprehensible.'

'Dreams! What use are dreams? They merely confuse people.'

His perambulation over, he came back to the fire and stood there fidgeting now with the china ornaments on the mantelpiece.

'What is the Sistine Chapel but the realisation of one man's dream?'

'Oh come, Father . . .'

'I don't credit myself with such noble dreams, but I have longed for so many years to see this defeated country rising from its knees. I dream of seeing the land, the actual land, soil, earth treated with enlightenment . . . burgeoning, serving us all . . .'

'Romantic rubbish . . . and you know it. Order is what Mother always longed for and you would never listen. Order is all important.'

'I will never live to see the trees grow.'

'What is all this mumbo jumbo about trees and the holy bloody land? You are prepared to allow disorder to take over and you excuse yourself by talking about dreams. Build your paradise if you wish and all the people will do is spit in your face.'

'That's a risk we all have to take.'

'Disorder, violence, death. Look around.'

His father moved uncomfortably in his chair and sighed.

'I deplore violence. Deplore.'

'Deplore.' Andrew repeated the word with contempt.

Miranda ran into the room followed more sedately by Harry.

'Dear Father, I broke a glass. A good glass. I'm sorry.'

She bent down beside his chair and took his hand in hers.

'It was the lightning. I'm so, so sorry. It was clumsy and idiotic of me. I got such a fright.'

'She always hated thunder.'

Andrew took the glass that Harry was presenting to him and held it up under his nose before tasting it.

'I don't suppose you'd remember.'

Miranda wondered if he were addressing her or their father. She held his fingers tight. Bony fingers, not a spare pick of flesh on them.

'She used to pull the curtains tight and sit in the middle of the room, her fingers knotted together. White knuckles. She prayed, silent words, no sounds, just silent words. It is the only irrational thing I remember about her.'

He took a drink from his glass. No one spoke.

'I remember.' Mr Martin spoke after a long time.

Miranda patted his hand and smiled up at her brother.

'I don't remember. Not anything like that. How could I?'

'I used to sit beside her. She didn't want me to say anything, just be there beside her until the storm had passed. Then she would open the curtains and the day would go on.'

He took another drink.

'I used to worry about her after I went to boarding school. Who minded her when there were storms? Silly really. Wasn't it, Mother?'

He spoke to the air. He spoke to her as if she were there listening with care to his words.

Miranda let go of her father's fingers and got up.

'You're as bad as Nanny, going on and on about the past. I don't want to hear about the past any more. I want to play billiards. Come on, Harry.'

She almost danced towards him, red dress swinging, and took him by the arm.

'There's so little time for fun. Let's have fun. Don't be broody, Andrew. Come and play billiards. You can play Harry and the winner can play me and we won't get to bed till all hours.'

'Billiards isn't a game for women, sister.'

He smiled though and moved towards the door.

Harry squeezed her arm tight against him.

'I think it's a sp-splendid idea. I look forward to beating both of you.'

Miranda laughed.

'Not a hope. I'm really good. Amn't I, Father? Will you come and watch.'

'No, no my dear. I'll just have another drink by the fire and then I'm off to bed. Sitting up till all hours doesn't appeal to me any more. I warn you both though, don't laugh too hard at her. If that scallawag says she'll beat you, she'll beat you.'

'Not a hope. When my hand and eye are steady I am unbeatable.' He took his sister's other arm. 'Even Harry's not too bad. We might put a bit of money on it.'

They went out laughing.

✻   ✻   ✻

I always liked to hear laughter.

That was Harry's great attraction. He made everyone laugh. I suppose he must have been like that in the war too, sitting in the trenches making people laugh.

Poor Harry.

How silly to say poor Harry.

Poor Andrew would be much more to the point. He was so afraid of all the things he didn't quite understand, of dreams, disturbing ideas. He wanted to see nothing for the future, only the steep ladder he had to climb for his own success. He truly believed in the importance of success, but the past troubled him constantly. It never seemed to occur to him that Mother's unhappiness could have been to a large extent of her own making.

I wouldn't excuse Father for his inattention towards her, but I do believe he cared. He just didn't have time for the frills of a relationship. Andrew was too young when she died to recognise that. Father became the evil demon of some fairy story to him.

It makes me laugh a little.

I mustn't laugh.

My pain comes when I laugh.

They become disturbed.

I don't want to disturb them. They misinterpret the signs.

Poor Andrew.

In spite of his success, his marriage, his charming children who will sell this place when I have finished with it, he was quite lost.

He spoke all those words with such apparent conviction.

Order. Discipline. Obedience.

Such hard words, all of them.

Frightened words and frightening words.

Poor Andrew.

Held together with string.

'Let me into your head, Andrew.' I said it once to him.

War-battered London was outside the window.

I was glad that Father hadn't lived to see such foolishness happen again in the world.

Trees in Hyde Park were beginning to bud with spring, grey war-streaked houses were unkempt and cold, even with the spring sun.

He said nothing.

He was just in the door that moment from the War Office in his pinstriped suit and his Brigade of Guards tie.

He stood beside me in the drawing room and said nothing. You could still smell war in the streets; dereliction and destruction held a smell that lingered for years. Flowers were beginning to grow through the dead houses. Maybe that will happen here. There it was a temporary phenomenon; here it will be permanent.

'Just for a moment.'

A child was skipping below on the pavement, crossing the rope and uncrossing it, counting to herself. I could hear the tap of the rope on the ground, but she must have been wearing soft shoes because her feet made no sound.

He came across the room to where I was standing and closed the window down.

'This room is freezing.'

His voice was irritable.

'I saw you coming up the road, marching up the road. You do march you know.'

He laughed.

'Why not, sister?'

'Well, I saw you marching, left, right, left right and then I thought . . . I'd like to get into Andrew's head.'

'Better stay out of it.'

We moved from the window towards the miserable fire, slatey coal that spat and smouldered.

'That's rotten coal,' I said. 'Can't you get better coal than that?'

'After all, there's been a war. We have to take what we can get.'

We never talked.

Never moved towards each other.

'When you retire . . .'

He laughed.

'Old generals never retire, they only fade away. We'll meet that bridge when we come to it.'

He didn't come to it. A motor accident took care of that bridge for him.

That was some sort of luck I suppose; like Father, he didn't have to wait for death.

'I just wondered if you'd feel like coming home at some stage? You know . . . I've minded the place well, but perhaps . . . ?'

'Home?'

'Yes. Termon,' I said in case he misunderstood me in some way.

He scratched at his little fair moustache before replying.

'Don't worry.'

'I'm not worrying. I just want to know would you think of coming home.'

'Nothing is further from my mind.'

'There's no need to be pompous and rude about it.'

'I – My life has always been here. It's such a stupid question to ask me. Nothing is further from my mind.'

He walked back towards the window and stood staring out across the road at the park.

'Nothing. You should know how I feel about things. I wish you . . .'

He still fought with his moustache.

'I do wish you'd leave me alone, Miranda.'

'I only asked you a civil question for God's sake.'

'No.'

'What do you mean no?'

'I mean no to your civil question. No to Termon. No to Ireland. No, no, no. Now, will you leave me alone?'

'Yes.'

He turned away from the window and bowed ironically in my direction.

I remember that ironic bow so well. His hair was still fair and thick. I remembered Father's hair.

Even sleeked as it was and cut to sit neatly under his absurd bowler hat, I could recognise that hair.

He held out a hand towards me and we walked towards each other in the chilly smoky room. I took his hand, cold from the street and held it for a moment against my warm cheek. Neither of us spoke.

I think that somewhere among the misunderstandings and the ghosts and the fear there was love.

Will you reject me, God, for not exploring the possibilities of love?

Maybe my self-imposed solitude was a sin?

It is so hard to tell whether we make the right decisions or the wrong ones.

I thought of You.

Yes, You, I'm speaking to You, God and of course to Cathal. I have to keep speaking to him. Neither of you have the grace to answer me.

I have to answer my questions for myself.

I thought there was no other way to repay . . . what a mean little word . . . repay; clinking of coins and rustling notes.

Repay is rubbish.

Words are so elusive at times.

Align my life with his death; that's dry, but more what I meant to do. Offer up my solitude.

I would truly hate to be rejected for that, God.

Don't frighten me now so close to death.

Would this not be an appropriate time for comfort?

A sign?

A word?

You're not like that, are You?

You've never given signs.

You wait.

I can wait too.

They come, quickly and quietly, the ministers, administers I should say, with their needles and their soothing words. Dimming shapes.

My players now have more reality.

* * *

Mr Martin's head nodded forward onto his chest, an ageing man nodding off to sleep. The glass in his hand tilted dangerously. A hand reached out and took the glass gently. The cold hand touching the warm skin awakened the dozing man.

'Oh,' he said, startled by the cold hand against his warm skin. He looked up. Cathal stood above him, water running from his hair, his face, his clothes, making lakes on the floor around his feet.

'I wasn't asleep. I . . .' He struggled to collect his thoughts.

'I was just . . . I wasn't . . . I must have dropped off. You startled me.'

'I saved your drink.'

'Thank you. Thank you.'

Mr Martin got to his feet.

'Charlie.'

'Yes.'

'How did you . . . well just arrive like this . . . just . . . How did you get in?'

He retrieved the glass from Cathal's hand.

'As usual. Through the door. You ought to lock your doors. I've been meaning to tell you that for a long time.'

'I've never known that door to be locked. Never.'

'It might be wise. Now.'

'Wisdom doesn't seem to be one of my strong points. I like to think of this house unlocked, welcoming, truly a sanctuary.' He laughed. 'The fools' sanctuary.'

His eyes seemed to focus on Cathal for the first time.

'My dear chap, you're soaking. Take off your coat. My goodness yes . . . your shoes if you so wish. Throw it down there on the floor. I've never seen . . . You're soaked through, right through to the skin.'

He bent and threw some more wood onto the dying fire.

'That'll blaze up in a few moments. You must have been out in the very worst of the storm. Let me get you a glass of whiskey? That'll warm you up a bit.'

'I won't have a drink thanks. Not tonight.'

'Take off your jacket too, don't stand on any ceremony.'

Cathal shook his head, shivered and held his hands out towards the fire.

'Is something the matter?'

Cathal stood silently looking down into the fireplace where the flames were beginning to grow, once more around the fresh wood.

'Sure you won't have a drink?'

'Positive.'

'Well sit down then. Pull that chair up to the fire.'

Cathal didn't move.

'I shouldn't be here at all,' he said at last.

'Can I help you in any way? You're in some sort of trouble. I can see that.'

'No. Yes. Trouble. Yes, trouble. Listen to me . . . you've got to get the two soldiers out of the house and away. Soon. Tonight. Soon.'

'The two . . . oh yes . . . I'm afraid I don't understand.'

'Orders have come.'

'Orders?'

'Yes. Orders. Don't waste time. I have wasted too much time already, foolishly standing out there in the storm. Just get them away.'

'What do you mean, orders? Whose orders?'

'Can't you guess? They are to be shot. Executed. Assassinated. Call it what you like. One word's as good as another. Gunmen will be arriving here before daylight. In their beds. Taken by surprise.'

'There must be some mistake.'

'That was the way it was supposed to happen. They have been under sentence ever since they arrived in Dublin. They're working for British Intelligence.'

'I . . .'

'There is no mistake. Believe me.'

'Charlie . . .'

'For God's sake look at the thing straight. Andrew isn't a schoolboy any longer home for the holidays, as he used to be. He's an officer in the British army. He's the enemy. You know as well as I do, we are a country at war.'

Mr Martin sighed.

'I've never been able to understand why people need to kill each other.'

Two of Cathal's fingers had gone dead and numb with the cold. He began rubbing at them with a sort of fury.

'This isn't the time to be working it out. Sometimes it's necessary . . . that's what they say. That's what I would have said . . . in order to survive . . . in order for freedom to survive . . . in order for sanity to survive. I'm as bad as you are for talking. Look it . . . what I'm saying is true. Will you go and get them . . . get them away to hell out of this.'

'There isn't a man round here, Charlie, would shoot my son. I'm sure of that.'

'Amn't I trying to tell you, it's from Dublin they're coming. They know nothing about you or your son, only that they believe he's dangerous. The dangerous enemy. They won't be talking when they come. They won't be asking any questions. My orders are . . . my orders are to show them the . . . to make the way easy for them. To . . . My orders . . .'

'That's enough. I have been blind.' He moved across the room as he spoke and poured a large glass of whiskey and carried it back to Cathal.

'Here. Drink this. You'll catch your death of cold without something warming in you. I am blind. Drink.'

Obediently Cathal raised the glass to his lips and drank.

'Four o'clock. I was to have the gates open for them at four o'clock, and the hall door.' He laughed. 'The bloody hall door. It never occurred to them they only had to turn the handle. I didn't tell them that.'

'What can I say . . . ?'

'I know what they'll say . . . Informer, traitor, a lot of very unpleasant words. I never saw myself in this sort of situation, everything has always seemed so . . . well . . . straightforward. It always seemed to me to be a just war. Don't say a word. I know you don't believe a war can ever be just, but there we must beg to differ. You've never asked me about this. I feel such gratitude for that. You never put me in the position where I had to justify myself to you. I . . .'

Mr Martin put his hand on Cathal's sodden shoulder.

'You don't have to justify yourself to me now either.'

'I have to talk. I feel diseased, plague-ridden in some way. I stood out there in that rain for hours trying to get up the courage to come in through the hall door. I swear I didn't know what I was going to say until I saw you there, asleep, about to drop your bloody glass on the floor. You looked so tired. You're getting on, you know. You should lock your hall door. If I hadn't been able to get in here and see you sleeping there I would have gone home. I would have let things take their course.'

'I still don't know what to say. Thank you seems miserably inappropriate . . .'

'Let's just get the pair of them out of here, then we can speechify all we want.'

The door opened and Miranda came in.

'I thought you were going to bed, Father.' Her voice was scolding. 'Oh Cathal. It was you I . . .' She stopped in the middle of the room and looked at them both. 'What is it? What's the matter?'

She moved again, quickly towards them, the red dress fluttering out and then clinging round her legs. She took hold of Cathal's arm.

'You're soaking. It was you . . . it . . . Father, what is the matter?'

Mr Martin hesitated.

'Tell her,' commanded Cathal.

Mr Martin cleared his throat before he spoke, putting off the moment.

'Ah . . . ah . . . Charlie here says that men are coming to get Andrew.'

Miranda looked puzzled.

'Get? Who? What do you mean get?'

'Shoot,' said Cathal. 'He doesn't like to use the word. Dead.'

'Andrew?'

Miranda's fingers gripped tight into his arm.

'And his friend.'

'Is this true? Father?' She moved beside him, stared into his evasive eyes. 'Father?'

'I'm afraid so. Yes it would seem to be true all right.'

A surge of energy seemed to take hold of her, shaking every part of her body.

'What on earth are you both standing here for? Why aren't you doing something? How utterly hopeless you both are. Go and bring round the motor, Cathal. I'll go and get the others. Luckily they're still up.'

The two men stood rooted to the floor, staring at her. She stamped her foot.

'Move for heaven's sake. Move.'

Mr Martin took a couple of steps towards the door.

'I'll get the motor.' He looked apologetically back towards Cathal. 'Sometimes you know, she's difficult to start. There's a knack you have to have. A flick of the wrist at the crucial . . .'

'Father!'

'Yes, yes, my dear, I'm on my way.'

He almost hurried out of the room and they stood in silence for a moment listening to the sound of his feet tapping across the hall.

'He's mobilised. Now tell me . . . quick . . . What is all this about?'

'I saw you in the dining room. I . . .'

'You're as bad as he is. This is no time for conversations of that kind.'

'He put his arms around you. You let him . . .'

'It was nothing.'

She stood close by him and put her arms around his neck.

'I was so frightened. Please, you hold me too, just for a moment. I am more frightened now. This isn't like the thunder. Please.' They clung to each other and she felt the damp of his clothes creeping through her red dress to her skin.

'I'm frightened too, Miranda.' He whispered the words into the softness of her bare neck. 'I've done the most terrible thing.'

'I don't know what you've done, but I know . . . we know, Father and I, that you could never do anything terrible. Cathal. Cathal.' Locked together they stood and the fire flickered, mellowing the air around them.

'I must go.'

He stepped away from her.

'I'd better go.'

'No.'

A wail like a peacock.

'Please. No.'

She grabbed hold of his arm.

'Please don't go. Stay here with us. Me. You must stay. I couldn't bear to think of you out there on your own. Cathal, Cathal. Cathal, please don't go away.'

'I'll stay.'

She sighed with relief.

'Good. Is that a promise? You won't slip away when my back is turned, will you?'

He shook his head.

'I'll stay.'

'I'll go and get the boys. Tell them.'

She ran out of the room.

Cathal slowly paced from the fireplace to a window, to another window, past the big round table loaded with flowers and books and photographs in silver frames to the fireplace again and then back to the long sweeping gold silk curtains and over to the piano. His feet were like lead, his head, his heart like lead. The piano keys were lit by a silver lamp on a tall stand. He began to pick out a tune, that never seemed to quite make sense, as his finger stumbled along the keys.

All around my hat I'll wear a green coloured ribbono.
All around my . . .

'I sup-p-ose it's too much to ask what's going on?'

Cathal was startled by Harry's voice. He quickly lifted his hand from the piano.

'Miranda has some garbled story. I g-g-ather we have to leave in a h-h-h . . .'

'That's right.'

The two young men stared at each other across the furniture.

'As you see,' Cathal's voice was almost conversational, 'I can't play the piano. I can't even get one finger to play the piano.'

'You're at the back of all this, aren't you?'

'Schubert, Beethoven, Chopin . . . They're all just names to me. I can't begin to fathom all those absurd little squiggles on those lines. So many books full of absurd squiggles.'

'Andrew's ranting and raving like a lunatic in the billiard room. I was winning too. M-Miranda . . .'

'Miranda can play the piano like an angel, can't she? I presume she's played for you.'

'I suppose I should get my gear together.'

'Has she?'

'She seemed to be indicating that we should leave in a h-h- . . .'

'Or hasn't she?'

'Yes, she has. As you say, she plays like an angel.'

Cathal turned back to the piano and let his fingers play a few random discordant chords.

'I wonder . . .'

'I'm bl-bl-bloody wondering too.'

'. . . if that sort of thing is important.'

'What on earth are you talking about?'

'Did you learn when you were a child?'

'The p-p — Oh yes. Five or six. Maybe younger. My father had a theory that we should learn to read music at the same time that we learnt to read words. Batty idea really . . . well, that's what most people would think . . . but to give the old man his due, it wasn't a bad idea at all. I can read an orchestral score and hear the whole thing in my head. Pretty amazing, wouldn't you say? There aren't too many people can do that. People who aren't professional musicians, I mean of course.'

'I suppose not.'

'I wish to God I had the technical ability to go with it. Or a spot of genius. I can tell you I wouldn't be in the a-ar — ar . . . but I haven't either, not an inkling. I strum.'

'Strum?'

'I'm not a patch on Miranda. Mind you, I'm very out of practice. Rusty fingers and all that. There is something serious up, isn't there?'

'Yes.'

Harry nodded.

'And I'd be right in thinking that you're at the back of it?'

'In a somewhat oblique way.'

A sharp explosion outside the window made them jump. It was followed by a series of quick rat-tat-rat-tat-tats.

'Wh—wh-wh . . . !'

Cathal slammed his fingers down impatiently on the piano keys.

'Oh sweet Jesus. It's the bloody car. He's . . .'

'Here.' Harry almost shouted the word at him. 'Watch that piano. It's a Steinway.'

'At this moment I don't give a damn what it is.'

Harry stroked the ebony case with care, almost as if it were a beloved dog.

'You have to hand it to the Germans when it comes to pianos. N-n-no one can touch them.'

'How do you stand with motors?'

'Motors?'

'If you know anything at all about them, I'd say you might be needed.'

Mr Martin almost rushed into the room, wiping his hands as he came on his white handkerchief.

'I got her going.' He spoke in the direction of the two young men. 'Mind you, I thought I was going to manage, I didn't want to get poor Paddy out of his bed at this time of the night. He's really the only person who can manage her when she's being temperamental. I get so impatient.'

He examined the state of his handkerchief and then shoved it into the pocket of his dinner jacket.

'Impatient. Yes. Anyway I got her going finally. It's the fine adjustments you have to make before you swing. We got as far as the front steps and then . . .' He waved his oily hands in the air . . . 'alas . . . alas.'

'She became temperamental again?' Harry's voice was sympathetic.

'Bang . . . she went bang. Didn't you hear her?'

'Yes,' said Cathal. 'We heard her.'

'There was a lot of smoke, I'm afraid. That's not a good sign . . . I'll have to go and waken Paddy after all. There'll be a bit of a delay, but it can't be helped. Paddy'll have her right before too long.'

'If I might h-help, sir? I'm actually quite handy with the combustion engine.'

'A man of many parts,' said Cathal aloud but to himself.

'Now, that's really very good of you. She's not old or anything like that. Only two years. She's just a bit tempermental at times. A Delage. Do you know anything about the internal workings of a Delage?'

'Just lead me to her. I'll have her going in a jiffy.'

They moved towards the door.

'My parents have a Delage. You know I wanted to go into the Royal Engineers, but they wouldn't hear of it. Not quite you know . . . you know . . .'

His voice floated back from the hall.

Cathal rubbed at his face with his hands. He could hear steps, movements everywhere, voices calling, the door slamming and the rain interminably flooding down from the sky. When he took his hands from in front of his aching eyes Miranda was standing in the doorway looking at him. She had pulled on a long black cardigan over her red dress and it seemed to cast a grey exhausted shadow up over her face.

'Andrew has gone up to change into his uniform.'

She just stood there in the doorway, like a statue, her hands forlorn by her sides.

'What on earth for?'

'He says he's not going to be chased round County Cork in his evening clothes by a bunch of gangsters. He's raging, Cathal.'

She took a tentative step into the room as if it weren't her room, her house even at all.

'He's had quite a lot to drink and it doesn't make him very reasonable. At first he wanted to stay here and shoot it out, but I . . . persuaded him how foolish that would be. So he's agreed to go.'

'Your father can't get the motor to start.'

'He never can. We'll have to get poor Paddy out of bed. He always says he can, but he never can. He's too impatient with it.'

'No need to disturb Paddy. Your admirer . . .'

'Cathal . . .'

'Your piano-playing admirer is dealing with the matter. He says he's a genius with the combustion engine. Did you know he could read music before he could walk.'

In spite of herself she laughed.

'That'll be all right then. I have great confidence in Harry.'

She stood looking at him uncertainly. The blue eyes very bright in her pale face. Her hands were no longer still, they twitched painfully at the front of the cardigan.

'You?'

She asked the question very quietly. Her voice only just louder than a whisper.

He shook his head, not wanting to answer.

'What will happen to you? We haven't begun to think about you. I

... we ... Cathal? Don't just stand there. What will happen?'

'What do you think will happen?'

She took another step towards him, just the one, the dress swinging for a moment.

'They couldn't do that? Why would they do . . . ? You've done so much for them. They know . . .'

He turned his head away and looked at the fireplace. The fire was burning bravely now.

'Nobody likes informers.'

'But you're not . . .'

'Nobody's going to stop and think what I am or what I'm not. I'm in the movement. I've had my orders. I've reneged. It's all very simple.'

Cautiously, almost like a child playing a game, she took another couple of steps towards him.

'But . . .'

'There are no buts. I can't bloody well work out why I did it. I can't stand your brother or what he's fighting for . . . It would be no skin off my nose if they were to shoot him . . . and his helpful friend. But I couldn't leave it at that. I couldn't get on with my job. Say nothing. Let the boys get on with theirs. Who would ever have known? Some bloody nonsense had to creep in.'

'It isn't nonsense . . .'

'Perhaps nonsense is the wrong word. Weakness might be better. No vision seeker should have a place in his mind for scruples . . . or goodwill come to that. That's pathetic corruption.' He put his hands up to his face again and stood for a moment in silence. 'You're lost the moment you forget that the end justifies the means. Lost. It all seemed so easy up there in Dublin. I had it all worked out. I thought I had the courage of my convictions. We all felt the same way. We had such pride in what we were doing, in each other. God.' His voice rose. 'Where am I now? I still know who my enemies are . . . but where's pride? Where's hope now?'

She ran the last few steps to him and threw her arms around him, holding him as tight as she could against herself.

'Stop it, Cathal. Stop it this minute. You can't fall apart on us now. Everything'll be all right when we get the boys out of the house. We'll hide you here . . . We'll explain to them . . . After a few days . . . After a while . . . It'll be all right. We'll explain.' Her voice had little conviction.

'How can I explain to them what I can't explain to myself?' He unloosened her hands from behind him and held them in his own.

'It's all right, love, don't be upset. I'll pull myself together.'

Andrew, dressed in his uniform, came in the door. He looked at the two of them for a moment before speaking.

'Before I set out on this idiotic journey, I need a cup of coffee. I looked in the kitchen, sister, but there's no one there.'

She disentangled her fingers from Cathal's.

'There isn't usually anyone in the kitchen at this hour of the night. I'll make you some coffee.'

'Large, black, with lots of sugar. My head is full of vapours.'

'You shouldn't drink so much.'

'Coffee, not advice, is what is needed.'

A smile glimmered on her face as she walked past him.

'I'll be as quick as I can.'

'So,' said Andrew, as the last of her skirt flicked through the door. 'Round one to philosopher Dillon. I must say you look remarkably glum about it. By the way, what's your rank in the rebel forces, just so that I may address you correctly.'

'I'm a Commandant in the Irish Republican Army.'

Andrew laughed delightedly.

'What a splendid rank. Straight from the Foreign Legion.'

There was a long silence.

'I'm glad you've decided to go,' said Cathal at last.

'A strategic withdrawal, old chap. I can assure you, we'll be back.'

'I have no doubt of that. With the whole damn army behind you. A sledgehammer to crush a mouse.'

'Perhaps. If it's a nasty foundation-nibbling mouse, a sledgehammer is quick and effective.'

'You're too late you know. The mice have done their work already. You don't have a few untrained rebels to crush any longer, you have a nation.'

'My dear chap, you misunderstand us. We don't want to crush you. You're all such emotional hotheads, you never stop and think, work things out. If you hadn't raised the national temperature by that ridiculous affair in 1916, the whole thing would have been settled by now. You'd have had your Home Rule and we'd all be friends. That's what you wanted, wasn't it . . . Freedom? What the hell is freedom anyway? You're a philosopher, give it a thought sometime. It's just one of those words guaranteed to make men reach for their guns.'

'Someone who has never known the lack of it is unaware of its importance.'

'You have to live by rules, disciplines.'

'Every nation has to have the right to create its own rules and disciplines.'

Andrew laughed.

'All you lot will do is fiddle around with what we've taught you. Make compromises. Believe me you'll come screaming to us for help when things go wrong. You'll cheat. Just you wait and see.'

'Why do you treat us with such contempt?'

'It's all you deserve.'

'Your father doesn't think so.'

'My father's a foolish, rather boring old man. He's passed all his life in a dream, a fantasy of trees and drains; he's never really thought about people; about how people behave or think or . . . hurt. Yes. He knows nothing about politics, don't be fooled into thinking that he does. He just wants everyone to settle down and plant trees. Paradise will exist on this earth, if we all plant enough trees.'

'I don't think you know what you're talking about.'

Andrew laughed.

'I know all right. Oh, I dare say he was nice enough to you. He encouraged you, listened to you, talked to you even; gave you some sort of confidence that you didn't have before. He's probably even paying your way through college, eh? Is he doing that?'

Almost imperceptibly Cathal nodded.

'Just another of his experiments. Look upon yourself as just another tree or perhaps a drainage scheme.'

Into the silence between them came the sound of a roar from the motor engine; it died into silence again.

'Let me mention one thing, Charlie Dillon. It's my money he spends on his experiments; my inheritance draining into his bogs and trees . . . and you.'

'Remind me to thank you sometime.'

'And Miranda's. Her inheritance too.'

'Don't let's bring Miranda into this.'

'You needn't think I haven't noticed the attention you pay to one another.'

He walked over to the window and twitched back the curtain. He looked out and down, peering to see the car. All he could see were the shining drops spattering the windowpane.

'Bloody rain,' he said, then turned back to look again towards Cathal.

'Perhaps that's the way your aspirations lie. You see yourself possibly as a country gentleman? Your just desserts no doubt after centuries of slavery. Sitting in my father's chair at the dining-room table . . . and Miranda. I'll tell you one thing, Master Commandant, I think I'll see you dead first.'

'We used to be friends.'

'We used to be children.'

The car coughed alive again and Harry's voice shouted something.

'Yes.'

'In those days there was nothing in our heads but swimming and ponies and climbing trees.'

'You used to call for me when you came home from school. Remember Miranda said that? Where's Charlie? Remember that. I remember the sound of your voice in our kitchen. I used to wait for you to come . . . to run down to our house. I had no better friend.'

'Summer friends.'

'I used to wonder what it was like in your boarding school. Did they slam you when you didn't know your work, like they slammed us? Did you sleep in a room with long rows of hard, narrow beds? Did you cry at night because you were lonely? I never asked you any of those questions. I was lonely for you when you were away. Did that ever occur to you? Not just summer friends. Do you remember we used to go with the men to cut the Christmas tree? Do you remember the dust flying out from under the saw, that rippling crash as the tree came down? That was always such a day, wasn't it? And your mother used to send me up the witch hazel tree to get the first flowers, that was just before Christmas, wasn't it?'

Andrew laughed suddenly. 'Do you remember the night we escaped out to try and catch the badger down in the wood by the stream? The blackness of it. It was the first time I'd been out in such blackness.'

'You were bitten. I remember the yells of you.'

'Yes. There was the most terrible row next morning. I got blood all over the sheets. I've still got that scar on my finger. Look.'

He held his hand out towards Cathal, his first finger pointing. Cathal moved closer and looked at it.

A pale tracery patterned the skin near the top joint. Tentatively Cathal touched it.

'Imagine that now, after all these years.'

'Your mother.' Andrew spoke softly. 'Surely your mother's not happy about . . .' He waved the scarred hand for a second and then let it drop to his side.

'They know nothing about me. About what I do. We're not that great with each other since I went to college. We don't really have the same interests any more, no talking points beyond family matters. I don't have to tell them what I do with my time. They're good people.'

'Yes.'

'Good people. There's a lot of things they don't understand.'

'Charlie . . . I asked them not to send me over here. You needn't believe me if you don't want to.'

'But you're here.'

'Yes.'

'That's what matters. That's why they want rid of you.'

'Yes.'

Miranda materialised beside them with two steaming cups of coffee. She handed one to Andrew and then turned to Cathal. 'I made one for you too, Cathal. I thought you might be needing one.'

'Thanks.'

Andrew took a sip. Hot and sweet as he had asked for.

'I hate this place. It's like a bloody quicksand. I have to fight all the time to save my . . . I don't know, integrity sounds too grand a word to use. I don't want to be like him. In forty years' time, I still want to have energy and hope and place. Believe me, Miranda, in forty years' time there'll be no place for us here.'

'Of course there'll be place. I will be here in Termon. I will have place, my place, our place.'

He shook his head.

'No. You'll have compromised yourselves out of existence. You and people like you and Father will never have the guts or the energy to stand up and demand your rights. You'll shut your eyes to what is happening. You'll acquiesce. Acquiescent people. Then one day, you won't exist any more. Maybe the country'll be better off without you. I don't know. I won't know. I won't be here to see. I want to exist. Once this war is over, I'm never coming back here again.'

The engine coughed and then throbbed and then continued, a deep healthy sound.

'The Englishman has saved the day,' said Cathal.

Two rich growling honks sounded.

'I knew he'd do it,' said Miranda.

'Good old salt of the earth Harry.' Andrew clapped his hands in ironic salutation.

They heard the hall door open and the wind scurrying through the hall followed by Mr Martin and Harry.

'The chap's a genius,' called Mr Martin from the hall.

As he came into the room he scattered patterns of rain around him on the floor. 'Knows more about it than Paddy. I told him he should start up a garage. He'd make a fortune. Listen.'

The car panted gently outside.

Harry followed him into the room looking modest and oily.

'Good old Harry,' repeated Andrew. 'Perhaps we should go now, before the damn thing stops again.'

'I'll just w-wash ... I'll pop upstairs and w-w-w ... The great drawback to the combustion engine is the oil. I'll collect my toothbrush as well. I never feel safe travelling without my t-t-toothbrush.'

'Get a move on.'

'I've wakened Paddy. I thought it the best thing to do,' said Mr Martin. 'He'll drive you to Cork. He knows the road like the back of his hand. You'll make sure he gets something to eat once you're there?'

'Of course. I presume he's reliable.'

'Paddy! Of course.'

Andrew sighed.

'I also presume you wouldn't know if he were or not.'

'Paddy's reliable,' said Cathal.

Andrew nodded thanks in his direction.

'I don't know what to say about all this,' said Mr Martin, taking off his dripping coat and slinging it over the back of a chair. Miranda picked it up and shook it and carried it out into the hall.

'There's no need to say anything.'

'It's all most unfortunate . . . ah . . . most . . .'

She laid the wet coat over one of the hall chairs, half-listening to their voices and half to Harry's steps on the stairs and across the hall. He carried a small case in one hand.

'Clean hands and a toothbrush. I've left some of my gear up there in the hopes we'll be coming back. Will you invite us back?'

Inside the room Cathal moved uneasily towards the window.

'They've done their homework very well, Father. I have to give them that. I am a sort of glorified spy. I can't say I like the role very much.'

His father merely waved his hands in the air.

In the hall Harry caught hold of her hand.

'Miranda.'

She wriggled her fingers, but this time he held fast onto them.

'You know,' said Andrew, 'when I get away from all this . . . this . . . I think I'll study the techniques of armoured warfare. Those tanks are pretty amazing, Father. Men galloping across the countryside in tanks. That will be the warfare of the future. Or airplanes of course, but the thought of being a knight in a tank appeals to me very much.'

Cathal plucked the curtains apart for a moment. The rain was slacking off. He could see Paddy clambering into the driving seat of the car.

'Why don't we run away and get married?'

Harry held her hand tight so that she couldn't escape.

She laughed.

'Why do you always laugh at me?'

'Because you're always joking . . . I presume you're joking?'

'N-n-no.'

They looked at each other.

Mr Martin and Andrew were suddenly in the doorway looking at them also.

'This time, I'm quite serious,' said Harry.

'We're not really very well acquainted.'

'Does that matter? We have fifty years or so to get acquainted.'

Miranda pulled her hand away from his.

'I'm sorry . . . oh Harry. I never know when you're being serious . . . I'm sorry.'

Andrew put a hand on his friend's shoulder.

'She's saying no, Harry, I'm afraid.'

'No?'

'I'm sorry,' she repeated. Her voice was gentle. 'I'm really very sorry, dear Harry.'

'You can hear my heart splintering inside me. Listen.'

Honk. Honk. Honk.

The three young people laughed nervously as the horn sounded. Miranda took Harry's arm and propelled him towards the door.

'I'm sure the young ladies in Cork are very good at mending broken hearts.'

'F-fractured ones perhaps. Mine is in tiny pieces.'

'Dear nice Harry, you are a most comfortable person. I have been so happy to have met you. We are going to be good friends, remember that.'

The car was waiting, Paddy at the wheel muffled against the rain and wind. The rain sparked in the headlights.

'We're not saying goodbye you know. I've left lots of my g-g-gear up in my room.'

'No. We're not saying goodbye.'

Mr Martin was at their side.

'Come along, my boy, let me introduce you to Paddy. With the pair of you in the motor, you should have no trouble getting to Cork. Indeed you could probably travel the world if you so wished. He also has your touch.'

'Father, don't go out in the rain without your coat.'

He paid no heed to her and hurried down the steps.

Harry took her hand and kissed it gently.

'M-M-M –'

'Go on, you dear silly thing.'

She pushed him out into the dark and stood watching from the doorway.

Andrew had stepped back into the drawing room. Cathal was standing still staring out of the crack in the curtains.

'She should marry a gentleman. She'll be wasted on you.'

Cathal turned and looked at him.

'Possibly.'

'Tell me, when you get your so-called freedom, what then?'

'There will be no more killing. We will build.'

'What a simple soul you are.'

Cathal said nothing.

'God . . . I'd give anything for a drop of whiskey.'

Cathal put his hand into his pocket and pulled out a silver hip flask.

'Here.' He moved over towards Andrew. 'Take this with you. It might come in handy on the journey.'

Andrew took the flask. It seemed full.

'Thanks. A real boy scout, prepared for any eventuality.'

He looked at the flask, turned it over in his hand, felt the weight, the smoothness of it.

'A nice piece of silver.'

'Your father gave it to me. He said every soldier needed a hip flask. You'd better keep it. I seem to have failed somewhat in my duties as a soldier.'

Andrew unscrewed the top and took a quick drink.

'A temporary loan.' He wiped at his mouth with the back of his hand. 'Until we meet again.' He pushed the flask into the pocket of his greatcoat. 'Philosopher Dillon.'

He made a gesture with his hand that was part salute, part wave.

'Goodbye Andrew . . . or perhaps I should say slán.'

'Would I appear too ignorant if I were to ask . . . ?'

'Be safe. After all you might as well be safe.'

'I'll be safe all right. I wouldn't like to guarantee your safety though.

The insecure deal very unkindly with those they believe have betrayed them.'

Cathal neither spoke nor moved.

'Come with us, Charlie. It's the only sensible thing to do.'

Cathal smiled.

'Sense,' was all he said.

'Andrew!'

Miranda's voice called to him from the hall.

'I'm on the side of sense,' said Andrew. 'For better or for worse. Coming.' He patted the flask in his pocket.

'Yes,' said Cathal.

'You're sure you won't come?'

'Yes.'

'In that case, I'm afraid I have to say adieu.'

He touched Cathal lightly on the shoulder and left the room.

'Cathal,' he said as he went.

'Thank you,' said Cathal.

Andrew's feet marched across the hall. Voices called, the car revved and then more voices called. It could have been any day, any time, any people saying goodbye. The car roared for a moment and then stuttered off down the avenue.

☆   ☆   ☆

Father looked so old at that moment. He took a step back into the lighted hall and his face looked ready for death, filled with a terrible resignation that I had never seen before.

'Will I lock the door?'

I had to ask the question twice before he shook his head and laughed. I hear his laughter now echoing in the hollow hall of my skull.

Why do we laugh when we should cry?

Here.

Is it only here in this sad island?

I suppose we might drown God with our tears.

Swim, swim, old bearded man. Keep your nose above the water.

Why do you allow us to torment ourselves the way we do?

There are no answers.

We always ask the wrong questions.

I always ask the wrong questions.

I.I.I.

'What use is a locked door?'

That was his question.

He walked through the hollow hall into the drawing room. His frame was stooped with all those years of leaning over books, searching for answers to his own questions.

He stood for a moment looking at Cathal. The distance across the room between them seemed enormous.

I watched.

I breathed so softly at that moment so that no one might hear that I was there.

He walked across the room and stood by Cathal and then slowly put his arms around Cathal's shoulders and kissed him on each cheek.

I had never before seen men embrace.

Cathal stood within the embrace and then put a hand up to touch my father's cheek.

They never spoke a word.

Then my father moved away and, bending down, threw some wood on the fire.

* * *

'What should we do now, Miranda? What do you think we should do?'

Mr Martin stood up.

The fire crackled.

Miranda came towards them.

'Wait, I suppose. There's not much else we can do, is there? Cathal and you and I? We'll just wait.'

'Quite.'

He sat down in his armchair.

'We'll wait here until daylight comes. Things never seem so bad in the daylight. If — well — if nothing — no one —'

He paused and seemed to search for acceptable words and then sighed.

'We'll be able to think more clearly in the daylight. We could sleep a little if need be. Here in this room, the three of us. I've always loved this room. My mother loved this room. I remember she had a palm tree in here for a time, over in that corner. Yes. One's mind functions better in the daylight. I've often wondered why that should be.' He steepled his fingers and stared over them at the fire in silence for a moment. He coughed, almost apologetically, and then spoke again.

'Just one thing. If the need arises, I will do the talking. Please both of you, young people, leave the talking to me.'

'No one will listen,' said Cathal. 'Your kindness, your goodwill are no defence against their weapons. That's all we have . . . people like us . . .' he smiled ironically as he used the phrase '. . . bloody goodwill.'

He dug his hand into the pocket of his trousers and pulled out a gun. Miranda gave a little gasp as she saw it in his hand.

'There.'

He emptied the magazine and threw the gun and bullets onto the table.

'No more guns. Amen.'

Mr Martin appeared not to notice.

'I will do the talking none the less. No matter what you may think. It seems to me to be the only thing to do. Meanwhile, as we sit here waiting for the morning, perhaps Miranda could play us something on the piano. A little Bach perhaps, my dear? It's a long time since you've played any Bach for me.'

'No,' said Cathal.

He took Miranda's hand in his and led her to the sofa.

'She's going to sit here with me.'

He sat down and pulled her down beside him, right close into his arms.

'Close to me. I will have that comfort at least. My arms around you, darling Miranda.'

She lay, her head on his shoulder, quietly in his arms. She could smell the dampness of his clothes and the heat of his body and the fear that lay all round him. His heart thudded as he kissed her hair and the naked nape of her neck.

'Did he sit like this with you?' he whispered the words into her ear.

'Foolish Cathal,' she murmured.

'Did he call you my darling Miranda?'

She didn't answer, just buried herself more into his body.

'Go to sleep, my darling Miranda, and tomorrow morning will come and we will all be happy.'

'That only happens in fairy stories.'

'Don't argue . . . don't say a word. Just sleep. I want to feel you sleeping in my arms, that peace. I want to know peace.'

She did sleep, because she was young; because she still believed in the inevitability of miracles; in the possibility of happiness.

He held her and stared at her and felt her breathing and the fire sank down and warm ashes were heaped in the grate and the air began to feel cold. The three figures were like statues and through the twitched corner of the curtains the darkness began to drain away from the sky.

'It's so many years since I sat up all night.'

Mr Martin's voice broke the silence.

'In fact I can't remember the last time. I must have been very young. It used to be such an exciting thing to do. See the dawn in.'

He got up very slowly from his chair and walked over to one of the windows. He pulled one curtain back, carefully tying it with its tasselled silk rope. The rain was over. It would be a clean and shining day. He pulled the next curtain with equal care. You could see the trees across the avenue silhouetted against the colourless sky.

'If that nice young man were still here he would play us a tune. Something lively. A bit of Gilbert and Sullivan maybe. I always enjoyed Gilbert and Sullivan. I sang in *The Pirates* once . . . oh . . . ah . . . long time, long . . . He had a great way with that engine you know. Said his father had one the same. Nice chap.'

He moved around the room to the next window. The rings rattled along the brass rail as he pulled the curtain open.

'I liked him. The sort of straightforward chap it's pleasant to have around. Uncomplicated.'

He sighed.

His hands trembled as he knotted the rope. His face in the dim light was grey with fatigue.

'I knew a Harrington when I was up at Cambridge. Wonder if he was a relation. Must ask the lad the next time I see him.'

He walked to the third window, the big one giving out over the terrace and the lawn below.

The yellow silk curtains were faded along the edges with the years of summer sun. She had bought those silk curtains in London, he suddenly remembered, the year after they were married; replaced Mother's brocade ones; green they had been, same colour as the palm tree.

She, Julia. Yes. Julia's yellow silk curtains.

For a moment his hands held their softness.

'He was an oarsman, if I remember correctly. Yes. Rowed for Jesus. I was an oarsman myself once. I think Harrington was in the Jesus boat the year we won the Bumps.'

He stood by the window frowning to himself, trying to hide the present in the veils of the past.

'Harrington.'

Fingers of blue light stretched out into the dark sky.

Below the terrace two men walked across the grass.

'Yes.'

He turned his back to the window, moved towards the two young people on the sofa.

His voice was brisk when he spoke.

'Tell you what we'll do tomorrow . . . today, I suppose I should really say . . . Your father and I, Cathal, will take you to see the new plantation on Knocknashee. Spruce. Doing very well now. Lovely new trees, fresh looking, only so high . . .' He measured with his hands. 'So high . . . but in five years . . . ten . . . We planted a shelter belt of pine in a semi-circle round the new trees. You know how bad the wind can get up there. Yes. We'll do that if it doesn't come on to rain.'

He stood beside them both.

'I think that storm has cleared the air.'

He put his hand quite lightly on Cathal's shoulder.

'One day,' he said, 'we'll plant forests all down the slopes of the West. Imagine, just imagine the bare hills covered with trees, just as they used to be in the old days.'

He stood beside them both.

'A romantic notion.'

A voice spoke from the doorway.

Mr Martin turned, keeping his hand lightly still on Cathal's shoulder.

Cathal could feel the trembling of the hand. He didn't move, didn't look round.

'Quite practical I assure you.'

Mr Martin's voice was calm, in spite of his trembling hand. A man wearing a long brown coat stood in the door, behind him in the hall two shadows. He moved slowly into the room. They moved carefully behind him. They had guns in their hands. The man in the brown coat took in the scene; the two men and the girl still sleeping, the pale irrelevant lamps, the warm ashes in the fireplace.

'It's Major Martin we're looking for.'

He spoke the words very politely as if it were some social occasion.

'I'm afraid,' said Mr Martin, equally politely, 'he had to leave. He and his friend were called away.'

'What a pity. We've come a long way to see him.'

'It's strange time of day to come visiting.'

'These are strange times, Mr Martin. Even living out here in the back of beyond, you must be aware of that.'

'I am aware.'

'You keep late hours.'

Mr Martin nodded.

'Sometimes. Not often. I am getting on in years. I was in fact saying only a few minutes ago that it is a very long time since I saw the dawn in.'

'You will be pleased to get to your bed then. Just a few minutes and you can be on your way.'

'I'm not in any hurry,' said Mr Martin mildly.

'But we are. Before the world is up, we have business to do. Come along, Dillon, don't let us keep the Martin family out of their beds any longer than is necessary.'

'Charlie is staying here. He is our guest, our good friend. Presumably you are aware of the name and meaning of this house?'

'I am indeed, Mr Martin. In the past . . .'

'He hasn't asked for sanctuary. I have offered it. Doesn't that mean anything any more?'

'Only to fools and innocents. The world is no longer as simple as you seem to think it is.'

'So my son tells me.'

'Your son knows what's what all right. There's no denying that.'

'I thought I might be able to tell you how good, how honourable, this young man is. I thought you might listen to me.'

'Informer. Traitor. Spy.'

'Oh dear me, no.'

'There are two sides to every coin, Mr Martin. I don't think you should interfere. There has been a serious breach of military discipline.'

'I know nothing about military discipline. Do you believe in God?'

'Hardly a relevant question.'

Cathal looked down and saw Miranda's open eyes staring up at his face. He smiled slightly and bent to kiss her.

'No,' she whispered.

'We just want to discuss a few things with you, Dillon. Are you ready to come?'

Cathal stood up.

'No.' She clutched at his hand.

'I can assure you,' said Mr Martin. 'Charlie has done nothing . . . nothing that cannot be discussed here in this room.'

'I'm ready,' said Cathal. 'Let's go. Let's go. Let's get this whole damn thing over with.'

'A sensible attitude, I must say. It's sensible not to ask for trouble.'

Miranda stood up.

'No. Please don't take him away. What can we do? What can we say? What can we give you?'

She moved towards the man in the brown coat, the red dress crumpled from her sleep.

One of the gunmen moved towards her.

'Go back please.' The man's voice was still pleasant, social. 'Back behind the sofa. We don't want anyone to get hurt. Contrary to what many people believe, Mr Martin, we don't like innocent people to get hurt. I believe you to be extraordinarily innocent.' He gestured with his head for Cathal to move towards the door.

Without a word Cathal crossed the room.

'Father! Don't let them take him.'

Her father waved his hands miserably in the air.

'He was right. Words have no meaning in this sort of situation. We are not your enemies.'

The man in the coat laughed.

'I am aware of your position, Mr Martin, but you must realise that breaches of discipline must be dealt with. Dillon has been quite foolish. I think that he would agree with me, wouldn't you?'

Cathal didn't speak.

'He swore an oath. We have to remind people that oaths cannot be broken. Commitment is until we have Freedom. Don't you think Freedom is a noble cause, Mr Martin? A cause to die for?'

He moved over to the table where Cathal had thrown the gun. He picked it up and put it into his pocket and dropped the bullets in after it.

'No point in leaving this behind.'

He smiled at Mr Martin.

'I'm sure a gentleman the like of yourself would have no use for it.'

'Anything,' said Miranda. 'Anything at all.'

Her father took her arm and held it close against his side.

'Your parents?' he asked across the room to Cathal. Cathal nodded.

'Just tell them any kind of decent lie. You'll know what to say. I'm sorry.'

'Out,' said the man in the brown coat. 'Take him away.'

Cathal nodded almost casually towards Mr Martin and Miranda and turned and left the room. The men with the guns followed him. Miranda picked up his coat from the chair where he had thrown it earlier.

'His coat.' She took a couple of steps towards the door.

'He won't need his coat.'

'He'll be cold. It's cold out. He'll . . .'

'We'll take care of that. Just put it down and stay where you are.'

He walked over to the door and turned.

'Thank you, Mr Martin. I don't like needless violence.'

He saluted and left the room. They listened to his steps cross the hall. They listened to the door open and close. Miranda ran to the window, there was nothing, no one to be seen, only trees against the sky and the sound of waking birds.

'Father,' she began to cry, to howl more like an animal. 'Father. No. No. No. Cathal. Oh God, God, God, God. Oh please God. No.'

The room was now almost light and she stood in the window, Cathal's wet coat clutched in her arms, the dim irrelevant lamps, warm ashes in the fire, shadows now starting to grow across the fields as the sun rose.

Doors were opening and closing, feet pattering, slapping, stumbling on the stairs; voices stumbling, whispering moved towards them, towards their silence. The girls, strange in their night clothes and their streaming hair, pushed their way through the door; stood gaping until Nanny moved her way through them to stand beside Miranda. She pulled the shawl from her own shoulders and threw it round the weeping girl. 'Something's been going on,' said the old woman. 'Give that coat here to me, child, you're all soaked holding it like that. Cars and men and people running in the darkness. The girls were frightened out of their wits. Give it to me, Miranda.' She tried to prise the coat from Miranda's hands, but her own fingers were not strong enough.

'I tried to warn you . . .' She stared at Mr Martin. 'But you wouldn't listen. You're not wise with all your years. Look at the state she's in now.'

One of the girls in the doorway began to cry.

Nanny turned fiercely towards her.

'Away with ye back to your beds, if you can't make yourselves useful. Mary, Kate, fill jars for the master's bed and Miss Miranda's. Stop that whimpering, Bridie, and take the lamps with you when you go, there's no point in wasting good oil on the daylight. You'll all catch your death of cold with the bare feet of you. Where's sense gone at all?'

She managed to pull the coat at last from Miranda's hand and let it fall to the floor.

'You're soaked through. Pull that shawl close around you. Come child, come here to the fire, come with Nanny, child. Dear heart, don't be crying like that.'

She coaxed Miranda over to the fireplace, to where her father was standing, like a statue, hardly noticing what was happening around him.

'I told you . . . Time and time again I said leave that boy alone to make his way as best he can. There's no good ever comes of interfering with the way things are. I told you leave him alone. Didn't I tell you that?'

'Yes Nanny. You did.'

'Where's the point in giving people notions? Shush your crying, my pet, my little darling. It will pass. God is good.'

'I hate God.'

Nanny took hold of her shoulders and began to shake her, gently at first, but then as hard as she could manage.

'Never say that.' She almost shouted the words as she shook.

'God is not good. God is terrible. Why? Why? Why?'

'Never, ever again, let you say a thing like that. He listens. He listens all the time. Never say it, Miranda. Such wickedness.'

'Why? Why? Why?'

The old woman lifted her hand and hit Miranda across the face.

'Highsterics,' she said in Mr Martin's direction.

Miranda stopped crying, stood for a moment in silence and then put her hand up to touch her cheek.

'Never again say a thing like that,' said Nanny sternly. 'Even and I'm not here to chastise you for it.'

'Why, Father?' She whispered the words.

Mr Martin shook his head.

'I have never found any answers,' he said.

He took her hands, pulled her close to him, kissed her hands, cold hands. Her face was bruised by tears.

'Is it our fault?'

He nodded.

'I suppose so.'

She began to cry again, quiet tears, rising and flowing.

His hands became wet with her tears.

'Could we have . . . could we . . . ?'

'I don't think so, my dear. I suppose we might have forced him to leave with the boys, but it wouldn't have helped him in any way. He knew that. Merely put off . . . merely given him time to think . . . Given him pain. Pain.' He pressed her hands. 'Go with Nanny now, there's a good girl. Go to bed. Take her to bed, Nanny.'

'I don't want to go to bed.'

'Yes, yes, yes, yes, yes.'

He waved his hands, dismissing her.

'Go to bed, child.'

'Father . . .'

'Come along, Miranda. Do as you're told. A few hours' sleep . . .'

'I won't sleep.'

'You never know what you'll do till you try.'

'I don't want to try. I want to stay awake forever. Father . . .'

He had turned away from her.

'I must go and wake Dillon. I – he – we must go to the police.'

'The police,' said Nanny with contempt. 'A fat lot of use that little Jackie Sullivan will be. Come along now, Miranda, leave your father in peace. Your bed'll be nice and warm and Nanny will sit beside you till you go off. You won't get him back you know, no matter how you go about it. Neither the police nor all the English army itself will get him back. Poor Mrs Dillon. You'd better hasten on below to poor Mrs Dillon and put your coat on against the wind. I don't want to have you falling ill on me as well as all the sorrow. Come.'

She led Miranda across the room. At the door she paused for a moment.

'When I have Miranda off I'll run down to Dillon's. Tell her that. She'll need someone there. Tell her Nanny'll be down.'

'I'll tell her, Nanny.'

He bent slowly and picked up Cathal's coat from the floor and then his sodden hat from the chair on which he had thrown it when he came in the night before.

How can I tell them?

What can I say?

Indisciplined words jostled in his head.

I will knock on their door and when they open it surprised so early in the morning, I will offer them such grief.

God give me gentleness and them the strength to hear what I will be saying. Amen.

Miranda's bed was warm and soft. Nanny tucked her in and smoothed her hair, pressing her head deep into the pillows, then as she had promised she pulled up the wicker chair and sat by the bed and sang.

' "I mbeal Atha na Gár atá an stáid-bhean bhrea mhódhuil, 'Bfhuil a grua marna caorthainn agus scéimh ina cló geal . . ." '

Miranda struggled against sleep; the betrayal of sleep; the inconstancy of sleep.

All I can do is keep faith, she thought.

'Ba Bhinne guth a béil-san ná'n cheirseach's ná'n smólach.'

Forever.

That is all I can do.

That is the only possible thing that I can do.

She forced her eyes open and looked up at the ceiling, striped now with morning sun.

'God, help me to keep faith. Forever.'

She had to say the words aloud. She had to have them witnessed.

'Sssh,' whispered Nanny. 'Sleep, pet, sleep.'

'Forever.'

''S ná'n londubh ar na'n coillte le soilse trathnóna.'

*   *   *

It was the song she knew I loved so much that she sang. The song about the fair maid whose mouth's soft music was sweeter than the thrushes or the blackbird's song. I can hear the echoes of it now in my head. I can hear the crumbling measures of her old voice quite close to me now.

If he had lived, what then?

Down all the years I have often asked myself that question. We might have outfaced the ghosts together; raised a spreading brood to fill this house. No idyll, mind you; idylls are for fairy tales.

On the other hand, that tentative love we had might have been dissipated by our separations. He might have moved towards politics, after the fight was over; shifted into that grey area where expediency nudges truth out of its way; where freedom becomes a slogan, rather than a possibility. I would have hated that. There was too much of my father in me for that to give me pleasure of any sort.

Such foolish speculation.

We have to live with reality.

I used to dream about his death; see in my mind the splintering bone, the blood. I heard no sound, just saw the yawning of his skull as the bullets broke into it.

Terrible dreams; but they softened with the years.

Sometimes now when I read the papers, hear the news on the wireless, I try to conjure up those dreams again, recreate the pain of the past.

I can't any longer.

My indifference to the events of the last few years, the restirring of the pot of violence, frightens me, even now as I lie here. I suppose I must have destroyed in myself the power to feel passion, pity, rage.

My one hope is that God will forgive me for the wilful destruction of myself.

If He remembers.

Had Cathal's body ever been returned, or even been turned up years later by some Bord na Mona machinery, or pulled from the sea, I might have reassessed my promise to God. I might have opened my isolation to some other person. Maybe not; a promise is, after all, a promise and I'll have Nanny if not God to face in the next world.

I have known the embraces of no man.

I wait now with deep impatience for the deep embrace of death.

I have played my play for the last time.

I am so tired.

The day Thou gavest Lord . . .,

Have pity on us all.